URG'S MILLION DOLLAR MUNICIPAL PIER.
Times
ST. PETERSBURG, FLORIDA, MONDAY, MAY
Germans Quit
To Allies At 8
ETERSBURG
FLORIDA
SUNSHINE CITY
V-E DA
s Here,
tersburg
e You, Too
vailable
vilian Visitors
IERICA PLANS
ERN CONTROL
VER GERMANY
ASHINGTON — (UP) —
occupation forces
their zone of Germany
an iron hand with the
akeable objective of
Push Back
Okinawa
age Fight
ASSOCIATED PRESS
d army divisions threw back Jap-
the southern Okinawa front yes-
ad in gains which put the Yanks
aha, the island's capital
Gulf Beaches Welcome
Army Group Increases
Mrs. Maxine Miller, her children, Linda and
Avedon, left last week for Freeport, Long Island.
the Gulf Plaza apartments.

St. Petersburg Times
ST. PETERSBURG, FLORIDA, FRIDAY, MAY
IARGES
ias' Sugar
uspended
GERMANS QUIT BY THOUSANDS ON WEST FRONT
PARIS —(AP)— Mass surrenders swept through German armies of the north yesterday as the fall of Hamburg sounded the knell of all resistance east of the great
Ernie Pyle and the Girl Wh
Visited, Wrote Up St. Peter
Ernie Pyle was as well known to St Petersburg and Pinellas county readers as to those anywhere in the world
Service 30c Children 14c
Evening 50c
FLORIDA
TIMES TODAY
THE BEACHES
wood Actor, Designer
on Ce-Sar Hospital
ALAN LADD
GAIL RUSS
ENJOY
MOONLIGHT Pleasure CRUISE
Play
STARTS TOMORROW FOR THREE
They're in the army
LANA TURNER
DAY
HIGHLIGHTS AT H
1 President congress lution aimed
IN EUROPE
1 Negotiations for Germany's sur be in progress. Munitions Min in broadcast over Danish radio hinges solely on Allied generosity opponent. (Page 1.)
2 Hamburg, chief German port, cross Kiel canal en route to German government may be esta mopping up "pockets" of fanatica ance. (Page 1.)
3 No trace found of Von Ribbentr ing prominent Nazis. Russians Hitler suicide report, search vainly (Page 1.)
RANDO
GYPSY
DINA
BOB
BEL
OF T
YUK
PLUS LATEST PARAMOUNT NEWS
PHEIL
9c
Rita HA
TONI
EVERY
No
A
Su

LEGACY:

The time is 1945, the final summer of World War II, on a tropical Florida shore washed by the Gulf of Mexico . . . a time when a place dubbed Hurricane House could stay hidden within its jungle growth, trapped in its brooding past . . . and a rustic, bayshore bar like Grouper Hole could draw a mix of characters, each with hidden passions and intentions . . .

Lelia Elliot – an exotic beauty at twenty-one, reared under the proper roof of a self-righteous Alabama uncle, arriving to find answers to the strange intuitive gifts she fears, but protects, behind a shield of calculated poise.

Kali – who came to this shore from Hawaii forty years earlier as housekeeper, now inscrutable recluse within Hurricane House, withholding her explanation of what happened here by telling Lelia, "Truth cannot be handed to another – it must be discovered."

Chuck – the remaining Elliot son, working as bartender at Grouper Hole, wry nonchalance covering bitter childhood memories of his mother's drowning, his father's disappearance.

Hazel – Chuck's wife, an impatient coiled-spring of a woman, scheming to oust Kali and claim the house as a beginning of postwar wealth.

Gil – an ex-Navy frogman, back on the waterfront as a fishing guide to pursue his single-minded vendetta or to cover his guilt over the drowning-murder of his fiancée.

Morris Alderman – Boston lawyer and bitter father of the drowned girl, returning to take his revenge.

Francie – impetuous young redhead, looking for romance away from her mother's surveillance, risking everything with an innocent's vulnerability.

Sgt. Tom Brockway – lanky deputy from the sheriff's department, looking for errant alligators as well as murderers.

J. T. Tingley – clownish itinerant newspaperman desperately playing sleuth to put together his longed-for "big story."

Evander Merrill – handsome, aging Hollywood movie star, hiding his own reasons for playing host to parties aboard his custom-built yacht, the *Silver Fox*.

Martha Critten – brassy woman bar owner who leaves Grouper Hole to nervous son *Bubba*, while she has other ways to make money off local servicemen.

Conch – powerfully built, aging black cook, whose stony silence hides what he knows about the waterfront's "two-legged" snakes . . . and his young wife *Cheta*, who has her own kind of protection.

Dummy – a slight, blond young man who lives as a deaf-mute beachcomber, selling shell jewelry to tourists.

Cap'n and *Skipper* – two old mullet fishermen, irreverent kibitzers from their favorite bar stools.

Legacy

Marian Coe

SouthLore Press

Legacy
by Marian Coe
SouthLore Press
One Blue Ridge Road
P. O. Box 149
Little Switzerland, NC 28749
Phones: Fax
NC (704) 765-1712
FL (813) 585-1481

Second Edition 1994

Cover and Interior Art: Paul R. Zipperlin
Cover Design: Therese Cabell
Interior Design/Type: Marilyn Ratzlaff
Price: $19.95
ISBN: 0-9633341-1-5
Price: $16.95
ISBN: 0-9633341-0-7
Library of Congress Card No. 92-64095

For Paul

With thanks to *The St. Petersburg Times'* files and the many St. Petersburg natives who shared memories of the Florida Forties. Also, thanks go to so many writer-group friends of the Florida Suncoast Writers and Wildacres Writers, including Doris Enholm, Flo Hallam, Alice Putnam, Marjorie Schuck, Bethia Caffery, Niela Eliason and Carol Perry.

BETHEL, ALABAMA
1930

PROLOGUE

On an Alabama summer night when a hometown street could still be center of a child's known world, Lelia Elliot first heard the secret about herself. Someday she would be crazy or evil.

"Marked" was the word the women used, their voices drifting down to her from behind honeysuckle vines. "That child has to be *marked*, don't you know, by the terrible thing that happened to poor Mary Emily Calhoun."

It was the night after Grandfather Otis Calhoun's funeral. Supper done, neighbors drifted to one front porch to do their talking. The men stood together at the far end of the veranda, cigarettes glowing, voices a muted rumble in the warm night, speaking of the Depression. Women took the rockers as they always did to talk of births and deaths and fates that happened in between. On this evening, they spoke of banker Calhoun, put to rest yesterday, when the flowers weren't yet withered on Cornelia Calhoun's grave.

Neighbor children played beyond on moon-spotted yards. Lelia sat alone on shadowed steps, watching a lightning bug glow messages against her palm. She was six. The women's voices floated out from behind the trellis of vines.

"I hate to say it of the dead, but pride killed those two, not pneumonia. Otis and Cornelia went to their graves without ever forgiving their own dead daughter. All these years. Stiff-backed if you mentioned Mary Emily's name."

They were talking about her mother. With sighs. Now one

was saying, "That child killed them both. And poor Mary Emily before them."

Lelia's fist closed over the glow in her hand.

"Did you see Tarrant's face? A strict man just like Otis. Tarrant will be his father made over in that house. Same as he'll be downtown in the First National."

"And that bride of his. Proud as punch looking at Cornelia's china. But fussing already about taking on somebody else's baby. Why Adelaide knows Mattie has always taken care of Lelia."

"That child! Too quiet for a natural child. Looks at you with those big brown eyes like she's seeing right in."

That's when the porch talkers said the word again, agreement as positive as the click of ice in their lemonade glasses. Hadn't they always said? That baby had to be marked by the terrible thing that happened to poor Mary Emily Calhoun.

"Not that Otis and Cornelia would ever say what happened, just that the boy had taken her down to some Godforsaken place in Florida. But it must have been worse than just any young bride has to, you know, face on her wedding night."

Lelia dropped the dead lightning bug and hunched over her knees. *Marked.* She'd heard the word before. Now she knew what it meant. Something strange had been hidden inside when she first began. Not when she was born upstairs on High Street, and her mother died, and she was put into the arms of the cook, Mattie. But before, in a house by stormy water in a place called Florida, where the Navy boy named Lee Elliot had taken Mary Emily.

A porch talker broke the hush. "Something unnatural." Murmurs of agreement. Didn't they remember now the girl looked when Tarrant brought her back on the train? Limp as a dishrag, white as a sheet in her brother's arms? A little bride, so sick with fright, no one knew for a long time their worst fears were answered. Mary Emily had come home in a Condition.

Lelia caught her breath. She knew what that word meant, too. She had been the Condition.

A rocker creaked. "Wait a minute. Little pitchers big ears, I think." The vines rattled. A face looked out. "Why Lelia

Honey, is that you down there all by yourself? Now you run home. There's Mattie now, out looking for you."

She ran toward the big dark woman waiting on the sidewalk. She let Mattie grab her hand, lead her back to the big two-story house on the corner, Mattie fussing all the way because she was so quiet. "Something eating on you, Sugar? Let's wash that pretty face and get you to bed, you hear? I'll let you roll biscuits tomorrow."

The summer went on as always. Twilight could still turn everything a magic color before dark. Lilac on the sidewalks, the oak-shaded gabled houses, the faces sitting out there after supper. From open windows, *Amos 'n Andy* fussed, Kate Smith sang like soft echoes up down High Street, and the night smelled of fresh-cut clover. Winter came again, bringing hot, close schoolrooms and new books, full of other people's secrets, like silent friends, helping her to forget her own.

But she had to know what terrible thing happened to poor Mary Emily. She had to know when the mark would show. It waited like a rustling noise behind a locked door. On a Saturday morning when rain pounded like sad knuckles against the windows, and the warm kitchen smelled of rising yeast rolls, Lelia went to Mattie.

"Look at that face." Mattie wiped flour from her hands, eyes shiny as the worn plush cushion in the kitchen rocker. "You been listening to folks again?"

"Am I evil, Mattie?"

"Who say that, Sugar? You look like some tangled-haired angel to me. One what needs a hairbrush."

"Uncle Tarrant, behind his teeth last night. His eyes always say that. You-are-evil-in-my-house."

"Lord help me."

"Tell me about my mother, Mattie."

"I done told you lots of times. Your mama was a sweet lil' thing, went off visiting a cousin in Norfolk, and met this Navy boy who musta been a fine, handsome young gentleman. She gave you his name, didn't she, right on her death bed. Goes to show she didn't blame him for what happened."

"What happened?" She was afraid to know, but she was

seven now and had to know.

"Lord help me. C'mere. Your legs got longer, but my lap's got bigger, too, so I reckon we can rock like we usta." Mattie sank into the rocker, pulled her close. "Lord, forgive this old woman for telling tales but a child oughta know about her own mama and daddy."

The rocker creaked against the linoleum. Rain drummed, a faraway sound with her face pressed against the soft front, the smell of cinnamon and snuff. Once Mattie started, the telling poured out like slow molasses that couldn't stop. Behind her closed eyes, Lelia watched it happen as Mattie told about Lee Elliot taking his bride down to the jung'ly place in Florida, on the train, to the house where he had been born, nobody living there but the old housekeeper who stayed upstairs. A big place on the shore where his own mother had drowned when he was a little bitty baby. He shouldn't of, Mattie said, but Lee Elliot had shown Mary Emily the grave outside. Then for two days the waves kicked up and the wind roared.

"That po' scared girl got up in the middle of the howling night. Came out in her long white nightgown to look for this boy she done married. Found him standing on the porch with his arms out like he was pushing away the storm. Only it was some billowing dark thing moving toward him."

"Don't stop – tell, tell."

"Shape of a woman out there, like an old black cloak blowing in the wind, she was walking toward that boy, her arms lifted and dripping with something wet and stinky and calling out to Lee Elliot, Son . . ."

"His dead mother?"

"Like she'd walked right out of the sea, seaweed hanging on her arms. Wet, smelly stuff touched Mary Emily's arm. Set her to screaming . . ."

Behind her tightly closed eyes, Lelia could see the Seaweed Woman reaching out, touching the thin blonde girl who was Mary Emily.

". . . screamed herself into a faint so's some doctor had to carry her off to town. And your Uncle Tarrant had to go way down there and fetch her home . . . Lord, have mercy, I'm answering this child, so she can forgive her poor scared Mama for running off leaving that boy."

Mattie's words went softer than the rain. "When Mister Tarrant brought her back home on the train, she was still shaking and crying . . . I had to bathe her off and bring up hot beef broth and settle her down. Your grandmama sat like an old stone in her room. Your granddaddy roared off to the courthouse to get an annulment. That's a paper that says it never happened . . ."

"Why didn't Lee Elliot look for my mother?"

"A paper came from the Navy saying that boy had drowned down there, same place, right after your mama got brought back home. Why or how nobody done told me to this day. You know Mister Tarrant don't allow his name to be spoke in this house."

"Mattie, what did the woman from the sea want?" Even as she asked, Lelia knew. The Seaweed Woman had wanted her, like evil godmothers in the storybooks, wanting to claim the firstborn.

Mattie stopped rocking, hushed by her own wonder. "Just goes to show a mama's love don't die in the grave. But don't you go telling. And you best be careful about letting on that you know what a body's thinking like I've seen you do. Folks in this old Alabamy town can't abide anybody being least bit different. 'Specially Mister Tarrant. Deacon or not, that man's got a dried-up soul in him."

But when the Preacher came to the house and sat her down in front of him, Lelia forgot to be careful. Who else should be able to understand her secrets and answer her questions? The Preacher looked so wise on Sunday mornings and when he came to dinner. He would know if other people had Knowings, her own word for the pictures that could flash in her head. Did they see shoulder colors, too, when people were angry or frightened or about to be sick? But the Preacher had leaned closer, the vein in his nose throbbing purple, dark yellow fear smoke blooming around his bent neck. His "Yesss" sounded like a hiss. "Yes, there are such things – cunning gifts of the devil! Get on your knees, Lelia Elliot!"

She ran from him up to her room. Tarrant had to yank off the covers to find her. She saw his hate flash from behind the shiny glasses. When he pulled loose his belt and raised his hand to punish her, she went far, far back into herself to hide.

When his footsteps faded back down the hall, she knew to never, ever let her secrets show. Silence would be her magic shield. Her voice left that night, like a bird choosing to fly off. It didn't perch back in her throat until later, when it was ready.

She told no one, not even Mattie, when the dream started waking her just before dawn. A strange woman, not ugly with seaweed, but with glistening white hair, stood by an open blue sea calling to her. Bethel had no water, only ponds by dusty country roads. But she knew this was the sound of waves, and knew the woman called her name like a whisper in her head and maybe the whisper meant, "Come to me."

Alone in her room that had once been Mary Emily Calhoun's, Lelia shivered in the high brass bed, trying to believe the dream woman was not an evil godmother, but a kind one who really loved her and wanted to explain about the mark. To keep the billowing Seaweed Woman from standing beside her bed some night, Lelia whispered back, "When I grow up, I'll come find you. I promise."

BETHEL, ALABAMA
May 1, 1945

1

Bo Rucker was back in town from Marine training, shoulders swaggering in the new uniform. On this raw spring night, every young person left in Bethel had gathered under yellow street lights. Volatile and restless, they piled into hay trucks to ride out to the Rucker farm.

"Look, even Lelia Elliot," younger boys whispered to Bo, to watch the hard grin on his face.

Later, down by the lake, the party had settled down, lulled by dripping hot dogs and chocolate cake when a sound on the plowed slope above them stilled their lazy murmurs. A loud crackle. Faces turned. Fire licked from a gaping barn door.

Crimson flames burst free, leaped high into the country night sky.

Like impatience bursting free, Lelia thought, watching, before she caught her breath, startled. Frightened. Had she caused the fire by saying "fire?"

The barn had been dark when she wandered up the slope to be alone. Then Bo had been there, the flat planes of his face too close, a cigarette glowing between his teeth. His hands gripped her arms like a vise, his voice like gravel. "Think you're so special, doncha, Lelia Elliot. Too damn special to let anyone touch that rosy body all those goddamn high school years. But you ain't looking at a kid this time."

He shoved her toward the open barn door. Hard dusty hay stopped her body. Rage tasted like blood in her mouth. With his face too close and his hands on her wrists, the words came from that other part of herself, unbidden, and instant. "Fire, Bo."

He froze. "Goddamit, where?"

She gasped it out again, "If the barn burns, your father will kill you."

His grip loosened. She twisted free, turned over, scrambled up and ran down the rough slope, back to the lake to the others. She sat apart, shivering, holding the sweater closed. When Bo sauntered back into the crowd, with a grim smile, he reached for the little Bailey girl who giggled a protest, glancing at Miss Willard. The chaperone wasn't looking. Don't little kitten, Lelia thought, but stared out to the dark lake thinking. Why did I come?

She had climbed into that hay wagon, as restless as the others, these people she had grown up alongside if not as one of them. She had her own reason. But she knew why these boys were simmering under their rowdy exuberance, why the girls were feverish under their flirting and posing. This was May 1, 1945, and here they were, when a war and a world was going on, out there, without them. Others had already left. She had stayed, even under Tarrant's roof. Trying to believe she would stay safe here. In Bethel she could refuse to believe in such things as family curse and being "marked."

But the dream had returned, the childhood dream of the woman calling from the open shore. Since her twenty-first birthday three months ago, the dream was always there on the edge of sleep. Someone on a shore was whispering, "Come to me."

Now the fire blazed on the slope. The party to welcome home new Marine Bo Rucker stood with blank faces, exclaiming, watching tongues of crimson leap high. Like a message, Lelia though, like the impatience smoldering inside herself too long, needing to burst free.

Shouts now. Bo was running down the slope, silhouetted by the orange glow. The Bailey girl scrambled in his wake, face stiff with horror, not at the roaring fire behind her, but at being caught in the barn with Bo Rucker in front of the senior class of Bethel High and two older brothers.

Bo ran toward them, holding up his pants like a man in a funny movie, only Bo wasn't being funny. He shouted in rage, "She did it! Lelia Elliot! She said it would burn! You bitch, you goddamned witch!"

She felt their faces turn to find hers. How she hated that careful, curious stare. Another commotion pulled their attention back. In front of them, old man Rucker waved his cane toward the flaming barn, dismay erupting into screamed obscenities. He lunged toward Bo, the cane shrieking down with practiced blows. The new Marine crumpled to his knees, fists pounding the earth, moaning in shame before staring faces.

Lelia walked away from them, alone. Beyond the gate, the dirt road stretched into darkness past open fields. She followed it into the ripe damp night until yellow headlights splashed her shadow on the road. A rattling red Studebaker pulled alongside.

"Lelia Elliot! It's me, Miss Willard. You're not walking ten miles home. Get in."

She dropped in beside the stocky little English teacher. The car smelled of dogs, the back seat piled with books. The Studebaker rolled on, only its rumble breaking the silence. Miss Willard finally spoke, a brusque voice softened by caring, "Lelia Elliot, why are you still in this town? You're a different breed of cat from the Calhouns. And this town doesn't allow one to be different. You must know that. I'll wager that stiff-necked uncle of yours makes sure you know it."

Lelia pulled her sweater over the torn blouse. Plowed fields, under cloudy moonlight, fell past.

"Know what I used to think about you, sitting back there in class? One of the best brains I've seen come through that old school. The girl's mind can flash like a diamond, I said, but she acts like a sleeping beauty and that was pretty damn frustrating."

"You're special, Miss Willard. You introduced me to books when I was a child, remember? That saved my life."

"When they thought you weren't going to talk any more,

sure I remember. But why in the name of heaven aren't you in college? Oh, not that excuse for higher learning for good daughters you went to. Honey, I'm talking Sweet Briar. I can't abide Mr. High and Mighty, but Tarrant Calhoun could afford to send you to the best."

"I want nothing from Tarrant!" Nothing but what he wouldn't tell. Where in Florida to find any Elliots and that house where her mother had gone. Yes, she had to find that shore. "I have my job at the library. I'm saving my money."

"To be Bethel's next old maid librarian? Oh no, Lelia Elliot. You may be silent to the point of distraction, but I know people. That wild mane of hair, those amber eyes of yours need some Heathcliff."

Lelia bit her lip and turned away. A train whistle moaned in the night. Fields rolled by, familiar as Main Street. Familiar as in safe. Safe as in comfort. Only it was false comfort.

"People say you can read minds. Or did when you were a kid. So maybe that's why you stay quiet. Well, I know a dreamer when I see one. But dream too long and you'll get stuck with somebody like Bo."

Lelia shivered. "No. I'm not staying here. I'm leaving. I've waited . . . to know just where I need to go." That answer was locked behind Tarrant's cold eyes and shiny glasses. She tried never to look into Tarrant's face. He issued orders in the house without looking at her.

Along High Street, Miss Willard let the car crawl, sass drained from her voice. "So easy to dream when you're young, waiting around for it to happen. But waiting turns into settling for what you can get. Most folks end up settling. I'm not sure how it is for a man, but for women just the giving-up to that takes a hard kind of endurance. I know."

"I'm not settling."

"You say." The Studebaker coasted to a stop in front of the Calhoun house. Miss Willard turned off the motor. "Good thing for you, the place is dark. Everybody looks all tucked in. Better sneak in quiet though, and not let that uncle of yours see how Bo tore that blouse."

Lelia flung open the door, but the teacher's rough little

hand held her arm. "Did you let him? Don't look so shocked. I saw when you ran from that barn. Not blaming you if you did. That boy has a body on him. About that fire . . ."

"You heard Bo! You heard what he said!" She spun out of the car and ran up the walk to the porch.

Inside the dark house, carrying her muddy sandals, Lelia padded up the stairs and down the carpeted hall. Thankfully, no sound came from the master bedroom at the far end of the hall. Tarrant and Adelaide slept, she knew, on opposite sides of the high bed, watched over by the carved relief countenance of the Virgin Mary, Adelaide's concession to her Catholic upbringing for becoming Baptist for Tarrant's sake.

Later, in the long fleece gown, she stood at the window looking down. High Street, familiar as the lines in her hand, wasn't hers tonight. It was her past. Even the scent of crab apple blossoms below the window came to her like memory. Then what now?

From downstairs, the phone echoed through the silent house. She waited, senses alert. The slippered footsteps went downstairs. They returned, not to the far end of the hall, but toward her own door. She stood frozen in the dusky moonlight watching the door knob turn. Tarrant, in his long robe, moved toward her. His face was pale with anger, his breathing audible as his harsh whisper, "You let that trash Rucker call me with that kind of tale!"

"Go away, Tarrant!" The loathing rose as he moved into the room toward her. Without the glasses, his eyes looked lost and wild. His hand gripped. Not a thick, hot grasp like Bo's, but with fingers long-boned and cold as his voice now, muttering curses that banker Tarrant Calhoun never uttered.

"You lured that boy of his to paw you! Then in some kind of vengeance, with some evil power —"

His hand trembled as he seized her thick hair before the hand loosened, dragged down her neck, down to the shape of her breasts. Oh God, how she hated his touch. The cold hand sprang back as though burned by her flesh. In the dim light, Tarrant's naked eyes went bleak with fear.

"Get out of my room, Tarrant!"

He stepped back, with a harsh whisper, "You are evil, born evil! Yet in my house, under my roof –"

"No! You hold me here. I've stayed, waiting on one thing – to know what you could tell me!" She had not said this to his face since she was young and punished for it. Now she said, "Tarrant, where did you go in Florida to bring my mother home before I was born? I know about her being frightened there. I've always known! Tell me where!"

Tarrant backed to the doorway. "If you must know – all Elliots seemed destined to drown." Dry words but his eyes gleamed. "All dead, I've checked. Except one, Charles Elliot, still there." His lips curled. "A bartender, I believe. All dead except one Elliot and you, of course." He wheeled away down the dark hall.

Pulse racing, Lelia got out a small satchel, a green velvet thing that had been her mother's. The southbound went through town in the morning. She stuffed in the satchel a roll of underthings and the roll of five dollar bills saved from library pay. In the dark, she whispered, *"Tell me! Don't haunt me, tell me where to go in Florida to find that house, that shore."*

There was one single possession she had to take: The framed picture Mattie had found in her mother's things. The last time Mattie trudged up the Calhoun stairs, she had brought the sepia photograph wrapped in a yellowed nightgown. The old picture showed a young couple in the dress of the twenties, each holding a small child. The Elliots, posed under a huge tree by a Florida house.

"That's the place," Mattie had said. "Only from what your little mama told me, they's all drowned or runned away. But it's your other folks' homeplace, and I know you're bound to go there someday, only I wish you wouldn't, Sugar."

The stoic faces in the picture seemed to look out with a silent message. At fifteen, Lelia did not want to feel its pull. She had hidden the photograph away in a bottom bureau drawer. Until now.

The hard cardboard frame was too big to go in the

satchel so she tore away its yellowed backing and took out the cracked photograph. Pasted on the back was a strip of newsprint about the Elliots in St. Petersburg, Florida, 1905.

With dreamlike motion, Lelia put the picture in a small volume of Robert Browning and the book in the bottom of the satchel. She would find Charles Elliot in St. Petersburg.

Waiting for the morning, Lelia watched shadows on the ceiling before closing her eyes. Behind dark brows, the dream started.

It was there again, a blue-green sea, a curving shore, sands opalescent in the strange light. The figure of a woman waited far down the water's edge, flowing hair glistening, garments vaporous as the foam at her feet. When the strange woman turned, the dreamer knew she would be an ancient creature yet beautiful, the eyes luminous.

The dreamer ran, straining forward as if moving forward through green water . . . to reach the ancient woman, who turned now, a billowing dark thing, calling her name.

SOUTHBOUND
May 2, 1945

2

In the chill May morning, the steel tracks gleamed alongside Bethel's small platform before they disappeared around a curve. The tracks hummed now. So did her pulse. Lelia paced, the green satchel held against the front of her camel's hair coat, the wind whipping her hair under the tam. The smell of coffee came from the open window of the tiny depot where station master Hawkins still watched his lone passenger for the southbound *Seaboard.*

"Place full of soldiers where you're going, young lady," he had grumbled, handing over the one-way ticket to St. Petersburg. Under his breath, he had muttered, "Lamb-to-the-slaughter?" Taking her ticket, meeting his gaze, she saw Hawkins was wondering how much lamb, how innocent.

Now the air hummed as the nose of the silver diesel appeared. Clattered in. Clanked to a stop. She climbed aboard the train and stood balancing in the vibrating aisle until Bethel fell behind, spring green oaks and streets giving way to countryside. How quickly it was gone.

She turned to the crowded aisle. Soldiers dealt cards. Some slept. Children whimpered against women's arms. Girls younger than herself jostled restless babies in their laps. The air smelled of peanuts and baloney mixed with tobacco. Just as surely the sense of mute sadness and silent hopes came to her in waves.

Alabama cotton fields moved by, faster now. She found a seat by the window. A heavy man in bib overalls sank down beside her. She moved closer to the glass, annoyed and alarmed at the pressure of his leg. Was she going to be afraid of people this way? Deep breathing, she suppressed the panic. She had to remember her childhood secret, belief in an invisible shield. She knew what it was now, a practiced facade of calm. But it worked like a shield. It saved her from feeling other people's energy.

At Mobile's midtown terminal, departure calls echoed like a monotone voice of fate. Newsboys paced, hawking their headlines, "BERLIN FALLS!" Their harsh gusto triggered a chill of joy – the war, coming to an end! Not yet in the Pacific but in Europe. In her mind, the war was a hideous stone wall blocking everything beyond. What waited on the other side? No image would come, not even her own future until she found out if she had one.

The southbound jerked and rolled again, moving free of railroad yards . . . hummed past spring-plowed fields . . . slowed again . . . a drab mill town now, the coaches clacking along Main Street. Women came out to wave, silent longing in their faces.

Countryside again. Trackside houses, windows hung with small white banners, blue stars or gold. Mantles inside, she knew, would be displaying photographs of boys her own age. Their fierce grins would be shadowed by new-issue garrison caps, faces caught forever in cheap frames, never to look like that again. Her throat tightened. She had never kissed any of them to send them off as girls in Bethel did, believing themselves in love, wanting desperately not to be left behind.

Four crew-cut, khaki-garbed soldiers on facing seats looked up from their cards, eyes narrowed. Their mouths showed crooked smiles but their gaze pierced too deeply. Men like that could trigger something hidden deep within the core of herself, like a dark red throb. Not passion, as the Bethel girls whispered about over their True Confessions magazines. Something else, more like rage. But she was careful not to think about it or allow it to stir.

The man in the bib overalls pretended to sleep, but his

heavy leg pressed against her hip. Instinctively, she concentrated chill into his leg. The leg jerked and the man pulled away. She didn't do that kind of thing often, wasn't sure how she did it, didn't want to think about how.

A raspy greeting came from the front of the coach. "Congratulations ever-body – J. T. Tingley's the by-line." A funny little man stood up there, holding onto a small black suitcase displaying the word PRESS labeled in white letters. He might have been a sideshow barker addressing the crowded coach.

"I say congratulations 'cause we're all headed for Floridy. Down to sunshine and good times and nothin' to shoot at but alligators and mosquitos. Right, folks?"

She watched this J. T. Tingley, a short, soft-bellied man in the sagging jacket and checkered pants, ruddy face shaped with grin lines. He might have been forty or fifty, yet the man's eagerness made him seem like a lonesome kid, eager to get invited to a party. Bemused, sympathetic because other faces turned away, Lelia found herself watching until the man's glance met hers. She turned away but back again as he kept on talking to the card-playing soldiers.

A mental image flashed, the way Knowings used to do, crazy pictures that made sense or none at all. She saw J. T. Tingley as a clown, a sad clown, grasping for balloons that would always burst at his touch. She watched him kick the suitcase down the aisle to the card players.

"Ain't that right, boys?" Tingley said, leaning in to four crew-cut heads, staying bent to their game.

"Yessireee, southbound in this U. S. of A. is the best direction going, considering the present possibilities, wouldn't you say, fellow?"

The sergeant shuffled the deck of cards. "Looks like old Lou Costello climbed aboard this here railroad train without his pard'ner."

"Nah," said another. "Costello's funny."

"Costello doesn't wear checkered pants and a goddamned pork-pie golfing hat."

"Hey, mebbe it's some strange outfit. Mebbe they wear

checkered pants and golfing hats as a disguise."

"For what? Go 'round ruining poker games?"

"Glad you asked, friends!" Tingley went on, beaming, ignoring scowls. "This hat was given to me personally by Sam Snead. Threw it at me, matter of fact, but as a friendly gesture, understand, on the greens in Augusta, Georgia. I see you admire the trousers. Trusted to me for safe keeping by a young man who right now could be in hand-to-hand combat on some Pacific atoll even as you ride along to Florida toward girls and home cooking. As for profession – "

"Bull-shooter," the sergeant said.

"Newspaperman. Permit me to introduce myself. J. T. Tingley's the by-line. Name a town between Virginny and Alabama, and I can tell you who runs the show. Also which gin mills can warm your gut or rot it. Right now, yours truly is headed to Florida for my new beat."

"Look out, Florida. Here comes a stupe who thinks he's Walter Winchell."

"Nope." Tingley's grin lines sagged. "I carry on for my buddy Ernie Pyle."

"Ernie's dead," the GIs chorused.

A skinny corporal looked up, "Got it from a sniper a few days ago. I was reading his last column when they told me. Hell, didn't you know?"

"Yeah. I know." Tingley straightened. For moments he studied the lonely, empty horizons bobbling past.

Lelia followed his gaze. A girl stood at a roadside mailbox on a red dirt lane, turning away, empty-handed, as the train hummed past.

"Yeah," Tingley said finally. "That's why I figured I couldn't wait any longer to come on down to St. Pete where things are happening, if not the shootin' – to do some real reporting like Ernie. It's personal, between me and him, see."

"Ernie Pyle know about this?"

"Well, let's say where good reporters go, Ernie's there looking back at the mess down here – so I figure he'll understand." With a solemn salute to the four, Tingley picked up his suitcase, but stopped again to blink at Lelia and the heavy man taking up too much of the seat. Tingley put a hand on the man's shoulder.

"Gentleman of the South, I hope? Your mama bring you up right?" At the man's surprised grumble, Tingley leaned close to his ear. "Then getcha bulk off of the lady here – now, that's a whole lot better."

Tingley found a seat across the aisle facing a frizzy blonde with a wiggling child beside her.

"You my daddy?" the boy asked.

"Nope – that's some other fellow." Tingley got up. Suitcase balanced against his belly and with a soulful grin for Lelia, Tingley weaved down the aisle.

Waiting for the bustling Negro porter to find her a seat, Lelia looked down the length of crowded dining car. Uniforms everywhere, Navy white and khaki shoulders turning, faces lifting, eyes speculating. At the far end of the car, a young girl wearing a peasant blouse, with red-blonde curls, stood in the aisle, waving frantically. The porter led Lelia back to the girl's table, interrupting what must have been a mother-daughter argument. The mother was a faded version of the daughter, a woman wearing a pale blue suit and pearls, plaited blonde hair coiled like a tiara.

Lelia realized how she looked in the woman's assessing eyes. The plain camel's hair coat, a schoolgirl's coat. Her hair wildly curled from the damp morning. The daughter stood there, full petticoats swaying, insisting, "Oh, join us. Those noisy old soldiers take up all the train, don't they?"

The redhead plopped back into her seat, patting the chair beside her. "I'm Francie Welburn and this is my mother, Elise Arnold Welburn, who is simply forcing me to take a rest from school. We're going to St. Petersburg. Are you going to Florida to get married or something?"

At the mother's curt nod, Lelia sat down, amused at this impulsive girl whose china blue eyes radiated a desperate signal.

"Francine, dear," the mother murmured. "Do stop making an unladylike spectacle." She rose and gave Lelia a tight smile. "Yes, have our table. We were just leaving."

Francie pouted. "I would just love another pudding, Mother. It just might make me feel better. This old train has been making me absolutely ill."

Elise Welburn left them, finally. Lelia gave the porter her chicken soup order, but Francie brushed aside any pudding. "Ugh! It tastes like library paste."

Francie leaned forward on her elbows. "You saved my life! I was simply dying of lectures. Mother is so worried and bossy anytime I'm around boys. She didn't know there'd be so many on the train. She's always watching. Stay and talk with me." The blue eyes implored.

Being with Francie meant listening. Lelia sipped her soup willing to listen, glad to forget herself as the train barreled on.

"I felt absolutely dragged off from home." The girl wrinkled her snub nose with its sprinkle of pale freckles. "And you know why?" She leaned back, shoulders making delighted little wiggles. "There was this keen Airman who looked like Robert Taylor, I promise you. Though Mother was right about him, kinda, because he did say 'ain't' and 'him and me,' which was so embarrassing when other people were around. But being alone with him, ahh – not that we did anything, really."

Francie paused, the pink mouth pensive. "You must think I'm the rudest old thing, talking about myself! Tell me about you. Lelia Elliot, you're so mature and exotic looking! You look like Jennifer Jones when she had all that wild hair and was a gypsy girl. Do you like movies? Remember Susan Hayward in *Foolish Heart* standing by the gate, so sad, knowing she was PG and her boyfriend was marching off to war? Oh! Can't you just imagine if that happened to you, wouldn't you just want to die? I know my mother would absolutely kill me first. Is yours like that?"

Francie bit her full bottom lip before rushing on. "Lelia, I just can't bear being stuck in St. Petersburg at my aunt's house with a bunch of married cousins and their little brats. For heavens sakes, I'm almost eighteen! If you're going to be there, maybe we could go to the beach together?"

"I don't know where I'll be yet, Francie. I have to find an uncle." For an instant, Lelia saw herself in those blue eyes, saw herself entangled in this impulsive girl's schemes. She couldn't risk that. She had other things to do.

"But we have to meet. It's fate! We'll do something exciting. Oh, no, there's my mother up there, tapping her foot. I have to go. Watch that cute Marine up front when I go past. Tell me later if he looks up." She leaned closer to whisper. "And you better watch out for those two old guys across the aisle. They've been watching us. The fuzzy-headed one with the tacky suitcase that says PRESS and the other one who looks rich and bothered. I'll see you tomorrow before we get off this old train."

Lelia looked back at the table across the aisle. Yes, fuzzy-head was the raspy clown, J. T. Tingley, gesturing over his coffee cup to a tailored-looking man who tapped his newspaper with impatience. The silver-haired man wasn't listening to Tingley. From behind the tortoise shell glasses, he frowned at her with bitterness in his eyes.

As if he recognizes me, Lelia thought. I must remind him of someone else. And this makes him angry. Or sad? Both. She turned back to the cold soup but listened, the way she had learned as a child.

"Yessiree," Tingley was saying. "We all have our reasons for heading down to Florida."

"Reasons, yes. Private reasons," the man replied coldly. "And how do you propose to get your `big story' out of people's private reasons?"

"I've got this theory. Professional fellow like you, Mr. Alderman, would understand. Florida's a get-away place, a somewhere-else kinda place. The Sunshine State, right, huh? All that water and clean sky and grapefruit hanging there for the picking. The kind of place folks dream about, an after-the-war dream. They're already coming, taking a look, hoping for a whole new life down there. They bring a hellava lot of stories."

"I assume you, sir, are one of the dreamers?"

"Yeah. Sure. I'm gonna be Winchell and Ernie Pyle and Lowell Thomas all in one. No, hell, I'm just going to get me a fine story, one that will make some old city editors I know look up with respect when they see J. T. Tingley's by-line. So what part of Florida brought you down, Mr. Alderman?"

"None of it. I despise Florida."

"Yeah? Well, yeah, you're right, it's the boonies if you're from New York City. Or Boston like you. Unless you're sitting around the Roney Plaza at Miami Beach, listening to Yankees boast. Sure, Florida has dive-bomber mosquitos and dinky cottages, scorpions in the closets, alligators in the ditches, and sand in your teeth. It's a boom-and-bust place where they can still sell you real estate under water. Just the same – "

Alderman's voice was precise and bitter. "I dislike the place for its flatness, its easy flamboyance, its naive cunning and whatever lure it seems to have for the innocent – or the stubbornly unaware."

Alderman continued, with cool vehemence. "My daughter, sir, the only thing in life I loved, came down to visit a Navy man against my permission. Two weeks later, I received a message from some idiot who called himself a sheriff asking me to come and identify her body. The sheriff would tell me nothing, not even the Navy man's name. That young woman across the aisle reminded me. I don't intend to speak of it again."

"So you're coming back to get that sheriff on the job."

"Yes. Also, to take my pound of flesh out of Florida."

Tingley said, "Huh?"

"I am an investor. I shall buy land, Because part of your – ah, theory – is true. When this war ends, so will the tolerance for waiting, for self-denial. People will want a marketable commodity called pleasure."

"You're right about that, yessiree."

"For reasons beyond logic, people associate sunshine with the good life. They equate it with satisfaction, health, opportunity, presumably waiting for them. As you say, like those grapefruit, ripening on the trees down there, ready for the picking. Yes. And they will need places to unpack their foolish bags. And houses to live in."

"Roger, Roger, I read you! You're gonna get in there and buy while the getting's good. Real smart, real smart. You fellows with money can do things like that."

Lelia stood up, counting out quarters on the table.

"Yessiree, Mr. Alderman," J. T. Tingley stood doing the same, gathering his suitcase. "Yessiree, Mr. Alderman, like I said, this train's full of stories all headed for the land of promises."

Lelia hurried up the aisle, trying to stay ahead of the clownish little man with the PRESS suitcase who followed.

GEORGIA NIGHT
May 2, 1945

3

The *Seaboard* moaned through the dark Georgia night, the window glass cold against her cheek. At a crossing, an Army convoy waited as the diesel rumbled by. For a moment, Lelia looked down into a young man's eyes gazing up from the first dusty windshield, blank-faced, in this no-where place between the known and the unknown. She wanted to tell him, I know how you feel. She carried unknowns within herself ever as the diesel moved her toward their uncovering. The rhythm of the rails was a heartbeat now, taking over her own.

She couldn't sleep though the crowded coach had long since settled down, peanut smells fading, babies whimpering into silence. Across the aisle, two quarrelsome soldiers had slumped into sleep, the skinny one's hands still fitful against his khaki leg. Thankfully, the garrulous little man next to her had finally talking. Pork-pie hat hung on checkered knee, feet planted on the suitcase, J. T. Tingley slept, head lolling against the seat. Beneath them, the soft clatter of rails went on and on, taking them into the night. Lelia pulled her coat tighter.

A barn sprung up and swept past. Now spectral trees raised limbs against gray-black sky.

She leaned back and glanced over at this J. T. Tingley fellow. The deep grin lines sagged now, but eagerness stayed etched on the forehead that extended to the thin ruffle of curly hair. Why, Lelia asked herself, why had she managed to avoid all those soldiers' eyes yet allowed this funny little man to attach himself from the moment they left the dining car.

Tingley had followed her down the rocking aisles, through coaches, talking all the way. He'd found them a seat together and proceeded to open the suitcase and pull out stacks of yellowed clippings, Ernie Pyle columns about the war and J. T. Tingley by-lines from a dozen small towns, his own name underlined in ink as if the viewer might miss it.

Yet she'd listened with benign impatience, even amusement. His persistence had charged past her guard of privacy. In a raspy monologue, he told her about going to Florida to find the best stories of his career. Under the boastful enthusiasm she could hear the hope and saw in his eyes a hunger to make it come true. Wet, brown eyes like some spaniel puppy's, innocent, eager. When he finally paused, she found herself telling him she would be looking for an uncle in St. Petersburg – a Charles Elliot who worked as a bartender there, that was all she knew. Tingley's florid face had beamed.

"Told you! Everybody heading for the land of sunshine has a story going. Honey, you're looking at the right fellow to help you. J. T. Tingley is a sleuthing reporter – what's more I know every gin mill in St. Pete. Yeah, I went down there three, four years ago. Aw, I been everywhere, east of the Mississippi, that is."

On impulse she had reached into the satchel and pulled out the old brown picture. Did he know anything about such a house on the gulf? Tingley's bushy brows worked up and down, studying the brown photograph of a young couple posed with two children under a banyan tree, the water showing behind the edge of the big house.

Tingley's stubby fingers tapped the picture. "Uh huh. Must have been rich folks. Not many three-storied homestead kinda places on those gulf beaches, lemme tell you. Family, huh?"

The Elliots, she told him. Her father's family. The baby in the picture would be her father, Lee Elliot, who had been in the Navy and had drowned a long time ago.

"Poor sonavagun." Tingley handed back the picture. "Died without ever knowing he had a beauteous daughter?

The other kid must be uncle, right? Honey, if he's all that's left of your family, we'll find him. A promise from J. T.!"

In the darkened coach now, Lelia turned back to the window. The diesel engine moaned into the night. A shuttered town moved by. Now a curving river twisted behind, falling back.

Whoever, whatever had whispered in her head as a child – did it know she was on her way? No answer. Only the soft clatter of rails. But then the Voice or the Knowings never came on demand. She could refuse them but could not command them to happen.

Across the aisle, the skinny GI bolted upright, moaning, twisting his hands. His buddy hissed, "Slack off. Go back to sleep, dammit! Dream about where you're going – the Don CeSar, fancy hotel. Bath tubs. Girls. Beaches. Girls." The nervous GI fumbled with his wrinkled pack of Lucky Strikes.

The coach quieted again. The *Seaboard* rumbled on toward the Florida border.

Dawn awakened her the way it sometimes did, as if its faint energy triggered the same in her body. She opened her eyes. Pale pink showed beyond a flat horizon of pine trees. She recognized the feeling and knew not to move if she meant to let it happen.

The sensation began with a tingling warmth low in her body. Not the other stirring which she feared, the churning in her core that had the feel of violence, like some alien passion laced with anger. This thing happening to her now was a rising of energy, a buoyancy that made her think of silver and high, lovely sounds, some secret kind of ecstasy all her own. How could it be evil if dawn triggered it, coming on the edge of sleep? It happened for only moments, but always it was like a gift, the opposite of loneliness.

So she sat unmoving now, eyes closed, allowing the silver stirring to rise, like something flowering inside, flowing warmth into the network of nerves . . . rising to her throat, hurting there as always like trapped tears. If it rose higher, past the throat, it could be a pale shimmering within her head, lifting her to the mental horizon that was the strange part of herself she had to hide from others and tried to deny to herself. But from that shimmering place she could ask any question and hear the answer. Sometimes she could see answers with her eyes open, if she held her gaze soft.

She turned her head to look at this man snoring softly beside her, this Tingley, not a clown grasping his balloons now. She saw him with dead eyes staring up under lapping water . . .

The silver-haired man from Boston, stalking now down the shadowed aisle, moved along in a haze of green sorrow, trapped in darker anger . . .

Across the aisle, the skinny GI flexing his hands in tortured sleep, she saw now, was trying to rid them of blood. His anguish twisted in her own body so sharply she leaned past the sleeping Tingley and called out to him, "Your hands are clean!"

The soldier's buddy bolted up, staring. Lelia pulled back, dismayed at what she'd done. The images dissolved. The buoyancy was gone. In its place was the fear of exposure. Tingley snored on.

She pulled her coat closer and turned to the window. New sun gleamed on a tin tobacco sign against a country store. She saw only the preacher from her childhood, his fierce eyes and the colors of fear like yellow smoke around his head, "Cunning gifts of the devil!" he had told her. He might have added – gifts that carry their own punishment.

She could still feel the soldier's confusion. His buddy's eyes narrowed with hard curiosity. She pressed her face to the window. The flat scrubby landscape showed shaggy palms now, glossy green against a brightening sky, a Florida sky. New, like the day. What was in her genes that made her strange? Old questions, lived with, suppressed but always there, awaiting answers. She closed her eyes and let the clacking rhythm of the rails say, *not afraid, not afraid, not afraid . . .*

ST. PETERSBURG, FLORIDA
May 3, 1945

4

As the *Seaboard* moved out of the tiny Clearwater station, the conductor marched through booming, "Saaintt Peters-burg!" Orange groves moved by. Now a streak of bay gleamed beyond. J. R. Tingley plopped back into the seat with his fresh newspaper – Thursday, May 3. "Look this, Miss Lelia Alabamy. Hitler's dead and the Ninth Army's about to go into Berlin. Eisenhower's waiting on the Russians. See what I mean? The war's gonna be over and everybody'll be itching to get down here to the land of promises. We got here first."

The train groaned to a stop beside a long shed of a station. The sun's glow bathed the platform and upturned faces, khaki and sailor whites showing among them.

Suitcase under his arm, Tingley disappeared into the milling crowd. Lelia stood still, the coat on her arm hot as a blanket. The warm air smelled of sea and something roasted, making her remember hunger. Two days had elapsed since she last sat down to one of cook's dinners at home. Home? Not any more.

Francie, the pretty redhead from the dining car, waved like a disappointed child before trailing off behind her mother. Morris Alderman, the angry father who thought she looked like his dead daughter, stalked away, a redcap following with two heavy bags.

Where to start? But here came Tingley, swaggering back with his bowlegged gait, chewing, and holding out a small brown paper bag. He thrust shelled nuts into her hand and nodded toward the ancient Negro at the edge of the crowd dressed in a black-tailed coat, white apron and top hat.

"See that character over there hawking his peanuts? Calls himself 'I-Got-'Em.' I oughta write a story about that booger. Bet I could make *Saturday Evening Post.*"

When she shook her head to more peanuts, Tingley threw the nuts in his mouth and grabbed up his suitcase. Under the Sam Snead hat, his ruddy face beamed, scanning the dispersing crowd. He turned back to Lelia.

"Well, let's go gettum. If that uncle of yours is tending bar anywhere in town, who do we ask? Bartenders. And you got J. T. Tingley here to do the asking."

The two of them started out down a tree-shaded street, Lelia carrying her coat on one arm, Tingley swinging along with the PRESS suitcase and her satchel. They passed rooming houses with awninged front porches, then a big store attracting and dispersing people with its round sign overhead claiming this was "Webb's City, World's Largest Drug Store."

Tingley huffed alongside with raspy explanations.

"You don't mind me calling you Miss Magnolia, do you, Miss Lelia Elliot? I can tell you grew up in one of those white-columned homesteads with Grandma's silver on the table and magnolias in the front yard. But I don't mean you talk like a southern darlin', dripping honeysuckle. Fact is, you sound downright me-lod-dious. How come?"

"Maybe I read more than I talked." She controlled her pace to match his.

"Now me, I can write the King's English better than I talk it. But when you're trying to get the truth out of some old geezer of a town commissioner, you gotta talk the same language."

From a doorway, two blue-haired women watched, narrow-eyed. Lelia smiled back, knowing why the women stared. They must make a strange pair – a tall girl in a long-sleeved, navy-blue schoolgirl kind of dress all wrong for this place, hair as wild as the dress was sedate, keeping pace with the bowlegged man who trotted alongside, a gnome of a guide in checkered pants, sagging jacket, and golfer's hat.

They passed a Spanish-looking building with a YMCA sign. Now a still grander stucco presence, the Florida Theater where sidewalk posters showed a glowering John Garfield in *Pride Of The Marines*. At a corner, Tingley's pace dragged.

"Down there's the St. Pete *Times* and the *Evening Independent* next to it. One of them's gonna want the J. T. Tingley by-line soon as I impress them with the possibilities."

Pure longing and a hint of desperation softened the raspy voice, the same hunger she'd seen in his wet, brown eyes on the train. This garrulous little man was here to find his "big story." Poor J. T. Tingley, are you going to find what you came here seeking? It didn't make sense that she cared. She mustn't get involved in his fate. She was here to deal with her own.

The next corner opened to a wide avenue, sidewalks lined with benches. Tingley put down the suitcase, satchel on top, to catch his breath.

"You're looking at this old town's main street, Central Avenue. Runs from Tampa Bay about eight miles straight across to where the sun's getting ready to set. Gulf of Mexico out there."

Lelia looked west down the sun-bronzed street. Out there somewhere, the Elliot house must be waiting. Whether the shiver she felt was anticipation or something else, she wasn't sure. "The sun looks like a giant orange ball poised at the end of the street," she said.

"Yep, sits on the horizon then slips right down under like a hot gold dollar. Heads for China by way of Texas." Tingley picked up the suitcase. "But we're going this way toward the bay, Miss Magnolia. Bars are down here."

Green benches lined the wide sidewalk, the gray-haired occupants like a seated parade watching them trail by. Lelia shifted the coat to her other arm, breathing away impatience at Tingley's running commentary. But she needed to know about this place.

They passed a Kress store with its bright red trim and gold letters, a larger version of the little one back in Bethel.

An ornate building on the corner had an open arcade, busy with a hot dog stand and a "Blood Pressure Taken Free" table. A hotel's lobby was open to the sidewalk, huge potted palms inside. In the next block, people stood at open counters drinking fresh orange juice from paper cups.

"Everything's open – like a county fair, right in town," she murmured, avoiding the stare of two Coast Guard officers.

"Eye-balling you. Can't blame them, Lelia Magnolia. You look like some hot-eyed madonna." His head dipped in apology. "Can't learn to keep my mouth shut."

"How much further?"

"That's Bayboro Harbor ahead. Gray ships you see are Merchant Marine. Coast Guard's down there, too. First time I saw this burg, three years ago, bay was full of ships. But St. Pete's still loaded with military. They don't stay long, but they've sure liked being here. Hotels with army cots beat foxholes. For that matter, this old town beats training at Fort Benning, Georgia. Fly-boys come in here, too, from Drew Field and from MacDill, across the bay in Tampa."

Tingley's grin twisted into a scowl. "You gonna have to look after yourself here. This is an old tourist town, but with all those guys here, well, it's not same as where you came from. Sonny boys back in hometowns still have the fear of God in 'em. Leastways, the wrath of the girl's old man."

She watched two bench-sitters nod at a pair of sailors. "I think they like having the soldiers here."

"Yessum. See, all St. Pete has to sell is sunshine and orange juice, so with the war and gas rationing they were pretty short of tourists – until Uncle Sam came in and took over most of the hotels. Uncle pays his rent – but on his own terms."

"For all the uniforms you see, war seems far away here." She saw the bay just ahead now.

"Well, they've had their excitement," Tingley said as they crossed another street. "Air-raid wardens keep thinking they see German subs out there in the gulf. No fooling. About six months ago, a sub musta let off a couple of U-boat fellows. They made it to shore and were all the way in town setting up their short wave when they were found. Got shot dead pretty quick, both of them."

"Germans, here?" She could imagine them walking along these busy sidewalks, wearing stolen khaki, their eyes taking everything in, getting smiled at by these old men leaning on their cane handles. Two old ladies emerged from the busy cafeteria and watched them pass.

"Old biddies!" Tingley sniggered. "The town's full of 'em. They go dancing like belles of the ball at the Coliseum."

He came to a halt. "Let's see – here's the Tarpon Bar, over there the Tradewinds, the Goody's around the corner. Or a fancier one, the Chatterbox on down the next block. Nope, I'll start right here." His pliable face stretched into a grin. "You got a nickel, Miss Lelia Magnolia? You wait right here, have yourself an orange juice while I go sleuthing." He handed over the green bag and swaggered into Mastry's Bar and Grill.

She waited, watching small live turtles behind a glass window. The train rhythm still vibrated in her pulse, exuberance becoming impatience. Each time Mastry's door opened and closed, the sound of loud male laughter escaped. In Bethel she'd never gone into a bar, but this wasn't Bethel. Shifting coat and satchel to one hand, drawing in a deep breath, Lelia walked into the din of raucous voices and heavy smoke.

The long narrow barroom smelled of beer and fried onions and throbbed to thumping rhythm from a glowing juke box. White and khaki shoulders crowded three deep along the bar. Along the opposite shadowy wall, couples leaned close over small tables. Lelia scanned the smoky haze for Tingley.

"Looking for daddy, honey?" The cooing voice came from a plump blonde in a polka-dot dress perched on the first stool just inside the door. "He don't wanna go, honey."

She spotted him at the far end of the bar, hunched on a stool, downing a drink as though gulping oxygen. A hefty sergeant gestured in his face, his khaki shoulders turning toward the noisy room to shout, "Hey – listen to this jerk! Says we can lick the Japs in six months after we finish with the Germans." The sergeant turned back to Tingley. "Fatso – you got any idea how many troops have to be moved out of Europe first? You got the re-mot-ist idea, Fatso?"

From the stand-up crowd at the bar, a voice called out, "Leave the blow-hard alone – we don't come to Mastry's to fight the war. Hey, Jonesy, here's my dime. Where's my hamburger? Here's another nickel. Slap on some cheese. I'm a big spender."

A GI turned from the bar, blank-faced until he saw Lelia standing there in the smoky gloom. Smiling, he sang falsetto over the babble, "Mama, don't cry for me no more. I just saw me a wild-haired angel come in through Mastry's door."

White and khaki shoulders shifted, faces turned. A sailor chanted, "Oh, Papa, come back home with me now. Mama is waitin' and the babies are hungry."

Their collective energy, male energy, came to her in waves, wild and evasive. Panic quickened her breath. She breathed it down. She mustn't do this, be afraid of strangers; she mustn't open to their energies either. She only wanted to find Charles Elliot, and these bartenders might know him. She looked over the noisy bar crowd to gaze at mounted fish and baseball team photos grinning from their frames.

"I'm looking for someone. A Charles Elliot who works as a bartender in town . . ."

"Miss Magnolia!" Tingley spilled off his stool and reeled forward. "I'm workin' on it, I am!" He turned back to his hecklers with a hoarse plea. "I got proof – ask this young lady from Alabama if J. T. Tingley hasn't left his by-line from the Carolinas to this Sunshine State, hell, anywhere east of the Mississippi."

A fresh whoop drowned out the boast. Tingley sank back on the stool. She had been right. He was the clown with the burst balloon.

"Chuck Elliot?" somebody spoke up from the crowded bar. "Yeah, Honeybun, he works bar at Grouper Hole – only that's way out on the beach."

"Only he's not there now. Chuck works wherever that chanteusy wife of his plays the piano."

"'Fascinatin' Hazel'? – I heard that dame last night. Tough lil' Frankie-and-Johnny type, but she plays a hot piano. Hey, she's still down at the Vinoy Park. You could try there."

The crowd chorused directions. Go right down toward the bay, turn left at a little yacht club, and follow along the water. The big pink hotel down that Bayshore Drive would be the Vinoy Park.

At the door, Lelia looked at the hot coat on her arm. Like Bethel, it was a hiding place, a thing from the past. She dropped the coat on an empty chair and without looking back, went out. Bronze light colored the sidewalks. She walked toward the bay with the kind of buoyancy known from her best dreams of weightless flight.

Beyond the yacht basin, the flat bay waters shimmered with gold. Further down, the imposing pink presence framed by tall palms had to be the Vinoy Park Hotel. She hurried toward the arched entrances that led into a long portico lined with rocking chairs. Just inside the high-beamed lobby, Lelia paused. Spanish tile, Oriental runners and big urns recalled Aladdin stories and history book pictures of Spanish or Moorish halls.

Where would Chuck Elliot, bartender, be in this place? An open ballroom spilled music and voices into this grand corridor. A crowd murmured and a bride stood pink-faced in her white wedding gown as a violinist dipped his bow in a plaintive "*Always.*" Elderly waiters dressed in black carried trays of clinking champagne glasses. But no bar.

Lelia wandered down the wide hall past potted palms and stiff-backed chairs where gray-haired women sat watching, drumming their jeweled fingers. Around a corner, wide doors opened onto a large dining room with massive white columns. A "Now Appearing" sign was posted by the doors.

The tinted photograph, stuck on the sign at a jaunty angle, showed a woman in a tight red dress, her small body arched in a teasing pose against a piano, a cluster of dark curls atop her head, red lips curved in a hard smile. "Songs by Fascinatin' Hazel, formerly with Herbie Ray," promised the glittery letters, tarnished now like a faded boast.

"Yes? May I help you?" A dapper little man attired in black stepped forward, obviously displeased with the presence of any windblown, unescorted female. His nostrils flared. "Your uncle, you say? Whatever. Yes, Chuck Elliot is behind the bar tonight. But not for long. You can wait for him outside."

"I'd like to see him now." She looked straight into the man's pale stare.

He wavered. "Come in, of course, if you like. But the manager is about to throw that woman out so I'm quite sure he'll go, too." The maitre d' turned back inside and she followed.

Heart racing, Lelia stood a moment studying the amber-lit dining room, a sea of linen-covered tables occupied mostly by men in dress uniform perfection. At the sudden piano dischord from the low stage, the muted hum of conversation and discreet clink of china stopped. A petite woman wearing a red dress stood at the baby grand, spinning sheet music across its polished top.

"Fascinatin' Hazel" was obviously having a silent tantrum. From the polished wood bar in the back, two bartenders watched the angry pantomime across the room. Lelia made her way toward them. The white-haired one gazed with impassive amusement, the younger one watched with pained attention, arms folded over a solid chest. When Lelia reached him, her voice came out a whisper.

"Chuck Elliot?"

He turned, still frowning and distracted.

Had her father looked anything like this man, now in his forties, close-cropped blond hair turning gray? A handsome, solidly built man, his square jaw set. Hearing his name repeated, he stared back with pale blue eyes.

"Yes?"

"My name is Lelia Elliot."

"Elliot? You don't say. What's that supposed to mean?"

"My father was Lee Elliot. I believe that makes you my uncle." She smiled into his frown and waited.

"Lee's dead. My brother's been dead – a long time."

"I know. My mother is too. I grew up with her family."

The man's gaze widened. As quickly, his attention swung back across the dining room. Moving toward them past bemused diners was Fascinatin' Hazel, a sassy movement in red. Like a tiny, brittle-boned bird in sleek plumage, Lelia thought. And she'll have long red claws.

Hazel stopped in front of them, teetering on chunky high heels. Under mascaraed eyelashes, gray-green eyes flashed from one to the other. The cigarette-husky voice demanded, "What's going on here?" Anger seemed to infuse the heavy scent of Evening in Paris perfume.

Chuck came from behind the bar. "Says she's a daughter of Lee's."

"Little brother Lee? Who said?" Hazel's spiky black lashes widened. "Well, what do you know! A lean, curvy beauty in a little-girl dress and a crazy mop of hair shows up and calls you 'uncle' and we gotta believe it? Well, pull the pot right out from under me without warning. What are you after, kiddo?"

"First, to find you."

Chuck looked uncertain. Hazel leaned back against the bar, her piano pose, red lips working into a smile.

"What about them marbles! Chuck, what if brother did plant a kid in that bride he took home? He couldn't have known it happened cause he got himself drowned on his honeymoon, didn't you tell me? Men are real careless bastards, aren't they, honey? Or have you found that out yet? You look kind of innocent."

Chuck frowned across the dining room. "What's this rhubarb with the manager? He's mad as hell up there looking at your mess."

"Let him clean it up." Her tiny nostrils flared. "We're getting out. I'm not about to sit up there and tinkle out Stephen Foster ditties like a Victrola record. Hell no. I've had enough of watching old fogies and snotty officers chew. I'd rather go back to Grouper Hole and play for sunburned asshole tourists."

"If Bubba will take us back. You told him off with some finality. You're the one who had us marching out."

"Ssoo? We'll march right back in. A tacky three-room trailer in the Cove is better than a tacky two-room dump in this town anyway . . . Cripes, here comes Mr. High and Mighty – let's cut out."

Chuck saluted his fellow bartender and followed Hazel's retreat from the dining room, grabbing up her sign at the door and nodding for Lelia to follow. Don't worry, I'm not going to lose you, she thought. Together they trailed down the corridor behind Hazel, the bare shoulders tensed but the red satin hips wiggling past startled old ladies in their straight-backed chairs.

Outside the hotel, against indigo sky and bay, the three of them paused, silent, until Hazel demanded, "Well, are we going home or what?"

"We've got to see what she plans to do here, Haz."

Lelia said quickly, "I came to find you and the house on the beach. This one." She pulled the old photograph from the satchel.

Hazel sputtered, "The house! Lemme see." She stared at the picture in the bluish light. "Gad! It sure as hell is. Same picture we have, Chuck baby. Look! This girl must not be whistling Dixie – she's a niece, get it, who wants her hands on that house." She turned to Lelia. "Listen, Honeychile, you're looking at the only Elliots left, and we don't live there. She does – the Spook."

Chuck groaned. "Let's not get into that tonight, Haz."

"Who lives there?" Lelia asked.

"The devil, as far as I'm concerned." Hazel's husky voice held venom. "Once, Kali was the housekeeper – until the lady of the house got drowned before her time, you might say."

The lady of the house – that would mean Lee Elliot's mother, her grandmother, Lelia thought. Drowned, yes. She knew that much.

"This Kali," Hazel said, "killed or ran everybody else away years ago when Chuckie here was just out of rompers. All the years since, Kali sits over there, dog in the manger, claiming the place is hers, not even letting us get inside the door to talk."

"Dammit," Chuck muttered. "Do we stand here all night?"

"She'll let me in," Lelia said quietly.

"Oh, yeah? You think so, huh?" Hazel looked interested. "What makes you so sure, Kiddo?"

"I came here to see that house – so I know I will."

Hazel considered that a moment. "That right, huh? Chuck baby, where are your uncle manners? Go get the car. Let's take this niece of yours home to Indian Rocks."

"We don't have any room, Lelia," Chuck said. "But sure, of course, you can come home with us tonight. Where did you think you were going anyway? Wait here, I'll get the car." He jogged off, the Fascinatin' Hazel sign riding under his arm.

When he was gone, Hazel's cat-eyes studied Lelia. "You must be some kind of innocent, hauling off, coming here like this. Innocent and young. What are you, twenty something? Gawd, to have those lashes and that skin – but that's beside the point. Let's lay it on the line, okay? What are you doing here? To get your hands on that beach front property? It's going to be worth something after the war, you must know that."

"I'm not here about property. I need to know about the Elliots – everything about the family."

"Yeah? You don't look like you're lying, Kiddo. So I'm taking you home. But let's get something straight. Help works both ways, I'll tell you what I know about the Elliots, and you help me get into that house so I can get Kali OUT. But you remember this, Honeychile, that property is mine. I mean Chuck's and mine. Don't you ever forget it."

PINEY COVE PARK
May 3, 1945

5

Hazel was a coiled spring of a woman, but Hazel was about to tell Lelia what she'd waited a lifetime to hear – who were the Elliots and what had happened to them.

Chuck drove up in an old blue Nash. Lelia sank willingly into the back seat, too tired and hungry to be impatient now, even when Hazel plopped in front and demanded they drive out to the Pier.

"Don't tell me about empty tanks and ration tickets, Chuckie baby. I'm starving. I want a Coney Island with sauerkraut."

The moon was out as Chuck turned off the bayfront boulevard and drove down the long approach that extended into the bay waters. Squatting at the end was a large two-storied pavilion. At the side, a serve-through window released aromas of roasting wieners and popcorn into the balmy night air.

Chuck turned around, explaining the dark pier. "Blackout. At the beach, you don't turn headlights toward the gulf."

Hazel sniggered. "They think Germans are sneaking around out there in the gulf. U-boats. Imagine!"

"So I heard."

In the dark back seat, Lelia listened to Hazel's tirade against the Vinoy and Chuck's wry condolences as they waited for the food. What a curiosity this pair would make back in Bethel. Hazel would be figured as a flamboyant hussy from a carnival show; Chuck would be suspect because an educated bartender with such dry humor wouldn't fit into any Bethel mold at all.

The whole place here was different. Along the dark seawall fishermen made content silhouettes against silvery waters. Inside the lighted pavilion, gray-haired people bent over their table games like serious children. And the air – soft on her face, lazy as the rhythmic lap of water against the pilings. She thought of Tingley's talk about Florida being a "land of promise" for post-war dreams. Maybe balmy air like this let you imagine something better could happen here, if not tomorrow – then maybe some other tomorrow.

The old question flared like a forgotten pain. Did she have a future? That's why she was here. To find out.

"Hey in the back seat! You going to sleep on us? We ordered you a Coney. Uncle Chuck here is a big spender."

They ate the hot, fragrant food in silence except for Hazel's happy little moans. As Chuck started the Nash, Hazel lit a cigarette and turned around.

"Okay, we're taking you home, Honeychile, but don't say I didn't warn you – home sweet home is a tacky little trailer."

"Piney Cove," Chuck said stiffly. "It's a trailer park on the mainland side of the bay next to Grouper Hole, where we work. That is, if Bubba takes us back."

"The dump where we work," Hazel said, sounding grieved. "A waterfront hangout full of smart-ass soldier boys. But this girl wants to know about the house, doncha, Kid? Well, from Grouper Hole you can look right across the bay to the beach. And down that beach, hidden in a bunch of trees, is a big, fancy place where she lives like the queen of the Spooks – in the house that ought to be ours."

"Can't that wait, Haz?" Chuck sighed.

Hazel exhaled smoke and impatience. "Chuck gets stuffy as hell when I mention the family skeletons – one of which, did you know, happens to be buried in the front yard of that house." Kicking off the red shoes, she curled up in the seat.

Tell me, Lelia thought. Tell me all of it.

For moments there was no sound but the cooler night

wind blowing in, whipping their faces. They left low buildings behind, but the wide brick street stretching west took them past an occasional gabled bungalow and stands of ragged palm trees. A lone car passed, the flash of yellow headlights outlining Hazel's sharp pensive profile.

A picture flashed in Lelia's mind showing her a thin, hungry child, sitting on a doorstep. The image faded but the impression stayed. This small-boned, husky-voiced woman had been that child. Tight red dresses and arched eyebrows and that topknot of curls were camouflage. Underneath was still that hunger, hardened into determination.

Hazel peered into the back seat. "You been in some snooty southern town all your life? In some big fine house I bet, not on my side of the tracks from the way you talk. And you never knew a thing about the Elliots?"

"Nothing." Nothing she could dare mention now. To break the tension between the two in the front seat, Lelia said, "Will I see the gulf tonight?"

Chuck answered quickly, "No. This Central Avenue goes straight west toward the gulf, but we're further north. We follow the mainland up through orange grove country. We're on the bayside up there. Indian Rocks, no rocks though, no Indians."

"Bayside or gulfside – it's all the boonies where you can still get away with murder," Hazel said. "You might as well know the risks, Kiddo."

"Past or current?" Chuck sounded grim.

"You're still worried about what happened to that little snit Susie?" Anger crackled in the husky voice. "Even if Susie winds up as fish bait like that Boston girl, I don't care. You know damn well what I mean about warnings. Lelia here came to find out about her daddy, so she'd better know what's happened to the Elliots. She has to know about Kali."

"Haz –" But Chuck leaned into his steering wheel, giving up the protest.

"I don't even know the names of those people in the picture," Lelia said quickly. "It was in my mother's things." So tell me, Hazel.

"Your mother died right after having you? Must not be healthy being married to an Elliot." Hazel whooped and punched Chuck in the ribs, but he didn't take his eyes off the road. "Well, I'm going to tell your Alabamy niece here some family secrets, so don't stop me. If she's Lee's kid, and an Elliot, she deserves to know about your family."

Hazel curled up in the front seat and tapped red nails on the back of the seat. "That picture you showed us? Made for the St. Pete *Times* society page. The boo-ti-ful couple, Bonnie and Don Elliot, of Indian Rocks, St. Pete, and Canada."

A street car rattled past, soldiers hanging out of the windows, shouting, singing in the night. Waiting, Hazel drummed her fingers, the long red nails like claws on the small hands. When the noisy trolley passed, she continued.

"We had an old brown copy of the same picture. The kid standing by the handsome young papa is Chucky boy here. Curled in pretty mama's lap is baby brother Lee. That makes Don and Bonnie, the famous Don and Bonnie, your grandparents."

As real as Cornelia and Otis Calhoun of Bethel. Those proper, disapproving faces still haunted Lelia in their own way. "Yes, I'm listening. Go ahead."

"Bonnie Elliot's father, Janus Sinclair, built that big house out there on the gulf as a wedding present for darling daughter." The husky voice turned wistful. "Some kind of wedding gift, huh? But this Janus was a filthy rich old buzzard from Montreal. He'd always given Bonnie everything she wanted."

Chuck interrupted. "He was one of the men who brought a spur of railroad into the mainland near Indian Rocks. It's not there now."

"Yeah," Hazel said. "He's the one I'd like to have known – with gumption about making money. Anyway, he built daughter a house as big and fancy as the best in town. Folks thought that was crazy since the beaches were just sand keys in those days, with nothing but cabins and birds out there. Mainlanders called it Hurricane House."

"Hurricane House? Why?"

"Old-timers figured the first blow would take it down.

When a big storm did come, it only built up more beach. So the house is still there, fifty years later, about the fanciest thing anywhere on that gulf front. Not that you can see it now. It sits in a bunch of palms and pines all grown up like a jungle."

"What happened to Don and Bonnie?" Lelia braced for the answer as Hazel's voice went on, wistful again, like the hungry child repeating the fairy story of the princess she envied.

"Bonnie and Don, gad, were just in their twenties, very social in town when they were there, that is. This was a rich girl who really liked to go places. I know because old timers have told me. I mean to New York or San Francisco or a ship to Paris because she could speak French. Can't you just see it? She wasn't about to stay parked in that house daddy built, way out in the beach boonies, having kids."

Another streetcar rattled past, heading back to town. Hazel took an impatient draw on a fresh cigarette. "From San Francisco, they came back with a couple of girls to look after sonny boy here. One of them stayed. A real heathen mind you –."

"Hawaiian, Haz," Chuck said.

"Well, natives, same thing. Anyway, from some island where they probably dance naked and chant funny things. That stuff may be showtime for tourists, but it ain't Christian so it's black magic in my book. My daddy was a hard-drinking coot, but he taught me that." She sighed.

"Anyway, when I was so rudely interrupted, I was saying this Hawaiian girl was hired to look after sonny boy here. You were about three then, weren't you, Hon? Now I don't blame Bonnie – I call her that – I don't blame Bonnie for wanting to go places. Lord knows she could afford all the servants she wanted, any color."

Hazel glanced at Chuck's grim profile but continued. "Bonnie and Don kept taking off, to Europe even, leaving that Hawaiian girl in charge of everything. Maylene, folks around the waterfront thought her name was, or maybe that was the one who went back to Hawaii, but then some old Swami type fellow showed up, some kind of foreigner, asking for Kali. He wrote down K-A-L-I when he asked. It means something awful. I looked it up once."

Chuck interrupted as the Nash turned off the wide street onto a curving brick road. "This is Park Street. Big place is Jungle Prada Hotel. A year ago, the Army put up a tent city around here. Had 15,000 men camping there."

Hazel tossed her cigarette into the night. "About that picture you have – when your daddy was born, that newspaper announced the young Elliots had themselves another baby. And of course, that old Spook Kali was still there to look after the house and both kids when they traveled. Well, back then of course she would have been a young Spook, but don't they get meaner with time – any kind of heathen hexers? Anyway, she killed Bonnie soon after."

"Haz, I don't care to hear this," Chuck said quietly.

"Okay, your mother drowned, but not of her own choosing buddy boy, and not facing that fact doesn't change a damn thing. Well, as I was about to say when I was interrupted, Chuck here was four and Lee was still a baby when it happened. Bonnie washed up right on the beach, all entangled in something."

"Seaweed?"

"You guessed it. Doesn't it give you the creeps? An old fisherman found her and ran off to get Doc Miller – he was the doc on the beach then so I know that story's true. Ask anybody."

"Why do you think she was murdered?"

Hazel snorted. "Here she was, rich with this doting daddy and a handsome husband who'd follow her off whenever she took a notion to go. Everything in the world a girl could want, right? And she didn't even like the water or boats unless it was first class on the *Queen Mary*."

"Walsingham Road," Chuck murmured. "If the tank goes dry, we can walk from here."

With an annoyed look at Chuck, Hazel continued, "They buried Bonnie right in front of that house, back from the beach. We know that for sure because Chuck remembers watching from an upstairs window. Baby brother in the house bawling. I add that part because it figures. Chuck, don't look like that! Lelia wants to know how it was."

The road narrowed now, passing thick tropical growth on both sides. Hazel sighed and went on, "Chuck was this little kid watching his daddy and this Kali throwing bougainvillea on the grave, mind you. The doctor was there too, this Doc Miller. That's important because he's still around, in St. Pete now, and that means there's still one person who knows the truth, besides Kali."

"Why would he withhold the truth?" Lelia asked.

"Yeah, why? Because Kali must have spooked him as she did everybody else. Don Elliot just up and disappeared. Drove out of town like a wild man, the story goes. Never came back at any rate, not even to see his kids. That really loused up Chuck's view on life. I tell him – you don't know for sure to blame your old man. Maybe Kali hexed him to make him help her do the dirty work. Don Elliot had to run away – stop groaning, Chuck."

Lelia's pulse thudded louder in her ears than the night wind blowing in the car. So the Elliots had been young, rich and restless, but not mad. So madness had been done to them. She waited to feel relief, but it didn't come.

"Hazel – what do you mean 'hexed'?"

"You know – some devilish kind of power that makes people do things the hexer wants them to do. Listen – Bonnie's daddy, old Janus Sinclair, showed up from Canada after Bonnie died and Don went away. He went to the house. Chuck was about five then, but he remembers his granddaddy clear as day. He was sent out of the room so they could talk, his granddaddy and this Kali. From there, did old Janus go to the police? And tell them his darling daughter was dead and buried and his son-in-law had run away leaving two little kids? Did he complain about this Hawaiian girl still there acting like she owned the place? Nope! Kali must have hexed him, too, because – know what he did? Deeded Kali the house and left town!"

"And the boys? The grandfather didn't try to take

the children?"

"Nah, he was pretty old then and you can figure he didn't want to take on any little kids," Hazel said. "But still he didn't bring in the police. So Kali had to have done something weird to old Janus to get him to give her the house and leave Doc Miller money for the kids before he left forever."

Chuck kept his eyes on the road. "He left a trust fund for both of us. We grew up in a boarding school — Florida Military in town."

"That trust fund was no skin off her back," Hazel said. "In fact, it kept them off her back and out of sight except a few summer visits back to that house, which I take it, weren't so happy. Doc Miller handled everything so she must have spooked him, too, for him to stay quiet or else she paid him off. What's important now is that property. Chuck here claims he doesn't want to go near the place, but it's rightfully his — ours — I'm not going to miss out on what's due!"

The doctor must be the one who looked after her mother until Tarrant came for her. Hazel couldn't know anything about what happened to Mary Emily Calhoun in that house — the touch of a dead woman. Did Chuck know? She would have to find out later.

"What about Dr. Miller?"

Hazel drew on a fresh cigarette. "Still in St. Pete, still doctoring matter of fact, at seventy. I have been there. You'd think I was some gold digger off the street — he wouldn't see me. I keep trying. And I made Chuck go with me once to the house. The Spook wouldn't let me in the door. I get so stinking mad I could spit nails! What makes you think she'll let you in?"

"I can't tell you, I just know."

"We're here," Chuck said.

Just ahead, a bridge showed in the moonlight, the bridge to the beach, to the gulfside. But the Nash turned off the narrow brick road onto a sandy drive.

"Piney Cove Trailer Park," Chuck announced. "Further down by the bridge is Grouper Hole where we work. It's the local watering hole for GIs and fly-boys. We still get tourists, too."

"Run by a slob named Bubba," Hazel added. "That is, he's supposed to be running it for his mama. Martha Critten is the old bag who owns it. Maybe we can fix you up with a job there. They need a girl, now that Susie's among the missing."

Chuck frowned. "Forget it. Not a good idea."

The Nash's headlights followed the hard sand road, past silvery metal trailers crouched at random under tall pines and gnarled oaks.

Hazel sounded desolate. "I warned you. And another thing, if you plan to stay around here, you ought to know about the local wildlife. Besides mosquitos and rattlers, we have horny soldiers and fishermen with no last names from God-knows-where. Hey –" the husky voice warmed. "Speaking of waterfront characters, look who I see. Tall, Handsome and Unfriendly."

The Nash's pale headlights caught a lean man in white dungarees and shirt, striding ahead on the sandy path.

Hazel whipped around. "This guy is a loner who lives in a cabin on the bay. Stop frowning, Chuck – she ought to know. Lelia baby, this Gil's the only good-looking male around here who's not over-the-hill or in uniform and heading some place else. That's including Evander Merrill, a fancy movie star who docks his yacht here. But what I'm saying is – steer clear of this one if you want to stay healthy."

"Hold it, Haz," Chuck protested as the car rolled to a stop under the pine trees. "The man's only been here three months. You don't know a damn thing for sure. That's gossip."

"I know what I know. Gil's got to be a Section Eight." She pointed to her head and made little circles.

"I've told you, Haz, it's a man's own business why he's in or out of uniform."

"Par-don me. Lelia, your uncle is real touchy about not being a war hero. Okay – calm down, lover."

Chuck turned off the chugging motor and stuck his head out. "Hey, Gil, wait up!"

"What did you do that for?" Hazel fumed, fumbling

around for her shoes.

"Gil will know how things are going at Grouper Hole." Chuck slammed the door and walked toward the man who turned and waited in the spotty moonlight.

Lelia didn't move. She sat looking at this strange place where she had landed, a windy grove smelling of pine and palms. She sorted impressions as Hazel poked at the wispy hair loosened from the topknot and fussed about this Gil. The lean man with tousled sandy hair stood out there with a lazy grace. But Lelia saw the tense shoulders. He was a loner. She knew all about being a loner. "Don't worry," she murmured. "I didn't come here for that."

Hazel got out of the car, shoes in each hand, waving one toward the nearest trailer. "This is it. You're looking at the Elliots' lil' cabin door." The sarcasm was edged with sadness. "Well, you coming?"

"Coming." She stayed a moment longer in the dark shadows, breathing in sea smells and pine. Hazel minced on across the straw in her stocking feet and tight red dress, swinging the shoes at mosquitos and groaning, "Damn, they love my body," until she reached the two men and struck a pose in front of Gil. "Calling on the folks of Piney Cove?"

"Gil's telling me the bar's a mess over there," Chuck said.

"So what's new?" Hazel said, eyebrows arched, hand on the red hip.

As Lelia took a deep breath and moved from the shadows toward them, Gil was saying, "Sure, Bubba needs you back. Not that the poor slob will admit it —" He stopped, as though startled, to stare at Lelia, even as he muttered, "What are you doing here?"

"Hey! Is that po-lite?" Hazel fumed. "This is Chuck's niece come to visit. But don't let it be anything to you."

"Sorry. Of course. Sorry."

His eyes were cold blue picking up the light yet the gaze reached into her like heat. In that moment, there was no reality but the breeze stirring leaves and this man, planted in her path here, like a challenge she didn't want.

"I'm Lelia Elliot – and why are you here?"

"Yeah," Hazel purred nastily, "we never do catch your last name."

Gil looked away toward the dark woods then back with a wry smile. "Hello, Lelia Elliot. You surprised me for a moment. You must forgive me."

The odd moment was over. His easy baritone resumed, bemused, as he talked about Grouper Hole.

"Golly-gee," Hazel interrupted, "thanks for the news. Now if you've stared long enough at the visiting relative, we have to re-tire to the family mansion here."

"I'm going," Gil said, looking at Lelia.

He touched her arm, a gesture of apology, but it reached into her, nothing like Bo's hot, sweaty grasp or Tarrant's cold grip.

With a curt nod to the three of them, Gil turned and stalked away into the grove of trees. As Chuck went back to the car, Hazel said, "What did I tell you? Handsome dude like that – but he gives me the heebie-jeebies."

"What does Section Eight mean?"

"Don't you know? That's when a guy gets out of the service by going bananas. We see them at Grouper Hole all the time, from the hospital on the beach, the Don CeSar, a fancy hotel before the war. They act real quiet – they don't go around telling anybody they've been looney. Natch, I'd keep my mouth shut, too. Still it figures. Why else would a man like that – a healthy-looking, educated fellow – must be under thirty – why would he be working around this old waterfront with the war still going on? Why would he be living in a cabin down on the bay and acting like a clam?"

"What does he do?"

"Fishing guide. Calls his boat the *Strike*. Does water taxi work for the movie star's yacht sometimes."

Chuck came back, suitcase under one arm, the Fascinatin' Hazel sign under the other. He kicked open the trailer's stuck screen door. "Cut the gossip, Haz. Let's find Lelia a place to sleep."

"Didn't you see what was going on just now? Wolves

always smell fresh meat, even the ones in fishermen's clothing. Well, Honeychile, what are you waiting on? Come on in, if you're going to."

Chuck disappeared into a bedroom at one end of the trailer. Lelia followed Hazel into the tiny closet room, slinky gowns and bright dresses hung on a line stretched across the small space, towels dumped in a corner. But the room had a cot and the transom window let in the piney breeze.

Hazel stood in the doorway, the husky voice tired, mouth thin and pale without its red lipstick. She snapped out instructions.

"We're not taking in free boarders, understand? But I'll do for you if you do for me, remember that. Tomorrow you bury that dumb hot dress you're wearing. See these pastel cottons bunched to one end of the line? You can have them. Chuck bought the whole lot from some traveling salesman. He should have known they're not my type. Too long. I've got good legs. So there. The shower and john's outside, a community thing. Don't worry. It's private. I'm telling you all this now because don't expect me mornings until you see me moving."

Later, stretched in her slip on the cot, listening to pine boughs sigh against the metal trailer, images swirled behind Lelia's eyes. The loner Gil's face burned again through her fatigue. Morris Alderman had looked at her with that same bitter recognition thinking of his dead daughter. She must forget them both.

The Bonnie she heard about tonight – the grandmother, murdered as a young woman – had she become the Seaweed Woman who frightened Mary Emily? Had Bonnie whispered somehow from the grave into her mind when she'd been that frightened, lonely child in Bethel? Then and later, the woman who called to her from the dream shore – was this Bonnie, too?

Lelia drew in a breath of balmy night air to clear her mind. Hadn't she always believed her dead grandmother – or whatever Bonnie had become – was a benevolent energy? Not an evil one. Now thinking of Hazel's story she had to wonder: Did Bonnie draw me here to do vengeance on her murderer? Has this been waiting for me? Is this the mark? Vengeance as a legacy? Whatever was the truth, she had to find out. Not to know had never been an answer.

INDIAN ROCKS
May 4, 1945

6

In pale dawn light, Lelia dared open her eyes to see what whispered and moved overhead. Shadowy forms weaved and sighed like disembodied dancers. Hazel's costumes, yes, hanging across the room, stirred by the faint breeze. The sighs came from pine boughs outside. She was in a trailer, in Florida, minutes away from the open gulf shore.

She sprang up in the slip she'd slept in and looked at the crumpled navy dress. It didn't matter. The cluttered room didn't matter. This first day waited like a package to be torn open. Hazel had offered the cotton dresses hanging there with the sassy costumes. Plucking one from the line and wrapped in a towel from the heap in the corner, she slipped out of the silent trailer and headed for the grove. In the dank bathhouse, shower stalls smelled of sulphur but the rusty pipes released cool water like a baptism into a new world, fecund and natural.

She pulled on the yellow cotton dress and looking in the bathhouse's cracked mirror blinked at someone Bethel didn't know. Not that quiet Lelia in dresses severe as the old head librarian's. This pale yellow might have been a summer nightgown except for the petticoat lining. So soft, it took the sash to give it shape. No, her body did – as it had for the Bethel girls who wore batiste and voile with ribbons in their hair, floating around summer lawns at ice cream suppers like butterflies, pretending to be unaware how soft pale fabric shaped high young breasts. On this humid morning in a

Florida grove, she was grateful for Hazel's thin cottons.

When she came out to towel her hair, the sky had turned pink and blue high above pine branches. A welcomed breeze moved over her skin like a caress. She knew, for an exquisite moment, how it felt to be totally alive, maybe like the bird up there, no past to regret, no future to fear.

The breeze had a salty smell. The bay was close and beyond the bridge would be the Gulf of Mexico and the Elliot house. Hurricane House, Hazel called it, warning her not to go "nosing around." Quietly, not to arouse Chuck or Hazel, Lelia left the rolled towel and brush on the stoop and headed down Piney Cove's sandy drive past the silver trailers. The parked Nash brought back the memory of last night of Gil. The look of sudden consternation on his face, so quickly covered up with an ice cold stare. She blanked him out.

The path led out to the narrow brick road. Spotted with early sun and shade now, it led straight to the bridge ahead.

Someone was walking toward her, a barrel-chested, slim-hipped man, hands deep in his pockets, head down. Chuck Elliot. He looked up, called out, and picked up his pace, reluctantly, Lelia thought, but she waited, studying this uncle who was the last of the Elliots. A man with a wry smile and unhappy eyes. A defense against what? Bitterness for not being in the war as Hazel had said? Or haunted by whatever happened to his family? Last night he had listened in tight-jawed silence as Hazel told about his mother being drowned and his father running away. Or did Chuck know more than Hazel?

Her arrival must have upset him. But why? To have someone besides his bossy wife wanting to go back to that house, expecting him to do something about it?

When he reached her, the smile was genuine, the eyes curious. "Surprise niece. Lee's daughter. I still can't get used to it. You're out early."

"And you. I didn't want to wake anyone."

"Hazel doesn't show her face till noon when she puts on the war paint. I get out early and walk down to the groves and back. Talk to myself. I'm an excellent monologist, inclined to be masochistic, but who's to know?" The grin faded. "This time I kept wondering if I'd dreamed that a beautiful young female showed up last night and announced kinship. Lelia Elliot." He ran fingers through the close cropped curls that defied a crew-cut. "Damn if I don't recognize the amber eyes — Lee's, I guess. Shakes me up. So tell me, what are you up to?"

She'd have to be patient to learn what he knew. "Right now? Wanting to see where I am." She looked around at this new kind of morning with its bay smells and the hum of motor boats churning under the bridge ahead. "I've only read about seashores, never seen one." Only dreamed of this one.

"So I'll show you." He seemed relieved she hadn't mentioned Hurricane House. "Those boats you hear are commercial fishermen. Let's go watch — just don't listen to the language. Ready?"

As they walked toward the bridge, "So Hazel dumped all of those dresses on you? That's fine, I'm glad. Wrong type for Hazel — I should have known. She likes to think of herself as a satin doll, God knows, not sweetly innocent."

She knew he wondered if she were sweetly innocent.

"With that long hair of yours, Lelia, and those — that little waist — you look like something out of *Midsummer's Night Dream*. Damn — I can't get over it. Lee's daughter. But then he was a handsome guy, moody —"

"Tell me more about him." How could he blame her for asking that?

"Sure, you'll want to know." His square jaw tightened. "We'll talk about that sometime. Right now, I'm showing you this old waterfront. I warn you, it's not anything like a good white-washed Alabama town."

A low wood building hugged the brick road to the left. The weathered sign on the top said GROUPER HOLE RESTAURANT AND BAR. Chuck paused. "Here's the dump where we work as Haz puts it. Early morning like this, it looks like an old sea turtle crawled down to the bay."

"Are you going to see this Bubba?"

"He won't be awake yet. Fellow's a pain in the a - - neck, but he generally hides when there's work to be done. Which keeps the bartender busy."

"That's you. And Hazel?" They stood a moment longer by the low, weathered building.

"I'm not complaining. Work has its therapeutic advantage." The wry smile flickered. "Hazel does her thing at night at the piano. Keeps her happy, sort of."

"Do you hate it here, Chuck?"

He looked surprised. "No. I grew up in town at school but spent summers on this waterfront. The place pulled me back in spite of everything. Grouper Hole is a job. Actually, it's more than a dump. Call it an important watering hole and gathering place for the local characters. Not to mention our uniformed boys on weekend pass. Fly-boys from Tampa. Coast Guard fellows. A mix of locals and the sandy crowd. That's what I call town folks who come out to the swim pavilion across the bridge."

She followed him onto the wooden bridge. Chuck showed no intention of walking across to the beach side. He leaned against the wooden railing, expecting her to do the same. A huge gray bird settled down a few feet from them.

"Pelican," Chuck said, "graceful in flight, awkward things touching down."

Beyond the narrow channel of greenish bay, the gulf beach showed as a long, horizontal silhouette held down by the expanse of pale morning sky. She wanted only to go to the gulf, but she had to be patient with this man. And yes, she had to know everything about this waterfront as well as the Elliot house. With Chuck, she leaned against the railing, looking down on Grouper Hole's back screened porch as he explained this was the dining room. A narrow dock extending out into the bay was empty now except for pelicans. All the motor boats sputtering up the channel were going under the bridge, under their feet, to the other side of the bayside embankment.

"That's the dining porch down there. You plan to stay around, Lelia?"

"Yes."

"Then you need to know about this waterfront even

before you go hunting that house over on the gulf. I'm not accustomed to this uncle business but I know it means there are certain warnings I have to pass on."

Chuck rubbed his jaw and fell silent. They watched two more motor boats slow and disappear under the bridge to the docks on the other side before he said, "Under this bridge six months ago, they found a dead girl. Boston deb, turned out. A tourist. Here to meet some Navy boyfriend."

"I know. I heard her father talking on the train."

"Yeah? There's more." He nodded again to Grouper Hole's screened back porch below. "A local girl, skinny little spitfire named Susie worked down there, bar girl and food girl for old Bubba and his mama. And me. Susie's been among the missing for a couple of weeks now."

"So what are you trying to tell me?"

"I hope she's hiding out. She has reasons. Susie shot at some lieutenant-lover in town. Missed but his wife walked in, and Susie ran and the sheriff is looking for her."

"Why are you warning me?"

"I'm saying soldier boys on weekend pass all look the same and that's the danger. Especially for someone who looks like you. Gad – this is tough, this uncle business. But trust me. There are other native characters around here, too, who probably haven't seen anything like you except in their dreams. They're the ones you hear roaring in under this bridge right now, to Al's Bait House on the other side. Take a look."

They crossed to the opposite railing and looked down. The wide dock extended from a weathered shack clinging to the embankment. Motor boats bobbed there. A dozen grizzled, sun-leathered men ambled around on the dock.

"Big Al's Bait House," Chuck said. "Commercial fishermen down there. They'll hang around long enough to drink lousy coffee, swap lies, and buy bait before heading out to the gulf."

The bridge rumbled under their feet. From the beach side, a car was rolling across, noisy against the planking, passing them, pulling off the brick road to park under the trees above Al's Bait House. Two men got out with shiny fishing poles, white knees showing under their baggy shorts. They headed down the slope to the bait house dock.

"Tourists," Chuck said, grinning. "We still get those, too. Usually they're here to visit sons. We even have a movie star, the one Hazel told you about who comes in like a grand duke aboard his custom-made yacht. But we're looking at the local wildlife now."

He nodded to the dock below. "These fishermen are tough old salts. Some are not so old. Hazel calls them no-last-name-Joes, meaning they've skipped out from someplace else from stuffy jobs or bitchy wives or the hometown draft board. Who knows? It's their business."

"The two old fellows sitting on the crates?"

Chuck grinned. "The scrawny one in the yellowed captain's hat – that's Cap'n. Picks up gossip and dispenses it like an old woman. Hangs out at my bar. The big one hunched there next to Cap'n like an old buzzard is his crony, Skipper. Both of those old water rats are among my most faithful clientele. They keep me humble."

Lelia looked down at the men prowling the dock, each with a hand wrapped around a blue tin mug of coffee. Images came of how they must live in some bayshore cabin, rolling out of a bare cot in predawn darkness to squint into a cracked mirror at a stubble beard, pull on yesterday's pants. The picture faded. Had one of these fishermen killed the Alderman girl?

"Look at that," Chuck said. "Our two tourists – proud city fellows that they are – are right now foot-shuffling foreigners trying to confront the natives in their own habitat. Watch. They'll be ignored until Big Al comes out to the rescue."

With the boats silent now, the fishermen's growling and guffawing rose up to them on the cool morning air. Lelia shushed Chuck.

"I'd like to listen." She knew how to listen well.

On the dock below, the chubby-faced tourist repeated his question. "Ah, what kind of bait you folks recommend this morning?"

"Bet Tiny has somethin' for you soon's he finishes his coffee." Cap'n asked with a crackle. "Doncha, you big palooka?"

"Aw, AWW!" A hulking fisherman dug a finger into his coffee mug and looked around. "Which one you sonnabitches put a roach in my coffee agin? Aww, Cap'n, you ain't gonna grow up if you live to be a hunnard."

"Hope not. Ain't that right, Skipper?"

"You already a hunnard and five," from the solemn-faced crony.

The impatient tourist spoke up. "Is anything biting around here this morning besides the mosquitos?"

"Bobby Earl can tell you about a lil' old gal in Crystal River does a pretty good job of bitin' but he can't show the scar, can you Bobby Earl?"

A big red-faced man ducked out of the bait house and pitched smelly water into the bay.

"I'm Al. What can I do for you gentl'men?"

The two tourists grumbled their questions.

"Good idea. Take on breakfast first. Fellows, you heard about old Conch's cooking. You wouldn't forget his smoked mullet or crab cakes either. That's Grouper Hole, opposite side of the bridge here."

"Well, they didn't look open when we came by."

"Won't be until you see Conch going in the kitchen door. Bubba runs the place and he's gotten mighty independent lately, hasn't he, boys? Takes his time about opening up since he's been getting the Hollywood trade."

"Hollywood?"

"Evander Merrill. A big movie star, matinee idol they told me," Al said. "Docks his yacht, the *Silver Fox*, over there real often. Don't ask me about movie romeos, but I can tell you that 62-foot Chris-Craft looks like the *Queen Mary* in this bay."

Both tourists laughed, their charity and self-image restored. "Why indeed should one special customer slow down an operation?"

"Does for Bubba. When that yacht docks over there, it draws women like flies, from town, the Inn and beach cottages. Bubba has to put out lunch now, not just crab cakes to go with the booze."

Cap'n slapped his knee. "They got Conch making itty-bitty sandwiches. Wimmen show up ever time they hear Old Handsome's gonna be comin' in."

Al nodded. "You ask these two old farts anything you want to know around here. Cap'n and Skipper claim to be mullet fishermen. Mostly they hang out over there watching the action."

"Don't you folks realize?" The chubby-faced tourist was addressing every man on the dock. "After the war you'll have more tourists than you've ever seen? If you're ready for them. If you want any progress here. This Bubba person – doesn't he want to make money?"

"Mebbe. You have to know Bubba."

"Naw. You hafta know his mama," Skipper drawled. "Martha Critten owns the place."

"And lordee, that woman sure likes money."

"Betcha the old gal's made more bucks off Uncle Sam than a couple of smart fellows put together."

The chubby tourist wanted to know, "Is she the local, ah, female hermit, one hears about?"

"Naw." Cap'n again. "Martha's no hermit. She's an old belle of the ball once she gets behind the bar."

"He means Kali," a fisherman droned.

Big Al's voice boomed up from the dock. "We got us what you call a re-cluse. See that large strand of trees over there? With a dock on the bay? A big place inside that green. Hurricane House, people call it. Owners disappeared way back. That's Kali you've heard about. She's the local hermit. Knows how to set good crab traps though. We leave her be."

Cap'n explained. "Folks come around asking to buy that house now and then, but they can't. Even that movie star fellow wanted to. But Kali won't let anybody come near. Maybe she's got more dead bodies over there."

"Aw now, Cap'n." Al looked at his two customers. "If you want, go over and have your breakfast. When the *Strike* hauls in, I'll set you up with a fishing trip this morning. Gil's an independent cuss, but he'll look after you fellows."

"Just don't introduce him to any pretty daughters," Cap'n jumped up and slapped his leg with glee.

Lelia looked over at Chuck leaning on the railing. "The man we met last night. Is he one of these fishermen? He didn't seem to be."

"Gil? He's been here three months, works for the yacht and as fishing guide for tourists. Those whites he wears look like Navy issue, without insignia, of course." He studied her, lines creasing his tanned forehead. "Hazel has decided he's Section Eight. We don't know that he is. You don't go around explaining trouble like that. If the guy is putting himself back together by hard work in the gulf sun, that's his business. Just stay clear of him, okay? That is if you do intend to stay around here."

"Chuck, do you know how long I've wanted to find some Elliots – and this place?"

"And what you've found is the last remaining adult male in this ill-fated family. Poor as the next beach bartender. Which brings up a point. If you do stay, you'll need a job in town. That's the reality."

"I intend to. Don't worry. I can run a library or teach. But I want to stay here, not in town."

"Great. And I can lecture on the Renaissance. An unfinished thesis gathers dust under the bed at this moment. But I tend bar at Grouper Hole. What could you do here?"

"Work with you at Grouper Hole. In Susie's place."

"No. Lelia, it's not for you, running food for a bunch of tourists and loud-mouthed GIs. You wouldn't like it."

She looked out toward the beach. Further down, the dark patch of green had to be the jungle that hid Hurricane House. So close. Waiting. But this morning was about step one, getting a job so she could stay this close.

"There goes Conch." Chuck said, looking back toward

the brick road. "Come on. I promise you the best breakfast on this old Florida west coast."

"And a talk with Bubba?"

"That, too." He pretended to groan. "Let's go."

GROUPER HOLE BAR
May 4, 1945

7

A side driveway led off the brick road around to Grouper Hole's front. Beyond the sun-bright sandy lot, scraggly palms continued along the shore. Senses alive to this new place, Lelia stood looking at the glittering bay beyond the dock. Peaceful as it was here, some message prickled her arms. The notion gave way to eagerness to go inside, meet this Bubba and get the job.

"Ready for this?" Chuck waited at the screened porch door.

Past the pool table, they entered a large pine-walled room that smelled of last night's beer and smoke. In contrast to the dark barroom, another screened porch, the dining room, was bright with morning sun from the bay.

"'Bout time you showed up – who's she?" The high-pitched voice with a whine belonged to the fleshy man, about thirty-five, who stood there blinking at them. He held a tray of food braced against his aproned belly.

"Bubba, my good man, you're staring at my niece. Lelia Elliot arrived on our shores from Alabama last night. I was surprised, too. Hey, you're spilling your biscuits."

Bubba grabbed the tray closer to the khaki apron. The round, moist face looked her over.

"Hold on," he said and stomped out to the dining porch where the two tourists from Al's Bait House waited.

Chuck grinned. "Hazel warned you."

They stood watching Bubba slam down the plates, pull

out a towel, mop his face, stick the towel back into his hip pocket before coming back in from the porch, groaning, to drop into the booth where his breakfast plate waited.

"Damn fool tourists." He began forking in the food. "If they come back looking like boiled lobsters, serves them right. My grits and eggs are getting stone cold. Well, sit, sit." He kept on talking and chewing, the bulging eyes looking up with furtive glances.

Lelia waited until Chuck slipped into the seat before she perched on the edge. How could she stand working for this whining, nervous man? Lounging against the wall, Chuck looked amused, saying, "Bubba hates tourists and all our brave boys in uniform, Lelia."

"Smart-aleck GIs are worse'n tourists." Bubba dunked a biscuit into a puddle of syrup and shoved in a big bite. He smiled, eyes closed, like a man finding comfort. Chewing, Bubba grumbled, "Nothing but trouble 'round here lately. That little bitch Susie gone and people snooping around. Then Hazel getting on her high-horse like that, making you high-tail it off to town. Thought she could play it fancy at the Vinoy, huh. Well, I know you got fired last night. Mama found out."

"Oh, she did? Jesus, it looks like General Patton's troops moved through here." Chuck was looking across the scattered small tables to the long bar that dominated the room. "What did you do, Bubba? Let the high-in-the-sky junior fly-boys help themselves last night?"

"You plum outa your mind? Mama would kill me. Aw, you knew I didn't." At Chuck's grin, Bubba stopped eating to mop his face again.

"Damn your smart ass hide, Chuck. Awright, what you here for, to work or what?"

"Couldn't stay away. Missed your cheerful observations on life. But save them right now. A lady's present."

"You been gone five damn days. If you're just visiting, don't expect no free breakfast."

"Mine host, Bubba, is the soul of hospitality, Lelia, as you can see. We have an inexplicable kind of hospitality. Grouper Hole, where customers seem to interrupt the genteel tenor of days."

"You know what you can do with your fancy words."

Lelia stood. "I'm going to look around."

She moved away annoyed with both of them. Chuck was badgering the man like a smart kid heckling the dumb one. Bubba's bald stare made her think of some animal licking its lips for dinner. His body was like some sulking, intimidated bulldog, straining against his chain. The chain must be his mother from the worried way he quoted her. Maybe Martha Critten had to jerk the chain.

She wandered around the dark, woody room looking at the scarred upright piano in one corner. Hazel's stand probably. A Wurlitzer juke box sat near the front door.

"Don't bother to read the jokes," Chuck called out as she paused by framed and faded cartoons, more dumb than ribald. Khaki and sailor hats seemed to have been flung on the wall and caught there. From a tattered poster, Betty Grable smiled over her shoulder, her bottom scrawled with names. A huge mounted fish arched elegantly against the pine wall.

"That's Moby Flounder." Chuck called out again. Bubba's stare reached her.

She moved on, rubbing her arms, her skin prickly, pulse quickened by the energy she was picking up. Restless male energy maybe, strong as the smell of last night's beer. And some other message? She reasoned, I'm not accustomed to bars. Or being around someone like Bubba. How could she work for a man who watched her with that blinking stare?

"Go ahead, swing on a bar stool," Chuck called out. "It's safe on Friday mornings. The sandy crowd doesn't show till noon. The troops don't take over until eight."

The bar that began near the dining porch opening ran down the side of the darker room. It looked old and fancy as something out of a western movie. Wooden stools and tarnished brass foot rail, a Schlitz clock, like a giant pocket watch, dangling overhead. Behind the working alley, a yellowed mirror ran the length of the bar.

"Time, salt air and smoke does that to it," Chuck called out again, explaining the mirror. "Customers get a mellow view of things. From the working side, I have to look at them – and that's reality."

Lelia swiveled onto a stool. Elbows propped on the dark wood surface, she studied the reflection of the barroom behind her, a fractured view through the array of bottles at the mirror's base. How horrified Tarrant and Adelaide would be at the thought of a Calhoun in such a place and working for that nervous sweaty man. The thought of their dismay made her smile.

In the reflection of room and bottle clutter, something caught her eye. A Mason jar with scrawled label: "The U.S. Armed Forces' Susie Fund." Green bills and coins showed inside. A cheap bracelet, dangling with tiny pink hearts, encircled the jar.

Susie? For an instant, the image of a freckle-faced girl flashed so clearly the face seemed to be looking at her out of the mirror. An urgency in the eyes was a call for help. Susie, whose place she'd be taking? Was it the girl's left-over energy here causing the body message? *Susie, where are you? You did leave. And I do need this job.* In this place, close to Hurricane House and the gulf.

Yes. She meant to work here in spite of Bubba. Or Susie. Or Chuck's reluctance. She swung off the stool and went back to the booth to look into Bubba's moist face. "You need help don't you? I'm ready to go to work."

Bubba managed to grin. "You're mighty right I need help. But you pigeons are trouble."

"Pigeons?"

"Bubba is referring to females, the young and pretty," Chuck said dryly. "The town's daughters flock out here for Mr. Handsome Movie Star's yacht parties and to meet soldiers. Their folks don't like it."

"And Mama don't like them coming out," Bubba mumbled. "You two want some breakfast? Chuck, you go in the kitchen and get it. Conch's in there."

"Wait," Lelia said. "You need someone to work here. And I'm ready. Why don't I start now?" She faced Chuck's scowl.

"Can she handle these Joes, Chuck? Susie could handle

them and look what happened."

"Susie," Lelia repeated. "Tell me about her."

Chuck sighed. "I told you about Susie. She ran away."

"But there's more. You started to tell me."

"Okay. I'll make it brief. Calm down, Bubba. Lelia has to know our little problems – and why the sheriff's department has Brockway showing up around here."

"Go ahead," Lelia said.

"Six months ago this Alderman girl was found under the bridge. Right out there. Head injury before she drowned."

"I knew about Nancy Alderman. This is now. What about about Susie?"

"Since then," Chuck said, "any time some local daughter turns up missing – taking off with a soldier, what else? – their families get excited. Because of Susie's trouble, they have barged out here with Deputy Brockway in tow, blaming Grouper Hole for providing sinful opportunities for their innocent daughters."

Bubba's fat eyelids blinked hard. "Like I'd have anything to do with those pigeons. And how come folks think we're responsible for what those damn weekend-passers do? Mama can tell you. We got more MPs around here on a Saturday night than they got downtown."

Lelia persisted. "Did Susie shoot the lieutenant here?"

Chuck shook his head. "In town, at his apartment. Susie ran. She's been gone for a month. Not that you can blame her for not writing home to mama or showing up for work – she's wanted for attempted murder. We don't know where she is." He ran his fingers through his close-cropped hair.

"Freckle-faced?"

"Did I say that?"

"I had a feeling," Lelia said. "She's around somewhere close." Alive and angry. Yes, the eyes in that face were angry. "But she's not here and I am and you need someone. Why don't I start right now? I'll go bring out our breakfast." She looked into Chuck's frown then into Bubba's stare. Yes, she breathed into their eyes. *Say yes.*

"What about it, Bubba?" Chuck shrugged as he had giving up to Hazel the night before. "Lelia says she can take care of herself."

Bubba looked at his empty plate. "Awright, girlie, it's your party."

"Lelia, the name is Lelia Elliot." She didn't soften the stare until he blinked comprehension and gave a contrite nod. "Awright, Miss Lelia Ma'am, but before you go hippety-hoppin' in there – you know, doncha, this Conch you gonna run food for is an old coon. Probably meaner than a rattlesnake if you tangled with him. He catches those things right in the palmettos. And that wife of his – well, you won't have to fool with her, she's not around much. But old Conch's the best damn cook anywheres."

"That's the kitchen door, end of the bar," Chuck said.

Midway across the dark barroom, Lelia slowed to look out toward the sun-streaked porch. The two men were collecting their gear and talking to someone on the boardwalk just outside. She recognized the lean man in white, the shoulders, the sandy hair. Gil, the fishing guide.

She turned toward the swinging kitchen door. For a flash moment, the way it could happen . . . as though seeing everything at once from some other vantage point . . . she saw her mesmerized self, following some plan like a puppet who was not aware of the source of the strings.

The door swung open to the aroma of ham and a narrow kitchen galley that ended with a window on the bay. Against the long wall, at a flat-top stove, a powerfully built man was frying the ham, his arms dark against the white shirt. Except for the frosting of white hair, he might have been young. Conch turned. The solid brown face studying her made Lelia remember library pictures of ageless native chieftains, staring stony-faced at encroaching white men.

"Can I hep' you, Miss?" The bass tone was rhythmic but had no warmth.

"I hope you will, Conch." She moved into the room past its single wooden table and cane chair. She looked around at the deep metal sink, an old icebox painted white.

"I'm going to be working here," she began, ignoring his stony coldness. "So I'll need you to tell me what I'm expected to do."

The big Negro turned back to his stove, his silence solid as armor. She walked to the window and looked out at the bridge, waiting. Of course, another white girl bouncing into his kitchen was an unwelcomed challenge. Back in the Bethel, Mattie had confided more than once about colored folks having to hide what they felt with white folks. She needed his help. She needed to be here.

Conch wiped his stove top. "Who you working for, Miss? Mister B or his mama? Miz Critten, dot's who gives orders." He glanced at her with narrowed eyes.

"Bubba. I haven't seen his mother. But I don't expect him to be very helpful."

A flicker of a smile. "Dot right?"

"I hear you're the best cook in the county."

"Best snake man, too."

He ladled a mound of creamy grits onto the waiting plate, added a touch of black coffee from the pot to the big skillet of ham drippings, and poured the red-eye gravy over the grits. "You got a customer waitin'?"

"Just my uncle and myself—oh, this is your breakfast, isn't it?" His glower told her she was right. "Sit, sit down and eat while it's hot." When he hesitated, she added, "I need to look around. Please. Sit down and eat."

Silently, Conch added three biscuits from back of the stove. He padded over to the long wooden work table and sank down. When she walked away, he began eating.

From the window at the end of the galley, she said, "I like it in here – sunny, the bay out there – I'm not accustomed to dark barrooms."

This was obviously Conch's domain. The open wooden shelves stacked with white plates and sacks of corn meal. A hamper of red tomatoes on the floor. A car rumbled across the bridge onto the brick road. The walls vibrated behind the stove and sink.

"Dot's Old Noisy, dot bridge." Conch muttered over his

eggs. "Why you want to work here, Miss?"

"I need the job. I came here to look for my uncle. The Elliot family used to live here. Do you know about the place people call Hurricane House?"

Because his bushy brows went up, she said, "Tell me about it." Yes, behind that big brown face was something she needed to know.

He shook his head and studied his plate. "A man doan get this old and be healthy telling all he knows, Miss."

"Conch – please don't call me Miss." She came back and stood by his table.

He sopped the biscuit in red-eye gravy. Carefully, "Why you say dot?"

"Because my name is Lelia. And I'm not an old lady needing any title. And because you hate saying Miss."

He looked up with a faint smile. "You some special lil' lady to come 'round here." He got up with the empty plate, set it in the deep sink, and started cracking eggs in a bowl, whipping them to a golden froth. "For you and uncle bartender – he come bok, huh? – two Conch specials. Sooon come!"

"Soon come?"

"Jamaica talk." The bass voice warmed. Turning the eggs gently, Conch told her he was born in Kingston, but his mama dragged him to Key West, tippy end of Florida before he came up here to this waterfront and got himself a patch of land, old palmetto and scrub land down the road apiece. Good enough for his hogs. Bought 'em with rattler skins. That's why folks got the best ham in Florida from this kitchen, Conch said, the words full of pride. Too bad scrub land didn't grow coffee beans, or he'd have something that tasted better than the awful stuff that came with ration stamps.

"Conch, how long have you been here?"

"Don't count years. Just wives." His laugh rumbled over the sizzling ham. "Outlived one. Another ran away bok up north. Cheta's the best. A young one, came from New O'leans. Knows secrets."

"Secrets?"

"Folks say black magic and doan let her work. I say 'stay

home,' I make the living but she's stubborn."

"It's not easy knowing secrets people don't like." Tell me more, Conch, things I need to know.

He spooned grits onto the two plates. "She's stubborn woman, Cheta. She sells her bread over to dot house where nobody else goes."

"Hurricane House. Then she knows this Kali?"

"Dot's the one." Conch piled on scrambled eggs, adding curls of ham and the browned biscuits, put them on a tray, and added a bowl of fig preserves from the icebox. "You come bok for coffee. Conch doan trot out food. When Mister B doan have girl-help, he has to do the delivering hisself and that makes him mad as a trapped mutt." The big face turned to brown stone again. "If you work here – you watch out for yourself, Lil' Lady."

"I intend to, Conch."

GROUPER HOLE
May 4, 1945

8

At 10:00 a.m., a big sedan pulled into the hard sand yard in front of Grouper Hole. Five women piled out to peer toward the sunny bay and empty dock.

Inside, at the Wurlitzer, Lelia watched her first customers parade onto the front screen porch, five flustered women protesting to the solid figure in the big brimmed hat.

"But he isn't here!" and "Jessie, this is a bar, you know."

The instigator of this visit remained calm. "Now, girls, let's go in just the same. Maybe we're early. We did see his yacht moving up the bay."

They swept inside, a flurry of flowered dresses and sun hats, chins high, eyes averted from the bar stools occupied by a lone GI slumped over a cup of coffee and the two old fishermen from Al's Bait House. The women didn't stop until they reached the bright screened porch where they sank into wicker chairs.

The GI lifted his head. "What's that all about?"

Cap'n sniggered. "Wimmen. More wimmen 'bout to pee in their bloomers just to see that movie fella. Ain't that right, Skipper?"

Skipper's soulful gaze stayed on Chuck's movements, cleaning up the bar. "Mess, ain't it? Where's Bubba?"

"Sleeping in that cubby hole room of his, I betcha," Cap'n said.

"Or whatever he does in there." Skipper's long face adjusted for a smile.

"Madam Palm and her five daughters, heh, heh." Cap'n beat his yellowed cap against the bar in pure delight.

Chuck dug into the ice chest behind the bar. "Watch it, Cap'n. Or you'll find that brown onion head of yours in a ringer." He filled a pitcher, motioning for Lelia to come over.

Cap'n made a face. "Aw, now, me and Skipper just got through saying we're glad you're back. And you brought us another girl." He grinned as Lelia joined them. "Pretty, real pretty. Honey, we had a spitfire before. Bartender here had better keep you locked up nights. We got some horny fellows round here."

"Drop it!" Chuck ordered. His tan deepened. "For a scrawny old fossil, Cap'n, you have a real big mouth. Lelia here is my niece. Watch your language."

Cap'n whistled through his gapped teeth. "Lordee, didn't know you had any niece." He grinned. "Anyways, one you'd let work for old Bubba."

She acknowledged their greetings, admired Cap'n's hat, sent Chuck a reassuring nod as he finished dumping ice in the pitcher and pushed the tray of glasses toward her.

"Take the ladies their lemonade." Chuck said. "And now if you two old buzzards will hush, we can hear the news." He turned up the small brown Philco stashed among the bottles. H. V. Kaltenborn's sonorous voice filled the place:

"Hitler's Eagle Nest in the Bavarian Alps is still smoldering from RAF bombings a week ago . . ."

"They find that devil?" Cap'n bounced on his stool.

"Not yet," Chuck said. "Not yet."

On the porch the women's moist, powdered faces kept scanning the empty dock and bay as they chattered over their tall glasses of lemonade.

"This place isn't so bad – now is it, with a nice girl like that waiting tables? And Evander Merrill might still come in for lunch. And we'll be here first!"

"But isn't that bridge the very one where they found that Boston girl caught underneath?"

"She'd gone to some beach party likely. I wouldn't let my

daughter come out here for one. Oh yes, I know the nicest people have beach places and entertain soldiers out of the kindness of their hearts. I've had two boys at my own table. But when you have a whole *crowd* of them, well, you can't be sure."

"Not out *here*, with an open beach – and bushes." The speaker's face flushed.

"What about Evander Merrill's parties for the soldiers on that big yacht? My dearest neighbor let her daughter go."

The women considered that with pursed lips. The confident face under the big hat brim settled it. "I've heard the young officers invited have been selected by their commanding officer – or chaplain or whoever looks after social invitations like that. Remember, *famous* people have their public to think about. Those parties would *have* to be handled properly."

Their voices purred on, trying to remember if it was Evander Merrill or Douglas Fairbanks in that movie about the Foreign Legion. "Oh, Miss?"

Lelia stood at the screen, looking over the bay to the long flat horizon of gulf front with its ragged palms under endless blue sky. Was this the open shore in her dream? She waited for some answer, but the women were calling again.

"Tell us about him! Is Evander Merrill as handsome in person?" one asked as she walked over.

"I haven't seen him." At their vocal dismay, she added, "This is my first day here."

"Oh, well then." Their faces looked expectant again.

By noon, Grouper Hole's porch tables were filled with what Chuck called lemonade customers. The horizon was bright now with sun. The two tourist fishermen from this morning were back, sun-reddened and volubly pleased with their day aboard the *Strike*. As Lelia set down their lunch plates of crab cakes, she heard Gil's name.

". . . real helpful fellow but a closed-mouthed son of a gun."

"Didn't offer any reason for not being in uniform," the chubby one agreed. He studied his crab cakes before looking up at Lelia where his gaze lingered.

"Thank you, Miss, hope they're good as breakfast was. Ah, you know anything about this fellow Gil? We're here to visit our boys at the Don CeSar hospital. You understand, a man's got to wonder about this fishing guide, healthy-looking fellow like that, sounding like he's been to some ivy league school. Maybe with an old dad in Washington pulling strings."

"Your fishing guide has been in the Navy." She set their ice teas down quickly, surprised at herself. *Why am I defending him?* A motor boat churned up to the dock outside. She recognized the white dungarees flashing in the sun as Gil jumped to the dock. "He's coming in now."

She meant to gather her empty glasses quickly and disappear into the kitchen. When she turned with the full tray braced against her waist, Gil was there at the table, lean face shadowed by canvas hat pulled low. He set down a gold watch in front of the men. "One of you forgot this." As abruptly, he turned away from their effusive thanks, but stopped short when he saw her.

Again, the instant imperceptible recoil, then the blue gleam under the sandy brow. Gripping the tray, she hurried past him. The bar was noisy now with customers, the juke box throbbing with Gene Krupa's drums. Her skin knew he followed. A touch on her shoulder stopped her. She rested the tray next to the cash register and turned, close enough to smell the sun and sea on him.

"My apologies for last night," Gil said. "I must have sounded rude."

"As though you were seeing someone else."

"Perhaps." Something flickered in his eyes.

"I'm not that person."

"No."

"So I remind you of anger?" She turned away from his narrowed gaze, annoyed at herself for letting the thought come out. She had been more careful at home. Home? Not any more. "I have work to do. Good-by."

"No, wait." He touched her arm again. "A word of –"

"Warning?"

"Do you always know what someone is thinking?" His smile was quizzical. "I see you are working in Martha Critten's charming establishment while you visit. Shall I expect you to show up with other arduous females for a look at the movie star's yacht?"

"I'm here to work," she said, for some reason adding, "not to take Susie's place. I happened to need the job."

"Then take care of yourself."

"I always have."

She gripped the tray and pushed into the kitchen door. How many warnings did that make today? Chuck, Conch, Bubba. And now this man. Was she so obviously vulnerable? She knew how to protect herself. She knew to avoid this man who hid some secret thing ticking inside him.

In the kitchen, she went to the small back window in time to see the *Strike* roar off from the dock. It moved down the bay's channel, leaving its trail of churning foam in the dark green water. She closed her eyes and imagined how it must look below that green surface. It would be a sparkling emerald world at first, then a chilled, enveloping darkness. Fascinated, she allowed herself to feel it . . . This Gil was there, too, in green depths, his arms like steel and she, tangled in his arms, struggling, not with fear, but something else. She felt a scream rising.

She opened her eyes, the imagined scream still ached in her throat. The sunny bay shimmered peacefully out there. Beyond, the gulf gleamed flat and lazy under blue sky. Angry with herself, Lelia turned around. Conch at his sink had been watching.

"You got enough of Grouper Hole already? Goan quit on me?"

"No, Conch. Not quitting. I'm just beginning."

In midafternoon, Hazel swept into the kitchen, a bristling figure in a tight orange dress. "Come out of that window and listen to me," she told Lelia, dropping into the single cane chair and kicking off the chunky high heels.

"So you did it – got yourself a job. Well, I've been

working, too, Honeychile. This whole day has been the real pits." Her small sharp features looked pale under the makeup.

"All that gas and trouble to go into St. Pete and that damn Doc Miller wouldn't see me. Just you wait. When I do get that Spook Kali under the jailhouse or in a nut house where she belongs, that old man goes too. Just you wait!"

Wait? Lelia looked out toward the beach. With a sudden sweet clarity, she knew it was past time to wait for anyone's permission. She walked over to the fuming woman sprawled in the chair. "Hazel – I don't need Dr. Miller's information or permission to go over there."

"Hey, just a sec! This is our crow to pick. You can get your daddy-curiosity satisfied when I get into that house!"

"So? Then all three of us will go. We'll knock on Kali's door together. Now. Why wait?"

Hazel's penciled eyebrows went up. "You really mean that doncha, kiddo? Fix me an ice tea, Conch, I'm beat. Yeah, you really mean that. Like you lost something over there. All right. Long as you remember that house is ours. So all right. I'm game. We'll storm the old Witch's front door. Yeah!"

"This afternoon. Tonight at least."

"Chuck has to stay at the bar until five, then come back. It's Friday." She took the glass of tea. "Working in this dump means you have to be out there Friday and Saturday nights till God knows what time. That means you, too, kiddo."

"Then we'll go in between and be back by eight."

"Listen to Miss Sure-of-Herself. Okay – let's do it. Aw-reet!"

Chuck stuck his head in the door. "Haz? What's happening? Lelia, why don't you get out for a while? You, too, Conch. No more food till tonight. What's up, Haz?"

"Plenty." She set the tea glass down, crossed her legs, and struck a pose. "Get back in there and make me a double Martoony. I have news for you. We're going visiting tonight."

HURRICANE HOUSE
May 4, 1945

9

A breeze stirred through the piney grove, like a woman's sigh. Holding her hair off her neck to catch the coolness, Lelia paced in front of the trailer.

From inside, Hazel and Chuck's voices rose and fell in a lazy rhythm of practiced complaint. Her own pulse was louder. Fear? No, too late for that. Curiosity now. Readiness to plunge into whatever waited, had always waited.

Chuck burst out of the trailer ending her reverie. "She's into her war paints, and I'm not supposed to watch." He glared at her from the stoop. "Well, Lelia, so we're going to the damn house. Are you satisfied?"

"It's a start."

"What in the devil do you expect to find over there anyway – a family?" He joined her in the pine straw yard. "You're too late. It's always been too late. You'll only find ghosts."

She hid the shiver. "I know. But my father took my mother there."

Chuck fumbled for a pack of cigarettes, lit one, and squinted toward the grove. "Lee had a love-hate for that place, maybe I told you. I suppose that's why he brought her there, maybe to have a good memory for a change. I was at Duke at the time. But I heard Doc Miller took them back to town. I never heard anything more other than the girl left and Lee came back – and was drowned himself. I don't like to think about that because it was so damn crazy. He was still a lanky twenty-year-old, but Lee was no fool. A brooder, maybe, but not irresponsible."

Chuck's mouth clamped shut on the subject. She had to keep him talking. Calmly she said, "Hazel knows what she wants, doesn't she?"

Relieved, Chuck said, "She does, with a single-minded passion and determination of a General Patton. Getting that house is her cause. You have to understand Hazel."

Chuck darted a glance toward the lighted trailer before turning back, his voice brisk and low. "She was a dirt-poor kid and she's still angry as hell about that. Crazy old coal miner and preacher for a father. Singing got her out of a tarpaper shack at 15. Hillbilly stuff, on radio, then into some roadhouses around Kentucky. When I met her she was with Herbie Ray, not a name band, but a road band doing one-nighters. Well, you can't blame her for wanting something better now."

"I felt – something like that."

"Hazel will tell you she was going to be a big time vocalist, a Connie Haines or Bea Wain or Jo Stafford. She does have a quirky, husky voice. Plays a decent jazz piano. Just between us, the 'Fascinatin' Hazel' act is more make-up and brassy nerve than anything else. But you have to give her credit."

"I see that you do. Where did you two meet?" Keep talking, Chuck.

"Pensacola. Navy town. Haz was this tiny brunette babe, banging away at a piano in a roadhouse outside of town, singing and sassing the crowd with such damned energy." He smiled toward the darkening trees. "I was pretty high myself, sitting with a bunch of guys after a whole damn day of going through the physical. We were living it up, ready to be sworn in the next morning."

"You wanted the Navy."

"More than anything. Lee had run away to the Navy as a kid, too restless for college. Not me – I'd stayed on doing graduate work because I didn't know what to do or where to go next. Until Pearl Harbor. That night in Pensacola, my last civilian night – that's what I wanted, to get in. I ended up spending the night with Hazel, telling her a lot of bull about myself."

"But you came home." As she said it, she saw the flicker of pain.

"Sure. I was the joker who was 4-F the next day. They told me I had this inefficient heart, beating the wrong time. Hell, I knew that."

"The Navy turned you down, but Hazel didn't."

The wry grin flickered. "Hazel listened to my sad story and was all fired up to come back here with me. I'm afraid I'd made it sound too good the night before. She figured I had something of worth waiting here to give her. And I didn't." He opened empty hands, confessing, "I let her come back with me, knowing she expected more. Maybe that's why I put up with the little hellion."

"You're good to her. Almost gentle." A trait, Lelia knew, not appreciated by Hazel.

"Actually, I would like to please Hazel," Chuck went on quickly. "Bitch she is, still she'd fight for me like an alley cat – depending on her mood and the stakes. I'm no fool, understand. Haz may be fighting for herself. She's a bit older than I am, but don't dare mention that. She has a thing about loosing her looks and still being poor. She thought I was a ticket. But she does need me. I'm all she has."

And you need her, Lelia saw. "She's trying to get the house back for both of you."

"Lord, yes. She'd been to the courthouse in Clearwater as well as trying to get some clue out of old Doc Miller. The house is deeded to Kali, signed by my grandfather Sinclair. Kali manages to pay the taxes, so what can you do?"

"You don't like to hear what Hazel is trying to prove."

"That Kali killed my mother and ran my father off? Hardly. But for a kid, there isn't any really good way to get left behind. Left without any explanation, except the gossip everyone else on this waterfront knew. You can understand why I haven't wanted to set foot inside that house in the past 20 years. Hazel dragged me over there a year ago to make her little scene at the front door. Not much fun. I vowed I'd never go back."

She watched this forty-four-year-old man shrug off the

memory of a father who walked out on the child. But the resentment was there behind the tanned solid face. And more? He didn't know why his brother drowned and he didn't want to know.

"If Hazel can get Kali out somehow, what then?"

"Live there, I guess. Haz wants to look like a rich dame and I'd have to let her have that. She's built up a fantasy about the way Bonnie Elliot lived. It's quite a place if you enjoy a mausoleum, full of Oriental and Victorian antiques plus a few stuffed Florida critters thrown in. The house was well constructed of cypress. My grandfather had the materials barged in when there wasn't much out on those beaches but a few homesteading cottages. Sure, it's valuable property, but you see I don't want any part of it."

"When you feel so strongly about something, it's hard to be sure if it repels or if maybe it's pulling you." Places or people. She remembered Gil's touch and her response. Warmth or chill, she wasn't sure.

Chuck wheeled around to shout. "Hazel, prima donna! What's the delay?"

The trailer screen door opened. "Right here, Chuckie lamb." Hazel stood on the stoop, striking a pose. In the deepening shadows, the short strapless red satin glinted. The hard topknot of curls crowned the sleek upsweep of hair. Red earrings dangled against her thin throat.

Chuck groaned. "That get-up is too jazzy for Grouper Hole and a little weird for knocking on Kali's door right now."

Hazel stepped down into the yard. "Honeychile here will look innocent enough for both of us. Look at this, Chuck. This lil' old dress, tied at the waist. Looks like something from a ballerina's closet, a sweet ballerina pretending she only wants to dance by herself."

"I'm leaving the glamour to you," Lelia said.

"Come off it, you two," Chuck said. "If we're going, let's get it over with."

They headed for the Nash, Hazel fussing as her red heels dug into pine straw. Lelia heard the angry frustration, and something else. Fear, mixed with hope. Poor Hazel, how desperately she wanted that house. And how much Chuck hated it.

The bridge rattled beneath them as they headed across to the beach side, all three silent.

Straight ahead, a low frame swim pavilion sprawled to the left and a two-story inn sat under pine trees. In between, beyond the shadowed beach, the Gulf of Mexico rolled in, metallic blue under the darkening horizon. Not like the dream, but this had to be the shore. She had to come back here, alone, tomorrow.

Chuck turned right, past the inn, onto Gulf Boulevard, a narrow road that followed along the bay. On the side facing the beach, a patch of jungle growth loomed ahead. The Nash turned into a narrow overgrown drive and stopped. An iron gate, heavy with vines, blocked any entrance. Hazel wailed in disgust. Chuck muttered, "I know how to open the thing."

He got out. Lelia followed. Together they yanked at the rusted gate. A snarl from the other side stopped them. A huge black Doberman leaped at them, barking. Chuck stepped back, cursing under his breath.

"He doesn't like the car," Lelia said. "Once we calm him, maybe we can walk up to the house."

Hazel stuck her head out. "Not on your life. I'm riding. Hit him over the head. Do something."

Crouched down, Lelia talked softly to the dog until the Doberman sat on his haunches, allowing her hand to stroke his head. "You drive Hazel in, Chuck. I want to walk."

The pale headlights behind her, Lelia crunched ahead on thick pine straw, the Doberman slinking along at her side. The path tunneled through dense foliage until it opened to a tangled yard of tall pines and oaks thick with vines. It was like a small jungle, floored with low palmetto leaves, redolent with the smell of the day's sun.

I'm here. Does anyone know?

No answer, but a thought stirred, subtle as the rustle of branches overhead. *What has begun must be completed.*

The path turned. Hurricane House loomed in view, shadowed windows and cupolas looking down like heavy-lidded eyes. Sad eyes. In the fading light, the house was a pale presence, waiting. A slated wood boardwalk led across the sandy front yard to the screened porch.

The Nash rolled to a stop to one side under a huge tree. The banyan! Lelia recognized it as the huge tree in the old photograph. The gnarled limbs were thicker now, lightning had slashed down one side. Beyond, the gulf was a gleam of silver. She could hear its slow roll.

Hazel minced across the sandy ground toward the boardwalk. Chuck stood looking at the house, his face shadowed by thoughts and fading light. His shoulders sank. "Well – shall we try it?"

They trailed single file up the boardwalk.

"These damn wooden slats better not ruin my heels," Hazel fussed under her breath.

Bounding ahead, the Doberman nosed open the screened door and leaped inside the porch. They followed as the dog scratched at the heavily carved wooden door, grayed by years of salty winds. A chain of rusted bells hung there. Chuck pulled the chain once, then again. The dull clamor faded. Again there was only rattling fronds and the soft roar of surf.

Hazel fumed. "We're waiting here like a bunch of beggars." She reached past Chuck and yanked the bells harder.

A dim porch light came on, exposing them in a yellow glow. The door opened on a pale-lit foyer, stairs rising behind. A tall woman stood there studying them. Her purple robe fell straight from erect shoulders. Like an ancient priestess, Lelia thought. The woman's long hair, pulled back from a strong brow, coiled down over her breasts like spirals of gray smoke; her face so composed it might have been carved in stone. The deep-set eyes glinted.

"So, it is Charles." A contralto voice, like dark purple velvet, dusty from being long packed away.

Hazel sniffed. "Tell her, Chuck."

"We'd like to come in, Kali, and talk," Chuck said.

"We have somebody here for you to meet." Hazel sounded breathless.

"Indeed." The woman's gaze moved over them to rest

on Lelia.

"You'll want to see her, Kali," Chuck said.

At the low command, the restless Doberman trotted back into the yard. Kali studied Lelia again before saying, "Come in."

From the foyer, the three of them followed Kali into a high-raftered room. Dim light from the line of French doors captured the furnishings' ornate shapes. The musty air smelled of sadness. Greenery beyond the porch hid the surf but not its soft pounding rhythm.

With a chill of recognition, Lelia knew—my mother stood at those French doors. On that porch a dead woman spoke.

A richly colored Tiffany lamp sprang to life as Kali moved silently across the room. Now an orange fringed silk shade spilled pools of light on mahogany and faded brocade and Persian carpet. The room's paneled walls remained in shadow.

"Sit down." A softly spoken order. Kali sank into a high-backed Oriental chair, long fingers curled around the carved arms.

Lelia didn't move. She had intended to be open, to know what she should know here, but her senses might have been exposed nerves, picking up too much, understanding nothing. Yet the answers were here, somehow. Hidden in drawers? Locked behind doors? She saw the rest of them with the clarity of slow motion.

This woman Kali, so erect against that chair, still the high priestess, keeper of the dark castle, viewing interlopers found within the gates . . .

And Hazel, perched stiffly on the edge of the French loveseat, her red dress garish against pale brocade, mascaraed veiled eyes searching the room, taking in the gilt-edged, the lacquered and inlaid like the hungry, angry child who could only look at, but not touch the banquet table . . .

And Chuck, sinking into an old leather couch, running a hand over its faded red surface, his face unguarded for a moment, nodding, nodding. "I remember my father sitting here."

From nowhere, a Siamese cat leaped on a chair and

crouched down to study them. Hazel's husky voice rose to a squeak. "Keep that thing away from me!"

At Kali's soft order, "Nalo," the Siamese rose, stretched, dropped to the floor, and slipped away.

"Sit here," Kali said and Lelia obeyed.

"That old stuffed bobcat!" Chuck said. "The damn thing used to scare the wits out of me. But I pretended to be that bronze decathlon player over there." His smile faded. Silence again.

"So, Charles." Under the strong brow, Kali's shadowed eyes waited. "Why are you here?"

"And why not?" Hazel half rose but sank back. "Light me a cigarette, Chuck." Chin up after the first draw, she stared at Kali. "We have a right."

"Lelia wanted to come," Chuck put in quickly.

Hazel shrieked and sprang to her feet. "That cat! Keep it away from me!" She kicked a red heel after Nalo, sending the Siamese darting away again. "Had a clawing cat thrown at me when I was a kid." She eased back down, stiff lashes blinking. "We brought you an Elliot you don't know about."

"Lee's daughter," Chuck said.

"Is this true?" Kali turned to her. An ageless face, inscrutable in its stillness.

"Yes," Lelia said. The woman's gaze could penetrate her own quiet, her shield of protection. She turned away from Kali to watch Chuck's frown and Hazel's red lips pulling on the cigarette.

Kali murmured, "Indeed. Where are you from?"

"I grew up in Bethel, Alabama. My mother gave me my father's name before she died, but the family knew nothing about the Elliots. The name wasn't mentioned in the Calhoun house." She dared look into Kali's gaze. "I must know about the Elliots—because I am an Elliot." She saw the momentary gleam light up the woman's dark eyes.

"Yeah," Hazel said, "your favorite left some little southern daughter in a family-way and he took off. Did Lee really drown out there in some little old boat like his mama or did he just skip like his daddy? No answers here for his own brother."

Chuck flashed her a warning frown and turned back to Kali. "Lee married at 20. I'm sure you know that as they came here, I understand, from Norfolk. What was it for them – three days? I didn't know that much until I was informed his boat washed up after the storm. At any rate, Lelia was a big surprise to us when she came into St. Pete last night."

"Showed up without warning." Hazel snuffed out the cigarette against a china dish.

"We brought her home." Chuck looked uncomfortable.

"Home, hah! He means we gave her a place to sleep." Hazel sat on the edge of the seat, fingernails drumming.

Chuck said, "So we're here tonight for Lelia, not about the house –"

"For starters." Hazel was on her feet. "This girl sitting here means there are still Elliots around, besides Chuck, if you know what I mean."

Hazel sank down again, red nails digging into the brocade couch. "Chuck and I live in that dinky trailer park over there on the mainland as if you didn't know since that crazy Cheta must tell you everything. And since we've got to work to eat, we got Lelia a job at the same dump Grouper Hole where we slave away." With a ragged intake of breath, "So – it's time the remaining Elliots move into this place and live like we got a right to."

Kali's long fingers curled and uncurled on the chair arms.

"Right's right!" At Kali's leaden silence, Hazel's fuse of anger exploded in a wail. "You know this is Chuck's property. You think people have forgotten what you did? How you got possession of this house?"

Kali's face didn't change, only her eyes. "The greedy see only greed. Charles, do you let this woman speak for you?"

Chuck winced and stood up. "I'm speaking, goddammit. I'm saying we're getting out of here. I don't beg, Kali. Give me that."

Lelia stood too. She couldn't let it end this way. She faced Kali's hard silence. "We aren't asking for anything that is yours. Chuck has his rights. But I'm here for my own reasons. I have to know about my father."

Kali rose. "You may come here again, Lelia Elliot. Alone."

"Oh, no, she won't!" Hazel jumped to her feet. "She won't come without us, you hear? Not on your life!"

Kali turned to Lelia. "Do you see? I do not wish to have this woman's energy in my house."

"My energy?" Hazel shrieked. "I'm the only one in this family with any guts. You, you old spook – everyone knows what you are!"

"Let's get out of here," Chuck muttered.

They followed Kali to the foyer, filed through the door she opened and closed after them.

The porch light went off before they started down the boardwalk in the cloudy night.

Midway, Hazel cursed. "My heel's stuck in the damn slats!" Whimpering, she pulled her shoe free and took another minute to yank up the loose board and hurl it across the sandy yard toward the growling Doberman.

On the way back across the bridge, Hazel broke the silence. "Go over there by yourself, Lelia Elliot, and you're as guilty as that old witch. You'll end up dead on the beach like Bonnie and your daddy or spooked out of your mind yourself. My daddy used to say give in to the devil once and he's got you for sure."

The warning melted into breathy determination. "But don't you worry, Honeychile. Stick with Hazel. We're all going to live in that house, one way or another. I've made up my mind to that."

A juke box beat throbbed from Grouper Hole. Chuck parked the Nash under a tree on Al's Bait House side of the road. As they got out, he muttered, "Well, that was a disaster and here comes your first night with the troops, Lelia. Damn if I don't feel I'm leading an exotic lamb to the slaughter. But you wanted to stay around, so look after yourself. As far as food goes, Conch will show you the ropes."

They tracked across the road toward the back kitchen door.

"Don't worry, Honeychile," Hazel said with husky nonchalance, "Friday nights they bring dates. Guys who have one won't try to cop a feel. Their girls might look daggers at you anyway, but looks don't kill. I've tried it. Ha."

Once in the kitchen, Hazel swept past Bubba, out the swinging door, into the noisy barroom. Chuck followed. Lelia stood there trapped by Bubba.

"'Bout time you showed up." Bubba's nervous stare traveled over her, invading past the pink cotton dress.

He rocked closer, breathing through his thick pale lips, a nervous sucking noise. "Mama says give the bastards plenty of smilin' and listenin' but don't stay too long at any one table. We don't throw any of them out, except Dummy. You run him off if he bothers anybody." The meaty bottom lip stayed slack.

She wanted to run from this crude nervous man, but she wasn't running from this job. She faced him and sent a message deep into the blinking gaze. Stay away from me!

Bubba turned quickly to glower at Conch, silent at his stove. "Four fellows in the corner booth expecting those crab cakes and they're sitting here getting cold." Bubba helped himself to one from the tray and left.

"Who is Dummy?" Lelia asked when Bubba's door closed behind him.

"Skinny blond fellow. Don't talk. Mebbe he can hear. Don't know. Lil' Lady, once you get them fellows fed in there, you come bok and sit down to my crab cakes.

"What does this Dummy do – to bother people?"

Conch wagged his head. "Comes 'round with his shell jewelry to sell the tourist ladies. Daytimes. Not much when its mostly uniforms. Mister B oughta know but he gets flustered as a tied-up mutt."

Or a chained bulldog. Gripping the loaded tray, she pushed through the door and plunged into the smoke and noise of her first night at Grouper Hole, her mind still filled with Kali and the musty silence of that house.

GULFSHORE
May 5, 1945

10

Was this the shore?

In bright Saturday morning sunshine, Lelia stood for the first time barefoot by the open gulf, toes digging into the spongy, wet sand, salty breeze stinging her skin. The arcing horizon separated sky and endless glistening sea. It moved in toward her, on rhythmic swells that rose smooth as green glass before breaking into white foam, before surging on in as thin silken waves. The ebb and flow sighed around her ankles like a christening.

She looked down the curving shore. No ancient woman with shimmering white hair waited; no billowing dark figure with hollowed eyes. From the beach a formation of white gulls lifted as with one mind to swoop and dip and soar over the waves. Free things, riding some mysterious current they knew. She'd always envied such freedom, such knowing. She breathed in the live sea air thinking how sailors must know some of the secrets, at least some that land people never knew. I am no longer a land person, she thought, smiling at the thought because she had never seen open water before. And didn't even know how to swim.

A high voice called, breaking the reverie.

"Lelia Elliot – it's me, Francie!"

She turned. Oh no, it was Francie Welburn, the exuberant redhead from the train. The girl stood in the shade of the inn's Australian pines wearing a striped pink-and-white sunsuit and large brimmed sunhat, waving like a ten-year-old. Francie

Welburn was no child, Lelia thought, watching the girl run toward her now, holding down the hat, breasts like firm ripe fruit, face flushed with honest pleasure. She threw both arms around Lelia and stood back.

"I'm so glad to see you! Honestly." She yanked the sunhat further down over cinnamon red curls. "I'm already getting freckles. But you, Lelia! You'll get a tan out here and look like Dorothy Lamour. Exotic! You need a sarong bathing suit. Where are you staying?"

"I'm living on the bay side with an aunt and uncle."

"We came out here last night, Mother and Aunt Mo. Mother's allergic to something in Aunt Mo's yard. Well, I was so glad. To get out here, I mean. But already, I think I'll positively die of boredom."

"But you wanted to come to the beach – and isn't it beautiful?" Lelia waved toward the glistening water. A formation of sea gulls swept low over the waves.

Francie pleaded, "Come up under the shade and talk with me. I have to stay out of the sun. Mother would have a nervous hissy if I got burnt. I get a fever, and the burn turns into red freckles."

"I see five already. They're pretty. I'm out to walk, Francie. My first look." She meant to walk as far as Hurricane House.

"Oh, Mother's sleeping. I'll risk it." She kicked off her sandals and wiggled plump white toes. "Let's go."

Together they splashed along the surf's edge, Francie talking in quick little gasps of despair and enthusiasm. Small cottages sat from the water, crouched in the shade of cabbage palms and feathery pines.

"I wanted to come to the beach, sure," Francie said, "but not with both my Keepers. That's what Mother is, really! At least Aunt Mo will let me talk to a boy if Mother's not around. Oh, Lelia – with you right across the bridge, we could get together and do something exciting."

Under the big hat brim, Francie's creamy profile made a vulnerable image against the glittering gulf. Lelia stopped short with a sudden disturbing thought. Francie stopped, too, wide-eyed. "What's the matter? Oh, I talk too much I know I do. I didn't let you tell me about your uncle."

"No, something reminded me of a dream I had last night." Lelia looked away at a puff of dark cloud above the horizon. Had she dreamed of Francie last night? Or was it Susie? There had been faces, faces of young women, mouthing something before their images faded into a dark gulf.

They were past the small cottages. They both looked up toward the bank of low foliage bordering the sands. Behind the wind tangled seagrape bushes, tall palms and oaks became a jungle hiding Hurricane House.

"There's the spooky house they talk about," Francie said.

"What do they say?" Only the top floor of the house showed above the trees.

"Oh, just that some old hermit woman lives there. And people have died there."

"Let's turn around. You've had enough sun."

They walked back, Francie still talking. "While I'm at the Inn, we could go down to the Bath Club. Aunt Mo told Mother it's a nice place. Maybe we'll meet some cute officers."

"I have a job across the bay. Days and nights." Was Kali in the house watching them, she wondered.

"Oh – you mean that big old bar-place across the bridge?" The girl's pink mouth pursed a moment before she brightened. "Where the movie star Evander Merrill brings his yacht?"

"That's what they tell me."

"Then maybe I can get Mother and Aunt Mo to come over to see Evander Merrill. They're fussy but surely they'd like to see a movie star. But you've got to come over here, too. Promise!"

"I promise to try."

Francie was still saying "Remember," as Lelia left her on the inn's front porch and headed for the bridge. She didn't have time for the kind of excitement this impulsive Francie had in mind.

Midway across the old span, Lelia stopped to gaze down at the bay current below. J. T. Tingley hadn't been put off by her reluctance to talk. Francie was assuming friendship without the first notice of her own reticence. Both had barged into her life as if by some plan none of them knew about.

Why? Looking down at the water, Lelia saw Francie's face instead, the blue eyes startled, needing rescue but not from boredom. Quickly, she walked on denying that message from the strange part of herself, the part that could turn out to be madness unless she controlled it. There was enough to think about now dealing with this job at Grouper Hole.

Chuck had warned, "Tourists might hang around during the week looking for a movie star's yacht, but tonight – well, you'll see Saturday night is what Grouper Hole is all about."

She walked on. A pelican lifted from the railing and soared down to the dock at Al's Bait House. A boat churned down there, ready to pull away. The *Strike*. From the railing she recognized Gil's sure movements as he untied the lines. As though he could feel her gaze, he looked up, watching her for a long moment before turning back to his controls. The boat roared north up the bay.

In that dream last night, she had seen faces, Susie's and the dead girl, Nancy? And yes, Francie. Was Gil there, too? She hurried on toward Grouper Hole's back door and the comforting aroma of Conch's country ham.

By eight o'clock, Harry James' trumpet peeled out a brassy wail into the blue haze and beginning action of a Saturday night at Grouper Hole.

A scattering of middle-aged tourists sat at the tables. At the bar, old Cap'n's cackle rose over the low hum of younger male voices. Lelia glided quickly past the bar lineup of burr-headed men in their sun-bleached khakis with their "hot damns" and reaching hands. On the piano bench, Hazel rocked in her tight orange dress, red fingernails moving lightly over the yellowed keys. Waiting for the juke box to go quiet, she sang along with the Harry James tune, " I cried . . . for you" as Lelia brought her drink.

"Tell Chuck he's slow tonight but thanks, Kiddo. No don't go." Hazel sipped the drink and eyed the room. "Ever listen to those lyrics? Pure chit. Crying for what you want never changed anybody's luck. I found that out a long time ago.

When you want something bad enough, you have to figure out how to get it, that's a fact, pure and simple. Sit here on the old bench with me. You'll be hopping around enough tonight."

Hiding impatience, Lelia sat down to watch the long red fingernails dance over the keys. Hazel made her think of a coiled spring tonight, or a match ready to flare. The Evening in Paris scent waved out like bristling energy. But yes, she and Hazel needed each other for their different reasons.

"I can't start the 'Fascinatin' Hazel' bit until that kid gets away from the Wurlitzer." Hazel nodded toward the skinny GI. "He's been punching in every mournful tune. Glenn Miller twice, with that Sinatra fellow, what a snotty name, crooning he's never-going-to-smile-again. So tell me, Kiddo, you're still with us even after getting kicked out by the Spook last night. At least she was curious about you."

"I won't leave without getting in that house."

"Yeah? Well, you're looking at the one who's going to get herself in there to stay, not for a look-see at Daddy's homestead. One way or another – Hey, hold on. Chuck says to wise you up about good old Saturday night. I'm telling you this, Honeychile, since I can't be sure if you're innocent as a lamb or quiet as a clam. Your eyes look like you know a thing or two. But anyway, remember kids or men showing up here, the whole lot of them are primed for trouble. They're all looking for something to brag about Monday morning back at Drew Field or MacDill base or the Don CeSar hospital."

"I can handle it." She would block them out.

"Some guy is going to call you a long-stemmed, yellow rose in that sweet lil' cotton thing, but he'll be thinking of plucking those petals. Don't give me the cool eye, Lelia Elliot. Think you're so in control, don't you? Listen up."

Hazel set the drink down on the ringed piano top and started to improvise with the juke box beat. "Not bad, eh? Not bad. My minor chords are pretty damn good. Christ, that kid is playing 'Moonlight Serenade' again."

"You know it too," Lelia said.

"Yeah. These Dorsey and Miller arrangements put me right back there in front of Herbie Ray's band. That year on the road – most of it I'd like to forget. You stay in two-bit hotel rooms. You ride all day in a lousy bus. And one night we got stuck in a snowbank, hour before the gig." She did a chord and closed her eyes a moment, heavy lashes against a small, painted face.

"We never made it to the Aragon Ballroom or Glen Island Casino or Statler, but the beat was the same if the pay wasn't. Ballrooms are all alike, did you know that? In the daylight, the best of them are cold as those mirrored balls they always hang like a tacky chandelier. But in the dark, with that ball whirling, well, a ballroom is a beaut. Lights spinning all over the place, colors swirling on the dancers swaying away to 'Stardust' and 'Deep Purple' or flinging each other around with some jive number."

"I can see you up there singing in the spotlight."

"Yeah, I'd stand up there, skinny old me, acting like I was some long-legged sultry dame. Marlene Dietrich maybe. Or full of bounce and fire like Betty Hutton."

"After the day on the bus."

"Yeah, stomach queasy as if I'd swallowed some of the jagged glass on those lights. Damn tired. But some hard glittering thing in me . . ."

"Hope," Lelia said.

"Yeah, in the spotlight you can dream of the big time – getting where the real dough is before it's too late, before you get too old. Maybe even an easy studio job. *The Hit Parade!*"

"But Chuck came along."

"And look at me now. Beating this old keyboard in a watering hole for a scruffy bunch of GIs swilling their beer and acting smart. Some of them wet-behind-the-ears. If they look up at me at all, it's with this sneaky grin wanting somebody to see what a cute baby-faced girlfriend they've got curled up against them."

"You make them think you're playing for them."

"Yeah. Those babies. But look out for the hard-eyed sons of bitches, the sergeants and MPs you see coming in here flexing muscles and giving the old Clark Gable squint, acting like they are God's gift to women. Those swaggering bullies don't do a damn thing for me either. They're all brawn and no money."

"What about the quiet ones – from the hospital? The Section Eights."

"They're something else again. Their shrinks must okay their weekend passes. But who knows what nightmares those guys are carrying around in their heads? Same goes for the ones you guess about – like that loner Gil."

Hazel took a few gulps of her drink and picked up the juke box beat of "Tuxedo Junction."

"See that old bag coming in looking like somebody's grandma in a flowered dress? That's the boss, Martha Critten, in for her Saturday night inspection. After she gets through slapping backs and sits down to dinner, she'll want to see you. Isn't she something?"

Lelia watched Martha Critten maneuver around the room, leaving guffaws in her wake. "What's she like?"

"Behind the frizzy red hair and gosh-awful dress like cretonne curtains, she's the one who makes the loot here. Chuck does the work."

"Close to his radio," Lelia observed.

"Yeah, keeps his head in the radio listening to the damn war. Acts like he's General Eisenhower's driver and got left behind in these Florida boonies."

"But you came here knowing it was the boonies."

"I was in that club in Pensacola. Feeling lower than a snake's belly and there he was, real educated, not pushy, but as needy and sweet as a whipped collie pup. And he told me about some big family house on the beach in Florida. Where there's a big house, should be money attached somewhere. I didn't know till we got here he hated the place."

"Is he afraid of that house, Hazel?"

"So what if he is? Hey, you'd better get to work, they're coming in now. I'm going to start my thing." Hazel called over to the juke box player in a Mae West twang, "Save your nickel, General, and I'll give you the ree-all thang." She began the sassy beat introduction of "Fascinatin' Rhythm." Midway to the kitchen, Lelia turned to watch with a twinge of compassion.

Hazel's husky voice shouted over the din of voices, "My theme song, boys!"

Someone called out, "Hey, what happened to T. Dorsey?"

Hazel bent to the keyboard, making the rhythm brittle and furious.

Voices followed as Lelia threaded through the crowded room.

"Hubba, hubba, scenery's changing for the better in this joint."

"Oh, Miss, my name's Gilroy, and I been looking ever'where for you!"

"You a friend of Susie's? Where'd she go after she bumped off the guy?"

"Watch your mouth, shithead – she's no Susie. Anyway Susie didn't kill the guy."

"Maybe she shoulduv. Goddamn ninety-day-wonder loo-tenant."

"Hey, Darlin' – where you from?"

"I think she came from heaven. Or Bali Hi. Isle of me dreams."

When she passed the piano again, Hazel called out over the fast boogie-woogie beat, "Ain't this fun? Wanna do this all your life, I bet."

Conch turned around from his crackling iron skillet, his face remote again. "Miz Crit wants to see you. She's out on the porch with Mister B, waiting for this fried grouper."

"Bubba's mama."

"Dot's right. She'll be looking you ovah." He turned back to his stove.

Why the barrier again, Conch? She waited, willing him to talk. "What is she like?"

"She's the toady-shaped one with funny hair. You trot these cakes out and hurry right bok. The grouper'll be ready."

"She must be some kind of an ogre around here. But I didn't think you let people bother you, Conch."

"I doan mess in their business. I just cook. You just trot

trays and get yourself home."

"Good, I thought my trotting speed was disappointing you." She picked up the waiting crab cakes and headed for the door.

Conch turned again, his voice warmer, "Forgot. A fella's been in here, looking for you."

"Gil?" Why did she think that?

"Dot quiet fellow? Noo." Conch turned back to the frying fish. "Short fellow with a big red face. Come bouncin' in like his tail on fire and belly full of gasoline."

"Saying he's a great newspaperman?" Oh, no. It had to be J. T. Tingley.

"Dot's true. Said he's gonna write a story about me for the *Sat'day Evening Post.*" Conch turned around again, his slow smile showing how little he believed that. "Said he's coming bok."

In the barroom as she delivered the crab cakes to a crowded booth, the front screen door banged open, and over all the voices she heard Tingley's raspy salutations. He rocked up to her with his bow-legged stride. "Miss Magnolia! My, oh my, how purty." He looked happy, the ruddy face newly sunburned. "Been lookin' for you. Yours Truly is off booze, I swear. Got to talk to you."

She smiled at him in spite of herself. "J. T. Tingley himself. But I'm busy. Working." She bobbled the empty tray.

"But we gotta talk, Miss Magnolia. Serious stuff."

"Later." She didn't have time for this persistent character, this sad clown.

He followed her into the kitchen, rasping, "Conch, old man, I smelled your cooking from Johns Pass. Had to come back. And look at Miss Magnolia. I knew she was something else besides just purty first time I laid eyes on her. Already found Uncle Chuck and a job to boot. Nice fella, Chuck. Met him this afternoon before you came back." The grin wavered. "Lemme buy you a lemon Coke and sit down in a booth like a real dude. I got things to tell you."

"Later, Tingley. I really am working." She watched Conch set out the delicately browned fish, add sliced hearts-of-palm and red tomato on the side.

"Gottcha. Roger-and-over as they say. I'll be waiting at the bar. With a Coca-Cola."

Conch gave her a stony look. "Miz Critten and Mr. B are waiting."

The porch over the bay waters was blissfully cool and dark, lighted only from the dock outside. With her tray, Lelia stood in the doorway scanning the few occupied tables for Martha Critten and Bubba. Two couples danced in a cleared space to "Memories of You." Hazel's voice drifted out with the piano melody surprisingly rich with feeling. The dancers were two silhouettes, rocking with the music, curly heads against khaki shoulders, eyes closed, their steps a wistful sound brushing against the wood floor. Finally Lelia moved past, looking at the dark water, not the lovers.

"Over here." A petulant Bubba called from a table at the end of the porch. "We're waiting."

Even in this light, the woman's fuzzy hair showed beet red. For a fleeting second, Lelia glimpsed the once-young, once-pretty Martha, now a browsy old woman, the big breasts a sagging, heavy burden.

"Mama, this is the girl I told you about. Chuck's niece." Bubba sounded eager as Lelia set out the two plates Conch had taken such care to prepare.

Martha pushed the plate away. Lelia felt the gaze traveling up and down as if she were some commodity standing there for inspection. Over the half-glasses on her snub nose, the woman's large brown eyes assessed without revealing what she found.

"Uh-huh," She said finally, leaning back. "Real class. You did all right, Son." Bubba beamed and started on his food, but Martha grabbed his wrist. "So – you behave yourself, you hear?" When she let go, Martha winked up to Lelia. "Have to keep a growing boy in line, understand. Now. Tell me about yourself, Honey. What brings you to this old bayfront anyway?"

"My uncle is here." On second thought, she added, "My father was a child here. In what people call Hurricane House."

"Belongs to a looney, you know." The big brown eyes warmed. "Somebody ought to smoke her out of there – Wait, I'm not finished. Word of advice, Miss Pretty Lelia."

Martha leaned back, still studying her. "Waterfronts have strange fish, Miss Pretty. I've known a few, the bayou, the Mississippi, and this old Gulf of Mexico. All kinds of fish wash up on a waterfront. Both good eating kind and trash. Snakes, too, in these mangrove flats. Even in the nice sunny orange groves."

"Yes, I'm aware."

"But fish is for catching, too. Just make sure you don't swim with sharks or get careless with a catfish. You'd bleed easy." The smile faded. "And don't pull a Susie on me."

"I've heard about Susie."

"Yeah? Good riddance. We're talking about you, Doll. Don't tell me you aren't here looking for a spit-and-polish captain to carry you off to better things."

"I would go somewhere else for that." She looked away from the heavy-breasted woman, away from Bubba, who was chewing and watching. "I'm here because I want a job near the beach."

"Know how to handle these sons-of-bitches in uniform? Question bothers you then you shouldn't be here. Don't get me wrong. They're the best fish we've got when we don't have tourists. But don't go falling for any of them. They're just passing through, bastards all of them. Hear me? They get too much easy stuff. So don't think you're June Allyson duty-bound to send them off smiling. Life ain't like the movies." Martha turned back to her dinner plate, shoulders hunched in dismissal.

The dancers were gone. Lelia stood in the doorway with the empty tray, dealing with her distaste. Bubba's every gaze made her skin crawl. Martha Critten made her want to run out of this place and not come back. But she couldn't escape from herself. She would put up with the Crittens. She knew how. She would deal with them as necessary but would block out their energy. Taking a deep breath of night air, she walked back into the noisy barroom.

GROUPER HOLE

11

At the crowded bar, an airman's voice rose above the din of voices and Hazel's piano beat. "Shooting Stars, they call 'em. Those babies are gonna Fly at 800 per."

"Miss Magnolia!" Tingley leaned out from the line of khaki shoulders at the bar. "You been listening? This war's gonna be over yet. Old Il Duce has gone to that big spaghetti pot down below. The Russians and Yanks are marching into Berlin. You through working?"

"No – later. Do you still want to talk?"

"Do pelicans hang around bait houses? I got things to tell you. Don't worry. I've already explained to Uncle Chuck, that under this handsome exterior is an old fellow with honorable intentions. But it'll take time. You finish work. I'll wait."

Most of the crowd had filtered out, leaving behind bottle-cluttered tables and smoke when she made the last trip, kitchen to barroom. The Crittens had gone too, Bubba disappearing into his room beyond the kitchen. Chuck was polishing the bar when she came out, weary from this first Saturday night.

Tingley swirled off a stool, two glasses of Coca-Cola in his hands. He ambled to a booth, Lelia following. At the piano, two soldiers sat on either side of Hazel, watching her hands as she sang huskily about fools rushing in where angels feared to tread.

"That's me," Tingley grinned, leading her to the empty booth. "A fool in a hurry." He looked pleased as she thanked him for the Coke he pushed across the table.

Lelia sipped the strong sweet fizz and leaned back. "Ahh! I've just discovered how good it feels to merely sit down." Even the narrow couch waiting back in the cramped trailer would be welcomed tonight.

"Got to hand it to you, Miss Magnolia. Getting a job second day here." Tingley fished in the checkered pants pocket and brought out a crumpled pack of Lucky Strikes.

"A crazy job. Not much like the Carnegie Library in Alabama." She brushed back her hair with both hands and looked at him. This man knew something she needed to know. Illogical thought, but it felt true. "And you! Have you been to the newspaper in town yet?"

His brown eyes turned so bleak she studied the scarred table top and sipped her drink until he spoke again. "Well, it's like this, I'm going to go to the *Times*, real soon. I'll walk in there – when I have a good story in my hands to prove that I'm a damned good reporter."

Stubby, stained fingers tapped the flattened pack of cigarettes. "They won't give a – won't care if I have a suitcase full of J. T. Tingley by-lines from two-bit towns. All those who-when-whats are hack stuff anyway. Facts are so limiting, you know? It's people I want to write about, like my pal Ernie. Ernie Pyle. I have a deep down itch for the whys and the how-comes, too. You're looking at a sleuthing reporter, did I tell you? This schnozz smells when something's covered up, even before it starts to stink."

Tingley lit his cigarette, took a drag, tapped its glow hard against the pink sea shell already filled with ashes. "In the meantime, I have a job, of sorts." With a grimace, he pulled a folded tabloid from a back pocket and laid it on the table.

"*Gulffront Journal.* I'm selling ads and delivering papers up and down the beach. Temporary of course." The grin bloomed and wavered. "It'll keep me eating and on wheels for the time being while I work on my story. They let me use a '36 Chevy. It's pretty beat-up, but I've had it all day. It rolls."

She had to smile. Maybe the man attracted her sympathy. "All that in two days. Then you're doing all right, too." She watched him brighten.

"Aw, that's not my real news, Miss Magnolia." Snuffing cigarette ash against the shell, he leaned closer. "I've found my story. How 'bout that, huh? At this point, you're the one person I'm telling because – well, just hear me out." The brown eyes gleamed again. "Remember old Silver Bucks on the train? Alderman? Know why he's down here, hating Florida the way he does? His daughter drowned in the bay out here, six months ago."

"I know that." She didn't want to hear any more about Nancy Alderman.

"Yeah, guess Uncle Chuck would have told you. Did he tell you how up and down the beach folks are wondering if the murderer's still around, sure to press some other little white throat and throw the evidence in the drink like so much fish bait? Aw now, didn't mean to make you shudder like that. But I'm telling you things you need to know. There are a couple other local daughters missing, too."

"I know, Tingley. What if they've only followed soldiers off somewhere?" She was echoing Chuck now. But she didn't want to hear this. It made her wonder about Gil.

"Hey. You've heard about those girls. But that's not all."

"In two days you know everything that's going on?"

"Starting to." Tingley leaned forward, grinning. "I'm staying down at Johns Pass. Bunch of little cottages, for fishermen mostly. When you wanna know something about a town or a waterfront like this, you don't go ask some flunky in the sheriff's department. You get pally with a bartender. They are repositories of scuttlebutt and wisdom."

"Bartenders don't explain murders to the customers, do they?"

"Naw, naw. Like I say, you have to get pally and listen real good."

"So the Alderman girl is your story. Tingley, I'm tired. This was my first Saturday doing this job." She looked across the smoky barroom.

"No wait. That's part of it. Just one part of it. You need to know the rest." His blunt forefinger played with the spilled ashes on the scarred wood.

"This is unincorporated county around here, Miss Lelia Magnolia. The sheriff has a man out here, fellow named Brockway who is nosing around like he's in no big hurry. Supposed to be looking for that lil' gal who took a shot at a lieutenant, but everybody knows Brockway's scouting for the real dope on that Alderman girl. If he wasn't working on the murder before, he will be now. Silver Bucks came down here to kick the sheriff's ass – pardon my French, you know what I mean."

Lelia took a deep breath. "What do your bartender pals say about Nancy Alderman?"

"He says Alderman's darlin' daughter came down here to meet a boyfriend, a Navy fellow. They'd come into his place at Johns Pass. They all remember the girl, had a cocky Yankee attitude. A pretty long-legged, dark-eyed beauty. Like you. This girl got huffy with the Navy boyfriend one night and walked out. He tore out after her, mad as the devil. They are sure that's the girl."

Gil? He'd been around, out of uniform, only three months. Nancy Alderman was killed six months ago. "Go on," she said.

"Sooo – the jealous boyfriend could have found her and then – whatever happened, happened. He disappeared back into the Navy, but I can't check that out. Brockway can, being the law, not that he'd tell me. But you don't jump to conclusions on these things. Some other GI Joe could be around with his head messed up, doing in sweet young things."

She remembered the dream. The girls' faces mouthing some kind of message. But not a clear flash, not a Knowing.

"No more bodies have shown up, Miss Magnolia, but –"

"Bodies, oh, Tingley." She shivered in annoyance and apprehension.

"But this one little gal in particular is missing and I'm curious. Well, she used to work here, you've got her job, Miss Magnolia."

"I know about Susie Holms too, Tingley." She wanted to stay out of this. She looked over toward the yellowed bar mirror, almost afraid to see the girl's face. Only Chuck was there, smoking and listening to his war news.

She remembered the Knowings about Tingley. "Be careful with your sleuthing. Don't grab at empty balloons. Or loaded ones."

"My nose is twitching all right." He looked toward the bar. "What else has Uncle Chuck told you?"

"Parents have come out here, complaining. The Crittens are uptight about criticism. Especially since they have what Chuck calls the lemonade trade now. Tingley, don't girls go off with soldiers all the time?"

"Makes the world go 'round. But I found out those two girls disappeared without a toothbrush and without telling a girlfriend or mama. I figure they looked into some soldier boy's eyes in the dark and got surprised."

"I hear women talk. They blame the house parties people give for the soldiers. Do you know about the big yacht that docks here?"

"Evander Merrill. Yeah, the Hollywood dude with the big boat doing his bit for the boys. Ha. The yacht's gonna be part of my story – gives it some juice, big fancy boat like that on this lil' old waterfront. But the movie star fellow wouldn't need to fool with any jail-bait daughters. He could have all the St. Pete dames he wants."

Tingley's forefinger pushed the ashes together to a little pile on the table. "See what I'm getting at – that rich Nancy and missing Susie and those two gone girls might tie in together to make one big story. What do you think of that?"

"I'd say you were trying to make it one-big-story." But she wasn't sure at all.

"Yeah. Maybe you're right. Maybe the other girls are in some tourist cabins in Georgia, hoping the fellow will take them to a preacher so they can write home and tell Mama it's all right."

"Yes!" For an instant she could see their faces. Maybe it was because she wanted to believe they were alive. "They're staying away because they are –" She waited for a word to come, "ashamed, I think. And Susie is angry." Yes, she'd felt that. "Are you going to warn me, too? Everyone else has. Do I appear that naive? Don't worry. I have always looked after myself. I wear an invisible shield. Men stay at a distance." She laughed, making a joke of the truth.

"Glad to hear that. Knowing why you're here, I figure you'll need protection – and not just from the young and handsome in uniform either." His face was serious.

"Then you are warning me. Do you figure me in your story, too? Tell me, because I have to go now."

"That house you're looking for is the big one on the gulf. Has Uncle Chuck leveled with you about that place and the hermit woman?"

"Yes. I know. Hurricane House." She wanted this to end.

"Old timers around here say she got rid of the Elliots." His grin lines tightened to a grimace. "Know about your daddy drowning, too?"

"I know that much." It came out a whisper. Did Tingley know more, already? "You've probably heard all the gossip about Kali. But that's the past." For you, but not for me.

"If I'm going to do a story about strange happenings on these bucolic beaches, I'll start with the past as background and go on from there. New murders, soldiers all over the place, and now a fancy movie star yacht – makes a story about these beaches every tabloid and wire service will pick up."

"Kali won't like that," Lelia said quickly.

"Naw, I guess she wouldn't at that. That's why, Miss Lelia Magnolia, I wanted to tell you to stay away from that old woman. I know you were curious about seeing your daddy's house. But no fooling – stay away."

Silently, she watched Tingley's stubby finger push the spilled ashes into one pile.

"There's one more thing I gotta tell you. Something I found out this afternoon about Alderman's daughter. Heard it on the Inn front porch. She came down to see the boyfriend all right. But she stayed by herself at the Inn for a whole week. And she'd walk down that beach, nosing around that big house. She was real curious and interested, telling folks at the Inn she wanted Daddy to buy the place. Maybe she went inside and got herself in trouble there."

It felt true. She looked away, concentrating on Chuck talking the last two GIs into leaving. Hazel had gone. A tall jet black woman in a flower-sacking dress came out of the kitchen and with slow and idle grace began cleaning off tables. Cheta, Conch's wife, Lelia guessed.

"Right now, it's just a bag of worms. But I'll figure it out," he said.

She stood up. "I know how it feels to want something you can't grasp or prove. Maybe it makes us imagine more than is really there."

"Aw, you think I'm some kind of a nut." The heavy clown eyebrows went up and down. "Maybe I am. But I've got good instincts. You'll see." He balanced the pink sea shell on top of the little pile of ashes and got up, too.

"Tingley, I'll tell you something. You're going to find your big story regardless of what anybody says. And I'm going back to Hurricane House, no matter what anyone says. Good night now."

She walked out. In the silent, humid night, she started running toward Piney Cove and the lighted trailer.

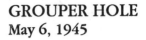

GROUPER HOLE
May 6, 1945

12

Midday Sunday, sunburned tourists and the khaki crowd poured into the smoky barroom and throb of juke box beat. Earlier Chuck had promised, "Sundays are different from Saturday nights. The sandy crowd shows up in a lazy stupor from too much beach sun."

By noon, they knew this Sunday would be anything but ordinary.

The small Philco behind the bar chattered with the news. On this May 6, 1945 – any hour now – the war in Europe was about to end.

Racing from kitchen to porch to booths with plates of crab cakes and trays of pop, Lelia enjoyed the energy of the place for the first time. Subdued energy as yet, but crackling like hope.

Pink-nosed girls, their bathing suits rolled in wet towels, stood around the Wurlitzer, feeding in nickels, and drinking lemon Cokes. Dinah Shore's voice flowed out again and again, the yearning notes smooth as cream, "You'd Be Sooo Nice to Come Home To."

Middle-aged tourists wandered in, faces flushed with unaccustomed sun; balding men in their baggy shorts, their wives in sundresses gazed around with half-smiles, taking in pine walls hung with nets and hats and mounted with the hard shapes of dusty fish. Today they wanted to smile at noisy GIs at the bar. When Lelia brought their ten-cent sodas and three-for-a-quarter crab cakes, their expectant faces held her, needing to talk.

"Look at this pretty girl here on this old waterfront."

"Honey, have you ever seen Miami Beach? White-gloved doormen down there on Miami Beach –"

"Not like this coast, but sleeping's fine in that dinky cottage over on the beach, windows open to the sweetest breeze and the sound of surf."

"Like I told the better-half just now," a portly fellow beamed up at Lelia, "One of these days, I wouldn't mind just packing up and moving down. Have an orange tree in the front yard. Let life be as simple as that. You could live longer down here, no worries."

Two couples from Lansing had Lelia take their picture. They stood close under Moby Flounder, beaming toward their Brownie camera, chorusing "V-E Day" as the juke box wailed, and Lelia snapped the picture.

"Thanks, honey. We won't ever forget this Sunday, just like we won't forget December Seven four years ago. We'll say we were in this old waterfront place, way down in Florida, looking at the prettiest girl outside of the movies, a whole assortment of GIs and waterfront characters hopping up and down at the bar –"

At the bar, Chuck shouted. "Lelia, pull the plug on the juke." He turned up the bar radio to a vibrating squawk as Artie Shaw's clarinet went quiet. Lelia sat down at Hazel's empty piano bench to watch the room. Murmurs faded to listen to the radio voice, solemn and triumphant:

> "After five years, eight months and six days, the European warfare, greatest, bloodiest and costliest war in human history, is about to come to an end. . . . General Eisenhower is now in headquarters at Reims, France, to meet with the Chief of Staff of the German Army."

A young Coast Guardsman sloshed a spiral of beer suds with his leap. "I'm going back to Kansas and marry Florrie Putnam. If she's not around, maybe Dottie Enholm. But never gonna set foot in anything bigger'n a rowboat." His face held his grin, undaunted by the volley of hoots and protests exploding from the swiveling stools.

"Forget Kansas, Sonny – there's a lil' geisha gal or a Yokohama mama waiting for you . . ."

"After we whip Hirohito's ass first."

"Why do you think we're here, being inoculated by Florida mosquitoes? Getting ready for the Pacific where they're big-ger'n hornets."

"Not funny, McGee. You're talking about real hellhole spots in the Pacific . . ."

Artie Shaw's clarinet resumed its wail.

In the kitchen, Lelia watched Conch fill a tray of crab cakes. "What do you do – when you're not here?" she said finally.

"Told you." His rattling pans sounded angry. "I got my place ovah in the palmettos 'cross the road. Got me a good woman, no matter what folks say."

"Cheta. Who goes over to Hurricane House?"

"Sometimes she goes."

"The girl who used to work here, do you know where Susie is?" Last night she'd dreamed of that girl's face again, Susie and the others. "Do you know anything about her? I keep feeling her around."

Conch's back straightened. He took his time turning around. He's hiding something about Susie, she was sure. The big brown face stayed a careful mask. "That youngun played risky and got herself in trouble. You goan hafta be smarter, lil' lady."

"In what way? With any one in particular?" Yes, he knew more than he intended to tell. About Kali? Or the person who murdered Nancy Alderman? Talk to me, Conch.

"Live long as I have, and you know all about snakes. They slink around where you least expect. Two-legged is the worst kind. Lord forgive me if I look the other way. The ones I catch are worth my catching. Their skins goan buy me more land to plant me some grove."

Back into the barroom with her tray, Lelia watched Francie sweep in, wearing a peasant blouse and billowing blue cotton skirt, the red curls tucked under a white straw hat. "I'm here!" Following behind, two women in pastel linens, disapproval written on Elise Welburn's patrician features, curiosity radiating from the one who must be Aunt Mo.

Lelia led them past the bar and out to the screened porch occupied by other sun-hatted chattering women. Francie trailed behind, steps lagging at the sound of a low whistle from the bar before she dropped into a wicker chair, wearing a smile of rapt innocence.

"Mother and Aunt Mo aren't silly about movie stars like I am. But I told them they really should see Evander Merrill or at least where he docks his big old yacht all the time." Francie looked up, the blue eyes beaming a warning to Lelia. "I also told them that you were doing this for a summer job."

"Very industrious, a summer job," Elise Welburn murmured. "But of course a young woman should be aware of the type of situation in which she places herself."

"I have plans, yes, but right now, I have to be here," Lelia said.

Aunt Mo's breathy voice was more kind. "Francine says you two are friends. Now I think that's lovely. Elise, we could easily stay a few more days at the Inn."

"Don't encourage her, Sister. We're not staying, I told you that."

When the trio finally marched back through the bar and out the front door, a flushed Francie darted back inside to grab Lelia's arm. "Isn't Mother a snob! But I'll be back. Listen – I saw the most gorgeous man at the dock. Better looking than Van Johnson. And he was really staring at me. His boat is the *Strike*. Do you know him?"

"I do – and I don't." Oh, Francie, go find some other gorgeous man. Your mother and I would both disapprove of this one.

Sweeping toward the screened door, Francie collided with the blond boy coming in. Dummy, surely. Shells spilled over the wooden floor.

The redhead squealed, "Oh! I'm so sorry; let me help you." Dropping down, blue skirt billowing around her, "Do you sell these things? They're so pretty!"

The boy stooped down too, his silent unsmiling face inches from Francie's as he scooped shell jewelry back into the tray. He bounced up and walked quickly out to the dining porch where smiling women waved. "There's Dummy! Over here!"

At the door, Francie huffed. "Well! He could have said something. Lelia – don't forget, you've got to come to the Inn before we go, please?" Sighing, she ran out into the sunny yard where the blue Packard waited, motor running.

Lelia watched the skinny young man in his baggy fatigues wander about the porch. Martha Critten wasn't around. She wasn't going to run the boy off. He moved like a dutiful prisoner of his own silence, pausing now and then to let women finger his tray of wares and maybe hand him some coins.

What a cruel name, Dummy. Surely he must read lips. She felt his loneliness so acutely that she had to turn away, impatient with the hurt of it. The place was quieter now. She had to get out alone, to the beach.

"I'm leaving," she told Chuck without waiting for an answer.

The two-piece bathing suit, an orange latex discard from Hazel, tight as skin, left her body free. Lelia dropped the towel and ran down the wet, spongy shore, hair flying, trying to keep up with three pelicans sweeping across the color-streaked surf. She stopped to watch the huge gray birds settled on the waves, rock with them. That's what I must do here, she thought. Ride with what's happening. I must be patient. Stay controlled. Hadn't she always been controlled?

The late sun slanted across the lapping waves. Footprints in the sand made purple shadows, the beach open and empty of anything now but sea gulls and the little birds picking at the surf's ebb and flow. No, someone knelt at the water's edge in front of the swim pavilion. A long-legged boy stood up. It was Dummy, in swimming trunks, not the baggy fatigues. She saw he was not a boy, but her own age or older, a wiry body but with a man's muscled shoulders.

As she watched, he left the box on the shore and strode into the gulf . . . paused an instant and plunged into a wave. His lean body cut through the water with swift grace. How much she'd like to do that! Some urge pulled her toward it, but caution held her back.

Passing the metal box, she glanced at the fresh collection of perfect shells, the kind he used for the earrings and necklaces. This was the way he lived, trapped in his silence. Obviously though, he was happy in the waves, out there like a blond fish, moving freely.

Down the beach she picked up her towel, intending to go, but stopped. A beginning sunset streaked a wide band of gold across the water toward her feet in the edge of the surf. Overhead, a lavender and blue sky colored the incoming waves, roaring softly like a sighing invitation. She dropped the towel and waded into the water, then gave herself to it, waist deep.

The waves came to meet her. So did the blond head, popping up close by, shining in the dull gold sun like his slim face. She smiled back, rocked in the surf, sand oozing under her feet. This beautiful boy made a funny sound, shook his head, and motioned for her to follow.

"I can't swim that well," she called out over the roar, repeating it with a shake of the head and arm motions of swim strokes.

He dove under, moving swiftly just below the surface. Popped up again, his arms encircling her waist, forcing her to stroke the water.

"Hey – are you teaching me to swim or trying to drown me?"

His smile didn't change but he let go, swimming around her, a playful sea animal, bidding her to follow.

She did. With an ease that followed the initial daring, she swam alongside him, with long easy strokes, both of them rising and falling with the waves. So this was how it felt to let go, abandon fear, trusting your body to surge ahead . . .

Until, looking up over green swells, she saw only open

horizon, no land. Her feet went down to seek sand and found none. Sputtering, she tried to turn. Powerful waves pushed her down into the green surging world. When she came up, salt seared her nose and throat, and the blond head was far away, appearing, disappearing in the waves.

Breathe, remember the stroke, remember the rhythm of it, trust the water, use the current. Yes.

Gasping, she swam again, struggling toward shore. Rough, shallow waves knocked her the final distance, slamming her down against hard shells and solid sand where she sat, rubbing her legs and regaining her breath. Out there, Dummy's head and arms still flashed, swimming with power back toward the pavilion where he'd left his shells.

The waves had angled her farther up the beach in front of the jungle that hid Hurricane House. Legs still trembling, she stood a moment to look. The dull glint of the top floor windows showed above the green. Did Nancy Alderman take that path in from the beach through the seagrapes? Was that the girl's mistake? Or did she meet up with someone like Dummy? Shivering again, she had to wonder – would Dummy have let her drown out there? Or was he just a lonely deaf-mute kid, trying to share his one joy, swimming?

She found her towel, put it around her wet, chilled body and ran back toward the bridge. Forget Dummy. And Gil. This morning's buoyant hope came back. Something was about to happen as well as V-E Day. Another door was about to open.

GROUPER HOLE
May 7, 1945

13

Monday afternoon, and Grouper Hole hummed like a Saturday night. Hazel burst in, blinking behind her dark glasses. She had pulled on red shorts and a yellow top and tied a scarf around her head, not taking time to pin on the topknot of curls.

"Hey, Chuckie, Lelia – I got news!"

Behind the bar, Chuck muttered to Lelia, "I knew it'd take the end of a war to get Haz in here before dark." He continued to pull drafts of beer for the noisy stand-up crowd.

Hazel swung onto the end stool. "Wait up, dammit. Let's talk."

"Later." Chuck slid down a ginger ale and bourbon. "Lelia's running all over the place. Bubba had to go after more ice. Martha's on the warpath in the kitchen." He strode back down the alley to turn up the radio for the next bulletin blare:

> ". . . announced officially after German broadcasts told the German people that Grand Admiral Karl Doenitz had ordered the capitulation of all fighting forces and called off the U-boat war . . ."

"Well I'll be damned," Hazel said. "Is it really over?"

Cold pitcher in one arm and headed for the crowded porch, Lelia handed Hazel a newspaper with its black headlines.

OFFICIAL V-E DAY
WAR IN EUROPE OVER!

Francie and her Aunt Mo were on the porch expecting her to sit down. Impossible. She wished devoutly Francie would stay out of this place. Of course the girl wanted to share in this excitement too. The redhead had shown up in a cloud of pink-and-white dotted swiss, face flushed and with subdued delight, explaining her mother had to go home to see her doctor. She would be staying at the Inn with her aunt.

Dummy came in, no happy blond fish now, but again the silent lost soul in his fatigues, carrying his tray. He retreated quickly to the empty piano bench and sat there. Like an outsider in a strange land, Lelia thought.

On the porch, Francie must have been watching too. The girl jumped to her feet, waving white plump arms, demanding his attention. "Here, out here!"

Dummy walked to the porch as if mesmerized by the gesturing, dancing girl with the red-gold hair. At the table, Francie flung her arms around his rigid shoulders and hugged him. As quickly, she drew back and plopped down in her chair. The giggly laugh was part sob.

"I just had to hug somebody! Nobody thinks I care. And I do," Francie wailed to the faces watching from the crowded porch. "I've never known a day when boys weren't going off. Oh, don't look at me like that." She turned a flushed face to Dummy. "Sit down with us, please. Aunt Mo and I are going to buy all your jewelry, aren't we, Aunt Mo?" She stared until Dummy sank into the chair, no change on his own face.

You are strange, Lelia thought.

Tingley swaggered in, waving the newspaper. "Read all about it. The radio's good for 'Amos 'n Andy' and bulletins, but not news. You gotta read it with your own eyes." He slapped Cap'n on the back. "Chuck, listen to this. 'In St. Pete air-raid sirens proclaim the welcome news that V-E Day is officially declared.' Now get this: 'Liquor and package stores will be closed for a 24-hour period.'"

At the moans and razzes, "Naw, that's good. Huh, Chuck? All the celebrating will be going on out here on the beaches, from Pass-a-Grille to good old Grouper Hole, Miz Martha Critten's famous house of repute."

Cap'n came off his stool to jab Tingley with a skinny elbow. "Here she comes now."

Martha Critten sidled down the bar alley, stopping midway, arms folded over the big flowered breasts. From over the glasses anchored on her snub nose, the woman looked at her noisy customers.

"One round on the house for everybody." With a nod toward Cap'n and Skipper's bald heads, "even you two old pirates from the Spanish-American War or was it the Crusades. And include Fascinatin' Hazel down there, but not any clown who can't hold his liquor." She glared toward Tingley. "Now when the rest of you whip the Japs, come back, and I'll make it a double."

The minute Martha Critten marched out, Hazel jumped up. "Bartender – over here, dammit! And wait up, Lelia! I've got news too."

"What's the problem, Haz? Lelia, let's see what's on her mind."

"I've won!" Hazel dropped back on the stool to look at both of them from behind the dark glasses. "I've finally won. Not like I planned it. But listen."

The husky voice went silky with satisfaction, telling about the phone call in the phone booth in the trailer park from Doc Miller in town.

"The old cuss wanted to speak to Lelia, but I said he'd have to talk to me first. He was at Mound Park Hospital, calling for the Spook herself."

"Kali? In the hospital?" Lelia asked. "Why?"

Hazel shrugged. "She fell Friday night after we left or the next morning. That loner Gil found her early Saturday and got her into town."

"Gil," Lelia murmured, "Did he find her in the house?" *Does he have reason to go into that house?*

"No – out in the yard on that damn board walk."

"Where you pitched out the plank," Chuck said.

"That's not the point of this news, Buster." Hazel lit a cigarette, fingers trembling. She answered through the plume of smoke. "Anyway, she's there in the hospital with a broken leg or cracked hip or something, and Miller says she can't go home alone, soo – now get this."

She leaned close, beaming behind the dark glasses. "Kali tells him to call Lelia to come over and take care of her. The nerve! You know she has that weird colored gal Cheta going over there regular. The old Spook has some gall asking that. Of course, I said no-way."

It's happening, Lelia knew. Another locked door was opening.

"So?" Chuck sounded grim. "What's the good news?"

"I told him we weren't about to let Lelia go over there alone in some kind of service to that old witch. But I said she might – if we ALL went over. I mean move in, one hundred percent. There!" The red nails drummed the bar top.

"Go on," Chuck said.

"So he leaves me hanging on the line ten minutes and comes back sounding stiff, but saying yes. Kali agreed."

"You haven't asked Lelia," Chuck said.

Hazel took off the dark glasses revealing gray-green eyes naked and defenseless without the black mascara.

"You game, Honeychile? Maybe that old woman likes to do in sweet young things. Maybe she wants to finish off the rest of the Elliots. You and Chuck are the last."

Chuck groaned. "Thanks a lot. Lelia, looks like it's up to you. Maybe Kali only wants you to bring up her food or something. She lives upstairs. Always has."

"How soon can we move in?" Lelia asked.

"Tomorrow." Hazel grinned. "He's bringing her back to the house at ten in the morning. We can come after that." The dark glasses went back on. The red smile widened. "Don't worry, Honeychile. We'll be there, too, watching if she tries to spook you."

On the last night she would sleep in the cramped trailer, Lelia woke, still heavy with the dream that held some message. Willingly, she followed the sense of it back in . . .

Into darkness and rain, lashing at a carved weather-beaten door . . . Hazel crouching by the door, wind tearing away her long lashes and the topknot of curls . . . Chuck stands, face in his hands, waiting for her to open the door . . . Why does she turn away? Gil is there in the blowing rain. She reaches toward him even as the dark ache stirs and rises in her core . . . He is holding a girl in his arms, her wet body trailing seaweed . . . Is it Francie? . . . Hazel is angry, red mouth working, saying, "Open the door. . ."

Inside, someone stands at the top of the stairs, a girl, strangely familiar. Is the girl herself? . . . She climbs the stairs and follows an endless hall past so many doors yet to be opened . . . one opens to a room with no walls . . . dark waves surging below calling her name.

On the couch in the trailer, Lelia surfaced again, heart pounding, before falling back into exhausted sleep. When morning light woke her, she searched her memory tentatively, but the dream from last night had faded. Only anticipation remained.

GULFSHORE
May 8, 1945

14

Kicking the screen door open, Hazel burst out of the trailer, skinny arms wrapped around a box of old stage costumes. She wore a red playsuit and heels, the topknot of curls pinned on askew, held by a scarf.

At the Nash, Lelia helped force in the final box of wrinkled satins and black-beaded gowns, sad looking in the bright sun.

Hazel muttered, "Ought to dump this stuff. Some day I'm going to dress like a goddamn lady. Now – if Chuck will get his ass over here so we can go. He walked over to the office. Whatcha bet he's making a deal not to give up this dump of a trailer just in case we have to crawl back."

"I could leave now since I'm walking."

"Damn his hide. Making me wait like this. Oh, don't gimme that look and tell me you've waited, too. For what? To get your nose in the Elliot homeplace. Be sentimental all you like, Kiddo, not me. I don't give my folks a thought."

"Except your father." A gaunt-faced man who would strike the thin child. Anytime she studied Hazel, that image could flash.

"What's Chuck been saying about my old man? No, don't tell me. Anyway, Pa had more guts than Chuck'll ever have for all his brawn and book smarts."

They stood silent in the sun-spotted shade, Lelia breathing down impatience, Hazel leaning against the hood of the parked car, smoking furiously.

"I got news for everybody. I'm not coming back!" Hazel said.

"You won't. You won't be back here."

"Miss Sure-of-herself. You'd better be right. And don't forget for a minute who that place belongs to once we do get the witch out."

"Chuck doesn't want to move over there. He's proud."

"Stuffy pride maybe and soft backbone." Hazel sighed. "He's really a sweet guy, but it galls me how he blames everything that's gone wrong in his life on his daddy walking out – even more than his mother getting murdered. And yet, look at him, a big, tough-acting guy but afraid to face up to Kali who did his folks in."

"What else do you know about Don Elliot?"

"An artist, when he wasn't traveling off someplace with Bonnie. Had a studio, Chuck says, in that third floor tower room. They were rich with her money like I told you. What more to know? They were rich and young and beautiful, and then she was dead and he was gone. Nobody left but Kali and two little kids she shipped off to school. Holy Mackerel, do you realize we're about to move in with that woman who's killed off all the Elliots she hadn't run off?"

Hazel dug the cigarette butt into the sand with a red heel. "Aren't you worried? You're so damn calm. Or maybe you're a dumb dreamer. Oh, go ahead and start walking. I see him coming."

Lelia reached midbridge before the shiver eased in her shoulders. How little Hazel or anyone knew of her fears. Hiding them was a matter of control. On the bright beach, swimmers filtered out of the swim pavilion. The gulf rolled in, flat and glittering as she headed past the Inn toward the house in its patch of jungle.

From the Inn's piney shade came a squealed greeting. Oh, no, Francie, not now, Lelia thought. But the girl was running forward, sunhat held down with both hands, white legs pumping under the pleated shorts. Up close, Francie's face glowed pink with sun and pleasure. "Lelia, wait! I have the craziest news. Come back and sit with me."

"I can't now, Francie. We're moving into a house on the beach today."

"How marvelous. I'll walk with you. Aunt Mo is downtown at the celebration. Which house is it?"

"Behind the jungle."

"That spooky old place? Is it really haunted like people say? You're not going to live there with that hermit woman, are you?"

"Tell you later. Walk with me. So what's your crazy news?"

Splashing barefoot along the surf's edge, Francie explained in a rush of breathy confidence. Auntie had gone to town this morning to hear speeches in the park but had let her stay out here, which meant a wonderful chance to wear the new bathing suit and get into the gulf before the sun got bad, so she wouldn't burn of course.

"Well! I almost drowned!"

Lelia stopped short. "You're not joking."

"I just meant to kick around in the shallow part. Actually, I'd love to swim like Esther Williams and for that matter skate like Sonja Henie."

"Back to the almost-drowning." Hurry up, Francie, the house is near. They walked again.

"I got this little old cramp in my foot, and with the waves pulling me and knocking me around, then I felt something nibbling at my feet, oh – anyway I just screamed. And here came my rescuers."

Francie quickened her stride to match Lelia's. "Do you know they BOTH swim like fish? There I was, gagging, ugh, salt in my nose and eyes and my hair pouring down over my face when poor sweet Dummy came splashing up, grabbing me, and I was so frightened, but then there was Gil helping him. He'd seen us and dived right out of his boat!"

"Go on, Francie." She watched the girl's face, radiant in the hat's pink shade.

"First, Dummy was grabbing me, then Gil popped up out of the waves, shouting to Dummy and holding me up, my face right up against his chest and those curly hairs and big brown shoulders. The way he looked at me! Not grinning like stupid boys do." Francie sighed. "Well, Dummy was sweet, too, thrashing around, swimming alongside as Gil pulled me in. You know Dummy doesn't talk, well, not any sounds you can understand so he couldn't explain he was trying to save me and not trying to drown me, for goodness sakes."

"And then?"

"On the beach, Dummy ran away, but Gil stayed and lectured me like a meanie." The pout eased to a minxish smile. "Gil is that terrific-looking man I asked you about before."

With calm she didn't feel, Lelia replied, "I'm glad you're all right. We're here. You get out of the sun."

She returned the girl's hug and watched her run back toward the Inn. For a moment, Lelia stayed at the surf's edge, studying glittering gulf, breathing deeply. Should she have warned Francie about Gil? No, the girl needed a listener, not more keepers. Then why the tight chest now? She knew, of course. Lelia studied the seamless blue sky until the flicker of dark fire in her body subsided, until it could be pushed far down, denied, ignored. Calm again, she turned from the gulf and headed toward the seagrape path that led into the jungle around Hurricane House.

The path to the house led through a low tangle of wind-gnarled seagrape bushes overgrown enough to discourage any curious beach-walker. Except perhaps a determined one like Nancy Alderman? Sandals dangling from her fingers, Lelia picked her way slowly through the knee-high growth. Sandspurs made sharp surprises for her bare feet. No sound of the Nash came yet from the other side of the house. Good. She needed time, alone.

The path ended in a narrow clearing. Clumps of blue periwinkles grew unattended from the yellow sand yard in front of the porch, the same place where her mother had been frightened on a night twenty-three years ago. Now the low porch was a long platform of weather-bleached planking. She sat on the edge to brush sandy feet and put on the sandals.

Palm fronds rustled and stilled again. Surf sounds came in, muted.

What am I supposed to know here? Breathing in, exhaling, she opened her senses to this place, eyes closed, hands opened on the rough, sun-warmed boards. An image came, a sunny porch with banisters, wicker chairs, a child, a small boy with pensive face. In a flash it was gone.

She opened her eyes to the present. Her father had been a child here. Had she seen him or imagined him? It was the twenty-year-old Lee Elliot she needed to understand. Why did he return here after his bride was taken away back to Alabama? Why did he go out in that boat and drown? The wind rose and fell into silence. But she knew. He had come back here for answers. Just as she had.

She stood, rubbing chilled arms in bright sun. Where in all this greenery – the front or the side – was Bonnie's grave? The vine-wrapped trees and low palmettos made a dense jungle to one side of the house. The grave didn't matter anyway, she thought. Not if the spirit of the woman could reach out over time and space into her mind and at least once, materialize.

"Are you here now?" Lelia whispered.

She felt the house watching. Or maybe it was Kali in there watching. Lelia looked up at the grayed and weathered presence. Gables and balconies gave it lidded eyes, gazing out to sea. A sad, proud face, hiding its secrets. The third floor was the tower room, Chuck had said. Years of salt-spray deadened its window-eyes. But along the second floor, partially open French doors gleamed back the sunlight. They opened to a wrought-iron balcony with a stairway that curled down to the side yard.

A rustle, and the Doberman was there, growling until she called to him sharply, "Orion! Remember me." She stroked the sleek dog. He followed her around the side of the house.

In front, a trim little man in a seersucker suit and Panama hat stomped at the boardwalk, putting the loose plank back in place. Under the banyan tree, leaning against a big sedan, waited a brawny Negro man in white, a hospital orderly, Lelia guessed. The man on the walk turned to look at her. Behind wire-rimmed glasses, his features were as precise and gray as the rest of him.

"I'm Lelia Elliot. You're Dr. Miller, aren't you? My uncle and his wife are on their way over."

The thin mouth tightened. "So you're the one." His voice was dry.

She tried to read behind the eyeglasses of this man who must know everything that had happened here. He got out a linen pocket handkerchief, touched his face, and wiped his hands in a brooding reverie. She had to ask a second time, "Kali – how is she?"

"We just took her up in a wheelchair. Ankle sprained and the right hip fractured. It may be months before she can go downstairs. But she insisted on being brought home. Against my approval, I must add. She is quite strong-minded." He gave the board one last stomp with a polished shoe before looking at her again. "The most independent of creatures has to accept help in some circumstances. So she has allowed you to come here."

The only reason? "Will Conch's wife, Cheta be here, too?"

"She comes when she pleases." Dr. Miller shrugged. "Are you willing to do what is expected of you?"

"And what is that? I work over at Grouper Hole, and I need the job. I'm not asking anything from Kali."

"But to live here? I understand you left home and came here to find this house. I hope not with the same tenacious purpose as your uncle's wife."

"This was my father's home. But you know that, don't you, Dr. Miller. So what is expected of me?"

"I cannot speak for Kali. But you are to prepare and bring her breakfast and dinner. I can warn you she eats very simply and strangely. Grains and fruit and herbs mostly. A great deal of the fruit grows on the grounds, so this should be no problem. There's something else. About the living arrangements –" He stopped to stare at the Nash chugging into the yard, parking now behind the waiting sedan. The seersucker shoulders stiffened at the sight of Hazel emerging from the car.

Quickly, turning back to Lelia. "You must know Kali is a strange woman, living alone so long. And I am a strange friend for such a woman. Nevertheless – I have tried to protect her." His lips tightened on that admission.

Chuck plodded over. Hazel sashayed behind him, heels digging into the sand, her red smile set. "Is she here?"

Dr. Miller directed his crisp answer to Chuck. "I brought her home, and I'm here to give you instructions. Lelia is to live upstairs. You two are to stay downstairs. It's the master bedroom as I'm sure you know, Charles. You are to look after yourselves. Kali doesn't wish to see anyone but the girl."

Hazel blinked, then smiled. "That's hunky-dory, Doc. Couldn't suit us better. We get the whole downstairs to ourselves. Lelia, you go on up and announce yourself. Chuck and I'll be moving in."

She's relieved, Lelia realized. She won't have to deal with Kali. I will.

Inside the weathered carved door, Lelia stood in the foyer, looking up the stairway. No figures waited there, only a shaft of sun lighting the second floor landing.

"Go on – go on up." An impatient Chuck brushed past, arms loaded with Hazel's boxes. He stalked through the silent living room, hesitating a moment in the darker paneled hall before disappearing toward the master bedroom.

She climbed the carpeted stairs, already knowing how the carved wood railing would feel under her hand.

A wide hall ran the length of the second floor. The shaft of sunlight came from the only open door in the center. A contralto voice called, "In here."

Just inside, Lelia stood still, absorbing this room of sunlight and shadows. The French doors, open to the balcony, framed the open gulf, brilliant in midday sun. At one end of the long room, a wall of books. At the other, an alcove with a tapestry covered bed. Over the bed, a huge painting, a seascape, swirled with pale sunrise colors.

Something gleamed from the pedestal table that centered the room. A perfect crystal ball sat high on its gold stems above its mahogany base, catching the sunlight, sending out needles of colored light.

This room was a hideaway, a sanctuary. From what? A low voice broke the spell.

"So. You are here." Kali moved into view. Even in the high-backed wheelchair, the woman once again gave the impression of an ancient priestess viewing the intruder into her kingdom. The long hair was pulled back and coiled over the erect shoulders. A woven cotton robe the color of old wine flowed down to the toes of the Oriental slippers and bandaged ankle.

"Chuck and Hazel are downstairs." She met the woman's gaze. Dark eyes, shadowed in the poised, amber face.

"I heard."

"I spoke with Dr. Miller. He told me about your fall. Are you feeling pain?"

Kali looked away to the gulf horizon beyond the balcony. Her voice blended with the sound of surf below. "I intend to heal quickly. Now, we must talk, to know if you are to stay. I have been alone for a very long time."

"I understand."

"Why are you here, Lelia Elliot?"

"You called. You invited us."

"I invited you. I allowed them. That is not why you left Alabama to come to this waterfront."

"This was my father's house. You must understand I want to know about him – and the Elliot family."

"The past. And you are young in the present."

"But I came from that past."

"Yes." Long fingers tapped the wheelchair arms. "Choices once made give shape to the present and seed the future."

"You mean 'sins of the father – visited upon those who come behind?'" So it was true, all her fears.

"It means there is an inexorable law of consequences – what is put into the universe, returns in time, in kind. Like a boomerang."

"Irrevocably? Like fate? It doesn't seem fair."

"There is another law which does not contradict – new

choices have power, too," Kali said. "You are young. You can make your choices."

Lelia looked beyond the balcony to the bright gulf. She wanted to say, How can I choose to live and love if some kind of madness has been planted in me? But she knew to be careful with this woman. Learn but not reveal. Aloud she said, "I want to know about the family. I have a right."

"So you come demanding answers, Lelia Elliot. Truth cannot be given to another; it has to be discovered." The dark eyes burned, the velvet voice lowered to a whisper. "I shall tell you this. I live with the past in this house. I accepted this. You must be sure you wish to know the past."

"All my life, yes. And as for Chuck and Hazel, they have been living in a trailer and Hazel wants —"

"I know what Hazel wants. Speak for yourself."

"I am. I wanted to see the house where my father brought my mother and where I began."

The dark eyes studied her. "Is that all you know?"

Lelia nodded. All that she would tell.

"You are not here to help that woman? Make your choice. Your own purpose, or Hazel's."

"My own." It was true, yet she was making a promise here not to help Hazel. Did she imagine a flicker of satisfaction in the controlled face? She wasn't sure, not sure of anything.

Kali pushed the wheelchair to the pedestal table and opened a slim drawer. "You are to have the room at the end of the hall on this floor. The others are to remain downstairs."

"They know. Doctor Miller told them."

The long fingers extended a paper, written in a fine hand. "Read this to know the food I shall require. One tray soon after sunrise and a second tray at sunset. I eat very simply. You will find everything answered here. Now, leave me until then."

With the paper in her skirt pocket, Lelia went downstairs. She found Hazel and Chuck in the living room.

Hazel held up a tarnished silver goblet, husky voice kept to a whisper. "Would you look at this stuff! Worth a mint. What did the old Spook have to say?"

"Hazel's going to play house," Chuck interrupted, "but

we've got to get back over the bridge, Lelia. Our movie star is due in. Place will be crazy."

"Hold it!" Hazel put down a china figurine. "I want to know what happened up there." She gave Lelia a warning look. "We made a bargain and don't forget it. The sooner we find out something on that old witch, the sooner we get her out."

"I only have to bring her an early breakfast and dinner at sunset," Lelia said. "It won't be difficult. You two have the downstairs to yourselves."

She couldn't tell Hazel she had just made some kind of pact with Kali.

GROUPER HOLE
May 8, 1945

15

Gliding down the narrow channel of Boca Ciega Bay, the *Silver Fox* made an imperial presence against mangroved shores and an occasional wooden shack. The yacht approached the bridge with parade grace, white hull gleaming.

From the embankment above Al's Bait House, Lelia watched with Cap'n and Skipper. She'd never seen a yacht. A 62-footer the old fishermen said, respect in their sighs.

Cap'n's leather-brown face looked wistful. "Pretty, ain't she, Miss Lelia? Real filthy rich uppity pretty. But I'd be mighty proud to sit in that pilothouse and take her into blue water, wind up to ten knots, one hand on the wheel, other on the throttle." The old man sighed.

"No chance," Skipper said

Cap'n shrugged his skinny shoulders. "That runty captain might let us come aboard sometimes. Maybe when the movie star's busy fighting off the wimmen and getting himself some of Conch's cooking. But naw, not when that first mate Sloan's around."

"Looks like a bouncer I saw oncet."

Cap'n glanced at Lelia. "Sloan guards Mister Movie Star like he was the Prince of Wales."

A young deckhand, polishing the mahogany railing, grinned down at them as the yacht waited at the bridge.

"That gooney kid," Skipper said. "Wouldn't have him on my yacht."

The three of them watched the bridge-tender trot out

with a long bar. The key, the old men explained. See, the fellow unlocks connections at both ends of the bridge then rides the center span around until it's parallel with the shore.

"Why is it here?" Lelia asked as the *Silver Fox* glided through, angling toward Grouper Hole's dock.

Cap'n pushed back his yellowed cap. "Oh, she sails between here and New Orleans when she wants to. Must have two 250-horsepower, Chris-Craft motors in her with a full 16-foot beam, besides those teak decks and fancy salons. Could sleep a dozen if that movie star wants that much company. He's got a crew of four on there. Doesn't do a lick of work himself, I betcha."

"Chuck says we'll be busy today," Lelia mused.

"Yeah, some wimmen and that loud newspaper fella are already over there. That Tingley's going to bite down on some bait he can't chew. He's around asking about them missing girls."

"What you tell him?" Skipper droned.

"Well, I told him all I knew about girls was I hadn't had one since I was fifty-nine and I forget how long ago that was. Aw, come on, let's go over and watch the wimmen show up and make Bubba sweat."

Conch's stove crackled with frying fish as Lelia came in. The big cook looked up from his hush puppy batter. "Glad you come bok. We got Mister Honsome today."

"I saw." She stood at the kitchen window, tying wind-blown hair back off her neck with a rolled scarf. Beyond the dock, the *Silver Fox* looked huge anchored out there. A big-shouldered man and a young one were securing the lines. "I watched it come in. Why are they here, on this waterfront I mean."

"Some folks like being a big fish in a little bay."

"And he comes for your food." But she felt Conch was right. Evander Merrill must enjoy the fuss he caused on this waterfront.

"Folks see the big boat acoming and they show up," Conch said, turning back to his grouper fillets. "Womenfolks, lemonade customers, the kind Miz Crit don't like. And everything has to be perfect for ole Honsome. When Mister B's worried, he's just more trouble under foot."

Lelia washed her hands at the sink, her body still humming, not from the fast walk over from the house, and not because of any movie star showing up. It was *happening* . . . As of an hour ago, she was now living in that house. Only a week ago, she was still trapped in Bethel. When locked doors do open and cracked walls start giving way, some inevitable force must sweep you along, too late to be stopped, even if you wished. Already she was caught between Kali and Hazel, but she would handle them both. She was in the house. The past waited there. Kali herself had said so.

She turned back to Conch. "Is Handsome on the porch yet?"

"Still on the boat." He looked up from the hush puppies. "Mister B says tell you they get the big round table in the porch corner. And use his mama's silver out of that drawer . . . But you still got time to pretty up the tomatoes."

Lelia carried washed tomatoes to the work table and started slicing into red ripeness, still thinking of Hurricane House. She'd left Hazel happy as a kid, ready to hang up the pile of clothes they'd dumped on the bed. Hazel, forgetting to be angry about anything, so pleased, turning around arms wide in that master bedroom, satisfied the whole house was practically hers, with Kali stuck in a wheelchair upstairs. What if Hazel knew Kali's upstairs seemed like a sunny sanctuary compared to the downstairs where musty air seemed like a caught breath? "That's a mess of tomatoes you're slicing, Miss Dreamer," Conch said, breaking her reverie.

Bubba burst in, fleshy face moist. "You got hearts of palm? He wants hearts of palm. There's three of 'em, without the captain. Him and that ape Sloan and Brockway. Shows you, any jerk can go buttin' in anybody's business when he's got a badge. Sheriff don't even give him a uniform, but Brockway's got that badge and his stinking nerve."

At the door of his cubby hole quarters, Bubba gave Lelia a pained stare. "They get the round corner table. And don't you be like that little bitch Susie and bug them about going on that yacht. You just smile pretty and keep 'em happy—and let them get the hell outa here." He slammed the door after him.

On this May Tuesday, with a V-E celebration going on in St. Pete, Grouper Hole buzzed with a subdued excitement, mostly soprano. Tingley watched from the bar between Cap'n and Skipper.

"Why aren't you downtown celebrating?" Lelia asked on her way to the porch with a checked cloth and Martha Critten's heavy old silver.

Tingley beamed. "The boys here are giving me the low-down before the show starts." He leaned out from his stool with a raspy, conspiratorial whisper. "Working on my story, Miss Magnolia, about these ole gulf beaches. I need a close-up look at this Hollywood fellow."

On the porch, a quartet of women from the Bath Club had descended on the round corner table Bubba meant for the Merrill party. Well, she wasn't about to make them gather up purses and hats and move. She set up another table next to the women. When she returned with the pitcher and glasses, all four were engrossed in watching who might parade down the dock from the yacht.

The first was a man about Chuck's age, but heavier, the burr head set rigid above the thick shoulders that were outlined in a tight sailor's jersey. Murmurs of disappointment from the women. "Who is that?"

"First mate Sloan, I believe," Lelia answered.

The women tightened their shoulders and continued to watch. Next came a lanky man in a rumpled brown suit following along with a loping gait.

"Sheriff's man, Brockway." It was Tingley at her elbow, beer in hand. Close to her ear, "If he's aboard asking a fancy movie star if his yacht parties are safe for local sweet young things, then he's a brave old cuss. But he might be just a good old country boy getting an autograph for mama and a free meal." He lifted his beer in salute and went back into the bar.

The women sat up straight. "That's him, oh, it really is!"

On the boardwalk just below the screened porch, Sloan and Brockway waited as Evander Merrill proceeded down the dock with the straight-backed assertiveness of a small-statured man, one who has learned to expect only welcome and esteem. Bright Florida sun gleamed on Merrill's golden tan, his silver pompadour and the white sharkskin suit.

The three men paused just below the screened porch before proceeding around to the front door. The women watched, exclaiming, "Oh, that face! Just like on the front of *Photoplay*!"

"Remember him in that picture with Madeleine Carroll or was that Douglas Fairbanks? I get them mixed up."

"Wasn't Rita Hayworth in love with him before she married somebody else? You don't read a thing about his wives. Has he had any?"

"Oh, one. Way back. She'd be old now."

"Well, he's no kid and he hasn't been in the service like Jimmy Stewart – but he helps morale, you know, around here anyway."

"Remember in that Donald O'Connor movie, Merrill played a four-star general? My husband hooted, but what does he know?"

"If he weren't a man, I'd say he's just beautiful. I bet this pretty girl thinks so, too, don't you, Hon? Oh – here they come!"

At the porch threshold, Evander Merrill paused in his white, tailored perfection. From behind the dark glasses, the tanned aquiline face turned, observing the screen porch audience of mostly women, then his own corner table occupied by four of them, upturned faces expectant.

Lelia saw the flicker of annoyance, saw how quickly he made it a smile. Evander Merrill nodded to the two men with him to proceed to the cloth-covered table. Was he going to ignore the Bath Clubbers' table so close? The elegant little man paused, and with a flicker of the *Photoplay* smile, murmured, "Lovely ladies." A tanned hand rested lightly on his blue shirt front, just above the trim waist, a promise of a bow. "It is our privilege to share the same view on this historic V-E day."

Merrill turned from their tittered response and took his chair, looking pleased with himself. The other two sat down, Brockway's long face fixed in a smile, Sloan's heavy features cold with displeasure for the seating.

Chuck brought their drinks and left as quickly. Lelia put down the plate of tomatoes and turned to go. Merrill's hand stopped her. A clammy hand, small-boned and insistent, for all its tan and flash of gold at the wrist and sparkle of diamond on the slim fingers.

"Look, Sloan, a lovely creature in place of Susie. Let me look at you, my dear." He said it *deah*, in his actor's voice, rich-toned and accented. Continental? Or honed during a dozen costume pictures on those Hollywood back lots she'd read about.

Evander Merrill slipped off the sunglasses to bestow the gift of his personal attention. The corners of his mouth lifted, along with his darker brows, making a pensive little smile. "You remind me of Jennifer Jones, my dear. In the native girl role, the fiery one. Am I not right, Sloan? It's the hair, and the face, with passionate depth behind the eyes. There are so many, too many empty little faces." A sigh. "Shouldn't we take her back with us?"

Sloan stayed silent with a look of grim patience. Lelia moved to go, but Merrill wasn't finished. "I must tell you this." The slim hand trailed the air, a gesture of eloquent sadness. "You don't want to offer that beauty to the crass, cruel film-makers. Stay here. Stay as you are." With a sigh, he returned the glasses to his face, held up his Scotch like a sad toast to himself, and sipped.

The Bath Club women who had watched, rapt with envy, looked at Lelia with uncertain smiles. They had witnessed her dismissal as well as theirs. *He's an actor*, Lelia wanted to remind them but walked away from the whole scene, amused, impatient to leave. Through the bar, she sailed past Chuck's sly smile and Tingley's wide grin.

"Yep, that was a real nice ride up from Johns Pass," Brockway was saying in his slow drawl when she returned with a tray for another table. "Good old waterfront we've got.

Nothing like you folks are used to in Hollywood. Makes a fellow wonder why you like it here."

"At present," Merrill answered with cool patience, "the yacht is home. When the war is over, I shall return to making pictures."

Brockway sloshed his drink around. "Tourists come down and think it's a lazy old place. Good thing they don't have my job. On top of everything, right now I've got this Alderman fellow from Boston on my tail, expecting me to check out every party for soldier boys anybody's been giving up and down this waterfront. Even the ones on a fine yacht like yours."

"So you told us," Sloan said.

Brockway looked solemn. "Understand why I had to come aboard and have your crew look at the girl's picture. Thought maybe they'd remember. Maybe they saw her having a fight with the boyfriend."

Merrill said, "And so you asked them." He looked bored. "Sloan?"

The first mate stood and signaled to the crewman on the upper deck of the waiting yacht.

Brockway didn't seem to notice. "Yeah, when I'm not shooting at some old alligator in a yard, I've got to be looking up these folks who give parties out here," Brockway explained. "Daughters talk them into it."

Merrill tapped his slim fingers against his glass. "We try to offer something special. A small gesture, of course. Hosts are not responsible for the hot blood of youthful ardor that happens elsewhere."

Brockway yawned and stood up. "One more thing, in appreciation of your hospitality – I oughta let you know there's this noisy newspaper fellow around who's hell-bent on making a story out of this Alderman girl. And all the parties, including yours on that fine yacht. Hope the fellow doesn't bother you."

Merrill waved the jeweled hand. "Sloan will tell you. I'm always besieged by the press. And not always fairly. It is the price one pays."

"Well, this Tingley fellow – the one in there a few minutes

ago, matter of fact – isn't looking for fan story stuff. I didn't want you to think Jim Brockway of the sheriff's department goes around half-cocked stirring up talk."

Lelia left the porch, eager to get back to Hurricane House but thinking, poor Tingley, you're going to get in trouble.

In the kitchen she told Conch, "Our Mr. Handsome is a good actor and a vain little man. But why should the Crittens worry about Brockway? He's slow as his drawl."

"All kinds of folks are good actors," Conch mumbled.

HURRICANE HOUSE
May 8, 1945

16

The Nash poked out of the overgrown front entrance, Hazel behind the wheel, dressed for the night, stopping to say, "The Spook's all yours, Kiddo. Take care, y'hear?"

In the middle of the bayside road, Lelia watched the car roll on toward the bridge, heading for the mainland. A jumpy Hazel leaving this early, dressed for the night, yellow hibiscus stuck in the hard curls like a flag of sassy courage, agitation strong as the perfume. Jumpy about spending the day alone in Hurricane House, even with Kali in a wheelchair upstairs, but not enough to give up the hard delight of being there. "A first step," Hazel had declared this morning as they moved in.

Lelia continued toward the house, into the rustling dark shade and patches of gold sun, followed to the porch by the silent Doberman. Why did she always hesitate at the front door? As if expecting to see – what? Nothing waited at the top of the stairs but a pale shaft of sun and silence. Fine. She had time to look around.

In the big living room, slanting sun rays glowed amber on carved wood, elegantly shaped old couches, lacquered surfaces and dark patterned Oriental carpet. A tall clock case, gilt and inlaid, French maybe, had long ago stopped counting time. Like the room? No, something seemed to wait here, suspended in time like these tarnished bronzes and dusty porcelain figures caught in their frozen poses.

Outside, waves hit the beach. The steady rhythm was the heartbeat of this house. "Are you here," she whispered, "whoever, whatever called me here?"

In the silence, her own heart throbbed to the same rhythm of the surf outside.

Knowings could not be forced. Messages from the strange part of herself could be denied, ignored, but not demanded. There was time enough, she told herself. She was here, in this place, by this shore. The truth about the Elliots waited somewhere in this house, and she would find it. She gazed around. These paintings must be Don Elliot's work. How alive they seemed. Seascapes mostly like the one upstairs in Kali's room.

Standing close to one, reading the signature released a shiver of delight. My grandfather did this – is this why I've always known the urge to paint? Over what was once a fireplace, another painting had been removed, the faded space showed. Was it the portrait relegated to the darkest wall?

She went over, stood below the burnished gold frame. Done in oils, a reclining figure looked down from a canvas dark and rich as an old master's. The young woman leaned back on a rose couch, a silken fringed shawl draped low over young breasts. Even here in the shadows, the shawl gleamed. Blonde hair cut in a 1920s style framed the fair, finely cut features. The tapered chin was lifted in confidence or defiance.

Bonnie Elliot. Bonnie Elliot in her twenties, more than forty years ago, then the rightful mistress of Hurricane House, now buried somewhere outside. But in this portrait, the eyes are so alive, Lelia thought. Restless eyes in spite of the curved lips. Was this impatience for having to be still for her young husband to paint this portrait? A slim white arm reached down, over the couch, toying with something. A cat, only its slanted eyes showing in the folds of the trailing shawl.

"Are you the one who called me, Bonnie? You or whatever you became?"

A soft thud made her wheel around. The Siamese had leaped onto a couch and settled there like a sphinx, watching.

"Nalo, Nalo, is that an ancestor of yours in the painting?"

The cat regarded her with lustrous blue eyes before it leaped off the couch and disappeared.

Quickly, Lelia went into the hall, then in the doorway of

the large master bedroom, Chuck and Hazel's quarters. During their hurried move-in this morning when Hazel had shown such open delight at the faded elegance, it had been easy to feel a rush of warmth for the bossy, brittle little woman. Warmth for Hazel and sympathy for Chuck.

How grim he'd looked, throwing open windows of the musty room as if trying to expel ghosts of his parents. No wonder Chuck didn't want to live here. Well, Hazel had definitely taken over this space, if not yet the house. On the big mahogany bed, garments were still piled on top of the faded rose satin cover, on the lounge by the windows, and even on the top of the carved salon desk, a lovely piece with an antique music box on top.

Panels of aged mirrors flanked the folding doors of closet space Hazel hadn't yet used. Bonnie's closet. Lelia shivered and went past to look into the high-ceilinged bathroom. The marble-topped dressing table was well strewn with Ponds and Max Factor and Lady Esther and the big blue bottle of Evening in Paris perfume.

Back in the bedroom, Lelia paused by the bed, again shivering. Mary Emily Calhoun Elliot had been here as a bride – a frightened bride. This was the bed where she had been conceived.

Lelia hurried back across the living room, colored now by amber gloom. The French doors to the porch – yes, this was where it happened, the Seaweed Woman out there in the windy night. It was just as well Hazel and Chuck didn't know.

She crossed the foyer, through a formal dining room, lifeless as a roped-off museum, the tall breakfront filled with tarnished silver and dusty crystal.

Beyond the heavy door, the kitchen was a big woody room, its musty smell lessened by the salt breeze coming in from the beach outside. A green lizard scampered across the stone floor, along the well-scrubbed wooden counters, an ancient yellowed sink, a bowl of grapefruit, still with some stems. Sink windows looked out on the thickest part of the jungle, and the back door opened into the sandy side yard. Only a screened door? But what outsider would wander in here?

She spread Kali's written instructions on the wood counter. The handwriting was as precise as her details. Each meal, morning and evening, must include fresh fruit, a cooked grain, and hot tea. Evenings might include a broth. She would find the grains, dried lentils, and the teas stored inside the wooden cabinets. Fresh herbs for seasoning would be found in abundance growing outside, also fruit from the trees – orange, grapefruit, avocado, papaya, and mango, whatever was ripe.

Lelia was studying a dozen Ball jars of dark dried leaves, pods, and seeds, finally choosing a tea when a sound made her wheel around. At the back screen door, a tall thin Negro woman watched, black and intent as an ebony statue.

"Cheta?" Lelia asked.

With a lazy grace, the woman sauntered in and took the jar from Lelia's hands. Frowning, she placed it back on the shelf. As silently, with a half-lidded gaze, Cheta scanned the other jars and handed one to Lelia.

"You gotta do things right for the lady upstairs."

As casually as she appeared, Cheta sidled out and through the darkening trees.

The tray was no problem. Barley, seasoned with savory and the butter found in the almost empty, ancient refrigerator along with a small loaf of fragrant dark bread, grapefruit, and the pot of tea. Balancing the tray, Lelia climbed the stairs, breath tight. If Kali was using her to stall for time against Hazel, then so be it. *I need time too.*

At the top of the stairs, she stopped short, remembering a dream of this hall, of a room that opened to a gaping dark sea. Dismissing the thought, she waited at the threshold of Kali's quarters, then entered. From the open French doors and gulf horizon beyond, sunset colors streamed in to bounce off the crystal ball. A green Tiffany shade glowed like an emerald near a leather chair by the bookwall. Beyond the open glass doors, in the high-backed chair, Kali sat on the balcony brushing her hair, her profile etched against the metallic gold gulf.

Lelia put the tray down on the pedestal table and waited. The hair brushing ritual continued. Was this how it was going to be? This woman inaccessible in her inner sanctum? I shall not be intimidated, Lelia vowed.

This was her chance to study the silent woman on the balcony. Something of the Hawaiian girl still showed, not in the almost aquiline features, but in the lean body, the tawny skin, the high cheek bones, the long hair almost glossy in the mellow light. The robe was dark purple tonight, different from the one this morning. So Kali was able to get in and out of the adjacent dressing room and bath to take care of herself.

Kali coiled the long hair back across her shoulders, turned the large wheels of the chair, and rolled herself into the room. A lift of the hand dismissed any help. Kali positioned the chair close to the pedestal table and tray before looking up. The dark eyes gleamed.

"One learns to be alone." There was no apology in the low contralto voice.

Lelia stood there, accepting the scrutiny. The half-lidded eyes made her think of dark purple petals, bruised but still potent.

"You know how to stay silent, that is good," Kali said. "Chatter is debris for the mind. I see you can follow directions."

"I had help. Cheta came in. She showed me which teas to use. Does it matter?"

"Herbs are natural substances with different properties. One must know when to use each." The poured tea released a sweet aroma in the room to mix with the faint sea breeze. Kali sipped and nodded. "You are curious about the room."

"The seascape over the bed – my grandfather painted that, didn't he? He must have seen such beauty out there. He painted upstairs, didn't he, in that tower room? Why did he leave it and walk away?" The questions burst out, beyond caution.

Kali's face was a mask. "We were speaking of what interests you here. Explore."

Against her rational wishes, the glowing crystal ball drew her interest. Certainly the library wall did. Books had been her only friends. "Did these books belong to my grandfather?"

"No. This is a collection owned by a man who sought no

less than the Elixir of Life. I have had them with me since I was a young woman. I had them brought to this house. You may look." Kali turned to her tray.

The mahogany bookshelves reached floor to ceiling. Dark leather spines, strange logotypes, some she recognized as Greek, German, and Oriental as well as English. They waited like hushed but strange voices, the kind she was drawn to and frightened of when she'd found hints of such voices on the dustiest shelves of Bethel Carnegie Library. But Bethel never had a collection like this: Descartes, Hermes, Masonic mysteries, Pythagoras, Quabbalah, Blavatsky, and Kumulipo, that seemed to be Hawaiian.

Lelia spun around, "Is this a library of the occult?" Pleasure turned to guilt and anger at her own interest.

"The word you use is defined as 'hidden.' Truth is always hidden. It must be discovered."

"In Bethel, they'd say –"

"These books are pagan?"

"Yes."

"You are distressed, Lelia Elliot. Do you allow others to tell you what to think? Words are only labels. They can be used to conceal and distort as well as to open and reveal."

"But your books use words."

"Words, yes, that attempt the impossible, to fathom levels of reality beyond the literal. Continue."

Lelia turned back to reading titles, still guilty with her initial pleasure. Tarrant's cold face flashed in her mind. You are evil, he'd said. And the old Rector's face, reddened with his warnings about cunning gifts of the devil. Both would consider this library like Eve's apple. Forbidden fruit. Evil, magic.

"You are troubled," Kali murmured. She had turned away from the tray and watched now from over the teacup.

"They're strange books."

"Strange or unfamiliar? Have you been taught to fear the unfamiliar? Select a book. Any one. Read to me."

"Which one?" Lelia met the eyes of the woman sitting so still in sunset afterglow.

"It doesn't matter. If you seek with fear, you must expect

to find what you believe is fearful. Pick any one at random, and we shall see what Lelia Elliot of Bethel fears."

She pulled out a volume and read the title. "*Magick, Theory and Practice* by Master Therion."

Kali's long fingers tapped the chair arms. "So—you found old Aleister Crowley. He fancied to call himself Therion. You're not pleased, I see."

Lelia glanced at the contents. Postulates, theorems, rituals. Hazel would be gleeful with this. She'd say, "See, the old witch even has books on black magic!"

"Read aloud what you have found. We shall see what concerns you."

The book's beginning was a page of verse. "Hymn to Pan." She obeyed and read:

"Devil or god, to me, to me . . .
Come with trumpets sounding shrill
Come with drums low muttering
Come to me . . ."

Lelia stopped. There was no sound in the room but the surf below. COME TO ME. How many times had she imagined hearing that whisper as a child in a lonely bedroom in Bethel. Was this a message now? From the grave?

Kali's fingers drummed. "Continue."

Lelia read on silently until the phrase *"lonely lust of devildom."* A warning? Did Kali want her here, sitting at her feet, for lessons in "devildom?" To be used against Hazel? She slipped the volume back.

"So you face your preconceived fears. Select another, at random," Kali murmured. "Read. Let me hear your voice."

Obeying, she reached and brought out a book, opened it, and read aloud:

"The power beyond language and creed waits in the vaults of your being. How is this? Thought, becoming choice, released by the focused will becomes power as it enters into universal currents . . ."

She returned the book to the shelf and faced the silent woman watching from the wheel chair. "The man who collected this library—did he find the 'Elixir of Life' is power over others?"

"Power. So that is what frightens you? Power can be used for works of hate or love."

"You have power, don't you, Kali?"

"It is not the power of others you fear, Lelia Elliot. It is your own. That is a greater fear."

Lelia picked up the tray. "I'm going back across the bridge now. To Grouper Hole. To work." But at the door, she turned to look at Kali, silent and erect in the chair. "I saw something else in your book on *Magick*. It said, 'Works of love or hate may recoil on the magician.' Isn't that a warning about power?"

"A warning, yes. Also a universal law. What is put out, returns in kind, in time."

Lelia heard melancholy in that low voice. So, Kali's actions had recoiled on her. Even so, this woman was not about to confess what she'd done to the Elliots. But given time in this house, she would find out, Lelia promised herself.

In the midnight darkness, a scream echoed in the house. Startled, Lelia spun around from the window where she had been standing, gazing down at the pale stretch of beach. She had been unable to sleep this first night in this corner room that once had been Kali's as housekeeper. A second cry came then faded. Now only the pounding against her eardrums and the softer sigh of waves from the open windows.

Barefoot in the long gown, she padded down the hall to the top of the stairs. Kali's door was closed. Below, voices – Hazel's husky whisper, Chuck's low muttering.

A single lamp went on as she reached the living room doorway. Chuck sat on the leather couch, cradling Hazel in his pajamaed lap. His bare chest muffled her sobs.

GULF NIGHT
May, 1945

17

"What happened?" Lelia whispered.

"She's here, that's what!" Hazel pulled out of Chuck's embrace and plopped back on the couch like a pinch-faced child in a slinky blue gown. "I swear I saw her in the room, on the lounge. Bonnie!"

"It was the cat," Chuck growled.

"He says," Hazel moaned.

Lelia didn't move. She wanted some message from this house, but not like this.

Chuck glanced back across the room to the darkened portrait. "When we came in tonight, Haz stood looking at that thing, talking to it. When we went into the room, she was jumpy as hell. Woke me up just now screaming and bolting out of bed."

"Jeeze," Hazel hissed, "anybody would have screamed! That was her in the room for a minute. On that chaise. I swear."

"The cat," Chuck muttered again. "Nalo crawling under a pile of clothes."

Hazel gave Lelia a reproachful stare and smoothed her own wispy hair with nervous red nails. "The next thing I see that moves is going to get one of these fancy statues thrown at 'em. You come prowling around here at night with that wild hair and long, white angel nitee, and you'll be in trouble, too." Slumping back against Chuck, "I want a belt of bourbon."

"We can move back to the trailer, Haz."

"Not on your life, Buster." She sat up again. "What I want

is to get rid of all the spooks in this house, dead and alive."

"In the meantime, let's get the hell back to bed." Chuck stood up, suddenly self-conscious in his baggy pajama bottoms. "Lelia, would you find that cat and throw it out? Let's go, Haz. In there or back to Piney Cove."

Hazel smoothed the slinky blue gown over her bony hips. "Yeah, throw the varmint out. And leave a lamp on." She gave them both a pale smile. "I'm not about to be scared off, you hear?"

Lelia watched them cross the living room, Chuck's arm still encircling Hazel's thin shoulders. She saw how really pleased he was having Hazel need him. Quickly, she scooped Nalo up from under a table and carried the cat, twisting in her arms, all the way to the kitchen before she let the Siamese spill to the floor. Nalo seized a green lizard and nosed out the back screen door, bounding toward the seagrapes.

How inviting the night air was. Sweet and cool. Yet under the long loose gown, her body was feverish and restless. Quickly, she stepped outside, then padded across the sandy yard and through the seagrapes. The surf roared softly like an invitation, as if some ancient being called.

On the path a sandspur stung, an exquisite little pain, before she plucked it out and went on, out to the open sands. There was no moon, only faint gray-white of the broad sands. She imagined a dark shape of a boat out there but no, the gulf was black infinity, the water flashing silver light. She had the beach to herself.

Jet black waves moved in, phosphorus-edged, reaching to shore, receding, calling her to follow, to forget uncertainty and nagging debate between the two parts of herself, the rational and the strange.

At the foamy edge, warm, live sands gave to her feet. A sudden wave lashed, leaving the bottom of the gown a warm burden around her ankles. She waded in deeper, watching the gown float up around her, the live water rising, shocking and pleasing her body. Stepping in further, waves lapped around her waist now.

Another surged higher, making the gown thick and heavy,

rubbing against her raised nipples. How lovely it would be to shed the thing, how free it would feel. She rocked in the waves, laughing at herself, this sea creature by nature, who couldn't take off her nightgown because she was also conditioned by Bethel, Alabama, where bodies must be kept nicely covered, even alone on a midnight beach. A sea creature who didn't yet know how to swim, not really, in spite of that strange afternoon in the gulf with Dummy.

But she could float, yes. Stretching out, face up to dark sky and faint stars, she could give herself to these buoyant waves, the gulf itself a great warm womb, rocking her. It felt as good as she'd imagined, to trust this motion and unfathomable darkness. It was a letting go of having to understand anything, and instead, becoming part of it.

A black image thrashed toward her. Instant alarm electrified her body. Angered at betrayal, she fought the churning water, lashing back.

Her feet found the sandy bottom, dug into it, but something had grabbed her shoulders. Not a fish but arms. Hard-muscled arms. Water closed over. She came up choking, sharp salt searing her throat.

Shells scraped her legs as vise-like arms pulled her onto shore. The man stayed on his knees, holding her, his chest hot against her wet gown. She stilled, as much from the moaned curses as his grip. She opened stinging eyes. Beyond his shoulder, a boat rocked at anchor in the dark surf. Freed suddenly, she inched back, chilled now, fingers digging into gritty sand, legs tangled in the soggy cotton gown. *Gil.* She recognized the shape of the bent shoulders, the shape of the head he buried in his hands. The soft lap of waves went on and on at their feet.

He stayed crouched there, a silhouette of remorse and mortification, as she watched, her own body shivering. Finally he said, "I saw you floating. I thought you were in trouble. You must take me for some kind of a fool."

Not a fool, not that, something else. A bomb of anguish or anger ticked inside the man. He sat down heavily on the wet sand beside her, elbows on his knees, face back in his hands.

"You were imagining the same girl again, weren't you?" She knew who the girl was. Gil had to be the Navy man who was here with Nancy Alderman before she drowned.

She wanted to run from him. She wanted to pull his hands away from his face and draw out his pain. Shivering in the wet gown, she didn't move.

"What happened just now?" Her fingernails dug deeper in the wet sand.

"How about temporary insanity." A self-mocking whisper. His shadowed face turned and tried to smile. "When I see floating bodies, I think I can rescue them, even –"

"Even if the girl has already drowned. Months ago." She stood up, arms folded over her breasts, conscious of the sandy gown clinging to her body.

"You've heard too many local tales." He sprang up too, still searching her face.

"One of the tales is about why you are out of the service."

"The Section Eight business? That crap?"

"You should go to someone," she said. "It's not shameful to need help."

"There are other medical reasons besides flipping out that can process a man out of the Navy." Now he was angry. "Besides, it's no one's damned business."

"Brockway will be making it his business. You know that, don't you? Nancy Alderman's father is here, insisting on an investigation. And there's a newspaperman too, trying to find out –" She was warning him. Why?

He stood close, searching her face. "There is something I have to do. Without interference."

She looked away to the dark surf. "Brockway and Alderman both know a Navy man was with Nancy. They'll learn it was you if they haven't already."

His hands slid up her wet arms and stopped, hot on her shoulders before they dropped. "I need time, Lelia Elliot. Time to find out who killed Nancy and threw her into the bay. I have to do it myself. I can't leave it to them."

She dared look into his eyes to see what was there. It meant opening to his energy, dangerous to do. The eyes, the lean planes of his face, the heat of his body told her – he believed what he was saying. With intensity. That was the time bomb in him. His need for vendetta. Or was it guilt? She didn't know.

"Get help, Gil."

A harsh whisper. "I've got to do this my way. The only help I need is for you to believe that and forget about tonight. Give me time."

"Does Nancy's father know you?"

"No, we never met." He stared into the lapping dark water. With quiet fury, "Alderman would have hated any man with his daughter. He was angry at her for coming down. He would not look beyond me."

"Why not go to Brockway before he comes to you?" She shivered in the wet gown.

"And tell him what? That I loved a stubborn, beautiful girl? And we had a fight before she walked out on me? That I had to go back to the base hospital to read about her death?"

Hospital? "Are you responsible for her death, Gil?"

"Responsible, yes, that's the hell I'm in. She'd be alive today if we hadn't fought. She left me angry. I tried to find her – too late. I've got to get the bastard who did it. I can't wait on some cracker sheriff's deputy. Have to do it, myself – I loved her, don't you understand?"

He gripped her wet arms again, his face close. "You're so much like Nancy. Strong. Only not the hot-head. Oh God, do you have any idea what it did to me, seeing you around here?" He looked away, mouth tight, then back. "You can hurt me. Or trust me. Give me time to do what I have to do."

What to believe? His pain was real. It would be as real if he were hiding the truth from himself. Possible, if he had loved the girl but had caused her death somehow, in anger, even in some tragic crazy moment. Logic told her all that. Yet the other part of herself, the strange self, stubbornly sure as a distant voice, wanted to believe Gil.

He glanced toward the boat, bobbing out there. "You know more about me now Lelia Elliot than anyone else. I've got to trust you."

He strode into the water and waist deep, plunged into the first full wave. When the motor roared up in the dark, Lelia turned away, ran toward the seagrape path, and around the porch into the kitchen. The huge pantry, stacked with linens, supplied a towel. The big house was silent. In her room, the hard spray of shower rid her body of sand, but not the feel of the pressure of his hands and the memory of the heat that had flowed between them.

INDIAN ROCKS
June, 1945

18

How easy to be the brave dreamer, how different to wake up and find people blocking the way . . .

On an early tide-washed beach, Lelia walked alone, thinking, June, already June, and the days were slipping through her fingers like a fist of grabbed sand. Sultry, warm days now, determined by other's expectations, not her own. And what had she learned? Only more questions.

Days with a rhythm, and she was caught in the rhythm. Mornings she took the early tray upstairs, Kali still a silent shadow in the alcove bed. No chance to talk then. But it was an opportunity to take another book from the shelves, one of the strange volumes she would read late in the night to forget the noise of Grouper Hole.

Why didn't she use the time to explore the house? Afraid to discover what she came for? There were doors down the hall she'd never tried to open. Also the third floor tower room. When she'd asked Chuck about Don Elliot's studio, he had flared, "Locked off for years. Why do you ask? Leave the past alone, Lelia."

She couldn't leave it alone. The past was in her. Even Kali had murmured agreement. One of the strange books from the shelves said the past could exert a pull in the genes, summoning the body to a place it was meant to be though the mind may not know where. She'd shivered reading that, remembering her dreams.

This morning she continued along this tide-washed shore,

comforted by being alone, but trying to sort out the distractions that filled the days now. There was Hazel to keep pacified. Hazel, who didn't appear until late in the day but could show up in the early morning kitchen in her orange silk kimono, small features looking drawn, the eyes defenseless without the mascara and penciled brows. A petulant Hazel, fussing that anyone would have to sleep like some zombie not to hear the night noises that kept her awake, and was Lelia sure Kali didn't leave her room? Always the complaint turned to angry demand. "When you going to get the goods on that old witch?" Hazel wanted to know.

"I can't demand a confession from Kali. She could still make us all leave. She has set up the rules."

"Rules?" Hazel had sputtered this morning. "Christamighty, what do you mean rules?"

"By her silence and cryptic answers. I know she's holding me off, but I must do this the best way I can." She didn't add, for my sake, Hazel, not just your greedy need for this house.

Walking the morning beach now, Lelia looked back at the place, hidden in its foliage. Each sunset hour she hurried up stairs with the tray, eager for the confrontation. Kali would be waiting in the high-backed chair on the balcony or in the winged chair by the books, silent as she came in but with that dark gleam watching from those deep-set eyes. Did Kali know why she was here? Drawn here somehow by the woman Kali had caused to die?

Always at these sunset tray times, they would talk but in a subtle ballet of wills, each advancing and retreating, each trying to learn the other's secrets without revealing any. She'd climb the steps to each meeting willingly, even aware of anticipation. Yet didn't she always run out into the late twilight with relief? Glad to be heading back to the noisy reality of Grouper Hole? Into the music beat and smoke. Yes, back to all those other faces with their own expectations.

Conch saying, "Glad you come bok. Lots of trotting to be done tonight."

And Chuck, "Take care of those old hens on the porch, okay?" Or warning, "Steer clear of that pasty-faced corporal who always sits alone. Don't like the way he watches you."

Bubba could march through with petulant orders, but thankfully he avoided her now. What had she said to him? Something. After one encounter in the kitchen alone with Bubba, she had looked deep into his blinking eyes and wet mouth and called up whatever words that seemed needed. "I know all about you, Bubba." The man had wheeled away.

Evander Merrill was a distraction for everyone when he showed unannounced, expecting adulation and instant service. Grasping her hand at the table, the silver head turned back, practiced smile working behind the dark glasses, "My dear, you are surrounded by provincials. You must – don't you agree, Sloan? – you must join us some night on the *Silver Fox.* You could report to the locals – and that irritating fellow who claims to be a newspaperman – inform these people, my dear, that good manners and hospitality are not suspect."

And Gil. Her own fault to allow him to be a distraction. They had not talked since that crazy night on the beach. Only twice had he come into the bar and left as quickly. Once he had spotted Morris Alderman, another time when he saw Tingley. In his quick glances, always the same question flashed. Could he trust her to stay silent? Did she believe his story of needing time to find Nancy's killer? Yes, Gil, I'm staying silent because I don't want to be involved with you or what you're looking for. I have my own reasons for being here.

"Tell me! Is the house spooky or gorgeous or what?"

After a week's absence, there was Francie, leaning against the bar across from where Lelia clanged away at the old metal cash register. Francie, foot tapping to the Benny Goodman beat, blue eyes shining with curiosity even as she promised marvelous news of her own.

"Tell you later." Lelia clunked ice in a glass and drew a fountain Coke, both annoyed and guilty with her impatience. Maybe this ebullient redhead was too much the reminder of something she'd missed herself – being so young and open.

Lelia pushed across the frosted drink. "Wait for me on the porch. You don't want your mother coming in and finding you sitting at a bar."

"I'm not sitting; I'm standing here visiting my friend. Look." Francie tapped a few steps and stopped. A hand fluttering over the peasant blouse before pulling her gaze back from the four GIs watching from bar stools. In a small voice, "I'm out at the Inn again with Aunt Mo and without Mother. Isn't that keen?"

"We'll talk – in ten minutes. I have plates to deliver."

In the kitchen, she wondered how much to tell to satisfy the girl's curiosity. Maybe about Don Elliot's paintings, and all the tarnished silver, dusty crystal, the exquisite figurines and stained glass in the house. About Nalo frightening Hazel into thinking she'd seen a ghost? Oh no, Francie would spread that story. And about Kali? As little as possible. Whatever the woman was , it was between herself and Kali. She would tell nothing about that night on the beach with Gil.

"I just love your hair pulled back like that," Francie said when Lelia returned. She'd waited, broomstick skirt swaying with the juke box beat. "It's real crazy, wonderful hair and you don't have to get a permanent or anything!"

"Small compensation for not getting red ringlets and peaches-and-cream skin–and your perseverance." Lelia rubbed a piece of ice along her bare neck. "I'll tell you about the house later. So what's your marvelous news? Besides your mother not being here." How could anyone not be charmed by this child-woman?

Francie's pink lips pursed a moment. "Well, not super-marvelous but just maybe. There's this group of local girls who get to go to parties for the officers at *nice* places like the Bath Club, not like this old Grouper Hole. They're called the Bomb-a-Dears. I'll be going – and you, too! You've got to get out of this place sometimes!"

From over Francie's shoulder, Lelia saw Gil walk in the front screen door. Her breath quickened. "Go on, tell me, Francie."

"Even my Keepers say I can go to the Bomb-a-Dears. Actually, the girls are surrounded by all these chaperones, ladies just like Mother and Aunt Mo. But they have real dances with men in dress uniforms."

At the door, Gil scanned the room before ambling to the bar. He slipped onto a stool next to Cap'n and Skipper and the four GIs.

"Go on." Lelia said. She made herself look at Francie.

"So you go with me to a little old tea party down at the Bath Club and you'll hear all about it for yourself. Promise? They meet on Mondays to look over new girls." Francie's gaze strayed again to the bar. She stood perfectly still.

"See him?" she whispered. "That's Gil who rescued me V-E day morning! Doesn't he look as handsome as Van Johnson? But more interesting, not like wicked old Errol Flynn. Sort of sweet and sad maybe like Robert Walker?"

"He's a fishing guide. You were talking about meeting officers." *Francie, don't get interested in Gil.*

"He's certainly not friendly, is he? Look at him ignoring us on purpose. Don't you just hate to be ignored? Or do you suppose he's shy or something?"

"Something," Lelia murmured. "Wait –"

But Francie marched down the length of bar to tap Gil on the shoulder. He turned, lean face cautious. She opened her plump white arms and gave him a big hug before stepping back to giggle. "That's thanks for the other morning – but don't tell my Aunt Mo what happened."

Oh no, Francie. Lelia watched the bar's reaction, Cap'n's whoop, Chuck's pressed grin. She saw Gil's tan darken even as his worried glance flashed beyond Francie over to where she watched.

Gil stood to glower as Francie, chattering now, pink-faced, explained, "I mean I don't want my folks to know I even thought of going into the gulf and having to be pulled out by two nice men." She grinned, happy again. "I forgot my water wings that morning."

Tension eased in Gil's face. Lelia saw his hand raise as if to reach for the girl's white arm, but instead rubbed a fist against his thigh as she chattered on. *He wants to touch her.* He wants to put his hand on that bouncy red hair, on those breasts, that white neck. The thought carried an anguish she didn't want to recognize.

"And what is Dummy's real name?" Francie was saying, "I think it's perfectly awful to call a nice boy a name like that even if he can't hear. He was real dear pulling me out, same as you were so strong. So I've wondered –"

"Francie, I can't tell you anything about Dummy," Gil said clearly. "Just stay out of the gulf, all right?" Turning back to the bar, he slid his quarter toward Chuck and drained his beer.

Francie walked back to Lelia at the cash register end of the bar. The juke box was quiet, her voice bell-clear in the silence. "So as I was saying, you must go with me to these lovely parties and meet some real officers with nice manners."

"I might do that," Lelia said. "I see a blue Packard out front waiting on you." Leave, Francie.

She watched the redhead sashay to the door, pause, and glance back once again toward the bar. The solemn pout gave way to something else. The girl's face glowed. Triumphant. Because Gil had turned to watch. He sat there studying her with a slow smile. Beaming, Francie wiggled her fingers in a wave before running out to the waiting car.

Haunting, gut-level blues drifted in from the barroom that was supposed to be empty. Slumped in the kitchen's single cane chair, waiting to ride back to the beach, *that's how I feel,* Lelia thought. Tonight the pasty-faced corporal who worried Chuck had tried to whisper things she didn't want to hear. Now all of the crowd was gone including the corporal, but Chuck insisted she ride with them. She waited, aware of the piano chords that seemed to read her own mood.

Cheta pushed through the swinging door, carrying her stacked tray like a trophy, lean flanks undulating all the way to the big sink. The slow smile was directed to her, not Conch, hanging up his canvas apron. "White boy out there yours? He can jive."

Conch nodded. "Real hurting, low-down blues. Not sassy kind, not like Miss Fascinatin'." He stalked out the swinging door to take a look. Lelia followed after Cheta.

They found the shadowy room empty except for Chuck

slow-polishing his bartop and Hazel, leaning against the piano top, watching the man at the keyboard.

A tousled head and broad shoulders bent to the music. Gil, immersed in his playing, like a man remembering something he loved. He didn't look up as they all moved closer.

A wild minor chord ended it. He sat looking at the keys. Hazel spoke up in her sultry voice, tinged with accusation, "Ha. I knew you weren't just a dumb fishing guide. Where'd you learn to handle a clunky old bar piano like that?"

"Around," Gil said mildly. "At various clunky bar pianos. And earlier, listening to some fine stride piano where they know how, along Bourbon Street. Ever hear of Yellow Willie?" He looked up.

Lelia met the direct stare, not surprised at its impact. *You still wonder if you can trust me, I know.* He turned back to his playing, a fast rhythm now, before he stood up. "The Duke does that one," Gil said. "It's called 'Things Ain't What They Used to Be.' Bit of observation there."

Hazel looked miffed as the screen door slammed. "I warned you, Honeychile, look out for that one. That chip on his shoulder could be a grenade ready to blow."

On the way back to the beach, the Nash crossed a bay achingly beautiful in moonlight. Curled in the back seat, Lelia fought a strange need to cry. She never cried. Never allowed it. Gil's piano blues rode with her, and she tried to block it out. She could not allow herself to open to any man's energy. It would trigger dark red anger in her core, this foreign passion that had been part of her fear always. Control was her safeguard. She was controlled now, wasn't she? And tired. Then why this feel for tears? It was something else tonight. For the first time, she let herself say the word. Behind her safety shield, she was *lonely.*

HURRICANE HOUSE

19

A faint light showed from Kali's room as Lelia turned toward the house from a moon-bright beach. What if she refused to play Kali's waiting game and just walked in now and demanded, *Tell me what I have inherited from the Elliots – madness or curse?*

At the end of the path, she sat on the single marble step to put on sandals. Something shone in the tangle of seagrape bushes. Nalo's eyes, catching moonlight. The Siamese darted out and ran toward the house. Something else, flat and white showed, too, there in the foliage. A slab marker. Bonnie Elliot's grave, long hidden just off the path.

The sight caused a swift fatigue. She didn't want to think of Bonnie now or confront Kali either. Sleep, that's what she wanted, hopefully free of faces mouthing some silent cry. Every morning the images still hovered. One thin girl's face always. Susie's.

At the top of the stairs when the contralto voice called, she hesitated a moment but went in.

Moonlight shaped the crystal ball but didn't reach the alcove. A small bedside lamp lent faint color to the seascape painting on the wall and the woman in the bed. Kali sat against high pillows, long hair coiled over one shoulder, a gauze-thin sheet pulled to the waist of the woven thing she wore. "I see you find the gulf a pleasure." The voice seemed warm.

So she watches me, Lelia thought. But she obeyed the gesture and sat down on the folded tapestry cover at the end of the bed. She accepted the offered cup of tea. Two cups there. Had Cheta been told to bring two? Cheta, who came in and out of the house at odd times like a languid shadow.

"Tell me what pleases you about the sea, Lelia Elliot."

The swish of waves came up to them like rhythmic sighs. "That sound for one thing. Walking the beach restores me after noise and smoke."

"Yes, the body is sustained and renewed by energies from earth and sea. Few are so consciously aware," Kali murmured. She leaned back against the high pillow. "You would appreciate the beach of my girlhood, in Hawaii. This gulf can be deceptively placid. My shores are wild and beautiful; Hana, on the remote and rugged side of Maui."

"I can imagine you as a girl in that kind of place," Lelia said. The tea seemed to relax her.

"I was Kala then, a name meaning life, joy."

"Not Kali?"

"Someone – a teacher who came looking for me a long time ago – charged me with that name, which I accepted."

"Then Kali has its own meaning?"

"Many. Hindu goddess of time. A symbol for cosmic force. There is another – Kali, as Terrible Mother destroying to build." The thin purple lips tightened.

Kali, at last speaking of herself. She must stay alert and listen. "Your sister came with you, didn't she, to work for the Elliots?"

"Yes. Maylene."

Don't turn away Kali, don't stop talking. "Young Kala, what was she like, in Hana?"

"She ran with grace and power on that shore. She sat at the feet of wise teachers. One, a scholar from the world of doubters and seekers – his books, as I have told you, here on the shelves."

"Philip Seaton. I've seen his name and his margin notes in the books." The Englishman who sought the Elixir of Life. What had he found? "There were teachers on your island?"

"Kahunas, they were called. Elsewhere they would be known as shamans, healers, seers, teachers of the Ancient Mysteries."

"Of magic you mean?"

"You fear that word, Lelia Elliot, so you cannot hear the answer."

"I want to know."

The answer came like low music. "Down through the ages, there have been the few who have known the great secrets."

"Secrets?"

"Of working with the universal energies. In our islands, the Kahunas had their own words for the building of *mana* energy. When the missionaries came, these words and methods were misunderstood and therefore the knowledge had to be hidden."

"*Mana*?"

"An empowering energy. We have already spoken of focused will."

A breeze rose and fell outside. Lelia looked away. Is this how Kali forced Bonnie to drown, Don Elliot to run away? She didn't dare ask it now, but Kali seemed to guess.

"You fear power, do you not, Lelia Elliot? You mistrust it. If you had sat at the feet of my teacher, you would have feared neither life nor death."

"Your teacher makes your face wistful, Kali."

"Marriminde was the most revered Kahuna of all. Marriminde was known as the 'wise old woman of the sea.' The sea being metaphor for something greater and unknowable."

Because Kali fell silent, Lelia asked, "What happened to Kala?"

"Even the most natural of gifts can be squandered by the young who have exuberant arrogance before they are tried by life. Great gifts can be misused."

"Are you wanting me to learn your magic?"

Kali's face looked struck. "You speak out of presumptuous innocence, Lelia Elliot. One must be ready to learn before one finds a teacher. Wisdom is not imposed on another. It has to be perceived by the mind and spirit that is ready."

"Can't madness be taught? The mind can be poisoned

against its will? I've read . . ."

"You are troubled," Kali said softly. "In the Polynesian language there is a word *loa*. One of its meanings is passionate seeking. The Loa in you yearns to know herself. Lelia Elliot believes she is ready to know herself only she prevents the knowing."

"I know that my grandmother Bonnie drowned here, my grandfather ran away, my father came back and drowned, and my mother died of guilt or fright as soon as I was born—and you say I'm not ready to know why it happened? As though you're saving me from what more I could learn?"

"Yes."

She stood up from the bed, placed the china cup back on the bedside table, and walked out.

In her own room, Lelia looked down on moon-bright seagrapes that hid a grave. The night air was sweet. She remembered being six years old, sitting on Bethel front steps on a summer night, smelling honeysuckle and listening to voices say she was marked. Old wives tales but in some way they were true. And now, so close to knowing the truth, she was afraid to know. Kali was right. The realization made her angry at herself as well as this woman who knew she was vulnerable.

In her Chinese red kimono, Hazel paced the kitchen, "You've got to hear something. Same as I do. Every night."

"Old houses have to make noises," Lelia said. "Especially when they're sitting in a small jungle by the Gulf of Mexico." Was Hazel trying to frighten her? The agitation seemed real enough. She continued to stir a small pot of millet at the old stove.

"Well, Kiddo, I lay there in the wee hours scared out of my skin, hearing noises. Is that old woman upstairs pulling one on us about needing the wheelchair?"

"She still uses it. She walks with the cane. But I haven't seen her out of the room."

"Does that damn cat or the dog trot around upstairs any?"

"I don't think so. Nalo seems to stay downstairs or out.

Orion is outside most of the time. Always at night."

"Lelia, you're *sure* you're sleeping good, like some innocent child?" Hazel's pinched face looked annoyed.

"Not as an innocent child, no. Being on one's feet dawn to midnight assures sleep when one gets around to it." Had she dreamed again last night? Yes.

"Chuck says he sleeps. But I swear he must go back to the trailer and sack out afternoons. Says he walks. Yeah. Well, I figure he's alone there at any rate. He's got better sense than to risk anything with those young chicks who come in. Except I didn't like the way he got suckered in by Susie. What I'm talking about here is the damn sounds. If it's not Kali – then it's her, Bonnie."

Lelia put down the wooden spoon. "I found Bonnie's tombstone in the seagrapes, sunk in there." She didn't want this conversation.

"Makes no difference where she's buried. That portrait in the living room, those eyes, I swear she's watching what goes on here."

"Don't, Hazel. Imagination is a risky thing. I know. It can seem so real. You don't know what to believe."

"I swear, Lelia, I thought you were a dumb-innocent from a sweet lil' Alabamy town. But maybe you're as weird as the spook upstairs."

"Don't say that!"

"Gets your goat, huh? Never saw you mad before. Remember we're not here for our health, and it ain't getting healthier. I'm all for calling the sheriff to come haul Kali off to the county nut house."

"You can't – without proof."

"That's where you come in and don't you forget it."

She picked up the tray and left Hazel trailing behind, feathered mules flopping. At the foot of the stairs, Hazel glanced upstairs and whispered, "I see you take up two cups for that teapot. Real friendly."

"I have to talk with Kali, remember, when I can."

"Better you than me, Kiddo." Hazel shivered and headed back to her room.

BAYSHORE

20

"Our local protector from the sheriff's department is looking for you," Chuck said as Lelia brought in the two plates of early supper to the empty bar. "You know, lanky old Brockway. I didn't help. He ambled on out."

"Thanks, I don't have time for him now. I have to get back to the house."

"You don't hate that duty?" Chuck contemplated a hot hush puppy from the plate of red tomatoes and fried fish. "You hurry out of here every afternoon to serve that woman upstairs."

"It's the agreement." She avoided his frown and began to eat. Chuck waited, expecting more, so she said lightly, "It's not much work, really, taking up her food. Fruits, grains, and tea, that's all. And Cheta's bread. And Conch's butter, thanks to their cow."

He began to eat slowly, so she talked to divert any more questions. She told him about her beach walks with Francie, making it funny. But Chuck frowned into his plate, still curious. "Hazel's pushing me to push you. What's the old gal like up there in her lair? I hated her as a kid. I was sure she was going to drown us, too. Not that we stayed around long enough to find out. And you go in there twice a day."

She couldn't tell him that the mention of Bonnie Elliot could darken Kali's face and silence her. She said, "Being around Bubba is no easy matter either. But we do." With a smile, she gathered up the plates. One last trip to the kitchen then freedom until tonight.

Just inside the kitchen door, she ran into trouble: Bubba's trouble. Slumped in the cane chair, he looked up, grateful for the interruption. Martha Critten stood in the middle of the kitchen, brown oxfords planted solidly, arms folded over the big flowered bosom. "And I want words with you, too, Miss Willowy Beauty."

On the work table in front of Bubba, like evidence of his latest failure, sat the Mason jar filled with coins and a few green bills, labeled "The U.S. Armed Forces' Susie Fund," still draped with the heart necklace.

"You caught me just in time," Lelia said, crossing to the big sink with the plates where Conch scrubbed at a pot, his back turned. "I'm on my way out."

"My paid help just walks out? Same as this lazy son of mine?"

"Yes," Lelia said cheerfully, washing her hands at the sink. "I know you must be glad I live so close and can do that. It means I can leave and come back and you don't have to pay me for being here breakfast to midnight."

"Listen to Miss Smarty," Martha Critten crooned. "See there, Bubba? Gumption. You ought to try some. Hey, I'm not finished. Let me look at you."

Lelia stood, patiently nodding at the frizzy-haired woman but concentrating instead on the hamper of tomatoes on the floor, dishes on the shelves reflecting sunlight. She had learned how to deal with both mother and son; ignore the unwanted impressions that might glimmer from their voices and eyes. This was only a job.

"Classy little dame, aren't you?" Martha Critten crooned. "Real officer material as they say. But nothing wrong with giving the burr-heads something for their money too." From behind the heavy glasses, the big eyes narrowed. "Bubba tells me you folks moved over there into Hurricane House. Well, well. Some call it the 'murder house,' you know. What's it like living with that old woman? She drowned any sweet young things lately? Don't tell me. I don't wanna know. I've got my own problems."

And I have mine. She turned to go.

"Hold your horses, Miss Pretty. Answer me something. That long drink of slow water named Brockway from the sheriff's department—he's been hanging around again. Know anything about that?"

"I've seen him come in. He's a big fan of Conch's cooking."

"Ha. Well, that old excuse for the law has been asking Bubba here about Susie. He been talking to you?"

"No." She'd avoided Brockway for her own reasons. He might ask her – warn her? – about Gil. But she said, "Why would he talk to me? Susie left before I got here." She watched Bubba's thick fingers flip Susie's heart necklace from the jar.

Martha glared over her glasses. "I don't like him asking around in my establishment. What will the customers think about this joint? I'll tell him or anybody—who cares where the girl is? That little chit was nothing but trouble."

Bubba popped the cheap necklace apart, scattering small pink hearts. They spilled like tiny pleas for help, Lelia thought.

"Yeah," Bubba said, "Brockway's asking like we're hiding her or something."

Martha exploded, "What did I do to deserve a fool son? Bubba, we don't want him asking 'cause it stirs up the paying customers. Empty that damn money jar into the cash register this minute and throw that dime-store junk in the trash. You hear me?"

"See you tonight, Conch," Lelia repeated to the cook's solid back. She let the screen door bang behind her.

Across the brick road, a lanky man in a brown suit stood under a tree, smoking a cigar. Brockway, waiting for her, and not to be avoided.

"Howdy, Miss Lelia." Brockway tossed the cigar away. "Been waiting to talk with you." A slow, tobacco-stained smile creased his long face.

"I'm on my way across the bridge."

"Mind if an old fellow comes along for a ways? It'd be a real pleasure."

They walked onto the wooden bridge above the narrow bay, Brockway's pants flapping against his long legs, Lelia holding up her hair to catch the breeze. A pelican lifted and soared away. They watched, squinting into the late afternoon sun.

"Ugly old critter till he gets flying," the deputy observed. The brown suit, like his breath, smelled of tobacco, but his manner was courtly and unhurried, saying, "Well, well, so you've been here since V-E Day. Sure must be different from wherever you came."

Lelia found herself confiding in the man, at least telling him the surface truth. Yes, Bethel was an old and proper Alabama town. She'd been a librarian. Everything was different here. She'd come, hoping to find out about her father's side of the family, the Elliots. She had found Chuck. And that's why she was working here. She watched his nodding profile and wondered what he knew and how much they could tell each other.

Together they leaned on the wood railings bronze-colored in the afternoon sun. Brockway pointed out the mangrove shores, talking tides and birds like a man sharing what he loved.

"We got another kind of bird around here, too, snowbird tourists." A soft guffaw. "Come down here and get so sunburned it's a shame. Some of them come back and retire and want to be mayor or councilman in one of these little old beach towns. Then they're against any more tourists 'cause they want everything to stay the way they found it."

Was he going to mention Gil?

"Miss Lelia, you're a real special young woman. I've watched how you handle yourself with those soldier boys, keeping them happy but at arms' length. Real good sense, that. I notice you don't talk too much chit-chat, but that means you got a head on you and you probably listen good. Am I right?"

"I listen. Everything here is new to me." Waiting, she looked back at Grouper Hole, crouched low by the bayshore.

"Guess you know why I show up now and then. I've got a big area to cover. These beach towns, some of them have police chiefs, some don't. All kinds of things to look after, Lord knows. This morning had to corner a hungry alligator coming out of a neighbor's ditch. But I don't like it a bit when somebody tries to get away with killing around here."

"I know about Nancy Alderman. Her father was on the train with me coming down."

"Guess you've seen us talking at Miz Critten's place. That Conch cooks a fine mess of fish. Yessum, Morris Alderman is one angry papa. It figures."

Brockway looked down into the flowing water. "Alderman's a smart Boston fellow used to bossing people around. Well, I appreciate his feelings, but in spite of this kindly mug, I got this turtle shell hide on me. I have to do things my way." Frowning, "You know this Tingley fellow?"

"He was on the train, too."

"Bumbling fool. If he's a friend, you might tell him I don't let anybody interfere with my investigations, including rightfully angry papas. Or pretty-faced movie stars or their bozo bodyguards for that matter."

Lelia smiled. So, behind that slow drawl there was a stubborn Brockway who was no fool. "I'm sure Tingley and Alderman realize you're the sheriff out here."

"Work for the sheriff. Don't even have uniforms but we're the law. We got the responsibility."

She pulled in a deep breath. "Have you found out anything yet about what happened to Alderman's daughter?"

Brockway pursed his lips, studying the bay below. "He says his daughter came down here to meet a Navy fellow. Doesn't know the name, a fact that makes him all-fired madder, so naturally he's sure that's who killed his girl. Well — possible."

"But she could have met so many people here. Just because they had been together —"

"Yessum. 'Course when the papers ran the story all over because she was this rich Boston deb, no Navy gentleman got back to her papa with any condolences and grief, if you see what I mean."

"Oh." She looked away. "I must go now."

"Here's the thing," Brockway went on. "That Alderman girl is dead. Can't change that. Give me a little time, and I'll find out who did it. But something else is smoking on my griddle right now. That's what I wanted to speak to you about since you're a good listener. You know about this little gal Susie Holms?"

"I heard."

"Took a pot shot at a two-timing married lieutenant. I've got to bring her in for that. Naturally, she'd rather not show up. But I'd like her to know she'd be a lot better off if she'd come in to Clearwater with me than wherever she is."

"Martha Critten is upset that you've been asking about Susie at Grouper Hole. She says it looks bad to the paying customers."

"Critten." A flicker of a smile. "I'm asking you, Miss Lelia, since you're a good listener and all. Have you heard where she might be hiding?"

"No. I came after she left."

"Susie didn't get far. I know that much. She's around here someplace, in trouble. I got a feeling she knows something that's not good for her health, if you know what I mean. I'd like to find that little gal."

"Is she a clue – to the other?"

Brockway rubbed his long face. "Well now, that would be something, wouldn't it? And clues should be live ones. With all kinds of folks, soldiers and all, coming into Grouper Hole, you just might hear something. I'd appreciate you letting me know."

So he still hadn't decided it was Gil. Lelia felt relieved but curious. Brockway wanted to find Susie. An urgency there. She thought of the girl's necklace, all those pathetic little hearts.

Brockway beamed a wide, yellowed smile. "By the way – you getting 'long good with those folks who run Grouper Hole? And the old cook Conch?"

"It's a job. I want to be on this waterfront."

"Wish I had a daughter pretty and smart as you, Miss Lelia. You're a real confident young woman. But you'd have to be, to move into that Hurricane House with that woman Kali. My, my, never thought she'd let anybody in there."

She wanted to know more, whatever Brockway knew of the old gossip, but the lanky man was intent on telling her something else.

"You're one of us now, Miss Lelia, so you should know about this old waterfront. We used to be all homefolks with a few honest rum-runners thrown in for vinegar and spice. Now besides the tourists and a few land-sharks and what-all, we've got all kinds of soldiers from everywhere. Some folks even believe this coast has German U-boats sneaking around out there." He grinned but sobered as quickly.

"Anyway, young lady, I wouldn't want anything to happen to you by being – ah, too trusting. You know what I mean? You listen real good. So remember, you hear anything you think I should know, you call me. I'd be much obliged."

He dipped in a courtly good-by. She ran toward the beach road. Susie. The girl was somewhere near, Brockway said. A flash image came and went as quickly: a cabin in palmettos, near water. Hazel had said Gil lived in a cabin on the bay.

I'll find out, Susie. I'm going to look for you.

BATH CLUB

21

Tingley barreled in from the sun-bright yard, whooping with relief, "Too hot for the devil out there." He made his bow-legged way to the bar where Lelia was scooping ice into the lemonade pitcher.

He swung onto a stool to watch, eyebrows wiggling up and down in admiration. "If you don't look like a blooming magnolia today. This old watering hole doesn't deserve an angel on duty, but how about pulling me a Coca-Cola with a shot of ammonia? Notice I'm leaving Uncle Chuck to his war news down there. J. T. Tingley is on the wagon. All day – till dark. This sleuthing business is tough in this heat, lemme tell you."

For the first time, she was really glad to see him. She needed a ride to the Bath Club but had to wait until his talk slowed down. The man's clown act was as automatic as his breath. Underneath was a fifty-two-year-old man doggedly determined to prove he wasn't a clown.

He gulped the cold drink. "What's up today? You look party-purty."

"Do I?" She turned and studied herself in the yellowed mirror. Her skin did have a golden tone now, and the dress showed white and cool against her arms and throat. One of Hazel's discards, the thin seersucker cotton had a bertha col-lar and petticoats underneath.

Turning back to Tingley, "I'm about to take my first afternoon off if I can get to the Bath Club. Hazel keeps the Nash. I thought—are you still driving the *Gulffront Journal* car?"

"Right outside. Didn't you hear all the racket? That lizzy is held together with bailing wire and cussing." His grin lines spread. "You need a ride to the Bath Club, you got it. I'm heading for Johns Pass and the Bath Club's half way there. Whatcha up to?"

She rang up his dime. "Francie wants me to meet her there in about thirty minutes if I can make it,"

Tingley groaned. "That pink marshmallow with the girlish glee? You going down to keep her out of trouble?"

She laughed. It felt good. "I thought I'd try some girlish glee for a change. It's a party, a tea, for girls who get invited to the dances for the soldiers, the chaperoned dances. The girls call themselves the Bomb-a-Dears." She winced at the name. "Give me a minute and I can leave."

In the wooden cubby hole of a ladies room, she brushed her hair high, tied it with a ribbon, applied the orange Tangee lipstick, tucked the tube and a tiny coin purse back in her skirt pocket, and hurried out again, actually feeling eager about this. Tingley and Chuck had their heads bent toward the bar radio.

> *" . . . three million men coming home for redeployment to the Pacific . . . And now, turning to the home front, good news . . . Production of cars, refrigerators and washing machines will begin in six months . . ."*

Chuck flipped off the radio and lifted his beer with a sigh. "Everybody happy? At last, new Frigidaires." He took one swallow, slammed it down and studied the sunny afternoon bay.

The parking lot was hot this late June day, no breezes from the bay.

"You understand, Magnolia, why Uncle Chuck stays testy. He takes it hard sitting out the war from the back of that bar. Partly the reason I joke around about Ernie Pyle. Here we are alive and kicking on this old waterfront with the war still going on." He opened the door of the rusty Chevy and threw yellowed newspapers into the narrow back seat. "I'm glad you needed a lift because I've been wanting a chance to talk to you, private."

On the beach side, the Chevy turned south, picking up a noisy momentum. From the open windows, salty breeze whipped their faces. To her surprise, Tingley stayed hunched behind the wheel, eyes tight under the brim of the pork-pie hat. Was he going to tell her something about Gil? Whatever, she had to listen. "I'm glad I came," she said over the blowing wind, "I've seen so little of the beaches. You know about them. Tell me."

"See those mangrove islands?" He nodded toward the patches of green in the bay to their left. "Birds get them started. It's all muck underneath, Know what they're talking about when the war's over?"

"No, tell me." Already her hair had blown free, so she tied it back again.

"They're going to pump in sand and make land of that muck. Fingers of land sticking out in the bay, for houses. That means instead of mangroves, you'll see streets and mailboxes and kiddy-cars at the front door. How 'bout them apples?"

He slowed for a pothole. "You got a ride back with the Redhead?" At her nod, "Okay, but sometime, Magnolia, you hafta look at this whole gulf front. From Clearwater Pass just north of here, you got twenty-five miles of beach, all the way down to the tippy end at Pass-a-Grille."

She leaned back, determined to enjoy this freedom and not think of dark questions and secret hopes. She looked out at the passing gulf, glittering out there under a bright blue afternoon sky that dwarfed everything else, people, trees, the occasional low cement block structure with its motel sign.

"Past the Bath Club," Tingley went on, "you've got Johns Pass in between two lil' old beach towns. Johns Pass is where yours truly bunks. Tourists hang over the bridge fishing, but real fishermen live around there. Folks who know what's going on up and down this old waterfront."

"Where's the hospital, the one they call Flak Hotel?"

Tingley nodded, "Big fancy place, one of those boom-time hotels, called the Don CeSar, down at Pass-a-Grille. Army and fly-boys all over the place. I hear the Army's moving out soon. Not gone yet, you can tell. Busiest juke joints are down that way."

"Busier than Grouper Hole on a Saturday night? I thought we were headquarters for weekend passes."

Tingley wagged his head. "The guys show up at Mama Critten's when they want to get away from the rest of the pack, for reasons soldier boys have. Getting a beer is just one. But they sure found out you're a lady."

"What are you telling me?"

"Aw nothing. You see the fellows. They bring in local girls from the beach. And heck, they like to chow down on Conch's fried fish, sure. And then there's the house parties up that way."

"Tell me about those." She wanted to know what Tingley had learned.

"A lot of folks from St. Pete and Tampa have beach houses out there. Not as big and fine as that one *you're* in." He gave her a reproachful look. "You didn't tell me you had moved in with that old hermit."

"It happened fast. Tell me – do those men with battle fatigue, do they get passes too?"

"You're serving them Conch's fish cakes every weekend. But in a crowd, naw, you wouldn't notice. If a guy starts acting up at one of the bars, an MP just taps him on the shoulder like a brother and takes him along, without any fuss."

Tingley laughed and hit the steering wheel. "Other night, down at Pass-a-Grille, a pack of five fellows were getting pie-eyed. Know how a sergeant got that crew collected and back to the Don? Marched them back down the street, shouting cadence all the way."

He wrestled the wheel over another pothole. "Local mamas and papas figure these boys are away from home and need some fried chicken and chocolate cake and Glenn Miller on the record player."

"So?" She challenged his mugging face.

"So all they get their hands on is the chocolate cake and

a drum stick. Then they pile in at Chuck's bar to swap ah, condolences."

"I'm wondering if Nancy Alderman went to one of those parties," Lelia murmured. "And met someone –"

"Who took her into the shadowy palms for a kiss and she never came back, huh? Possible. And if so, that lover could be long gone. Or still around."

Lelia gazed out at the gulf, hair stinging her face in the wind.

"You shoulda told me you were moving into that house," Tingley said again.

"Why? Hurricane House doesn't have anything to do with those missing girls or Nancy Alderman. That's the past."

"When you're looking for answers, you have to know what happened yesterday to understand what's showing up today."

She sighed. "I know."

"Magnolia, I'm a damned good reporter. Believe it or not, when a story's concerned, I don't go off half-cocked. Last thing I want is to come up looking like a damned fool." He looked grim. "That stucco spread up there, that's the Bath Club."

"So what is it you wanted to tell me?"

"Questions first. How does that deaf-mute fellow act when he's in your place? Anybody that sneaky quiet makes me wonder."

"Dummy? He acts like a lost soul." Lelia remembered the wiry, strong arms holding her in the water. But Gil's grip had been stronger. She shook both images away, glad the rattling car was pulling to a stop.

Tingley cut off the motor. "I'm sure the person who left Alderman in the bay is still around. Those folks with missing girls are keeping quiet hoping daughter has run off. I don't think so. If I find Susie, I'll have my big story, Lelia Magnolia. Because that little gal knows what happened to Alderman."

"Brockway doesn't like you interfering with his job, J. T. Maybe you should tell him if you know anything about Susie. I hear you're getting yourself in trouble with everyone."

"I have a tough hide, Magnolia. But that brings me to what

I had to tell you. If you hear anything, let me know. But while you listen, pretend you aren't. I see you doing that all the time." He grinned.

The door handle was hot but she told him, "I know this. The girl is frightened. I'd like to find her myself. I've dreamed about her."

"Magnolia, that's what I'm trying to tell you – stay out of it. It's too late to stop you from moving in that house, but take it from J. T. Tingley, don't get mixed up with this Susie thing. If anyone asks about that little gal, you play dumb. Don't sound interested. You could be in line for the deep, too."

"Thanks for the ride and the warning. Take care of yourself, J. T."

She stood a moment in bright sun watching the Chevy rattle away, then ran toward the awninged entrance.

The small carpeted lobby led into a windowed lounge, pink walls hung with green ferns that moved in the soft breeze from a ceiling fan. From their card tables, pale-haired women glanced up, curious. Lelia looked around for some evidence of Francie's party.

There. On a shaded terrace beyond the windows, waving, was Francie in a lime green linen dress too straight-lined for her curves. Bursting into the lounge now, exclaiming, "You missed the dumb refreshments but at least you're here!" She grabbed Lelia by the arm. "Oh golly, you have a comb? I have. C'mon."

In a corner away from the bridge tables, Lelia obliged by calming her wild hair. "I rode up with Tingley. Am I here to pass inspection?"

"You look simply exotic and that's the problem. Mrs. Strickland is out there. And don't mention working at old Grouper Hole, okay?"

"Francie, I spent years avoiding white-gloved tea parties. All right, I'll tell them how my maternal grandmother was a Daughter of the Confederacy and my paternal grandmother was murdered on their very own beaches, how about that?"

Francie's momentary dismay gave way to a nervous giggle. "You must think I'm a snob just like my mother. But it's so absolutely necessary I get to be a Bomb-a-Dear, and you must too. Mrs. Strickland out there looks like Kate Smith about to sing 'God Bless America' but that old fatty is checking everyone out." Behind the giggle, the girl was intense.

"Francie, what's happening with you?"

"It's just that I've *got* to have an excuse to get out, especially now. C'mon."

On the shaded terrace, the large woman, addressing the party-dressed girls seated in a semicircle of wicker chairs, paused over her clipboard. Francie plunged into the introduction of "my friend Lelia Elliot from Alabama." Mrs. Strickland resumed her speech.

Under her lashes, Lelia studied the scene. Beyond the terrace, green lawn framed a busy swimming pool glittering in the sun. Further down, umbrellas made spots of shade on a bright beach. A different world from Grouper Hole. What was she doing here? Escape, maybe. Creating her own distractions. But why was Francie fidgeting with impatience?

In the wicker chairs, eight polite faces stayed turned toward Mrs. Strickland's droning speech. Some of the girls young as Francie, some her own age, dutifully poised in their voile summer dresses, patent leather pumps crossed primly, ID bracelets glinting at the ankles. The same Bettys and Sues and Debbies as gathered in front parlors and wide front porches back in Bethel for bridal showers. Yet it must be different for these here with a backdrop of an endless gulf horizon, not a single downtown square and neighborhood streets where everybody was a Mrs. Strickland and knew your family history without asking.

"Remember, my dears," went the concluding reminder. "You represent your city and your parents. You are to conduct yourself as *ladies* we can be proud of. And do not forget – it is against Bomb-a-Dear rules to date the service men you meet there."

At the rustle of subdued protest, Mrs. Strickland's plump hand went up, admonishing, "Now – if your parents wish to invite the young man to your home, well then, our responsibility has ended."

The murmurs faded. Smiles bloomed, but stayed suppressed.

"One final word. It pains me to say so, but I cannot stress too strongly, some girls – only a few – have not conducted themselves *wisely*, and with *grievous consequences* I must add. However, I'm sure everyone here will remember what is expected." With a sigh of relief, Mrs. Strickland with her clipboard bustled into the lounge.

The gathering, like a stiff bouquet, burst free. The newly approved Dears sprang to their feet, stretching, yawning, chattering before dropping back into the wicker chairs to talk.

"You know what she's so nervous about." A petite brunette included Lelia and Francie in her glance. "She's talking about those girls who met service guys at house parties and *never showed up again.*"

Chairs were pulled closer.

"Maybe the girls eloped?"

"I know one who did. She was so tired of St. Pete she had the heebie-jeebies to go somewhere, anywhere else. Now she's living on some awful base in Texas with two babies already. Ugh."

"How dumb! I wouldn't believe a one of those boys."

"What about that captain you thought looked like Jimmy Stewart! You liked him, tell the truth!"

"Don't remind me. All I have to say – watch out for the shy and lonely types. They make the best liars."

"Let me tell you a funny! This Coast Guard fellow, real cute like Audie Murphy, said he was just dying to swing on a front porch and put his feet under a real home table. Well, he shows up with this pound of butter as a gift and Mother was honestly thrilled but guess what? It turned out he'd snitched a pound of *yeast*. But he sat down and ate everything in sight at the dinner table –"

"What happened on the front porch?" Francie asked, slumped in the chair, one patent leather pump tapping the floor.

"Oh boy, it wasn't very romantic. He had terrible breath." A sigh.

Lelia spoke up. "Have any of you been to the parties aboard Evander Merrill's yacht?"

Eyebrows raised, glances exchanged.

"Just Georgianna here. Go ahead and tell, Georgie."

"I just went once."

"Well, tell!" A chorus of urgings.

"Oh, it's a real beautiful boat. Lots of lounges, you'd be surprised."

"But the parties."

"Oh, food and real drinks," Georgianna told them, coloring. "Everything real *sophisticated*, with the crew in their uniforms serving you. There's a tiniest wood floor in the main lounge for dancing."

"What does *he* do, Evander Merrill?" Francie insisted, looking at the jeweled watch on her wrist.

Georgianna shrugged. "He's smooth and friendly. He'll take you around to see the yacht if you like, top deck to galley. I didn't want to go, so he just put his arm around that silly boy I was with and off they went. To tell the truth, it wasn't all that fun, except going out from the dock and back. A peachy looking guy took us out in his motor boat, but he wasn't very friendly."

Gil, Lelia thought.

Francie jumped up, announcing they had to go now. Lelia rose, too. Breathy with a flickering smile, the redhead announced, "You can tell Mrs. Strickland I'm going to be the sweetest little old rule-abiding Bomb-a-Dear she could want." The confession burst out like a delicious secret. "Because I'm already in love."

Francie wheeled around and disappeared through the lounge door. Lelia had to follow. She knew, or feared, Francie was talking about Gil.

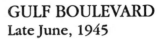

GULF BOULEVARD
Late June, 1945

22

The blue Packard hummed up the boulevard, Francie embracing the wheel, avoiding eye contact, chattering about their flurry of shopping. "I just love to buy things and give presents, and you needed something really peachy to go to a dance. Besides, you're my friend."

Lelia patted the package on her lap. A chiffon dress, color of pale hibiscus blossoms, off the shoulder with a full ballerina length skirt, both innocent and provocative. From that fast retreat out of the Bath Club, Francie had pulled her into a small beach store across the road.

"I love the dress, I really do," Lelia murmured. The girl's generosity was genuine. And once she got around to it, Francie would be as honest about the favor she expected.

"I made you spend all your own money on matching pumps, but you'll look like Jennifer Jones and then some." The Packard lurched down the uneven road, Francie frowning over the big dashboard, launching into a distracted account of Bomb-a-Dear parties.

Finally, Lelia interrupted, "If you're so happy, Francie Welburn, why are you so jumpy and driving so fast?"

No answer. The wind whipped in against their faces, smelling of roadside pines. Lelia waited for the girl's quick look before she spoke into those blue eyes. "I know. You need me as an excuse to get out, away from your aunt. So you'd better tell me what you're getting into."

"Oh, Lelia. Let me drive you home." Past the Inn, the

Packard lumbered into the overgrown drive and rolled to a stop under the banyan. Orion appeared, growling at the car until Lelia sent him slinking back into the foliage. Nothing stirred but palm fronds around the house. "Gee," Francie murmured, "It *is* spooky!"

She turned to Lelia. In a trembling whisper, "Have you ever done it? I mean – you know."

Lelia turned away sharply, throat constricted.

"Oh, I'm awful to ask. You don't have to tell me, it's just that you look like you *know*. Even if you don't talk about it. My mother and aunts must think I'm not supposed to know, ye gods, not even *wonder* a darn thing until I get in my going-away suit, throwing the bouquet."

Lelia waited. This confession wasn't going to be silly romantic musing. "Tell me."

"Mother would absolutely die or want to kill *me*, I swear, if I let a man – if I did *anything* before I walk down the aisle in white Belgium lace with ten bridesmaids. And the people on his side of the church will have to be just as stuffy important as my side of the church."

"I know all about expectations, Francie. I grew up in a Queen Anne house, the walls lined with proper Calhouns, great-aunt faces staring down at me." And the town watching, yes. "Not unusual, Francie."

"But you're not usual, are you? And Lelia, I'm not either. I may sound silly, but I'm dying to know more than my friends seem to. They whisper about some girl leaving town because she was *past due*. You know. Then they go right on talking about their silver patterns and their hope chests, and all the time I'm thinking, wondering, about life and all. I don't know *anything* and I'm scared."

"What's this about being in love?"

"It's crazy." Plump pink fingers flexed on the wheel. "It's absolutely unexpected and utterly crazy. All before, I've had fun with boys and that cute serviceman back home – but I never let them *do anything*, understand? Frankly, I was too scared – of Mother, more than them. This is different. It just happened."

"Already?"

A ragged sigh. "Not yet. But it's going to any night now. I can't help it. I go out and meet him on the beach real late when no one could know. I *want* it to happen!" She circled her arms on the wheel and hid her face before looking up, the blue eyes brimming. "Lelia, how can I be so miserable and happy at the same time?"

"Who, Francie?" *Not Gil. Don't let it be Gil.*

"I can't tell. Please don't ask. You're my only friend and you're a real woman, so please understand – I *promised*. For his sake. It's very important!"

"What about *your* sake? What do you know about him?"

She shook her head. "This is going to sound crazy – but I know just enough to understand he can't have people wondering about him, even noticing him. He's trusting me with his life! So I've given my solemn promise."

"To protect him. I take it this is happening around Indian Rocks?"

Francie let out a shaky breath. "Yes. So you see why I just have to stay at the Inn. Why I need a friend."

"What can I do, Francie?" So it was happening, as if she'd always known it would. "I can't be responsible for what happens to you."

"That's not what I'm asking!" Her fists hit the steering wheel. "Everyone around me spends their whole life being responsible for me. I want to be responsible for myself. I'm going to be eighteen next month." She stopped, bit the full bottom lip. "Just be my friend. That's all. Please?"

You don't know what you're asking of me, Francie. It's Gil, isn't it?

"I promised not to say anything to anybody, Lelia, but I had to tell someone at least that's it's *happening*. Who else could I tell?"

No one, of course. She looked at the girl's flushed face, then away, dealing with her own feelings. Gil had asked her for silence, too. Obviously, he'd asked the same of Francie. Only this impulsive, love-hungry girl was ready to give more. *Don't let her, Gil.*

She slipped out of the car and came around to Francie's window to look into eyes vulnerable as blue periwinkles. Francie couldn't know everything about Gil; he wouldn't have explained torment about loving another woman. But he must have won her willingness to protect his identity. If I have chosen to trust him – and Lelia realized she had, from her sensing self, not the rational – if I trust Gil, then what right do I have to turn Francie against him? And hurt this girl so hungry for love?

The answer swept through like a wave of nausea. Jealousy? Oh no, she thought, not Lelia Elliot. Control was her armor, her protection. Francie had leaned into the big steering wheel, her head cradled. Lelia reached in to touch the red curls. "What should I tell you?" Francie looked up, the pink smile faint.

"I know – in the words of dear Mrs. Stickland – be wise! Oh, Lelia, you're so calm and sure of yourself, but just wait till you feel this way too. But I'm glad I told you. I knew you'd understand."

The Packard churned out the drive.

She set the sunset tray down on the pedestal table.

Kali stood, hand on the cane, looking tall in the straight purple robe. "So. We do not have Loa tonight, but Lelia Elliot, unfocused and disturbed."

The low voice stopped her from walking out.

"Stand against the balcony light. I wish to look at you. Yes, in the solar plexus and lower chakra, a churning of trapped energy. You shake your head. Denial does not stop the pain."

I know. Stay out of my mind, Kali.

"Blocked energy shows dark red in the body's aura, in the lower chakra. What happened to you today?"

"Everyday. I work at Grouper Hole, remember, for a revolting man and his irritating mother." She couldn't say: while I keep Hazel calmed down and while I wait on you, Kali, to tell me what I need to know.

"The dark red shows desire, thwarted, Lelia Elliot."

"Desire, Kali? I have only one thwarted desire. And you

know what it is."

"Ah, Loa speaks again. But Lelia-Loa, you will learn nothing about yourself as long as you deny any part of yourself."

Without answering, she ran from the room.

Deck lights of the *Silver Fox* glowed just off Grouper Hole's dock as Lelia reached the bridge, running all the way from the house and Kali's words. Tonight she welcomed distractions. In an almost empty barroom, Hazel bent to her piano keys, a minor beat like her mood, as Chuck wiped up his bartop.

"Party night, Lelia. Nothing much doing inside when the parking lot's filled. Come on out and watch the embarking of the Invited. It's a show. Your pal Tingley is out there with our resident kibitzers."

She followed Chuck to the porch and sank in a chair. The yacht's spotlight sent a shining path to Grouper Hole's dock. "Is Gil ferrying tonight?" She ignored Chuck's quick glance.

"Usually does when they have to wait in the channel. I guess the guy makes a buck where he can. Sloan handles the *Little Fox* and runs the whole show, of course. That idiot deckhand Jellybo was sent back for more food for the whole crew tonight. Conch had to stay and cook again. You're quieter than usual tonight, Lelia Niece. Not even the Mona Lisa smile."

She shrugged.

"Look what you get when you've got bucks and a famous kisser." Cap'n sounded wistful.

"You mean women knocking on your cabin door?" Tingley asked. "You still interested, Cap'n?"

"You don't need no females for satisfaction if you've got a seagoing si-ren like that beauty."

Car doors slammed on the bayside lot. Baritone and soprano enthusiasms spiked the night air as couples came around past the screened porch and down the dock.

Chuck murmured to Lelia, "This is always an exercise in chagrin for me. These uniformed guys—Lord, if they don't look like ROTC boys to me. And the sweet young things on their arms make them nervous." He laughed, making truth sound like a joke. "Hazel, you may have noticed, gets bitchy jealous of anything young."

Tingley came over. "Glad to see Miss Magnolia is not impressed with old Handsome. Smart girl."

"I'll go sometime just to see if the yacht is done in mirrors. Merrill must need them to practice that smile."

With Chuck, the two old fishermen and Tingley, she watched the parade of summer ruffles and tailored twill shoulders going by to fill up the platform end of the dock, waiting for the short ferry ride to the yacht.

"Who gets invited to these deals?" Tingley rasped.

"Mostly young lieutenants," Chuck said. "No real brass. No lowly GIs. They bring dates or not. Some Special Services U.S. Army Air Corps captain checks them out."

"Mama's darlings without Mama around to watch, think of that," Tingley mused. "Tell me, Magnolia, you think these young gals go for old Handsome? I mean, are they afraid he'll turn out to be Errol Flynn? Or do they kinda hope he does? I'd like to know."

Watching, taking her mind off Francie, she found herself thinking of Susie again and Nancy Alderman. Had Nancy been on that boat? Is that why Gil worked for them? But what could he find out now? And who knows what other young officer could have met her there, followed her off?

"What do you think, Magnolia?" Tingley insisted.

"It's not Merrill they've come to see," she said. "They are happy because of the whole night, being part of something. But *he* needs *them* to be there. I don't know why he needs them."

"Sure you do," Tingley said. "And it ain't any war effort. It's ego. Necessary for an old has-been movie star."

"Warning, Sleuth," Chuck said. "If Sloan hears you slandering the boss, you'll be in more trouble. Look at the guy out there, those shoulders. But he's sharp. You don't tangle with him."

"Ain't much of a job for a real man, playing nursemaid to a puny old dandy," Skipper said.

Cap'n snickered. "Maybe he has to wrestle down those wimmen who gush on Old Handsome's pretty shirt."

"Sloan and the crew live well, of course," Chuck said. "Sloan puts away enough food for a battalion."

They watched Sloan in the 14-footer *Little Fox,* giving orders to the first couples stepping on from the dock. Once loaded, the boat puttered toward the yacht. Now the *Strike* moved in. Gil tied up and took on the next couples waiting.

"I'm going back to the beach," Lelia said. "You don't need me tonight."

But she stood watching the *Strike* come back for the last two couples on the dock. As always, she sensed the impatience hidden under Gil's quick, efficient movements. The girl holding his arm stepped down, squealed, and fell against his chest. He grabbed her in an embrace and as quickly swung her aboard and turned to help the next one waiting.

She remembered that chest, the turbulence it hid. Did the girl feel it? See in his eyes torment over a woman who was dead? Did he confide this to Francie or only that he had reasons to hide his identity? Impressionable as she was, that would have been enough to win Francie over.

The *Strike* pulled away toward the yacht. She left the men on the porch and went into the barroom. Hazel sat at the piano playing and singing for herself, something about sugar daddies.

She left the front way, avoiding the kitchen and Bubba. From the bridge, the lighted yacht could be seen moving slowly down the bay. Its music echoed faintly across the water. A car rumbled over the noisy boards. A woman's face looked out with a secret smile before turning back to the man's shoulder. Lelia walked on, hugging her arms, thinking, Francie wants that, the giving up to another without question. The girl needed love and was taking it. *But I can't.*

As she passed the Inn's shadowy front porch, rocking chairs creaked and contented voices murmured but there was no sign of Francie. *Am I spying?* A shudder of disgust at the thought. Francie had said, *I go out there late, when no one will know.*

The gulf glittered darkly as she walked, concentrating

on the sucking, sighing of the ebb and flow around her feet. Tonight, the rhythm wasn't calming. It echoed her own restlessness.

Someone strode along the beach toward her. A young man in a flapping fatigue shirt and baggy pants. He walked head down, not seeing her until he was near. She recognized his finely chiseled features.

"Dummy?"

He stopped, a rigid figure for a moment. What could one say to a deaf mute to assure him? She reached out a hand, "It's me, Lelia!"

He backed away, mumbling a protest, and ran past her.

So, he could make sounds. She turned and looked until he was a faint movement far down the dark shore. A Knowing hovered, something about this blond boy. She grasped at it, but her thoughts were too jumbled, her body too restless, and the impression faded.

Still sleepless long after midnight, Lelia stood at the open bedroom windows. Below, faint moonlight carved a pale curve of shore, a secret world down there for night creatures only. No, someone was running from the direction of the Inn toward the house.

Francie? It had to be, moving like that, arms swinging free, veering in now, toward the seagrapes, slowing as her feet plowed the deeper sands. Yes, Francie, passing the house, stumbling toward the far end, arms open to someone . . . merging now with the shadow that waited, both disappearing from view.

She wheeled away from the window, her body chilled and shivering under the long gown. She knew where they'd gone. Into the edge of the jungle. Lovers had been there before. She'd found an old Army blanket and palm fronds molded into a nest inside that screen of foliage.

Her body trembled with self-loathing. The feared thing was rising, spreading, until it filled her chest. Tarrant's face flashed, mouthing the words *evil, born evil*, hate in his breath.

Only her feet knew what to do. Flexible, bare, they took

her into the hall. Beyond Kali's sanctuary, there had to be another corner room with windows. She would get in somehow and wait and watch. She would look down on them when they came out. See them together. Self-disgust would punish her back into control.

Once in the hall, she stopped short, hearing her name, a whispered command, "Come." She stood wavering in the dark, listening, fighting the silent scream that threatened to rise.

HURRICANE HOUSE
June night, 1945

23

The words came from Kali, not her own mind. From the hall, Lelia watched the purple shadow move from the balcony into the dark room and sink into the wheelchair. Again the invitation came, a softly spoken command from the woman who waited. "Come, Lelia Elliot."

Like a numbed sleepwalker, she obeyed. In the dark room, the crystal ball was a dull glow, and only Kali's eyes reflected light. The sound of surf went on, and on, but the beach would be empty now, the two people hidden in that nest. The two shadows she had seen down there, merging, would have been Francie throwing herself against his chest, Gil's arms closing over.

"Did you intend to watch them?" Kali's voice was a melancholy sound in the dark.

She couldn't answer. Inside the long gown her body trembled, unable to stop the other thing, the whirl of angry colors rising up from the deepest part of her. Red as dark blood, the alien rage, coiled and trapped with gray repulsion. A silent scream filled her chest, leaving no room for air. Never had she let it rise this high. A scream always there, but held low. To deny it was to hold onto reality, onto sanity.

Kali's voice reached her, soft as a sigh. "Such anguish shows in your energy, Lelia Elliot. Yet you wished to watch the lovers down there?"

She dropped to the leather ottoman, the nightgown spilling over her feet, arms hugging the aching chest. "I wanted to see them together . . ." To shame herself back to control.

"Pain fosters cunning solutions, does it not? But the cunning mind can be a grinning trickster. Self-punishment does not end desire, only twists it into something else, Lelia Elliot."

"I don't allow myself to desire – anything I can't have." She rocked on the low stool.

"The disturbance in the lower chakra grows. Such trapped energy can become turgid and dissonant. It causes one to be closed off and separate from others."

Separate, yes. Her shield. For safety.

"You are afraid of passion. This chakra energy is the life-force."

"Afraid, yes."

"It is true this energy, distorted, mixed with insane perceptions, can possess the mind, consume a life, destroy."

"You frighten me, Kali."

"What you deny frightens you."

She rocked again, hurting. She shouldn't be here, shouldn't let Kali see her fears.

The wheelchair came closer. "Allow your Loa self to hear this. This energy is the life-force still in its unknowing, primal state. Rising, expanding into the heart center, this energy becomes love. Still higher, it is the divine force that opens horizons of the mind. Intellect for some. Wisdom for others. This life-force is not to be feared, but allowed to refine the spirit within the body. Does your Loa self hear?"

She thought of the strange buoyancy that could happen at dawn, like a silver energy rising, free of fear or any need. Almost joy. But this was a dark thing, a danger, waiting inside like a vial of poison kept hidden, not yet broken but about to break now.

Long fingers lifted her chin. "We know, do we not, Lelia-Loa, how to hide secrets from others. We protect ourselves. Yet to hide truth from oneself is another matter. Denial gives life to fears, allows them power. From their hidden place, they will master you."

"You hide so much, Kali."

"From others. Not from myself. You came here to know who you are, Lelia-Loa?"

She couldn't answer.

"Those two lovers down there are only catalysts. Don't hate them. They force you to look within yourself."

She was in the high-backed chair, giving in to a great lassitude that eased the trembling. From behind her, Kali's fingers stroked her forehead. Cool, electric fingers eased the clenched jaws, pressed the throbbing pulse on each side of her neck. Again she obeyed the low voice and released the long inhalation.

"Such turbulent energy. Beneath the fear there is body guilt. Deeper than guilt is rage, rising like virulent poisons from the seed of their beginning. It is the seed you want to uncover."

The beginning, Kali? My beginning was in this house.

The fingers continued tracing her temples, gentle and sure as the hush of waves below.

"The tide brings in debris, leaves it on the beach in view. Another wave can take it out again. But first you wish to look and see what is there. I will speak words to you and you will see."

Faint words, rhythmic as music. Polynesian syllables. Kali's magic? But she willingly followed where they led, not to the Elliots but back to Bethel.

The images came clearly in focus. High Street, inside the house, the hall, Grandmother Calhoun's chandeliers over the dining table, Tarrant seated at the end with his newspaper, Adelaide at the other.

"Whose eyes do you see?"

"I try never to look at those eyes."

"It is safe for Loa to see. Allow her to see and hear as it happens."

The smell of spruce in the big house. A party downstairs, Christmas night. She is fifteen, almost sixteen. Then the creak of the step in the hall outside her room. She hates the sound of that creak even when the steps turn out to be Mattie, or an aunt . . . Tarrant comes into her room. Tarrant Calhoun, rigid as his beliefs. Banker Tarrant Calhoun, the teetotaler, drunk on brandy, and angry.

He is saying that downstairs she made men look at her. . . let one touch her hair . . . wives had noticed . . . Adelaide furious . . . How dare she live under his roof and be carnal, evil, a temptress, wanting men; he could see that she did! She should be punished again.

"Get out of my room, Tarrant!"

She said it aloud in the dark room where the gulf washed in below.

"Go back," Kali's low voice was saying. "What punishment. Look at the first time. You were a child then?"

The electric fingers moved like balm against her temples. Again she was back in Bethel in the house on High Street, watching herself at seven running upstairs from the preacher's red-faced fear, "Cunning gifts of the Devil . . ."

She heard Kali's voice as in her own mind. "See that time. The child is there, left alone to be frightened forever. Go back to her. Watch from safety and help her."

Again she was that frightened child running upstairs, getting into a nightgown and hiding under the covers. The hall creaks outside. Someone is coming. Tarrant is there. His eyes cold behind the shiny glasses. Standing by the bed, his mouth twisted, saying she had killed them all by being born. She had forced him to come back to Bethel to harbor a child with evil gifts. She must be punished. . .

Lelia stopped. The dark red anger she feared stirred now like a sickness. Always it tightened her breath. She rocked on the stool, wanting escape.

"Go back." Kali's voice, a soft command in the dark. "The child needs you to see."

Again the room high above High Street. The child who is herself sits in the middle of the bed, clutching a pillow to her chest. Tarrant unfastens his belt, the buckle flashes in the light as it pulls free, the cover yanked away, the child pushed on her face, the gown shoved up. But the child twists back around, grasping the pillow in front for protection. She sputters words to Tarrant, terrible words because they stun the uncle who stands over her, arm raised with a belt. "You want to look at my body, don't you, Tarrant?" She watches the hand freeze on the belt, the eyes behind the glasses widen. Wild eyes. Then it is true, the child thinks, I frighten Tarrant, I am evil.

Kali's voice pushed her on. "There is a place beyond fear. Watch the child. And the man."

"My uncle drops the belt. His hand comes down so slow, down, down, his face whiter now. The pillow is pushed into my face. I don't fight it. It's better to hide . . ."

"But you see, you feel —"

"Behind the pillow, blackness, swirling with red . . ." Hiding there, needing to hide though there's no air to breathe, no breath to scream as Tarrant pushes up the gown. Icy fingers move, exploring. It's easier to go far away and remembering a boy once, bending over a dead bird, digging his finger into the dead bird on its back, not breathing, not owning its body any more.

She found herself rocking on the stool in this dark room above the gulf, the child receding, yet the red rage had broken free, filling her body. Kali touched her brow, repeating some question. "The child couldn't scream behind the pillow?"

No, no, no.

"You can now. For that child. Release her."

A pillow was in her arms, a gift from the dark. She seized it, buried her face into it, and watched the scream coil up from her depths, twist through her body, higher, a fury of jagged lightning ripping up until the clinched jaws lets its sharp heat burst free.

In the pillow blackness, she watched it go, a trail of sallow self-loathing tinged with crimson rage . . . watched it fade into a void.

How long had she been here, curled up on the end of Kali's bed, cradling the pillow to her chest? A faint streak of light showed above the gulf horizon. She stirred, stood up, weak, emptied of something. In its place an enormous sadness.

She found Kali on the balcony, seated in the wheelchair, head against the high back, eyes closed. In the gray light, the face looked drawn, the voice barely audible. "You can finish it now, with the man and the child."

"I want to forget them."

"Only if you finish it. Attend the moment in which you closed the memory down and sealed it beneath conscious awareness. Go back and see the child. It is safe now."

Lelia closed her eyes and looked again at the child sitting up in bed, watching the man straighten his clothes, tighten the belt, his hands shaking. She had seen the fear in his eyes. What had she done? He was warning her never to speak of this punishment if she were to live in this house.

She could tell Kali now, "Yes, I remember. He left the room. His guilt became mine. Silence was easy. My voice left me. Six months, I think. I didn't care. I felt safer that way. Tarrant and I avoided one another. After that it was just cold hate. I'm sure we both blocked out the memory." Until that one Christmas evening and that last night in Bethel.

Dawn streaked the sky. At the balcony edge, Lelia looked out to a gulf just beginning to appear. The air found new places in her body.

Kali murmured, "You are free of the fear of passion but not free of passion. Deal with that as you will."

Yes.

Kali's voice sounded strangely weary. "Loathing for another who has harmed you can be a dark pleasure, one that brews poison in the body. You have one more choice to make, Loa, to carry that loathing or to be forever free of it."

Lelia gripped the balcony looking down on beach sands growing faintly pink. Kali reached over and covered her hands with a warm palm of her own.

"I don't wish to think of Tarrant ever again, if that's possible."

As Kali sat back, she turned to look at this woman who had heard her own secrets and told none of her own. The strong face looked strangely drawn in the half-light. For the first time, Kali looked old. "Are you ill?" Lelia whispered.

"You are free of your hate . . . now I must free myself of it. Go!"

"Kali?"

"Leave now. I have my own cleansing to do. Go."

BAYSHORE
July 1, 1945

24

July now. Every afternoon brought a cloudburst cooling the hot day to a rain-washed afternoon. The waterfront moved at a lazy summer pace, but Lelia tied up her long hair and moved with restless, self-directed energy. She was going to find Susie Holms. Brockway hadn't found her and the girl needed to be found. Each dawn a dream woke her even as it faded. Had she dreamed of the ancient woman on the shore, or was it still Susie's thin face mouthing some plea? Was the message a trap? She didn't even know the girl. Illogical or not, finding Susie was something she had to do.

Bringing up the food trays, Lelia considered mentioning Susie to Kali. But since the strange session in Kali's room the other night, there had been little talk between them. The tawny, poised face seemed drained, inaccessible.

"She looks ill," Lelia confessed to Hazel, not explaining why. Thankfully, Hazel was absorbed these evenings, in a booth with Morris Alderman no less, drinking in lessons on buying land once the war was over.

"The old spook's probably deciding when she's going to do you in," Hazel had said. "Keep at it."

Today she knew what to do. Find Gil. Tell him Susie knew who killed his Nancy. Why do it alone, Gil? Susie's story could vindicate him. When the rain subsided, she'd go to his cabin, tell him to help her find Susie. Gil could find the girl better than Tingley or Brockway. She could face Gil now without fear of herself after that strange session with Kali.

Tarrant Calhoun had marked her past too, but now she was strangely free of him.

All afternoon rain pounded Grouper Hole's roof. She sat in a corner booth, alone, toying with lunch, impatient. At the bar, Chuck polished the plank in front of a lone GI and the two old fishermen. Tingley burst in, wet and elated. "Pour three big ones, Chuck, for me and my pals, Captain of the *Queen Mary* and Admiral Nimitz."

"Look what the storm blew in," Cap'n said. "Skipper, ain't this the gabby fellow hauled us down to Johns Pass couple nights ago? Didn't show us a dang thing we ain't got here."

"You really buying, Sleuth?" Chuck kept on rubbing down the bar top.

"Celebrating."

Skipper said, "Musta got himself a job. Eisenhower wants him to write up the war."

"You hear that, Chuck? No gratitude from the mullet skiff navy. Here, gimme that." Tingley grabbed the cloth and polished. "Go on, pour, I'm paying."

"How's the big story coming along, Walter Winchell?" Chuck set out the three steins.

"It's coming, it's coming. Details of which I cannot divulge to two old water rats who won't open up and share with a pal what little they know. Cackle all you want, Cap'n . . . Chuck, it's an honest-to-God story. Only I've got to be Edward R. Murrow, Drew Pearson, and Dashiell Hammett balled into one guy to stick the pieces together."

"Who you doing this for?" Chuck took back his bar rag. "The *St. Pete Times*? Do they know you're rattling around these beaches in their behalf?"

"My behalf." Tingley's ruddy face sagged. "And for a dead girl. And for that other one in trouble." The brown eyes narrowed, watching Chuck. "Susie."

Chuck's arm stilled. He put the rag away. "Know where she is?"

"Interested, huh?"

"She's a little fool." Chuck flushed under his tan. "Making

it worse for herself by hiding."

Tingley clicked down his quarters. "Anybody been in here looking for her? Besides Brockway? Like her old man. Big fellow they call Cracker?"

"Only half the guys who come in here. Look, J. T., save your interviewing for the docks. Not at my bar. You want news, I'll turn the radio back on."

With her lunch tray, Lelia swept past them, avoiding Tingley. He talked too much. He only wanted his story. He'd never find Susie that way. "I'm leaving now," she told them all. "The rain's stopped."

The sun was out as she ran down the brick road and into the sandy path that led through Piney Cove Trailer Park. There was still time to do this crazy thing and get back to the beach before sunset.

It was quiet in here. Under dripping trees, most all the trailers looked closed for the summer. She ran past Chuck and Hazel's old trailer, then into the still wet woods in the direction Gil had taken that first night. A cabin on the bay, Hazel had said. Low pine branches caught at her hair like doubts beginning to nag as she plunged through wet, pungent woods. Ahead, a small cabin sat inside the pines near the bay. She slowed, walking toward it. What if Francie were there? But she wouldn't be. Impulsive as the girl was, Francie wouldn't take her romantic notions to a sad little shack like this. A bower on a dark beach was different, hidden as it was, convenient for midnight escapes from the Inn.

A weedy slope led down to the new looking dock. Empty. But it had to be Gil's. Motor boat sounds split the quiet. That would be from Al's Bait House. She waited, confidence wavering.

She looked again at this place where Gil lived, where he *hid*. Two rooms maybe. Tiny dark windows faced the sagging wooden porch, screen door ajar. Something on the slanted porch caught her attention. Bits of red caught between the rough boards. She picked up what was left of a bracelet. A string of tiny red hearts.

The *Strike* cut its speed and sputtered to silence against the low dock. From the cabin's dark shade, Lelia watched, the heart bracelet cutting into her clinched fist. Gil jumped out, secured the lines and strode up the slight embankment, a slow preoccupied stride, head down.

Looking up, he stopped short, lean face etched with surprise. His mouth formed her name. He walked the last few feet slowly. "Lelia?" The intense blue gaze probed.

"I had something to tell you. But —" Her hand tightened over the heart bracelet.

"So tell me."

"No reason now. You must know more about Susie than I do."

He frowned down at her opened hand but as quickly wheeled around to squint toward the bay. A boat had cut its motors and was headed for the dock. "Lelia, listen to me." A staccato order. "No time to explain. Get inside." He gripped her arm, and even as she saw two men on the dock, Gil had pulled her with him up the single step into the screen door, and into the hot dim cabin. "Stay here!" He sprang out again.

She stood where he left her, obeying her own awareness of danger rather than his order. His cabin. This dark little place. A low couch of a bed covered with sailcloth. A scarred highboy dresser. A single deck chair. A bathroom door standing ajar.

Outside, heavy feet stomped on the porch. A drawling country voice challenged Gil. A second, with a different rhythmic cadence too low to hear. Two men, looking for someone. Gil's low answers sounded unhurried, edged with hard amusement. Derision in the answering laughter. They didn't believe him. They were coming in.

"Wait." Gil's voice sounded lazy as a shrug, "let me speak to the lady first."

He was inside again, his hand pressing her head to his mouth, his hot breath against her cheek. "Go along with me on this until I get them out."

The screen blew open. A barrel-shaped man in bib overalls and rubble chin strode in. Gil turned to face them, holding her so close against his side, her own body felt the furious pulse. The intruder stared with bloodshot eyes, thumbs in his pockets. Behind him a slight, olive-skinned man wearing whites. His jet-black eyes raked the small dim room.

The overalled man grumbled, "It's not Susie." He continued to stare.

"Meet Cage and Cracker, my dear." Gil sounded coldly casual. His grip stayed angry. "Rude sonofaguns, aren't they? Are you two satisfied?"

"Where is she?" Cracker mumbled. He rubbed the stubble chin. "Mebbe you got two." The man called Cage kicked open the bathroom door then turned back. His low voice had a sound, almost French. "Then what did you do with her? And who is this one?"

"You've overstayed your visit, fellows," Gil said. "Think twice before you muscle in on my privacy again."

Cracker's wet smile spread. "She ain't Susie, aw'right."

"New girl at Grouper Hole, aren't you?" Cage's black eyes probed.

Her own voice surfaced. "And who are you to ask?"

Cracker shuffled so close she could smell his sour sweat. "Sister, I'm looking for my little gal. Cage here is helping this old daddy look. And we coulda sworn this handsome fella could tell us a lot. If he was a mind to."

Gil's fingers tightened on her shoulders. "If she shows up and wants to see old daddy, I'll be happy to help. Now – get the hell out of here."

The big one kicked the screen open as they went out.

"Wait here," Gil muttered and followed the men.

She stood unmoving in the hot little room. Images, vague Knowings came and faded too quickly to be captured. The sound of motors revving up broke the spell. She pushed open the screen and was off the porch as Gil leaped up the slope. "Lelia, wait!" He reached her and gripped her arm. "Please."

She looked past him toward piney woods. *It's sunset, I've let sunset come, and I'm in this woods playing out some strange charade.*

"Lelia, for God's sake, look at me. Let me explain. I would not have subjected you to that – but you were here, and it had to be that way."

"And it helped to have a girl to show them. Because they knew one had been here. And it wasn't Francie – " His glower didn't stop her. "It was Susie Holms, wasn't it, Gil? And I had come to tell you this great news – that Susie knows who killed Nancy Alderman. I came to tell you the girl could be your answer – and your alibi if only you found her. But I guess you already had found her." She stopped. "You've known all the time about Susie, haven't you? She was here all the time Brockway searched."

"Not all the time. Listen to me, Lelia. She was here and she ran away about as quick, the little fool. I can't explain more right now. I didn't hurt her. But she ran."

"She got away, you mean? You're one of those looking for her, aren't you."

"I am, Lelia. For the reason you came to tell me."

"Why should I believe you?" She faced the hard blue gaze, felt its intensity.

"Because it's the truth." He released his grip. A vein in his temple throbbed. "That night on the beach when I acted a little crazy, you were willing to believe me. I'm asking again. I need time." He waited, too close. "I can guess you're here on this waterfront looking for some answers of your own in that mausoleum on the beach. Answers don't come easy, do they?"

"They don't come easy."

"Trust me, Lelia."

She left him there and without looking back, plunged through the woods. The path led quickly into the clearing of the trailer camp again. Past Chuck and Hazel's old trailer. Down the sandy path, she started running, out to the brick road, and across the bridge.

What to believe? Susie knew everything. If it wasn't too late to find her.

"Your desire is a different kind tonight, Loa." Kali had come in from the darkening balcony. The smoke-gray hair spilled damp and loose against the erect shoulders. The shadowed eyes probed. "Your energy comes from the heart center.

Your concern is not for yourself tonight but for someone else. And this troubles you?"

Caution melted. "Yes! It's Susie, a girl I don't even know who used to work at Grouper Hole. She's in trouble somewhere, somewhere close. I have to find her as soon as possible."

"So you shall find her. Focused desire has power. But it is diffused by annoyance."

"I didn't come here to get involved in other people's lives." Gil, Francie, Tingley, Susie. "Yet I've let myself get entangled."

"Entangled, you say. Perhaps they are a part of Lelia Elliot's own tapestry. Others can be a mirror for yourself."

"You, a recluse, telling me that?"

Kali turned a melancholy face toward the darkening water. "When I closed the door to this house so long ago—I had learned who I was."

At the door, the low voice stopped her. "You must have need to find this girl, so you shall. I remind you, Lelia-Loa, when you search for the truth, be ready to accept what you find."

PALMETTO WOODS
July 3, 1945

25

First mate Sloan marched out of Grouper Hole leaving Bubba groaning behind the bar and Martha Critten pacing the kitchen, asking Conch how many people could he serve. Evander Merrill wanted to give a party, a big fancy shindig, Bubba complained. Chuck shrugged sympathy and kept his head bent to the radio, listening to reports of B-29s firing on Guam.

When the Crittens finally left, Lelia brought Chuck a plate of hot crab cakes and sat down on a bar stool as he ate. Last night she had dreamed about a very small doorway. Susie was behind that doorway. Brockway said she was somewhere close on this mainland. She knew it was true. Where? Except for that crazy trek yesterday to Gil's cabin, she had not explored this wooded bayshore.

"July. Going to be hot now," Chuck said. "Something on your mind?"

She asked her question, making it casual, "What's back in the woods besides Sandy Cove trailer park?"

"Couple of fishermen's shacks on the bay. And more woods. Why?"

"You're the native and the morning walker. I still don't know the mainland." She ignored his frown. "What's it like back there off the road?"

"Orange groves." He shrugged. "Scrub land and snakes. Conch gets his picking of rattler skins there."

Her scalp tingled. "And where do Conch and Cheta live?"

"Behind Piney Grove. Swamp and woods back there. Why the interest in local geography?" Caution edged his curiosity.

"I was wondering where Susie would hide."

"Stay out of it, Lelia!" Chuck slammed down his fork, searched for a cigarette, but threw the pack down. "Too many people are looking for that crazy kid."

"I know. That's why she needs help. I think you care what happens to her too." She felt his alarm, which she ignored. Without knowing it, Chuck had helped.

The big cook was clearing his sink before leaving for the afternoon when she came back into the kitchen. Conch had been a silent dark thundercloud for two days now, she realized. *You know something about Susie, Conch. Are you hiding her?*

She sat on the cleared off work table. "How did this mainland and beaches look when you came here?" *Talk to me, Conch.*

"Jungle. Old scrub jungle." At the sink, he drew himself a jelly glass of water. "What you want to know dot for?"

"I wondered – how it was here then for a young woman, the one who was my grandmother. The stories say she liked to sail on big ships with grand ballrooms and go to Paris. But here she was in that big house on the gulf, away from everything, and having babies. I've wondered what kind of a place it was for Bonnie Elliot." *Talk to me, Conch.*

"What dot lady wanted not in the same world as any long-legged colored boy from Key West." He rubbed his big hand over the frosted white head. "My mama dragged me up here to this old place. Hated it at first. I got Jamaica blood, you know. Told you."

"But you stayed."

"Collecting coon oysters and selling them. Those days they washed in thick and fat on the mud flats. Land was a dollah an acre then. *Sooon come, sooon come*, dot boy promised hisself. Gonna get me some old scrub land, clear it off, have me an orange grove. I got my scrub. Got no tractor yet. Too busy cooking. Gettin' old." A half-smile. "Still hoping, before I die. So I don't want any trouble I don't need."

Don't go yet, Conch. "And what's your scrub land like back there off the road?"

He untied his canvas apron and stood holding it. "About the same. Hammocks of cabbage palms and palmettos, both sides of this old bay. Roads different. Some you see now—trails then, made by old razor-back hogs." His shoulders eased in the remembering. "The first lil' gal I married up and died. The second high-tailed it out and went nawth. I stayed. Cheta's a good woman." He hung up the apron.

"Conch, where do you suppose Susie Holms would hide if she were around here?"

He stopped still. "I'm gone now." And he was out the back door heading down the brick road.

He knows! She ran out after him.

The dark face turned, guarded. "Miz Crit show up? You tell her I'm gone."

"No. May I walk home with you, Conch?

He stayed rooted as an old oak.

"I must talk to you – and Cheta."

"White girls don't come visiting." His face a dark thundercloud. "Dot's trouble."

"But if one came running to you from *other* trouble, wouldn't you hide her if she had no where else to go?"

"Why would I do dot?"

"To help her if she asked you to, I'd think."

A car rumbled by, occupants' faces staring at the two of them, stepping off the road to let it pass. Conch shook his head and groaned. "Females are sure stubborn critters."

"Trust me, Conch."

He studied the empty road. "I doan go through the trailer park. My path's further down. You can follow, if you stay behind me."

A narrow path led off the brick road into a cathedral of tall pines. She followed behind Conch's broad back, her sandals sinking into powder white sand. Conch stalked ahead, poking a long stick at low thick palmetto fronds on either side that were still sending out the hot green smell from the day's sun. Now and then he glanced back to check on her. They trailed in silence except for the whack of his stick and the high whine of insects.

In a clearing ahead, a substantial weathered cabin sat alone, shaded by two huge oaks. Someone leaned in the shadowed front door. *A small door.* The figure was not a skinny freckle-faced girl, but a languorous dark shape in a flower-sack dress watching their approach. Cheta sidled out on the slanted wood porch, planting her bare feet at the edge to look down at the two of them. "What you want?" The jet eyes were narrowed to slits.

"To talk with you. Cheta, you know who I'm looking for."

"Yeah. A skinny speckled gal with tin cans tied to her tail."

"Susie. Tell me –"

"Somebody's trying to set fire to that tail."

"I know. She's in trouble and I want to find her. If she's hiding here, tell me."

Cheta lifted her strong shoulders in an eloquent shrug. She dropped to the porch edge, long bare legs swinging. Still rooted in the sandy yard, Conch said, "I let you come so's you can see. She's gone."

Beyond the dark girl, through the open front door, Lelia could see the room, walls papered with a crazy montage of magazine pictures. The warm smell of the herb bread drifted out. Above, oak branches made the only sound.

"She was here, wasn't she?"

Conch kicked the sandy dirt and folded his arms over his chest. "Dot little gal showed up a week ago like some scared rabbit. But she ran away." He looked hard into her face.

"I believe you, Conch. Please tell me about her."

"Came with her likker bottle and her shaking and her tin cans rattlin'," Cheta said.

"Somebody wants to kill her, don't they, Conch?" She looked at both of them. "That's why she runs."

Cheta pursed her full lips. "I coulda tied worsen tin cans to somebody else's tail, I coulda done that – only that gal too scared dumb to listen."

"Where did she go when she ran again? What did she tell you?"

"He gonna help hide her better, she say." The full lips pressed in a smile. "Some fella."

"Who? Did you see him?" *Tell me what you know.*

Conch sat down on the porch edge and stared at his shoes. "She was here a week, curled up scared. Ran away two days ago."

"Somebody came for her, didn't they? *Who*, Conch?" Who are you protecting?

"You better go now, white gal," Cheta said.

Conch's dark gaze bore into hers. "I let you come so you'd know the truth about Cheta and me. Doan ask me anymore. You best go now. Just you take a stick going back to the road."

She left them on the porch and followed the sandy path through hot, hushed woods. She wasn't giving up. Susie was still close. So was the one who meant to shut her up.

A glimpse of a trailer made her turn abruptly off the path and whip her stick through underbrush into Piney Cove's clearing. Pulse quickening, she walked past the rooted trailers. So many were deserted now. Where better to hide? She stopped in front of Chuck and Hazel's old trailer. Chuck had kept it. Hazel accused him of sneaking off and sleeping here afternoons.

The door was always unlocked. She pushed it open and went into the hot, musty trailer. Another small doorway stood half opened on Chuck and Hazel's old bedroom. Skin chilled, Lelia stepped in. A pink chenille spread trailed from the end of the bed to the doorway. On the floor, she saw a paper plate and what was left of a single dried up crab cake, like the ones from Grouper Hole's kitchen.

On the rumpled bed lay a small empty jar, the one that had been the fund for Susie.

Martha Critten had ordered Bubba to throw that thing away with the bracelet. Did Bubba retrieve that bottle and find out the girl hid here?

No, it was Chuck, wasn't it, Susie, who gave you a place to hide, who brought you food and that bottle for you to see.

The air felt like a strangled breath; the faded pink chenille stretched like a silent struggle. *You were here, Susie, and taken away against your will, dragged out, hand clutching that spread.*

She ran from the trailer. Under scudding clouds she ran along the road, past the Nash, Hazel waving from the Nash. In the silent kitchen, she worked automatically preparing Kali's tray. *I tried to find you, Susie, I tried.*

It had been safer before, being the dreamer, the observer behind her invisible shield. Lonely, but safer.

Why did Chuck hide Susie? She remembered the concern he hid under brusque impatience. Some kind of guilt there. Conch had protected him. Maybe Chuck cared for the girl. Certainly he'd have to hide that. Hazel would be livid.

That awful man Cracker hovered in her mind, made her skin give its danger message. But if he was Susie's father, he had a right to look for her, just as the girl must have wanted to run from such a father. No, that wasn't why Susie was running. Bubba loomed in her mind and this time she didn't block him out. She looked at his sweating insecurity and furtive gaze and waited for a Knowing. It made no sense. She saw him afraid of Susie.

Gil? Why did Susie run from him? Only Susie could tell her that.

Glancing out to the beach, she saw someone come from the seagrape path. From Kali's balcony steps? She ran into the yard and saw Dummy's wiry shoulders shining in the late sun. He strode to the beach and disappeared from view.

Upstairs, she set down the tray and went to Kali on the balcony. "That was Dummy in the yard. The deaf-mute boy. Kali – do you *know* him?"

"He takes fruit – with my permission." Kali's smile was faint. "The exiled find one another. We have much in common. Lelia-Loa should understand that very well."

"I don't understand anything right now."

"You have not found today what you sought? Perhaps you are afraid of what you'll find?"

"No, I've tried!"

"The day isn't over."

At Grouper Hole that night, Chuck worked, grim-faced, refusing to meet her eye. At midnight, Lelia ran out, took the beach way, welcoming the dark and the calming sound of surf.

Overhead, fast moving clouds rode over the moon, turning the beach hazy then dark. A motor boat echoed further down toward the patch of jungle. She hurried toward it. Gil? No, a smaller boat, pulled onto the beach. Three men stood there. She could see they were commercial fishermen, the sun-roughened men she saw around Al's Bait House. They crouched down at the surf's edge looking at something being washed by the waves. She pulled in a long breath and made herself keep walking toward them.

Slowly the three stood, blank-faced in the sudden moonlight.

"There's a body here, Miss. You don't wanna look."

"Maybe she'll know who it is."

"Saw it wash up against this beach so we pulled in. Miss – you sure?"

"Yes – I have to look," she said.

The three men backed away. She stepped closer to see what was sprawled there.

Waves lapped at the white legs and sand-crusted panties. The skirt had washed over the top of the body. A thin red braid showed, embedded in the wet shore. The open hand held seaweed.

Lelia stooped down. The cloth was thick and terrible to touch, but she brought the skirt over the legs and looked at the face. So elfin, so white. The eyes like pale blue marbles, staring up at the moon.

A single sob escaped. *Susie, Susie, I heard you calling.* "Jesus," one of the men mumbled. "We ought'n to have let her see. Here, Miss."

Warm, rough hands pulled her up. "You best go on now. We'll wrap her up and get her up to the sheriff in Clearwater."

She stood and managed to say, "Ask for Tom Brockway . . . Tell him you found Susie Holms."

Two of the men went to the boat and came back with something to cover the dead girl. The third looked up at a glint of light from Hurricane House. "Pore little gal. Washed up right in front of that old witch's house, too."

They moved away with the wrapped thing. Lelia ran toward the seagrape path. A light showed under Kali's door. Lelia pushed it open and stood there, breathing hard.

"Yes?" In the alcove bed, against the high pillows Kali looked up from her open book.

"She's dead. Drowned. On the beach in front of this house."

"The girl you were looking for?"

"Yes."

Kali's fingers pressed the book closed. "You found her. Now to understand what you have found."

INDIAN ROCKS
July 4, 1945

26

Oblivious to rain or death, Connie Haines sang in sweetly mournful tones. *What Is This Thing Called Love?* A thunderstorm rattled its fury against Grouper Hole, darkening the morning, a Fourth of July still quiet except for rain and the juke box.

On the bayside porch, Lelia shivered in the warm humid air, remembering last night, Susie's body there on the beach, blank marble eyes looking up, seaweed tangled in the dead fingers.

Tingley's raspy voice brought her back inside. Wet and agitated, he waved a newspaper. "You see this? Where's Chuck?"

She shook her head. Chuck had been missing all morning. Grumbling, Bubba worked behind the bar. Tingley pushed forward the *Evening Independent*. The photo from a high school album showed a gamin-faced girl with a minxish smile. Under the picture, the story said the body of Susie Holms, twenty-three, sought by the sheriff's department since April, had been found last night, washed ashore on Sand Key, discovered by three fishermen, on the beach near the place known as Hurricane House. The body was taken to the morgue in Clearwater. The girl's mother was unable to comment, but the father was calling it suicide and blaming the sheriff for "hounding his little girl for shooting at some guy who deserved it."

"You can bet they had to clean up Cracker's quote,"

Tingley said. "Dammit to hell – pardon, Miss Magnolia."

Chuck was there, dropping into the chair, pulling the newspaper over. Tingley and Lelia watched as Chuck read, a muscle in his jaw working, before he stood up and stalked away.

Tingley pulled the newspaper back and groaned. "My story in the damn evening paper."

"You're worried about that, Tingley? The girl is dead!"

His brown eyes looked bleak. "The hell of it, Magnolia, I kept my mouth shut and maybe I shouldn't of." He raked a stubby hand across his flushed face. "I didn't write anything because I didn't want to go off half-cocked. Now the girl's dead. Got in the way of a snake that's still crawling. Or a storm still brewing, not sure yet. She wasn't my whole story. Just part of it. Pitching her into the gulf was somebody's way of covering their tracks. I'm glad you stayed out of it. That somebody knows J. T. Tingley is onto them."

"How do you know, J. T.? Tell me what you know."

"Found a little gift in my cabin. Rot-gut booze in a good old Wild Turkey bottle. Woulda killed a lesser man than me."

She watched the grin lines turn to a grimace. The man was in trouble. He'd blundered into something. And Gil? He wouldn't blunder, but he would persist. Then he should be in trouble too. And anyone around him. That could include Francie. When the bar phone rang, it was Francie, insisting she go to a Bomb-a-Dear party with her that very night. Lelia looked around the barroom. "Yes," she heard herself saying.

The sun came out by eleven. By two, the sandy crowd began drifting in, girls clustered by the Wurlitzer feeding in their nickels. In her flowered dress, Martha Critten ambled through, like a pleased parade marshal. Hazel showed up, dressed for the evening in red beach pajamas, a white and blue ribbon tied through the curls sitting on the upswept hair. When she took her bourbon and ginger drink to a booth, Lelia slid in opposite, engulfed in smoke and Evening in Paris perfume. But she had to force someone to talk about Susie.

"No one cares," she said to Hazel. "A girl who worked here gets washed up on the beach and no one even speaks of it. Or wonders." She didn't add, even Chuck.

The black mascaraed lashes lowered. Hazel waved her cigarette like a shrug. "The nervy kid was hell-bent for trouble. I'm not going to lose sleep over her. She mooned around Chuck too much, like he was Big Daddy or something." Her attention went to the room. "Get a load of that old bag."

Together they watched Martha Critten slap a khaki shoulder here, pat a crew-cut head there, then stop at a table to whisper to three grizzled fishermen and leave them chuckling.

"She doesn't care Susie is dead," Lelia said. "She's glad."

"So what? Look at that hair. Like something out of the funny papers. You know – Maggie, Jiggs' wife, the one with the rolling pin. But old Crit gets respect where it counts. Down at the First National Bank. No telling what she makes on three hole-in-the-wall bars besides this place, and that's not counting the houses she rents out to officers, complete with maids. That part is under-the-table money, over and beyond what she's supposed to get with rent control."

Compact open, Hazel ran a new curve of red over the thin lips. "And what's doing with you and the witch upstairs, Kiddo? Don't expect me to be a damn patient fool forever."

"Or a fool by being too impatient – Chuck is calling me." She left Hazel glowering.

At the bar, she told Chuck, "You've said nothing about Susie." At the pain in his tight face, she said quickly, "I won't be working tonight. I've got to get out of here."

Low fireworks sputtered on the dock as she came back from the beach, dressed for the Bath Club dance. "Lordy, Lordy, ain't that purty," Cap'n said, following her in.

Behind the bar, she studied the fractured glimpse of herself in the bottle-lined, yellowed mirror. Who was this self anyway, hair brushed back off bare shoulders, Francie's gift of the peach dress shaping her breasts and waist above the full skirt.

Hazel leaned against the bar with a glass of bourbon and ginger. "Ha. I figgered you'd act normal sometime. Going to let some big military shoulders hug you around the dance floor tonight? Watch out. It's full moon time."

"It's a Bomb-a-Dear dance. I'm going with Francie."

"Lah-de-dah. One of those. With all that tanned skin showing, you'll have those good mama-chaperons lending you a crocheted shawl – so you don't get cold or something on this blasted hot night."

"Thanks for the warning."

The big blue Packard waited, motor running. A flustered Francie sat behind the wheel. The reason sat in the back seat: Aunt Mo, smiling.

Hiding her sharp disappointment, Lelia got in next to Francie's billowing skirt and the cloud of heady gardenia scent. So, there'd be no chance for honest girlish confessions from Francie on the way down to the Bath Club. No chance to deliver her own warnings.

The big sedan lumbered toward the beach side, Francie making a breathy explanation. "I *made* Auntie come along. I wanted her to see we're just *fine* going down to the Bath Club for these lil' old dances." Her quick glance pleaded apology.

Aunt Mo sounded uncertain. "I'm afraid of what your mother will say when she returns. You are the restless one, Francine! But Lelia, dear, I am glad she's had a nice friend like you to go along all these nights."

"All these nights?" Lelia murmured.

"Auntie wanted to go this *one* time to see how nice it is and all. She'll play cards."

"I see."

Aunt Mo's running pleasantries filled the silence as they drove south on Gulf Boulevard. Lelia studied the girl's profile, then looked away again at the moon-bright gulf. It was just as well they didn't have the chance to talk. She couldn't tell Francie that Gil may be a murderer, that he may have caused Susie Holms' death, too, to protect himself. *I don't believe it myself.*

What other reason could she give Francie to stop seeing him other than the woman he loves is dead and he's too old for her? But what right did she have to hurt the girl?

At the Bath Club's sprawling stucco buildings, the three

of them trailed in behind pastel-dressed Dears.

The exuberant swing beat came from behind double doors to the left. Aunt Mo trilled her good-by and turned toward the card lounge. Francie grabbed Lelia's arm. "Thanks for not saying anything to Auntie."

"But you can't depend on me as an excuse. Besides, an excuse won't save you from trouble."

"I know." The blue eyes had a desperate glint. "Tonight I just want to have a good time, a good, silly time, and forget about everything."

"Yes. I need to try that myself." She followed Francie in through the double doors. The Four Seasons room, awash with muted yellow light, pulsated with brass and the thump of bass.

"We're supposed to go over and act demure and say hello to Mrs. Strickland," Francie murmured, but they both stood there, just inside the door.

On the square of polished wood floor, a half dozen couples spun and whirled to a fast swing number. At the edge, more Bomb-a-Dears stood in clusters, watching, some as young as Francie, others like herself in their early twenties. Their petticoat-full skirts swayed. Their white pumps tapped. Their faces stayed animated, pretending they weren't waiting to be asked to dance,

At the other end of the room, commissioned officers made their own clusters. In their dress uniform perfection, they stood so carefully casual, faces stoic, yet their presence infused the party room with energy like the exuberant brass beat. She watched how their eyes scanned, wanting more than faces showed as the innocent lyrics bleated. *Don't sit under the apple tree with anyone else but me . . .*

"Have you been coming alone, Francie?"

"When I come, sure. At the big dances at the Coliseum, they have a band. But the records here are all the big bands. You'll be glad you came. See? Lieutenants and all. Different from old Grouper Hole, didn't I tell you?"

When a freckled-faced, gangly officer reached for her, Francie allowed herself to be led to the dance floor.

A clarinet's wail soared like a cry. Lelia stood alone by the door wrapped in the poignant sound.

"Dance?"

She shook her head.

Melody gave way to a shuffling rhythm. Francie waved and stayed with the lanky dancer. Couples crowded the floor now, polished shoes and pastel pumps moving faster to sassy, chorused lyrics, *You're undecided now, so whaddaya gonna do?*

A baritone hello made her turn. The freshly shaved face waited so close she looked straight into the pale eyes. Bland confidence there. Not ice blue eyes with hidden meanings, like Gil's.

The young man grinned and mimicked the lyrics along with the blaring record. Looking satisfied with himself, "How about it, Beautiful – are we still 'Undecided?'"

"Decided," Lelia murmured.

It meant less than his broadening smile assumed, but she let his hand lead her to the floor. After his arms, there were other arms throwing her out, bringing her back in, driven by the fast swing beat. Or holding her close with some crooning melody. The same facade of tailored twill each time, yet she felt their different energies, wooden or kinetic, each murmuring against her ear.

"You're so beautiful, but I got this girl, well, I did have this girl back home . . ."

". . . not from around here, are you? Not one of these mama's darlings, but a real woman."

Hot fingers moved her away and back to them like a possession, eyes saying more than their grins. "All that moonlight out there and we have to hold hands in here? Honey, I want to talk."

When the music halted, and the punch bowl waited to be refilled, the Dears trailed out into the cooler night toward the ladies' locker, voices blending, spiked with high decibel exclamations. In front of the length of mirror, bras were straightened, waistline profiles checked with pursed lips. Compacts snapped open and shut.

"Do you really think Woodbury facials help?"

"He wanted to tell me about Mussolini's 'love nest.' He said he saw it in Italy. It's an orphanage now. He kept telling —"

"And that short one with the glasses jitterbugs like a silly frog."

Francie grabbed her arm. "Let's get out." Not speaking, they crossed the fragrant terrace, back toward the music, beginning again with a mellow voice crooning *Falling in love is won-der-ful, so they tell me . . ."*

Francie stopped short. "I just can't bear to hear that. Do you mind if we get Aunt Mo and go?" The pink lips trembled.

"No. It's a good idea."

On the drive back up the boulevard, they were both so quiet Aunt Mo asked sleepily, "Didn't you two have a nice time? I looked in and thought, now that's doing more for those young men than a Stage Door Canteen with movie stars. You all looked like Cinderellas."

Or princesses at their own ball, Lelia thought, Daddy's Snow Whites and Sleeping Beauties, fearfully ready to wake up. At parties like this, they could smile sweetly and dance with the Frogs, but they waited for the possible Prince. They knew some night they'd look up and he'd be there, smiling, the band playing something so right like "All the Things You Are," and he would know it, too, and sing along with the words, like *promised kiss of springtime*. Hopefully, he would also have bars on his shoulder, maybe even be older, a captain, and he'd have a nice family back home ready for a daughter-in-law.

How innocent, how calculatingly innocent they were, Lelia thought. Even as a dreamer, she'd never been that innocent and now Francie wasn't either, but for her own different reason.

In the driveway at Hurricane House, with the Packard's motor still humming, Francie squinted back at Aunt Mo, snoring softly in the back seat. In an anguished whisper, "Oh, Lelia. Have you ever been in love? I mean so much you couldn't stop even though you knew it was dangerous and crazy! If only you knew, you'd understand."

Lelia got out of the car and stood in lonely moonlight until the Packard was gone.

Inside the foyer, she stopped, alert to a sound from the living room. A heavy wave onshore? It was habit to listen as she came into the house. She made herself step into the moon-streaked room. The light caught a moving figure.

"Hazel?"

Yes. Hazel in her yellow wrapper and head scarf, weaving across the room, cursing under her breath, gripping her flashlight. "Goddammit, Lelia, you scared the be-jesus out of me coming in like a wild-haired ghost when I was already scared."

"What's going on? What are you doing? You're shaking."

"Came home early without Chuck and went to bed. Then I heard something."

"And you came out to investigate? That's brave."

"I figured I'd come out and see if that sneaky Cheta had been in the kitchen. Not even the damn cat was around. But something was." Hazel turned the flashlight toward the portrait of Bonnie Elliot on the dark wall. "If it's not that woman upstairs, then it's Bonnie. Look at her, like she's waiting for something. She's watching us, sure as I'm standing here."

I don't want to hear this, Lelia thought. "Let's get to bed, Hazel."

Hazel swung her flashlight around, "Every night I hear something, but nobody believes me."

"Go to sleep. I plan to do the same. Good night," She waited until Hazel had trailed back toward the master bedroom before she looked up at the portrait. Don Elliot had been a master painter. Even from its shadows, the eyes seemed to reflect the moonlight. *Is that how you looked once, Bonnie? What are you now?*

She went to the open French doors and looked at the silvery white beach beyond dark green seaoats. Bonnie's grave was out there. She breathed in deeply and cleared her thoughts, The night's music was still in her body, like a lonely restless throb.

In the upstairs hall, Kali's door was closed. Her own door was open, but then it never shut completely. A strong sea smell greeted her, not from any moving breeze but a stench that waited. She scanned the room, not breathing. Moonlight shaped the dresser, the bed, the window sill. Something vile and slimy waited there.

Seaweed.

HURRICANE HOUSE
July, 1945

27

Hot July sunsets beamed against the second floor corner bedroom for days, fading the smell of seaweed but not its memory.

Lelia knew one thing. Not how it got there but that the slimy gift meant anger and impatience. She had to forget Francie and Gil and dead Susie. She had to discover her own fate.

Certainly she knew Kali played a waiting game with her, drawing her close, then retreating. Now Kali was a melancholy figure each night on the balcony, gazing into the horizon, murmuring, "Something is building. Do you feel it, Loa?"

"A storm? It's not yet August. I thought hurricanes didn't come until later."

"A storm comes when it is needed. Destruction for renewal. This is different —"

"You mean the silent storms in this house?"

"The ones we cause, you mean." A faint smile lit the strong face for a moment. "Yes, Loa, the whirligig of time returns our passions to us, like a boomerang . . ."

On this rainy early morning, Lelia sat in the gray light of the silent living room reading a volume from Kali's shelves. The strange book seemed to hold answers. She read with both guilt and fascination.

"Realities exist beyond the visible . . ."

It was true. The gulf this minute seemed obliterated by

gray rain but was still there, in all its mysterious depths and power.

She read on *". . .the subconscious or subliminal self is mysterious to the average man and thus called paranormal . . . Where emotions have been strong, the past can exist like a persistent memory in the psychic ethers of a place. It exists in another time-continuum, but there are those who have seen beyond these veils. . ."*

Seen? Yes. The yellowed pages told of recorded visionary experiences transcending space and time limitations.

"The process of 'seeing' takes place in the subconscious or subliminal self . . . makes its way into the conscious mind, into the brain which is primarily an organ of action for the thinker in the material world . . ."

Quickly, she skimmed past the warnings about *"ego and desire may alter what is seen and may leave its residue of pain."*

Again an early morning rain lashed in from the gulf darkening the musty living room. In the wing chair near the French doors, Lelia read the book one more time for courage. *"A kind of persistent memory remains in the psychic ethers of a place. The receptive mind of the sensitive person may tune in to and perceive what lingers. . ."*

Sensitive, it said. Not deluded.

Making sure Kali's door was still closed, she climbed the narrow stairs that led to the dimly lit third floor. The brass door knob to the tower room turned in her hand, but the door held. The dull thud of rain covered the sound of her shoulder thrust. With a harsh scrape, it opened to damp, fetid air and a long windowed room.

She stepped inside, closed the door, and stood close to it, scanning the long narrow room that once had been Don Elliot's studio. Something darted across the wood floor, a lizard, disappearing in the gloom.

Windows across the front, crusted with salt spray, lit the space with dead light. Yes, the past was here, suspended in this musty gloom. *Show me,* she whispered. Her pulse pounded in her ears louder than the drone of rain outside.

A shrouded easel sat in the center of the gray windows. At one end, canvases leaned along the shadowed wall. At the other end, a Victorian couch, piled with fabrics. Some had spilled to the floor. She moved toward the stacked canvases but stepped back, shuddering. The shadows were woven with thick cobwebs.

She avoided the shrouded easel and looked closer at the couch. Movement behind it. Her heart lurched but she stared. Figures showed in the gloom. Wild hair and pale face. Her own face. She was looking into a triple, dust-coated mirror leaned at angles against the dark wall.

She breathed again, hugging chilled arms. She must be calm, look around with eyes and senses open to what this place could tell her. This couch, piled with fabric . . . Bonnie must have posed here. The Chinese shawl, once red-gold, as in the portrait downstairs, lay crumpled, green now with aged mildew. A pile of grayish-pink on the floor must be the wine velvet dressing gown in the picture. She reached to touch the once-soft velvet but recoiled. Black roaches scattered from its rigid heap.

A woman's stiletto-heeled shoe lay on the floor. In the shadows, bits of glass, a broken Tiffany lampshade, now dull gray chips across the floor.

She went back to the center of the room, to the covered easel. Forty years ago, the sun would have streamed in here at sunset. The sky, pink and blue at dawn. This view must have been Don Elliot's inspiration for those ethereal seascapes and those joyous running figures. Why did he cover it and run away?

Tell me, show me, somehow . . . Why did you leave? Even in grief, even with Bonnie dead, why run away from two small sons? Were you guilty too, Don Elliot? Or did Kali cause you to run? What happened here?

The air with its wrenching sadness was hard to breathe, but she stood in the middle of the room, open to Knowing. Rain beat a minor key against the sound of her own pulse. She looked again at the couch at one end of the room. Yes, its litter was a frozen pantomime of rage. Someone was here, some presence in the room.

Show yourselves to me; I'm the daughter of your son. I have your blood in my veins. What should I know?

With soft-focused eyes, she imagined Don Elliot there at the easel the way he looked in the old photograph. Saw him there as a darker shadow in shadowy light. Yes, like that, at the canvas, long brush in his hand. She saw him now, in that grayness, saw how he wielded the brush, driven by anguish. Why? The vision faded. Wind moaned around the edges of the house like a woman's high cry.

Shaken, Lelia moved closer to uncover the easel but recoiled. The covering had hardened with time. But there were other canvases against the floor along the wall. With a long wooden paintbrush, she swiped at the heavy sheath of cobwebs. They whispered loose. Yellowed sketches fell back against the floor. All were beginning sketches of a portrait. An angled arm here, a tossed-back head there of a restless model. Bonnie. More sketches fell. Working sketches of the running figures, lines of exuberance. Telling her something, but what? Lelia went back to the draped easel.

The stiff covering cloth came off in a cloud of dust. A scarred canvas looked back, its colors still dark, brilliant of two women. No, the same young woman in a wine velvet gown, the ruby-toned Tiffany lamp in the background. One figure reclined, insolent, impatient. The second seemed to rise out of the first, blond hair in disarray, arms extended. The face looked out from deep gashes once made into the wet paint. By the artist? No. The painting had been slashed by a woman's narrow, sharp fingernails. Had Kali done this in jealousy? Kali, the Hawaiian housekeeper who must have been twenty-five to Bonnie's twenty-three in this house forty years ago?

Show me! Lelia backed away, daring to see. Her skin felt their presence. She felt their rage and despair, taking shape now into two figures, in this gray room, or in her consciousness. With some other sight, she saw them in a moving tableau, Don at his canvas, Bonnie rising from the couch, the red robe slipping from pale shoulders as she seizes the Tiffany lamp and crashes it against the floor. Advancing now, looking at the canvas, face distorted in a silent scream, before raking her nails down its wet surface, turning now to raise the paint-thick nails to his face . . .

The images faded. She was alone again in the airless room with the drone of rain. But she had seen the woman in the painting. She knew how Bonnie Elliot looked before she died.

Why did she have to be killed, Don Elliot? Did Kali make you help her? You were together, weren't you, in what you did.

Lelia closed the door behind her. Back in her own room, cobwebs still stuck to her skirt, the images clung to her senses. But already the sky was clearing. The gulf rolled in, a silver blue. By the time she dressed again and fled downstairs, the beach sands sparkled, motor boats hummed in the bay, cars rumbled over the bridge. What happened earlier in gray morning light seemed like a bad dream or something she had allowed herself to imagine.

She came into the room with the sunset tray, wondering if she dared say to this woman, it was you and Don Elliot, wasn't it? Together you caused Bonnie to drown.

Kali came in from the balcony, gripping the walking cane, the low voice barely audible. "It is building, Loa."

"The storm again?" But should she believe Kali – or Gil, or anyone – when she couldn't trust her own mind?

". . . building to a release that will be as beautiful as it is terrible." The dark eyes searched for something not visible. "No, I think not a release, but a beginning, a strange beginning. It must be about the war. Is there news today?"

"The war goes on in the Pacific, Kali."

"Yes. It begins there."

"I have to go." She ran down the stairs, grateful for fragrant twilight, the road, faces smiling from cars, the rumble of the old bridge. Kali's sadness had seemed real, but she didn't want to feel sympathy for this strange woman pulling her into her energy, with hidden intentions. Tomorrow the strange book would go back on the shelf. It was time to go about learning of the Elliots the rational way. Somehow she'd get into town. Confront Doc Miller. It couldn't hurt him to tell if Bonnie Elliot had been angry for a reason. For a spoiled rich girl to be wildly jealous at twenty-three was easy to believe. To be psychotic at twenty-three meant something else. Her life-long fear. Madness in the blood. Why now did she want to resist that evidence? The will to live must be more stubborn than the belief in death.

ST. PETERSBURG
July afternoon, 1945

28

Lelia slid into the blue Packard, Doc Miller's address in the pocket of her skirt. "I truly appreciate this, Francie. Hazel had the Nash."

"I was so glad you called." Under the new scattering of freckles, Francie's face was flushed and apologetic. "Will you ever forgive me for last night? Saying all those bad things about old Grouper Hole when you wouldn't go to the yacht party with me. Then running out like a spoiled ninny."

"And I was impatient with you. I'm sorry."

Impatience wasn't the word, of course. The images from that rainy morning in the tower room had surged back, co-existing with the realities of Grouper Hole, of Evander Merrill's yacht out there in the early night, laughter and voices on the dock outside. Francie had burst into the barroom, red curls awry, tears glistening, announcing she was about to jump out of her skin. Had to do something. Go somewhere. The yacht party maybe. Gil would let them go on the boat. Lelia must go away with her. No? Then Lelia was a stick-in-the-mud meanie.

Francie had flopped into a booth, clicking fingernails against the offered Coca-Cola, chattering with abandon about this old bar being a terrible place, running off people like poor Dummy, how cruel to call him that when he had a name . . . As quickly, Francie had interrupted that tirade to insist they both go out and join the *Silver Fox* party gathered on the dock ready to board. Gil would let them get on. No, Francie, no.

In the car now, listening to the girl's evasive apologies,

Lelia leaned back, relieved she didn't have to say anything about Gil. It must be over between the two at Gil's demand. Last night from Grouper's Hole porch, she had watched the distraught girl run out, down the dock, only to be stopped by Gil. Surely he was telling her to go home, to leave him alone, because Francie had wheeled away. She hadn't come back into the barroom.

Now behind the big steering wheel, a deflated and contrite Francie drove past orange groves, confessing, "I went back to the Inn last night like a good little girl. Maybe I'll try to stay that way." Her voice quavered, "It's almost August. I'll be leaving soon."

"You'll love again, Francie." It would serve no purpose now to tell this emotional girl that Gil may have been involved in Susie's death, too. "Did you trust him, Francie?"

"Of course! But let's don't talk about it!"

They were out on the county road now, still passing orange groves bright in the midday sun. "I'll miss you, Francie. And again – I appreciate this ride into town."

"Why are you so worried about seeing this old doctor? He should be happy to tell you about knowing your father when he was little."

"I don't think he likes to talk about the past. That's why I couldn't let him know I was coming."

Francie sounded wistful, "I can understand wanting to know what your father was like. I mostly remember mine in a gold frame. He was this really handsome Navy captain. When I was just a little old thing, we lived on the base, and I remember sitting on his lap. I was thirteen when he was killed right after Pearl Harbor. When he died, that's when my mother got so, well, like she is now."

Francie's hands tightened on the wheel. "Mother wants me to marry a new version of Daddy so she can just sit and watch us and be her life for heaven's sake. Well, it's true. She'd absolutely kill me if I did anything to ruin that for her."

"At least you know what your father was like."

"Have you learned anything about yours from that old woman who lives in the house? Or from your uncle?"

"A little. Slowly." They were passing small white frame motels with scrubby grass yards. "This morning, I listened to two old fishermen who grew up on that bay, sixty years ago – you know, Cap'n and Skipper. They knew about the Elliots, my grandparents."

"Imagine," Francie giggled. "What could they tell you?"

"Quite a lot, in fact. Local folks called her Queenie. They thought he was a kept man because he didn't work. I happen to know he was a fine artist."

Francie giggled. "Oh, I sound awful laughing. I don't mean it that way. I just know how you must feel. I'm not just the silly thing I sound like most of the time."

"I know, Francie. You're eighteen and eager and impatient for life, and you must think I'm afraid of it, but there are some things I need to know before – well, before I can –"

"Fall in love?" With a ragged sigh, "I don't think you can plan it, anyway not like my mother would have me do. It just happens." Sounding forlorn, Francie chattered on about her mother and having to go back to school soon. Lelia leaned back in the blowing warm wind, reviewing what she'd learned this morning on the porch with Skipper and Cap'n. She'd brought them breakfast, sat down, asked questions, looked into their weathered faces, and willed them to tell what they know of the Elliots. After some foot shuffling and elbow poking, the two old men told stories with relish.

Yessum, they remembered being kids on this waterfront back when folks were homesteaders and fishermen and city folks came in buggies on Sunday to the beach . . . As waterfront young'uns, sure, they had seen the young Elliots of Hurricane House, before *she* died and *he* ran away and the jungle grew up around that big house on the gulf.

"Tell me." They were alone on the porch, Chuck buried in his war news behind the bar.

The Elliots? Rich and uppity young folks, always seemed to be traveling off, big trunks following on a wagon sometimes. When they were around, their fine automobile would stop along the road where Cap'n's mama sold her eggs and milk.

Don Elliot, a tall young man, dressed in ice cream city suits, would get out to do the buying. Bonnie Elliot waited, high and mighty, in the front seat. Purtiest dressed-up lady Cap'n had ever seen until he went away for a spell to work on the docks at St. Louis. Womenfolks on the mainland called her Queenie and said Don Elliot looked handsome as those young men in *Ladies Home Journal* magazines, but they figured him to be a kept man for not doing any real work, just painted pictures . . . . Later, when Queenie washed in from the gulf, tangled up in one of those long, fancy dresses, women clucked about money and pride leading to downfalls.

"Did anyone see?"

A fisherman spied the body floating into the beach early one morning, then there was Don Elliot running out, the Kali woman after him . . . The skinny little doctor was seen driving lickety-split in his Ford over the bridge right after. They must have buried her the next day . . . Right after Don Elliot was over on the mainland looking frazzled, trying to sell his gold watch and some pictures. Next thing, folks saw his yellow Benz motorcar heading down the county road, the top up, stuff piled high, and that was the last anybody ever saw of Don Elliot.

"Was Dr. Miller the doctor who helped bury her?"

More head scratching and conferring between Cap'n and Skipper yielded recollections. Well, he was a skinny young fellow then, who'd hung up his shingle along a county road. He was the one who went to look at the body, then came back from town next day with the coffin saying that was what the husband wanted, for her to be buried right there. Doc Miller? Yep, that was the fellow. Finally moved to town.

"Did anyone question what happened?" she asked softly.

Oh, there was talk. But back then, folks figured it was a family thing. That long ago, no sheriff came around much. Yep, Queenie's rich old daddy came from Canada to see about the two little kids, but he went away and didn't come back.

"Didn't anyone worry about the baby and a four-year-old left with no parents?"

Sure, womenfolk on the mainland had wondered, but they weren't about to go over to that house or mess with that native girl. The colored washerwoman stopped going. Purely refused to go. Said the place was hainted. People shushed that, but they figured it was true.

When that skinny Doc Miller came and took those little boys away to school, a real fine military school in town, folks figured to leave well enough alone. Sure, the boys were around awhile in summers. Fact is, Cap'n had taught Chuck how to fish this old bay, but Chuck went away to school and got book-smart and sassier than before.

"And the youngest boy, Lee – what was he like? He was my father, you know."

Cap'n and Skipper had bobbed their heads in solemn agreement. Well, Lee was a handsome little fellow like his daddy, but a quiet kid keeping to himself best they could remember. After all he was living in a hainted house with a strange South Seas kind of woman. Ran off from that house and fancy town school when he was still a lanky kid. Joined the Navy.

"And that's all anyone knew of the house? Do you remember two native girls working over there? Kali and her sister who came too, at first. Maylene?"

More head wagging. Well, all they remembered was the one. Once the Elliots were gone, there was this native girl doing her crab traps, bringing them over in her little dingy to the bait dock to sell, and she'd leave as quick. Kali, the one who become the hermit woman.

Rubbing his brown shiny head, Cap'n had come up with one more recollection. Nobody ever went over there visiting far as they knew, but this one strange fellow who showed up years ago. Everybody remembered because he was one of those Hindoo kind of people, came driving an open touring car and looking for Kali. And now, Miss Lelia, Cap'n said, you're living right there with her! Lordy, Lordy.

In St. Petersburg, the Packard rolled along a tree-lined street past two-storied houses. Francie trilled an apology. "I've been doing all the talking, but you let me!"

Lelia studied the numbers on front porches. "Turn at the

next corner." They rolled past a huge banyan sitting in the middle of the narrow brick street. A sign in front of a white frame house read, "Andrew B. Miller, M.D."

Lelia said, "Here!" She squeezed Francie's pink hand on the wheel. "Park in the shade and wait for me."

She hurried up the steps of the front porch. He had to be there. She had willed it. And he wouldn't throw her out. She was beginning to learn the truth of something Kali had said. What was set in motion couldn't be stopped now even if she wanted it to.

The front door opened to a silent waiting room and faint medicinal smell. Stiff-backed chairs lined the walls under faded sepia prints. The place was like she remembered the man, the past persisting in the present. Only the neatly stacked Collier's magazines and *National Geographics* were current.

Light footsteps clicked down the narrow hall. He appeared, gray head bent, jacket to the seersucker suit on one arm, black doctor's bag in the other hand. He stopped short, his thin face studying her from behind steel-rimmed glasses.

"Dr. Miller, I'm Lelia Elliot." She smoothed her blown hair and took his scrutiny.

"So I see." The same dry, precise voice as that day he brought Kali home from the hospital. "Is something wrong out there?" Concern flickered behind the glasses.

"No. I've come to talk with you," she answered.

He stiffened, but she said quickly, "It's not about who owns the house, Dr. Miller." She waited until his eyes focused on her again. No wonder this brittle, old man was wary. What happened forty years ago had dried up in him, and she stood there, making him remember. A flush of compassion kept her patient. He must be seventy or more.

"Spend a few minutes with me, please." She eased into one of the hard chairs without taking her eyes from his face. "You knew the Elliots. I want to hear about them."

"Why? You are young. A beautiful young woman. Why care about the past?"

"You're a doctor. You should know why."

He sank into a chair, jacket still on his arm, the black bag on the floor. He sat upright gazing at the sepia prints like a disapproving patient.

"You were the doctor on the mainland out there, back then – and you delivered both children so – you can tell me about them then, when you were all young."

"Young." His thin lips tasted the word.

She touched his shirt sleeve, felt the thin boned arm inside. "Tell me, please." She met and held his gaze.

The dry voice began, haltingly, as if remembering for himself, not her.

He had been the lonely young bachelor, fresh from medical school in Durham, starting a practice in a rural place. And proud, yes, to be called to that household on the beach, as a doctor and also as friend.

She listened as she had done as a child, listened with her body and mind open to the glimmer of thoughts unsaid. An image came, clusters of bright coral hibiscus, then a hand reaching for the color but pulling back. When he paused, she prompted, "You loved going there. Maybe you loved someone there?"

His glance was stricken. "Why ask an old man such a question?" He stared away at faded wallpaper.

"What was *she* like? Bonnie Elliot." *Talk to me.*

"Perhaps you've read about the writer F. Scott Fitzgerald and his wife Zelda of the Twenties? They were like that, I think, not of the time but the temperament. Your grandfather was a fine artist. He could have been a great one. He would have been recognized."

She felt pleasure at that. "Then why –?"

"They traveled away often, for those days. Which is why they first brought the sisters back from San Francisco. To care for the child and house. Charles was an infant then." He glanced at her briefly. "A mistake. Kali – she was called Kala then – was 21 or so. Maylene, 19. Kala came only to protect her sister and send her home, back to the islands."

"What were they like then?" she asked softly. "When they first came to that house?" She waited, watching his silence.

"To the shy young man I was then, these were vivid creatures. I remember long dark hair, how it moved when they walked along the beach, how they ran –" He stopped, the voice becoming brittle again. "They were raised in totally different ways. An experiment of the father, an aristocrat, an Englishman. The mother was Polynesian."

Phillip Seaton was Kali's father? So the library had been his – even the strange pagan texts? The many notations in fine Spencerian handwriting must be his, too, questioning, discovering.

"How were they different, the sisters?"

"Let Kali explain that if she chooses." But as if the memory propelled him, "Maylene was like a flower that should have never left its own habitat. Kali, like a palm tree, powerful, resilient. The tree protected the flower. She came along to this waterfront only to send Maylene home, as I said."

She felt his discomfort. "Tell me about Bonnie. And the travels."

"Don took her to the south of France. She was happiest there. Once, she stayed and he came home, alone. It was – a good time for him. He painted as he wished to do."

She waited.

"Yes, I sat in his studio on occasion and watched him work. I ate from their table, always centered with bright hibiscus I recall – like a *joy* then. I watched what I couldn't have myself." He stirred, embarrassed before he went on. "I am a realistic man. I can watch another's happiness without rancor. Even then, young as that, I could see that loneliness is less painful than desiring and losing."

"You were Don Elliot's friend. You watched him being happy, you understood. But later, he wasn't happy, was he? No one in that house –"

She watched his thin lips tighten and she sensed his pain. "My father was born to an unhappy woman in a troubled household, wasn't he?" At his nod, she asked gently, "You treated Bonnie after the baby was born? Dr. Miller, tell me."

"Yes, I treated Bonnie. As best I could." Anguish in the dry tones. "Young woman, leave the past alone."

"Was she unhappy enough to kill herself?"

He took off the glasses, rubbed his face with a nervous hand, and replaced the glasses. "Enough of this. I must leave." A sad sound. But he seemed to have no strength to move.

"Maylene is the girl in the seascapes he painted, isn't she, Dr. Miller? He had fallen in love with her, hadn't he?"

"Any man would have."

Then you, too! "What became of her?"

"I told you, young woman. Kali knew she had to be sent away. Back to the islands she should never have left."

"Why didn't Kali go with her?" *Had she plotted to get rid of all of them? Did she want the house that much?*

He looked away. "It was too late for her to go. But I cannot speak for Kali. You must know that she is as strong as she is strange." His slim fingers picked at the seersucker jacket on his arm.

"But Bonnie died. And then he ran away. And I need to know why. Dr. Miller, I know you helped Kali and Don Elliot bury her. I'm not trying to hurt you now. I believe you were an honest guardian with the trust fund for the boys' school."

"Be content with that." He picked up his medical bag.

"Wait! There's so much more I have a right to know. You were the doctor who treated my mother when she was hysterical. You must have been the one who met them at the train when they first came. Why did they come here? I know my father had run away to the Navy at seventeen because he was unhappy here. Why did he go to such trouble to come back – with his bride?"

"I met them at the train and drove them out, yes. The beaches were remote then, '26, wasn't it? I remember a thin, blonde girl from Alabama. Too young. They were both too young."

"Tell me about them."

He shifted in the hard chair. "He called me from his Naval base, Norfolk, I believe, and said he would bring a bride the next day. He was handsome in his Navy seaman's whites. A tall young man with depth and intelligence. The girl, a timid little thing." A wry, brief smile. "Not like you."

"What did he say? What reason did he give?"

Dr. Miller studied his polished shoes. "He was drawn back. Young Lee had loved and hated that house. When he called, he said, 'I want to be happy there just one time, then I'll never go back' . . . and indeed . . ."

"What happened to him, Dr. Miller?" The room swam out of focus as she waited.

"He was upset when your uncle took the girl away. He got some kind of ride and went back out alone. A small boat was found north of the beach much later. It is believed he was drowned. It is difficult for me to tell you this."

A new thought flashed. "If you met the train and took them out that night as the storm started and if the storm stayed two days – then you must have been there still, in that house, *that night.* You would have *heard* her scream!"

"Yes. I had to stay. Out of their way, of course. As in the past, I used the small room beyond the kitchen, meant for the cook. Kali had long lived upstairs as she does now."

"But you must know what happened in the middle of that night to my mother. She woke alone and wandered into the living room looking for this boy she'd married. Found him on the porch or in the yard where she saw something that made her hysterical."

"You seem to know."

"I know it third hand, Dr. Miller. But you were there. I'm asking you."

He sat erect again and impatient. "I do not believe in ghosts, young woman. Memories can haunt us well enough. But to answer your questions, I heard the girl, her screams. By the time I reached her, Lee was standing in the living room, holding her in his arms. She had fainted. No one else was there."

His fingers tapped the satchel in his lap. "We put her in the car and brought her here, in town, that night. Before dawn, I recall. This is my home and my office, has been for forty-five years. She lay whimpering, threatening hysteria again. I had to keep her sedated the next day, too. Lee paced the streets outside like a crazed man. Her brother arrived, a young man of about twenty-five, severe with his indignation and arrogantly assuring me of his importance."

"That was Tarrant, my uncle."

"Extremely angry. I can understand why you know nothing of your father. The man threatened Lee never to come near his sister again. The marriage would be annulled, he promised. I take it she was a daughter of a proud Alabama family. But you know that. I can't tell you any more." He stood up and turned to the door.

Lelia followed. She sought his eyes behind the steel-rimmed glasses. Old eyes full of regret. "Dr. Miller, you must know the one thing I have to ask. It's about Bonnie, not my mother. I already know she was young and angry and jealous before she died, enough to rip up her husband's last painting. I found it in the studio. Was it more than jealousy? Is there something else I should know?"

She followed him out to the porch aware of turmoil underneath the old man's set face. The dry voice surfaced delivering a doctor's impersonal diagnosis, "She was dangerous at that point. To everyone around her. What happened, was inevitable. Again, I suggest, I insist, you leave the past behind."

"But the past reaches into the future, doesn't it? In one's blood, into the cells." Like a *mark*.

"So it does." He saw the parked Packard and stiffened, expecting to see Hazel behind the wheel. She watched him walk quickly down the shaded sidewalk toward his parked car before she left the porch and got in beside Francie, who whispered, "Well? Did you find out about your grandparents?"

"Quite a bit, yes." Her mind was racing, sorting out images.

The Packard pulled away before Lelia offered, "I'll tell you this much, Francie – people have been falling in love with the wrong people for a long time." They exchanged knowing smiles and each turned away, studying the street ahead, steaming now as the afternoon thundershowers began to pelt down.

Francie seemed satisfied. "Now you can make that old

housekeeper tell you more. I bet she stays quiet because you might be rich and not even know it, Lelia Elliot. Maybe that old woman is hiding some buried treasure or something."

"Something, yes." It didn't matter that Doc Miller had helped Kali and Don Elliot cover up what happened out there. The only thing that mattered was Bonnie Elliot. She tried to say it now, tried to believe it: *When my grandmother died at twenty-three, she was not only wildly jealous but also psychotic and dangerous.* But she had to hold that evidence away until she dared look, one more time, into the past.

HURRICANE HOUSE
August morning, 1945

29

The morning rain kept the sky leaden. With the early tray delivered to the dark sanctuary, Lelia sat down once more to read passages from the book that said the past could exist on other planes of reality. It was true, also the book's warnings were true. But she meant to risk it again. Did Kali know what she was doing?

Delivering the sunset tray last night, she'd found Kali standing at the balcony railing, a still remote figure in the purple robe, wind blowing the long, smoke-gray hair. The dark velvet voice still asking, "Do you feel it, Loa? Something building."

Are you trying to distract me, Kali? Did you guess I've been to see Dr. Miller?

Barefoot, Lelia padded down the dimly lit hall past the closed center door. As housekeeper, Kali had once occupied her own corner bedroom. Then the opposite end must have been Maylene's before Kali sent her away. Maylene, the rare flower, the nature child, who should have never been transplanted from her own island, Miller had said. His brittle voice had softened at her name. Could someone like Maylene have caused trouble in this house? Kali was the strong one, he'd said, who'd come here only to send her sister back to the islands. To protect the sister? Or had Kali been jealous of Maylene as well as Bonnie? Had she gotten rid of both of them? A sudden shiver told her some truth was there.

Here was another door she had to open. With effort, the

knob gave. She entered a corner bedroom, identical as her own, but no, silent as a tomb. The dead air, like a stifled sob.

Curtains, once lace, hung heavy and gray over the crusted windows. Next to a rocking chair, the curtain was pulled back by a hand gesture long ago. Now frozen there. Someone had sat by that window watching the beach and gulf below. A woman. Hiding? Or a prisoner here?

Above the oak bureau, a grime-covered mirror gave back a wavy image of herself, a cloud of dark hair, a pale oval face, shadowed, questioning eyes.

The single bed. A carved mahogany headboard. The covering sheet and pillow turned gray and rigid as a marble bier.

The top bureau drawer groaned as she pulled it open. Ancient mildew sifted like heavy ash. Inside, folded garments. Long pale dresses and undergarments. The odor of years stirred and invaded her breath. She closed the drawer quickly and yanked at another. A pale blue knitted thing and napkins lay folded inside. Lelia shivered and closed the drawer quickly. So this had been the nursery as well as Maylene's room.

She knelt on the gritty carpet to pull open the bottom drawer. Black palmetto roaches darted from beneath stacks of heavy paper. She picked one up. Sketches. Line drawings of a running figure, long, flowing lines of beauty, like those on the large canvases of Don Elliot's seascapes.

Standing, she rubbed her hands against her skirt. Images rose, elusive Knowings merging, fading. She felt like an intruder into someone else's sorrow, but she made herself stand there, open, willing to see.

Again the bed pulled her gaze, the grayed pillow with its indentation made by someone's head. Did long strands of dark hair once spread on that pillow? Yes, like that. She could see how it would be, spread there, but she couldn't see the face and the body. Because someone stood by the bed. A tall man, looking down, kneeling down, his movements gentle, now humble, stroking the long, dark strands.

In an eye blink, they were gone, the girl on the bed, the penitent man at her side.

The bureau pulled her again. A small compartment on top

held a narrow drawer that slipped open to her touch. A shallow, wood-scented drawer, its felt padding still green under a dark red, tooled-leather notebook. She pulled it out.

A feathery handwriting filled the yellowed pages. Poetry? The words scattered like leaves, some of them legible. Wistful and joyous words. She could almost hear them whispered as she read, *"Summer, 1905: Love lies in the soft earth of my body . . . like sunrise beginning to glow . . ."*

The entry faded. She turned the delicate pages. Now this one, done in bolder strokes like a cry, *". . . green-eyed, invidious . . . eats away at my soul. He is not mine, not mine, not mine . . . I want only to lie under Pele's fire to purge this hollow body . . ."*

She pushed the book back into its drawer, closed the door softly, ran barefoot down the hall past Kali's closed door. In her own room, she lay across the bed, inhaling deeply of new morning air. The impressions from that other room subsided but waited in her pulse like a whisper.

INDIAN ROCKS
August, 1945

30

By noon on this bright, hot eighth of August, a mixed crowd surged into Grouper Hole, elated and curious. Unlike the V-E Day's hoorays back in June, now incredulity subdued the voices. Was it true what the radio was saying? Yes, there it was in the morning headlines.

Chuck's bar radio sat on the plank, the volume turned high. From the downtown studio above the Pier, the announcer's voice read again another bulletin against the clattering sound of wire service machines:

> *". . . in his solemn announcement, President Truman made it plain that one of the scientific landmarks of the century has been passed and the age of atomic energy has come."*

Atomic? The word was a question left hanging in the smoky air.

Lelia leaned on the bar absorbing the news. At the first opportunity, she had to run back to the beach. Confront Kali. So the strange mood all week, like some melancholy trance, had not been a pose. Is this what Kali felt to be building? What the radio was saying now?

> *". . . a tremendous force for the advancement of civilization as well as its destruction . . ."*

A squid-smelling fisherman slid his quarter toward Chuck. "Heard it late last night. Can you believe a bomb is that powerful?"

"Right there, in black and white." A portly tourist pushed along his front page of the morning *St. Petersburg Times*, black headlines proclaiming:

ATOM BOMB DESTROYS 60 PCT. OF HIROSHIMA

Kali had said, *Something building . . . in the ethers."*

Big Al stalked in. "Never sat at a bar in the middle of a working day." He eased his bulk on a stool, solemn-faced, to read the paper spread out on the polished plank. He stared at the black headlines, then the newsprint face of the young U.S. Army Air Corps colonel with a caption that said pilot of the bombing mission has "Named the Plane For Mother. Parents at Miami Thrilled."

"You fellows know about a bomb like this?" Al asked a brawny sergeant on the next stool. "More powerful than 20,000 tones of TNT. Figure that!"

"Says here that's as powerful as a bomb load of 2,000 B-29's." The sergeant rubbed his stubby hair. "Buddy, I'm surprised as much as you are. Looks like I'm not going to see Japan the hard way, after all."

Tingley burst in, gripping a rolled-up *Times*. "'Fraid this old war's gonna get over without us, Uncle Chuck. Brought you the morning paper. Hiya, Miss Magnolia. Ain't this something? Glad I caught you here."

She spread his offered newspaper on the bar and read more of the story under the Guam dateline:

> *"The first atomic bomb dropped on Hiroshima completely destroyed an area of four and one-tenths square miles in blast that obliterated the city in a cloud of flame and smoke."*

What was the rest of it that Kali said? Something about a release that was a beginning, not an ending. She read on:

"Men of the Superfortress crews who unleashed nature's harnessed fury described the fearful effect of that one bomb . . ."

"You keep it," Tingley said. "I got more out there." Leaning closer and breathing hard, "How about moseying out to the Ford to get some more papers?"

His urgency made her look up. Tingley, never giving up on working out his big story. Was he over that bad whiskey someone gave him? But still getting himself in trouble, badgering the yacht crew, Chuck had said.

"Are you in trouble again, Tingley?"

The grin flickered and sagged. "Not exactly. It takes some explaining. Can't do it quick here. You gotta believe me." He stopped as the kitchen door swung open and Bubba sidled along behind the bar, bottom lip jutting in disapproval.

"Howdy, howdy, Bubba," Tingley beamed. "How's that big whing-ding party coming along? Going to get fancy for old Handsome?"

"You ain't invited, that's how it's coming along." Bubba sucked his bottom lip, blinking defiance.

Tingley wheeled around on the stool. "Miss Magnolia, hate to drag myself away from the hospitality on a day like this, but I'm off to local wars that are still brewing."

She watched him swagger out. In the bright sun, his shoulders sagged. *He is in trouble,* but she wasn't going to let herself care. She tucked the paper under her arm, escaped through the kitchen, and ran toward the beach and Hurricane House.

Bursting into Kali's room, breathless with the run, Lelia dropped the newspaper on the pedestal table. "Is this what you felt? The something that was *building*?"

Kale sat down and studied the headlines.

"How did you know, Kali? What did you know?" This was more proof of Kali's power, proof she didn't want. But she had to understand it. "Two weeks ago when you were saying those things, there was a test firing in some remote place in

New Mexico."

Kali brought out a magnifying glass and moved it slowly down the fine print. The black headlines expanded and distorted in the crystal ball.

"You said 'horrible and beautiful,' remember? Read what it looks like. A 'blinding flash more brilliant than the sun.'"

"So it happened."

"How could you *know*? This was a secret thing."

Kali looked away. "The power of creation has been made visible." For a long moment, she sat in silence then looked up, the voice barely audible. "Do you know the Bible story of Lot's wife looking back? Looking back into the face of God, we presume. Perhaps it was her arrogance in ripping the veils from the secrets. She plundered and was consumed."

"They're saying this will end the war. A horrible bomb to end a horrible war."

"Perhaps. Our actions seed the universe with our passions. The result can nurture or return to destroy us."

"But *how* did you know? Shut away here, all these years. No telephone, no radio, papers. Alone. How?" Her heart pounded with the need to know. "How does it happen – a message in the mind?" *Like the Voice that came to me as a child, and later.* "How?"

"One must be open to hear."

Or open to madness? "Tell me how it can happen."

Kali's fingers stroked the chair arms, eyes half-closed. "Loa will understand. You, Lelia Elliot now, are angry and in doubt. Hear if you will. The ethers in this universe can carry vibrations from one mind or a group of minds to another. It comes in as an awareness. The conscious mind can only attempt to translate the message. The translation may be only approximate."

"This was a *bomb* yet to explode. Not a message from another person. And you felt it building, you said."

"The minds of those who created it, those who made the determination to use it, those who prepared to deliver it. These were powerful thoughts seeding into the ethers. Perhaps this is what I felt."

Lelia looked out at the bright gulf. She was remembering a lonely bedroom in Bethel, Alabama. Those whispers that child heard, so they weren't fearful imagination. But who was its source?

Kali was saying, "The gulf movement you watch now, it never ceases, does it? There is a flowing stream of energy in the universe which also enterplanes our bodies, a construct of waves, of vibrations."

"Vibrations – heard as whispers, even words?"

"The inner construct is meaning. It must be that meaning enters the body's nervous system into the consciousness. The mind gives words to the awareness. Ah, yes, Loa, the message can be distorted by the receiving mind as it is filtered through the human senses, subject to desires of the personal ego."

"Then why don't others hear such messages?" Normal, intelligent people, not only strange ones like you, Kali, like me.

"They do. It is known as intuition. Ideas. Intellect. Realizations. Minds that cannot hear, refuse to hear, are those too filled with their own clutter to receive new thoughts. They reject what has not been deemed true by one's prevailing culture."

"I would think a mind so open to the ethers would be in danger."

"If the body's energies are not balanced, yes. One must accept the reality of the transient visible world as well as the power of the unseen. The unbalanced body, controlled by desire, is vulnerable to obsession and possession."

Possession. The word chilled her skin and tightened her breath. Possession by my dead grandmother, who pulled me to this place? Who may want me here now to do vengeance on you, Kali? But you, Kali, I still don't know what waiting game you play on me.

Quietly, she said, "I believe what you say is possible, about one mind reaching another. And it frightens me to know that."

"Of course. The unknown is always disturbing, therefore demands denial."

She watched Kali's face. "Hazel believes Bonnie Elliot is

here, watching all of us. Is that possible? Not just her imagination?" She didn't add, I want to think so, but finding seaweed in my room was not my imagination. She had to wait for Kali's answer.

"Imagination can be a perception of what is real. Or it can be distorted desire or fear. Wait, Loa. I must tell you – Hazel's greed feeds her imagination. She will draw to herself what she fears. You must stop this danger."

Or stop Hazel? Is that why you're warning me?

Lelia took the newspaper and hurried downstairs. Hazel, wrapped in her silk robe, opened her bedroom door. "Yeah? What are you doing here in the middle of the day?" She looked down at the black headlines.

"I know." Hazel took the folded paper and fanned her moist neck. "I've been listening."

"Do you know what it means?" The power of creation made visible, Kali had murmured.

"You're mighty right I know what it means." Hazel's pale lips stretched into a satisfied smile. "It means the war's going to be over, and this scrubby old coast is going to boom. And I'm going to be ready. Hazel Mae Elliot's going to be somebody."

GROUPER HOLE
August morning, 1945

31

"This damn party is coming up," Chuck said. "Don't get sick on us, Lelia."

"Why? Do I look – How?" An old memory flashed. Her six-year-old self, looking into mirrors wondering when the *mark* would show.

"Those amber eyes look haunted," Chuck said. "What are you doing out here?"

He'd found her on the Grouper Hole dock, holding her hair up to the breeze, face to the hot August day as if the day could blank out what still played in her mind, experienced in those closed-off rooms. Chuck gave her his worried frown. But he didn't want to hear what she could tell him – your mother was psychotic before she died, Chuck. Her presence is real in that house you hated. Even Kali hadn't denied that.

She flashed a quick smile. "I was studying sea gulls. Made for this place. When I was a little girl, I knew how it must be for a bird, caught in the wrong place and having to grow wings before it could fly away again – to where it was supposed to be."

"Well?"

When she shook her head, Chuck offered, "If Kali's getting to you, don't worry – her days are numbered. Sloan has talked to Haz about Merrill's interest in buying the beach property and house. Hazel's all fired up to get legal possession before they change their mind. She's talking about going to Brockway or somebody in Clearwater even if you haven't yet come up with any proof the sheriff would need."

"No! Hazel mustn't do that. Not yet."

"You protecting her for some reason?"

"No." But was she? "It's not time, not the right time."

True, whatever it meant. What if she told Chuck about Kali's premonition about the bomb? No, both Chuck and Hazel would call it a coincidence, a ploy, to keep her in control.

They crossed the hard sand lot, almost empty this hot early afternoon.

"Good thing you don't let Old Crit bother you either. Or Bubba. You'll be seeing a lot of both for the next week with that party coming up. Crit will be a General Patton. Conch will go into his shell. Bubba will run at a trot trying to please. And you?"

She shrugged. "No prob-lem, as Conch says. Awhile back, I frightened Bubba off somehow. He looks at me and runs the other way."

"Good girl." Chuck stopped at the front screen door. Questions still worked behind his tanned solid face. "Then is it Gil on your mind? I haven't said anything, but when he came in the other day, I couldn't help but notice sparks between you two. Or maybe it's daggers? I keep my mouth shut."

"And I haven't asked you about Susie."

Chuck groaned. "What could I have said?"

"Nobody mourned her. Not even you, Chuck."

"I tried to help her. I finally found her at Conch's. She was crazy scared, wouldn't listen to sense. So I talked her into hiding out at the trailer. Lelia, how could I let anyone know? Hazel would have shot me between the eyes and gone back to the piano to play 'glad when you're dead, you rascal you.'"

He looked away, confessing, "Maybe I loved that little alley cat. I thought I was helping, giving her a place to hide. And what did she do? Stayed there drinking like a wild cat before she ran out."

"Dragged out. She was murdered, Chuck. Don't you realize that?"

"You've been listening to Tingley." But he looked miserable. "Susie was tired of running. That charge against her — she figured she was headed for jail. The poor kid had a bitch of a life with that family of hers."

"Her father?"

"Stepfather. A hayseed bastard they call Cracker. Never came in Grouper Hole, but I know about him. Say, Lelia, I agree with Tingley on this one. Stay out of this. Leave it to Brockway."

As they went in, Chuck grinned. "Right now, we've got General Patton waiting for us."

"Mister Elliot and Miss Beauty. About time you showed up." In the sunny kitchen, Martha Critten's hair was the color of rust, the pudgy face flushed. "This is a meeting about the goddamned party. Go ahead, Conch, you don't have to stop what you're doing. But the rest of you stay put and listen."

Conch continued to scrub an iron skillet. Bubba, stayed slumped at the work table as his mother paced, arms folded over the flowered bosom, lining up chores.

A smile played at the corner of Chuck's mouth. "How do we know when to stage all of this? Sloan keeps changing the date."

"Sloan!" Martha spit out the name. "That leech doesn't run the show here. I give the orders."

"Fire away, General," Chuck said.

"Save the jokes for the customers. Date's Saturday night, whether it's V-J Day or not. We've got five days to rig this up. They want a big shindig and that's what they'll get. We're going to fill up the whole damn parking lot with tables. I've got it figured out."

She hates Sloan, Lelia thought, watching Martha enjoy herself under all the impatience. Could it be this tough, frumpy little woman was yet another fan of the elegant Evander Merrill? He never asked for Grouper Hole's owner when he came in for adulation and Conch's cooking.

"Chuck, you're going to set up the soda pop and booze on the front screened porch. Bubba here had better have all the ice we need in the barrels. Conch's going to cook his fish outside, do the bedsprings thing, and bring in his gal to help out. The yacht will be docked and Miss Beauty here – don't gimme the dreamy look – you listening? You're going to show the yokels this dump has class. That leech Sloan –"

"Wanted me on that yacht? Why?"

Bubba half rose from the chair. "Told you, Mama."

"Son here says you can tell what people are thinking – that right?" The big eyes narrowed. Conch's movements at the sink were the only sound until Martha continued. "But I got a fool for a son. Like I just said – I'm running this show. And you, Miss Cool Number with the hot eyes, you're going to circulate, give the guests some nice chitter-chat, and keep all the old bags from bothering the guest of honor. Get that?"

"Is that what he wants – to be left alone?"

"He'll be at the head table. Everybody can look all they wanna." Martha Critten smiled. "Bubba and I will be up there, too. I'm gonna enjoy this party."

In the barroom before the afternoon crowd filtered in, Chuck shrugged as he answered Lelia's question. "Why? Crit loves to make a buck. We need a celebration anyway."

The phone hidden behind the bottles rang. Chuck scowled into the black instrument. "Yes, she's here but no." He looked at Lelia. "Tingley. Insists he's sick, not drunk, and wants to talk to you."

She took the phone and listened to Tingley's rasping incoherence. Sick or drunk, the desperation was real. What he was saying was crazy.

"Yes, yes, I hear you, J. T. Keep talking." But he had hung up.

Chuck frowned. "Someone still feeding him bad liquor? That guy is a looser."

"He sounds sick." Or out of his head. But she had to find out. If she wanted distractions from the thing happening to her at the house, this was more than she'd asked for.

"All drunks have an excuse. That clown doesn't deserve your concern. Forget him."

She couldn't. But how could she get out of here and go to Johns Pass without letting anyone know? She thought of Kali's words, *focused desire*. Didn't she do that anyway when she dared send a thought into someone's eyes? In the kitchen, Martha Critten came out of the cubby hole office, fussing.

"Get moving, Bubba. Those flyers are ready down at Madeira Beach."

"Got no gas, Mama, no more ration stamps."

"Then I'll go pick up the flyers. I'll get Chuck's car," Lelia said. Madeira Beach was at Johns Pass.

"Yeah? Hear that, Bubba? This girl is useful as well as ornamental. Miss Beauty, you go down to Beach Printing and tell them to charge it. By the way, are you still living with that witch in the murder house?"

Conch spoke up from the stove. "Got your hot grits ready, Miz Critten. Busy woman like you needs hot grits."

Lelia thanked Conch with a fleeting smile. Once out, she ran toward the bridge in time to see the Nash roll past, Hazel at the wheel, waving. "Going to town, Honeychile. See you tonight."

The Nash disappeared down the road. She ran the rest of the way across the bridge. Francie, be there. Yes, the big blue car sat in the pine shade. And in front of the Inn, Francie, in a candy-striped playsuit, stood in the edge of the shade talking to Dummy over his tray of shells. At her approach, he wheeled away and tracked on down the bright beach.

"Lelia!" Francie spun around, surprised, then turned back to watch the retreating figure. "I keep buying his old shells. He has to have money to eat. Do you think I'm a dope to care?"

"I think you are a naturally generous person with everyone, Francie, and I'm hoping that includes me right now. Again! I have to get to Johns Pass. Hazel has the car. Can you drive me?"

"Sure." The girl sighed. "I'm about to jump out of my skin anyway. Why are we going?"

"Tell you on the way." But she would not tell Francie what Tingley had rasped on the phone. Something about a murder that hadn't happened yet. Another girl was due to be fed to the fish in the bay. Unless somebody figured out who planned to do it.

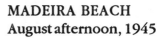

MADEIRA BEACH
August afternoon, 1945

32

A metallic blue gulf rolled under a cloud-streaked sky as Francie drove and Lelia explained, "I have to pick up flyers for the party. But first, I need to see somebody."

"Who?" Francie brightened.

"J. T. Tingley – yes, the noisy one with the grin. He has a message I need to hear."

Francie made a face. "You talk to the funniest people. But I don't care. Oh, Lelia." She sighed again.

"You can wait in the diner at Madeira Beach. Tingley is somewhere across the street. Stay and have a hamburger. I won't be long."

Beyond the Bath Club, the beach spread open again, then Madeira Beach with its roadside cottages, stores, and signs about deep sea fishing. Before reaching the bridge, lined with fishermen, they parked by the bright metal Peter Pan diner and went into the smell of frying onions and the soaring, subsiding strains of "Stardust" from the juke box. Francie settled on one of the low stools, sighing at the music.

Behind the long, narrow counter, a big blonde woman answered Lelia's question. "That gabby newspaperman? Sure. He's always promising to make my hamburgers famous. He stays in one of those cabins across the road. About the fifth one down, I guess."

Across the narrow boulevard, a small road, more like a dirt lane, led up past frame cabins shaded by scrubby trees. *Tingley, what am I doing here and can I believe you?*

The cabins were all alike. A tiger cat darted across the path and disappeared under a porch. Watching with sleepy-eyed curiosity, a leathery old man sat on a stoop, poking his yellow teeth with a long straw. She stopped and asked about Tingley.

"Two down." He went back to chewing the straw.

The door was open. From the small porch, she could see into the gloom of a room, musty as an attic though the back door was open to sun not twelve feet away. She could make out a bed and a bathroom door beyond. In the shadows, an old stuffed chair was occupied. Short legs in checkered pants stuck out, like a dead man's.

"Tingley?" She stepped inside. The place smelled of bourbon and defeat.

A soft snore and he jerked upright. He sank down again, covering a swollen face with his hands.

"You're hurt! Tingley, look at me. It's Lelia."

The hands dropped. A weak grin moved the stubble of beard. "Magnolia?"

She stepped closer. "Are you drinking, J. T.?" He looked terrible. Eyes puffed. Forehead skinned raw. Her disgust gave way to compassion.

The raspy voice surfaced. "Thought some wild-haired angel was standing in the doorway. Guess I don't look like my handsome self, huh?"

"You look like you lost the fight." She glanced around. No evidence of any food or kitchen. The small table, piled with newspapers and notebooks must be his desk. She turned back. "All right, tell me what happened."

"Gimme a chance." He pushed up with his elbows but sank back with a groan. "My bones hurt, but I'm not drunk."

She pulled the straight chair from the desk and sat down in front of him.

"Went ass-first off that dock. Worse part was holding on a piling, damn barnacles could rip the hide off an elephant. But those suckers came in handy. Current's strong in the pass. Coulda been in the gulf in no time." Squinting to focus her face, "Glad you had the gumption to come, Magnolia, even if you shouldn't."

"I have to pick up flyers for the party. So talk to me. What happened?"

"Two nights ago, I think it was two. At Johns Pass, Shanty Hogan's bar. This bozo named Cracker was roaring about no-good outsiders messing with the local girls. An act. I figure he's the big palooka's who left me the bad booze. When he left, I followed."

Cracker. She remembered the overalled bulk of him with Cage in Gil's cabin, looking for Susie.

"Surely you didn't expect to fight him. The man is heavy and mean."

"He oughta have some of his rot-gut poured down his gullet. Anyway, I followed to find out what he's up to, why he wanted to poison me, or who put him up to it. I keep telling you I'm a damn good sleuth. My nose twitches when I'm supposed to pay attention."

"So tell me."

"Followed Cracker to the docks along the pass, back from Johns Pass bridge. Dark as a witch's heart out there, which was a good thing since old Cracker was meeting somebody, and I wanted to hear what he was up to. Met another fellow, wiry kind, twangy voice, kinda like that Jellybo – ever heard that grinning kid deckhand on Evander Merrill's yacht? Only this fellow was no kid."

Cage, Lelia thought. "So what did you hear?"

"Heard a couple of names." Tingley blinked his swollen eyes. "Gil's, for one."

The small room was hot, but her body chilled. "What did you hear them say?"

Tingley groaned. "I heard some of it. Then some joker in a boat flashed a light around and they saw me. Next thing I knew, I was decked, hit by a coil of rope maybe, and there was Cracker yanking me up ready for the kill. I didn't get the full blow in the gut because I back-ended off into that stinky bay. Under the circumstances, the best place to go."

"They could have knocked you out. You could have drowned." She thought of the image she'd seen on the train, Tingley's eyes staring up out of water.

"That's what they figured. I had to hang on to those barnacles under that slimy dock for Lord knows how long until they finished muttering and left. Then I waited before crawling out." He turned his puffy hands over.

Quickly, Lelia covered his gashed and swollen palms with her own, the heat and ache searing into her hands before she drew back, rubbing them on her gingham skirt, dismissing the pain. "Just what did you really hear from those men?"

Tingley was beaming at his palms. "Feels better already." The smile sobered. "They're looking for a pigeon. That means a girl. A decoy. I figure she's going to be fed to the fishes to show up like Susie and Nancy Alderman."

"*Why?*"

"So they can prove – make it look like – Gil did it. Did all three."

He tapped his chest with a wrist. "Aw, Magnolia, don't look daggers at me with those almond eyes. It's bad on my ticker. What I wanted you to know is somebody is hatching a plan to prove Gil's the man, and I think you oughta know for good reasons. One is, I figure you've been sort of protecting him. That could mean trouble."

She ignored that. "You mean these two men are *going to kill someone – to frame Gil?"*

"Frame or catch, take your pick."

The raspy voice went on. "Personally, I like the fellow even if he acts like a clam. Who knows, maybe his girlfriend Nancy ended up dead by accident. Something he couldn't explain. Maybe he had to hush up Susie."

"Do you believe that, Tingley?"

He touched his raw forehead gingerly. "Let's say you can't afford to ignore obvious possibilities like maybe Gil's head was screwed up at the time. But to get to the truth, you don't stop at the obvious. You keep on asking questions."

"But to *kill* to trap Gil? Who?"

"Somebody with a reason, good or otherwise. An angry papa might have a reason. Cracker has made a lot of noise being Susie's poor old daddy."

"Stepfather," Lelia said. "He was the reason Susie couldn't

go home when she got in trouble. Chuck told me that."

Tingley nodded. "Silver Bucks Alderman is a man who gets things done and believes he can pay for what he wants. By now he has to know Gil is the Navy boyfriend his Nancy came to see. He is angry that Brockway seems to be taking his own sweet time doing anything about it." He watched her face. "That shock you – that Alderman would set up Gil?"

She remembered the dark green grief around Alderman. "He's angry and he's cold, but I don't believe he'd let another girl be killed to trap Gil. You don't either, do you?"

"Just figuring the angles, the connections. If that bozo Cracker isn't plotting for the devil of it, or paid by Alderman, then who?"

"The person who really –"

"Threw Nancy in the bay and Susie in the gulf?"

The stuffy room hummed with silence.

"We've got to admit," Tingley said, "Gil knew both those girls – and who else did? What about Martha Critten, that old bat? Or sonny Bubba?"

"What about them?"

"Susie worked for Critten not just as barmaid. You know about her maid service? To save your pearly years, Magnolia, I could put it this way. Listen to that touchy song Hazel sings. 'Love For Sale.'"

Lelia was silent a moment. "I'm not surprised. I've made a point of blocking that woman out of my consciousness. But Crit could have fired Susie any time she wanted. And Nancy Alderman had no connection with either Critten."

Bubba? The idea hovered and faded. "Nancy was never around Grouper Hole. Chuck would know and he vouches for that."

"Okay, okay." Tingley waved his swollen hands.

"What did you hear those men say?"

"About how timing's everything. They were talking about something happening a week from now. They said something about *front and center*. What do you suppose that means, front and center? What's happening around here at about then?"

"Only V-J Day celebrations everywhere. A big one at Grouper Hole."

"Evander Merrill's party, huh. Tell me more." Tingley managed a weak grin.

"It's going to be outdoors, with half the county invited." Lelia gave him a level look. "So? Merrill is an egotistical man, an actor who needs an audience, but vanity's not a crime, J. T. Don't try to imagine him a killer because you hate Merrill. I've heard how Sloan ran you off the dock down here."

"I've been insulted before. Goes with the job. I don't think they liked the publicity I got them."

He pointed to the stack of papers on the littered desk. "Look at that top paper. After Susie washed up, I had the nerve to go downtown to the *Times*. Wanted to sit down at a good, old Royal keyboard and write what I knew and let them take a look. City deskman thought I was a jerk. That figures. Didn't have any damn proof. But they picked up on the story. They ran their own. It's on top of that pile. Take a look."

The July 6, 1945, paper was folded to a gray and white photo of a gaunt-faced woman under the small heading, "Mother Grieves." And on the same page, a picture of the *Sil-ver Fox* yacht with Evander Merrill in his white suit, smiling from the deck.

"In her modest cottage in south St. Petersburg," Lelia read, "Nora Baskins grieves over the drowning death last week of her daughter Susie Holms, age 23. Mrs. Baskins, said she believed her daughter died because 'the girl got mixed up in those parties for soldiers out there' on the beach."

There was a side story, tone pleasant, about hospitality of local citizens for servicemen in the area, including private parties at beach homes. Mentioned too, the yacht parties given by famous movie star Evander Merrill for young officers and dates. The photo of Merrill had been taken when the boat first arrived in the area eight months earlier, the caption read.

She looked up. "You're really pleased about getting the yacht on the same page with the grieving mother."

The swollen, whiskered face nodded.

"Tingley! Is that what all your 'sleuthing' is about? Trying to embarrass those rude people? All summer that self-important little man has ignored you, had his bodyguard throw you off the yacht. Crit and Bubba insult you. But I believed you really wanted to find out who killed two women." When her indignant logic made Tingley slump deeper in the chair, she said more softly, "Do you believe the yacht is involved in any plot?"

"You said it, Magnolia, I didn't. I didn't say I had it figured out yet."

"Whatever you know or think you've heard, you must get to Brockway and tell him. You can't do this alone. Someone wants you dead, too, Tingley."

In the hot silence, she said, "What about all the soldiers who pass through here? Just one or two who hide anger?" She looked at his bruised face, result of Cracker's anger but then Cracker was an unfeeling, violent man.

"What do you know about Bubba, Magnolia?"

She shrugged. Bubba was a lecherous, nervous man, but his fear seemed to control him. "Do you know anything about the deaf-mute who lives on the beach? He's not angry, but shut out."

"Dummy is a story aw'right. I'm working on it." He waved a limp arm toward the papers piled on the table.

Lelia jumped up. "I'm going to have the diner send you some food. You're to eat and sleep but call Brockway and tell him what you've heard. Stay away from Cracker. I'm going to warn Gil, just in case –"

"Don't!" The sharp tone faded. "Aw, Magnolia, those eyes of yours make me spill everything I know. On that dock, Gil's name wasn't the only one that picked up these ears. They mentioned his girlfriend. They figure it's you. Mentioned your name. Said his girlfriend would be the perfect pigeon." At her silence, he said, "Believe me, Magnolia. Stay away from him and stay in the light. Keep your eyes open. Do that and I promise to 'fess up to Brockway."

Francie loomed in the open doorway in her candy stripes and big hat, blinking into the gloom. "Lelia? Hi, everybody. Lelia, I had trouble finding you."

"I'm coming, Francie. You were supposed to wait."

"I got tired." The redhead peered around the shadowy cabin. "These places are awfully, ah, cozy, aren't they?"

Tingley struggled to his feet. "You girls go along now." He made shooing motions with his hands. "You get your party flyers and go home and stay in the sunshine. You hear?"

Outside, Francie whispered, "What's that all about?"

Lelia shook her head. "I've got to figure it out." Her skin prickled even in the hot sun.

On the drive back up the beach, Lelia didn't have to explain anything to Francie. No chance. At the small printing shop where she collected the stack of flyers, a round little woman had descended on Francie with grandmotherly delight. "Love! I'm Ethel Biddle of Altoona, Pennsylvania. You know, staying at the Inn. Francine, you're an answer to prayer. Can Harry and I ride back with you two young ladies? Don't you know we ran out of gas just like I warned him?"

White-haired Harry, in palm-printed shirt and baggy shorts, came out of the back room, beaming, a stack of new notepaper for the bound folder in this arms. Mrs. Biddle explained why, with perky cheer, as the Packard headed up the boulevard.

"We've stayed at the Inn two months now while looking around for a place in St. Pete. Harry is writing his book, *So You're Coming To Florida To Live.* Tell these nice girls how it starts off, dear."

Harry demurred an instant, opened his big notebook, cleared his throat, and raising his voice over the salty breeze blowing in from the open windows, read to them in senator-ian tones:

"To those who have succumbed to the lure of Florida's climate, but who think it's only a playground for pleasure-seekers, here is a report from a newcomer here to stay. Leave snow and taxes and traffic behind. Nature has made Florida the healthiest, happiest place in all the world in which to live the good, simple, healthy life. Pure water, clear skies, peaceful days . . ."

Lelia turned around to look into Harry Biddle's pleased face. "You must come over to Grouper Hole some evening and talk to Hazel Elliot, the one who plays the piano. She loves to hear that people will be coming to Florida."

He beamed. "It's true! They'll be coming. A man can live longer here. I'm quoting a St. Petersburg banker who advises one should have a minimum income of $200 a month, but the sunshine's free. You don't need many clothes and maybe a little oil heater in winter. Mother and I are looking for a place in town. We can handle $10,000."

The couple's duet of enthusiasm continued until they reached the Inn. With her package of flyers, Lelia jumped out, blurting a question she had to ask, "Francie, where can I find Gil?"

She wasn't surprised when the blue eyes widened with usual innocence. "Goodness gracious, I wouldn't –"

"Forget I asked. And thanks for the ride." She left Francie and the Biddles and hurried toward the bridge. She looked in vain for Gil around the bayside docks.

Martha Critten was waiting. "Took your time. Looks like you rode a pelican back. Some hair you've got there." She sat down heavily, cussing under her breath about the party, but studying the top flyer with a satisfied smile.

"Look here, Conch, old boy, you're going to be famous. Listen."

Lelia watched the two, Conch coming over to look as Crit read aloud:

To celebrate Victory Over Japan
And thank the wonderful people of this waterfront,
Evander Merrill, star of stage and screen,
Invites you to a party, August 15,
Dockside, Grouper Hole Restaurant and Bar,
Famous for fried fish, drinks and music.
Mainland at Indian Rocks.

Conch stared down at the flyer. "Doan say who cooks."

"Now, Conch!" Crit's laugh shook the heavy bosom. "My

name ain't here either. We're just doing the work. Fancy-pants Merrill is giving this party. Well, what's the matter with you, Miss Beauty? You're too goddamned serious, you know that? Let up and wiggle those –" Crit clamped her lips shut and glared up at Conch until the big cook strode back to his stove in hard silence.

At the sink, Lelia drew a glass of water, drank slowly before turning to study Crit's frizzy head bent to the flyers. What was there to know here? An insensitive, brash, crusty little woman, but a survivor. Hates men, must have reasons; no patience with her own son, but protects him. What could this have to do with the murder of Nancy Alderman or a plot to trap Gil?

Watching Crit's face, she murmured, "Chuck says that newspaperman Tingley has run into trouble – hasn't come in lately."

"Yeah? Good riddance." Martha Critten stood up with her flyers. At the back door, she stopped. "Conch, we'll want that gal of yours to cook up enough grits to feed an army. Even fancy guests can be pigs when it comes to free food." And she was gone.

Tingley, you don't rate more than a shrug from Crit. What can I tell you?

Chuck stuck his head in. "Lelia? Glad you're back. Porch full of lemonade customers. Are you okay? You're sure?"

"Coming." Not sure of anything at this moment, Chuck, logically or intuitively. Tonight she'd walk the beach. Drop all questions. Listen to the surf. Then, calm again, she'd dare open to that part of her mind that whispered answers.

HURRICANE HOUSE

33

Seaweed. Again a slimy gift from the gulf waited on the sill like acrid anger. Again Lelia flushed it away, trying not to breathe its message or think how it got there. In pale morning light, the brackish smell still hung in the room, in her throat and senses. She dressed quickly and got out.

In the kitchen, a breeze came in from the jungle growth and rolling gulf. She pulled in deep breaths of air to dispel the other. Maybe something hot to drink, one of the herb teas Cheta brought in. She selected a jar and dumped leaves in a china pot, grabbed the whistling kettle, and poured. The boiling water rose and overflowed as she watched with numb distraction. With deliberation, she wiped up the counter top.

At the back screen door, she drank, both hands on the cup, watching an aqua, silk gulf ripple in beyond the seagrapes. Even as she watched, the water turned slate colored. A passing cloud changed what seemed real and unchangeable. Which gulf was real? What you see can fool the mind, the senses. What to believe?

She had to think of Tingley, not the live shadows in this house. His feverish story. Behind the bruised face of the jokester, she'd seen desperate need. To take his 'big story' to the newspaper in town? Whatever, struggling to make a pattern of pieces. She could understand that.

Her hands shook on the cup. Think clearly now. Today, go out and find Gil. Warn him what Tingley said may be true. A plot. Tell him to stay away from Francie, even in the dark.

Especially in the dark. Francie, hurry up and go back to town. In town you'll be safe. Stay there and all of this will pass somehow and you'll never know. You'll return home with no more tragedy than the end of a passionate first love.

She put down the empty tea cup with a shudder. Cheta's herbs could taste like bark or hay or flowers, but this one was bitter. At a sound, she wheeled around. Hazel came in, feathered mules flopping under the orange wrapper, head scarf framing a pinched white face.

"You jumpy too, Kiddo? Then you oughta believe it when I say I had one hellava night. It's not just that damn cat and this sore throat. Bonnie doesn't like me being in her room. You don't believe me?"

"Have some tea, Hazel. It's hot."

"Nah. Some of those leaves Cheta brings in here smell like the weed the band used to smoke. Give me bourbon anytime – except this being the crack of dawn."

The husky petulant voice went on, plucking at her own raw nerves. It helped to concentrate on slicing the dark bread, setting the tray. If Hazel knew about the seaweed, would she go berserk? Or gloat she was right, that Bonnie was in this house?

". . . so damn lousy, Chuck made me to go find a doctor in town yesterday." Digging into the pocket of the wrapper, Hazel came up with a small envelope and extracted a tablet. "He gave me this damn stuff."

Lelia poured more hot water over the tea leaves in the pot. She needed something strong and hot on her own throat. Hazel did sound hoarse. "What did the doctor say?"

"Flu. Look at this. Sulfa. Makes me feel lower than a snake's belly. No wonder they don't give it to military guys on watch." With glum distaste, she looked at the pill in her palm. "It's no damn virus. It's this house making me sick. And you keep pretending you don't know something's happening here. You seem pretty jumpy right now. Am I right or am I right?"

Lelia poured boiling water into a new pot of tea for the tray. "Busy. Have things to do." She left Hazel leaning on the counter.

Lelia returned downstairs, intending to get out of the house and walk in morning sunlight. In the foyer she stopped. The living room's stillness was a magnet, pulling her into its musty sadness. From the shadowed wall, the portrait eyes of Bonnie Elliot looked back into her own.

Are you here, Bonnie? What am I supposed to know?

The sound of surf came into the room, muted by the closed French doors but rising and falling like the breath of this room, cluttered with the silent past. She threw open the glass doors to breathe, to dispel the images that wanted to come. Twenty-three years ago, Mary Emily Calhoun Elliot had stood at these French doors, watching a billowing figure reach out to Lee Elliot and say, "Son . . ." With sudden longing, she spoke out loud, "I'd like to see you." Her flesh chilled. She saw for that instant a thin young woman in a ribboned gown, face frozen now in a silent scream. I've seen her picture, I've seen that yellowed gown, she tried to reason.

A fog covered the porch, a grayness from some other time. Rockers on the porch, behind white banisters. A small boy stood there in the fog . . . now a tall young woman emerged from the house, dark hair and long skirts blowing in a silent wind. Kali? A young Kali, head lifted, calling mournfully a name, not heard but echoing in her mind, calling the child, Lee Elliot.

The fog faded. Again the porch was the bare open platform. The planks bleached by time. Raindrops began to splatter the boards. She reached an arm out the French doors to make sure the drops were real. This was now, an August morning, 1945. She closed the glass doors and dropped into a wing chair, fighting vertigo. I'm open, I'm seeing and not afraid to see. A thrill cut through the disorientation as swiftly as heat lightning in churning clouds. Rain darkened the room, but she wasn't alone.

Dulled surfaces gave way to dark glow. Mustiness to faint perfume. On the stiff Victorian couch, hat boxes now and spilled garments. Shadows pulsated. Took shape. Became movement.

A figure swept past, diaphanous, a young woman, dressed

from another time in long taffeta that must be rustling . . . Bonnie, mistress of this house, pirouetting about in a homecoming . . . Someone followed, the spectral figure of a tall young man stood watching, the same man who had knelt at Maylene's bed upstairs? . . . Now a small boy's face waited in darker shadows, ignored by the shadow woman who danced, arms up, movements becoming jerky now. The man moved toward the French doors, his back radiating anger and despair. He threw open the doors. Turned back.

Lelia watched from the wing chair where she sat, heavy-eyed, leaden but knowing this was a homecoming. Needing to know more. *Bonnie, what should I know?*

The shadow woman moved toward her. The face, beautiful one moment, distorted the next.

Rain startled her arms. It blew in from opened French doors. Its scent was like new life in her lungs. In the musty, shadowed room nothing moved. They were gone. On the wall, the portrait smiled back.

Lelia got up. Had the doors blown open? Rain slanted across the bare porch. The roar in her ears slowed, became the steady thump of surf outside. She dropped back into the chair, waiting for the turmoil in her pulse to subside.

Someone stood in front of her. Chuck, frowning.

"Lelia? I wondered where in the devil you were. Were you asleep or in a trance? Do you know it's noon? Don't tell me you're coming down with what Hazel has."

She didn't try to move. "Not asleep."

He looked around. "Museum of a room isn't it? Always did hate it."

"Chuck – what do you recall of your mother?"

His shoulders slumped in resignation. "At four, you don't remember much. She was someone coming and going but usually absent." He squinted across the room toward the portrait. "I brought Hazel some food from Conch. She says this kitchen offers nuts and berries." He was studying her again. "Where's your tan? You look like some ivory sculpture. I can't handle but one sick female."

"Have you ever looked in the tower room? In the studio,

there's another portrait."

"Dammit, Lelia, I warned you – prowl the past and what does it get you? Lousy feelings."

"The past is still here."

"You and Hazel – get off that pitch, okay? As long as we have to live here. Look, the rain's stopped. I've got to get back. You coming to work?"

"Later."

In the kitchen, she bit into a piece of dark bread and drained the leftover cup of tea, not caring that it was bitter. She had to clear her head, make the chill go away. Maybe if she slept. In her room. No shadows there. Safe. When she fell across the bed, sleep was a dark tunnel echoing with voices . . .

Beyond the windows, an enormous ball of blatant orange vibrated above the horizon. She sank back on the bed. When she lifted her head again, a disc of dull copper was slipping behind the edge of the gulf. Now a gray metal sky darkened the room. Whispers filled it. The shadowed faces were behind her eyes, murmuring in her head.

She sat up. Bare feet found the floor. Clothes fell in a heap. Carefully, clinging to the sides of the small, deep tub she climbed in, splashed cold water on her hot dry skin. She crawled out, pulled a dress over her damp body.

In the dark hall, she looked back through the Kali's open door. Tray time missed. Already it was night. On the balcony, Kali, a purple silhouette.

The railing guided her downstairs. The kitchen counter was something to hold on to. If she ate, she could wake up, stop the faces spinning behind her eyes. Bonnie's face again, fading, surging, the eyes bright and demanding . . .

Her fingers groped but the surface was solid, no way out. Roughness against her cheek. Moldy wood and stone. Two slitted eyes watching. Cat eyes. Nalo, purring in her face. Why was she on the floor? She pulled up, sat against the cabinet, the whispers and the roar mixing in her head.

A hard shadow moved toward her, a face bent close. So dark it gleamed. Cheta? Yes. The woman's eyes gleaming like the cat's. Cheta mumbling. The sense of it couldn't reach through the blackness spinning in her brain.

Cheta's hunched shadow went away. Running footsteps now. Someone else, crouched in front, waves of tobacco smell and Evening in Paris perfume. A red mouth open, black eyelashes blinking over Hazel's widened eyes.

"Lelia, get up. Wake up. Oh, m'God, don't scare the living life outta me."

Now Hazel's running steps, clunking across the kitchen floor. Outside, the Nash's chugging sounds. All of them, running away. But she knew what to do. Get outside. To the water . . . to night air so soft and kind on the face. Where was the path? The jungle was so dark without a moon. Sandspurs now, but it didn't matter. Just ahead, the sound of waves, lapping, calling like the whispers in the dream. She would lie down on cool wet sand and let the wind from the waves cool the body and clear the head.

Did someone wait there at the dark edge? Not the ancient woman in the dream. Someone else, younger, darker, beckoning, telling her to come, to see . . .

She didn't want to see the boat. She only wanted to lie down . . . Is this what Susie saw, looking up? An infinity of blackness and retreating stars? Uncaring waves reaching and stinging, slapping your legs, shifting sands digging beneath you like a trap, like a grave . . .?

GULF NIGHT
August, 1945

34

The night sky was as immense as freedom. Only the gritty shore still sucked her down. No, it was the woman who meant to trap her, the woman standing here, beckoning, wanting her to see a small skiff rocking in the waves.

No, Bonnie, no. You are not real. I reject you.

A warm breath in her face now, calling her name. Hands of bone and flesh reached under her shoulders, the shape of a man's head bending close as she was lifted from the wet shore. Gil. Beyond his shoulders, phosphorous waves silhouetted a tall figure, a woman with long blowing hair. Kali? With Gil? For only a fleeting moment did she wonder if she should struggle or accept them.

Wet and shivering, she was held against the warmth of his chest, in his arms, carried toward the house, now up the dark outside stairway to the balcony above. A measured tread followed up the sandy steps. Kali.

When Lelia opened her eyes, she was on the bed in the alcove, the wet dress being pulled off. A sheet billowed over her and settled down. Faces surged and swirled behind her eyes. She clung to the reality of the room, to the voices. Now Hazel's husky distress. Now Gil's harsh whisper, "Cut the hysteria, Hazel. You're no help. Get out now."

Then Cheta's mumbling, "My herbs doan bring on no devils least you trifle in the wrong batch and mix."

"Go. All of you." An order from Kali, a vibrato of emotion in the low tones. Kali's fingertips touched her temples like fire, like ice, scattering the distorted murmuring faces behind her eyes. The images bloomed and receded to a perimeter of darkness where they waited, a garbled chorus.

Kali's fingers lifted. The images surged back. Imagined faces of those she'd ever called out to from that other part of her mind . . . the Navy boy who was her father, the Bethel girl who was her mother . . . Susie . . . but it was the portrait face of Bonnie who hovered now behind her eyes.

"Hear me, Loa." Kali's fingers again pressed her temples. "It was not only Cheta's herbs that did this, was it? The emotional body is in disharmony as well as the physical."

"Kali, I saw Bonnie, showing me a small boat."

"Loa, Loa, these are astral realms. You must leave them. You must come back. Breathe the cleansing breath. I have seen you do this. Breathe in prana."

"She's here, Kali, in this house. On the beach. In my head."

"You allow her life with your belief, Loa. Choice has power. Belief in helplessness is bondage. Imagine light dispelling darkness. I will work with you . . . something I have not allowed myself to do for a long time."

She knew Kali's hands moved above her, touching her temples, hovering, touching again, trailing a tingling coolness. The low voice intoned strange syllables, like spoken music. The phantom voices in her own head quieted, their faces faded back to a dark perimeter.

The room was silent when Lelia awoke. In place of the invasion of senses, an enormous lethargy. Gratefully, she gave into sleep again. When next she opened her eyes, the Tiffany lamp glowed emerald green. How long had she been here in the alcove bed in one of Kali's woven robes? Kali sat in the wing chair by the book wall. The smoke gray hair spilled down by the drawn face, the shadowed eyes.

Had Kali climbed those outside stairs last night? Behind Gil, yes. When next she opened her eyes, sunrise edged the balcony. Again, sleep drew her back into a tunnel free of dreams.

Morning sun was harsh in the room. Chuck stood at the end of the bed, looking grim.

"For God's sake, Lelia, I thought you'd never wake up. What happened to you last night?" He jerked around to face Kali emerging from the dressing room beyond the book wall.

She stood there, inscrutable, ashen-faced, braced by the cane, saying, "She is well, Charles. Perhaps a mix of strong herbs had a toxic effect."

Chuck shifted his weight in his discomfort. Frowning but curious, he glanced about the room, from the book wall to the painting behind the bed, then back to the crystal ball stung with light.

"See, Chuck, I'm fine." To assure him, Lelia swung her legs off the bed and sat up. "But I don't think I'll show up at Grouper Hole today." She smiled so he wouldn't guess she wasn't ready to stand. Drained, totally.

"To hell with working today." Chuck sounded gruff but relieved. "You scared the bejeezus out of Haz. She's feeling lousy enough with the flu and finding you last night made her go haywire. At least she had the presence of mind to go out and find somebody close by. Gil. Sure you don't want to come downstairs?"

She had to get him out so she could sleep. "Are you busy over there?"

"Will be." Chuck jammed fists in his pockets and glanced over at Kali. "Don't know if you're aware of it shut away up here, but the Japs have surrendered. Truman announced it yesterday. The war is over."

Kali nodded. "Yes. Now the future begins."

Chuck turned back, uncertain. "Okay. Take it easy. This is Thursday. But we're counting on you Saturday. That's the big day. Evander Merrill is playing his grand farewell to the natives, as if we could forget." He wheeled out of the room almost colliding with Cheta.

On bare feet, the lanky Negro girl in the cotton sack dress walked in, balancing Kali's morning tray with easy grace, glowering toward the alcove bed. "Your tray's in your room. You git on in there. And you best watch out next time you mess around with my herbs."

She padded down the hall, lightheaded, to sit on the side of her own narrow bed and spoon up some kind of hot cereal sweetened with honey and sliced bananas. The tea, a thin amber liquid, fragrant as spring flowers. She sank back in the bed, gratefully.

When she looked again, clouds raced across a gulf sky, streaked with gold. Gold now, but a storm is coming. The thought flashed and was as quickly lost. Someone moved about the room. Kali's tall, robed figure, shaped by the sunset's amber glow now from the windows. Dark fire showed through the hair spilling over one shoulder. Kali was looking around at this room that had once been her own. Turning, she said, "I have brought you a gift."

The seaweed had been a gift of anger and impatience. From Kali? The answer came with clarity. No, not from Kali.

What day was this? She had eaten from Cheta's tray this morning and fallen back, swimming again in deep sleep. Now sunset again, waves of faint color shimmered against the lathed white ceiling. She was too tired to think clearly but no longer heavy, drained. She watched the ceiling movement and floated with it.

"You have rested well?" Kali, still there.

"Can't wake up . . . why?"

"Rest must replenish psychic energy that was drained away."

Drained and possessed. "What's happened to me?"

"Toxic substances, toxic thoughts."

"The herbs – that bitter tea?"

"It was an answer for Charles at the moment. Whatever, you entered forbidden veils, Loa."

"I saw the past – happening." And once it began, it wouldn't stop.

"You saw residual fields of energy. You gave them life by belief."

"No, I was being shown – things happening."

"You saw within the astral realm."

"Astral?"

"The first plane of nonmaterial existence beyond the physical and visible."

"Then the past must exist there."

"There are higher, finer realms of awareness. But we speak of what defies definition, and you are not fully awake."

"You brought me back."

"You were in danger."

"In danger of learning what I had to know? What you refused to tell me?" With effort she focused Kali's face. Shadows made dark hollows under the high cheekbones. More shadows, no, hazy smoke the color of sadness, hovered around Kali's shoulders, but the low voice remained composed.

"You glimpsed into the astral. And this holds a fascination, yes. But perception is distorted when interpreted through conscious desire or fear. One can be lost in these realms, unwilling or unable to return to the natural plane. And it is here we must function."

"Madness, Kali?" The warm hand on her arm drew away.

"Always your fear, isn't it? Yes, you were in danger when we brought you in from the beach. But I speak now of delusion."

"Bonnie a delusion?"

"Loa understands. Lelia Elliot questions. It is often so, the conscious mind must reject what the unconscious perceives. Both are gifts. One illumines the other. I have waited for you to accept both before I told you other facts."

"I have been to Doc Miller."

"I know."

She needed to talk but this strange lethargy drew her back toward sleep. Did Kali do this? Yet it had stopped the invasion of her senses. "I haven't told Hazel what I learned. She intends –"

"I am well aware of what Hazel intends. But I will leave this house in my own time. And that time is close, for my reasons, not for Hazel's. I shall return to my own shores. To Hana. You are surprised. You wonder why I have stayed. That I will tell you, too. Later. Sleep again. It restores. I have brought you a gift."

She was asleep before Kali's footsteps faded.

In the deep of the night, she woke up, instantly alert, freed of the voices and the lethargy. A new moon raced behind clouds over the dark gulf. A large thin book waited in the chair by the window, a note on top. In the yellow light of the small bedlamp, Lelia read the precise script. Kali's handwriting. "This is my own gift to you from the past."

The notebook was an artist's sketchbook. Figures and comments were scribbled here and there. Don Elliot's sketchbook. She could almost hear his voice speaking those lines. None had to do with Bonnie. Or Kali. Or Maylene. These notes spoke of technique and depth of seeing and about trusting one's self. At one full page, she read with mounting comprehension and gratitude:

> *". . . the artist must live in peace with both reaches of his being, the conscious intention which weighs and chooses and the unconscious which is the source of genius, the font of creativity, when he reaches into something higher than himself to glimpse the inexplicable . . ."*

Don Elliot never knew that she would exist, yet she ached with pleasure now holding his gift and knowing her own mind and fingers held his kind of passion and maybe his talents. This was an inheritance too, as well as whatever she carried from a long line of Calhouns. She gulped in new morning air, like freedom, smiling at the thought. Yes, she was marked as surely by the Calhouns' need for self-control and conformity, as by Elliot blood. Talent and madness.

Don't try to claim me, Bonnie, she whispered in defiance. *I am part of all of you, but I am myself too. I won't allow you to live through me.*

Dawn was coloring the sands pink and lighting up the dark gulf. Kali had said there was power in choices. Watching the day begin, she made choices now. She would not tell Hazel what she knew of Kali, of Don Elliot, of Dr. Miller. Whatever happened, they had acted to protect Maylene. Bonnie must have returned home before they could send Maylene away.

No, she would not expose Kali. That meant she would have to leave, no matter how much she'd come to love this old waterfront. Even the house, in spite of Bonnie's felt presence. But why should she stay? Hadn't she discovered what she had to know? But she couldn't go until she knew Francie was safe. Tingley too. And Gil? Yes. They are part of your tapestry, Kali had said. You needed them to know yourself, Lelia-Loa.

The sky brightened to a glare. This was Saturday morning. Chuck counted on her being there to help with the party. Tingley's bruised face and warnings came back now, bringing a chill. He'd said timing was everything and something about front-and-center. If his plot theory was right, what better timing than when everyone up and down the bay would be partying on Grouper Hole's lighted waterfront? The full moon gone, tonight would be dark. Evander Merrill wouldn't even have to know his party was being used to cover a murder.

Lelia closed her eyes, cleared her mind, and brought up the image of the dapper movie actor, saw the silver pompadour bent over filing his nails, the diamond ring glinting. Saw a handsome, aging man whose hands would never dirty themselves with murder. As she held him there in her imagination, the heavy face of Sloan loomed in behind a nervous Evander Merrill.

BAYSHORE MORNING
August 15, 1945

35

On the bayside road, the Nash honked behind her and Lelia stopped. The open window was already hot to touch when she leaned into the car's shade to smile into Chuck's frown.

"Do you know how worried I've been?" he said. "No sign of you from these upper quarters. You realize what day this is? Saturday. The damn party tonight. I've been putting Crit off, swearing you'd show."

"I'm on my way now. See?"

"Better ride over. It's going to be a long night. The place will be a mess all day, setting up. Get in?"

"No thanks. I need to walk. Chuck, before we get over there, tell me – have you seen Cracker around? Or talking to Morris Alderman? Do they know about the party?"

"What kind of a question is that? Everybody on the waterfront knows about tonight. The war's over. Look at the traffic this morning. Gas rationing's over. If Merrill hadn't ordered the party outside, we'd be having a crowd inside anyway."

Because she waited, he said, "Have I seen Cracker? He's no customer. I've seen Crit hiss at his name. I'd like to drown the son-of-a-bitch, for Susie's sake. Alderman? I don't think of that guy and the hayseed in the same breath. Why do you ask?"

"What about Brockway – has he been around? And Tingley?"

Chuck's fist hit the steering wheel. "That joker. Tingley's

called you couple or three times, sounding out of his gourd. Or drunk. I told him to get lost, not to bother you. If he shows up, Crit will have him thrown out, and I'll have to do it. As for Brockway, Crit has sent him and the sheriff a special invitation. How about that?"

"Wait, Chuck—J. T. has a theory about tonight. He thinks someone is planning to frame Gil for Nancy and Susie's murders. He says a third girl will be found somewhere on the bay." At Chuck's grimace, she said, "What better time for something like that to happen? Everyone will be celebrating V-J Day at Grouper Hole."

"And you believe that? I swear, Lelia, sometimes you sound strangely wise, other times like a total, trusting innocent. You have to know J. T. Tingley has a pathetic need to be the hotshot reporter. He's been hanging around the yacht like a mongrel yipping at the heels of the Great Dane who wouldn't give him the time of day. You're the only one who'll listen to the joker."

Lelia looked away at the mangrove banks in the bright sun. "I want to hear what else he knows. If I can't go find him, he'll be calling again."

"We're blocking the road. Are you riding over the bridge with me or not? Okay, see you there."

The Nash turned onto the bridge, and Lelia ran to the Inn's front porch. Francie wasn't in sight, but she had to make sure. Every chair on the long porch was filled as guests rocked at a quickened pace behind the opened newspapers. Asking for Francie, Lelia accepted a paper and read the huge black headlines:

WAR IS OVER.

"The second world war ended tonight. All fighting has stopped. A formal armistice will be signed by the Tokyo government in a few days . . ."

The future has begun, Kali had said.

"Francine?" A gray-haired woman beamed. "Oh, you must be the friend that sweet girl is so anxious to see. Left in such a state when the aunt had to return to town. But they'll be back here this afternoon."

Oh no, Francie. Stay away. "Please tell her to call me," knowing she couldn't depend on that, she'd have to get out of Grouper Hole long enough to find her. And find Gil.

Walking across the bridge, pressing against warm, rough railings for cars to pass, she searched the channel for Gil's boat. No sight of the *Strike*. Further on, Al's Bait House docks were empty except for Cap'n's little *Sea Bitch* bobbing down there.

Voices echoed from Grouper Hole's waterfront. Shouts and whoops now. From the bridge railing, she looked down at a dozen bare-chested GIs racing around on the hard sand lot, putting together tables from boards and saw horses. Like a troop of oversized Boy Scouts setting up camp, they were making a party out of helping Martha Critten with hers.

In the kitchen, Conch bent over his tub of ice and silver mullet. He nodded toward Bubba's quarters. "Miz Crit in there making Mister B call up the ice truck folks again. He's sulking like a whipped dog. And the Army done landed out front."

"I saw from the bridge."

"Those boys need reminding to keep tables away from my fire pit," Conch grumbled. "Miz Crit's got me cooking crab cakes for the whole bunch before they get gone."

"I'll tell them."

The barroom was in disarray. Tables scattered. Two GIs crouched behind the pulled-out Wurlitzer, arguing over how to wire it to the speakers they had attached to the roof outside. Watching from the bar, next to Skipper, Cap'n dangled his little feet from a stool.

"There she is."

Chuck looked up. "Take a pitcher of ice water out to those guys, okay? Crit promised all the beer they could drink, but tell them they'll have to come in to get it."

"They ain't expecting no water out there," Skipper warned.

"Glad I ain't old and blind as you," Cap'n said. "Those boys'll see a plum angel of mercy with the water pitcher."

Lelia stopped on the screen porch, clutching a stack of

Dixie cups and a pitcher of cold water against her chest. Tables covered the hard sand lot. Fifteen or more bare chests sweated in the sun out there. Clowns all of them, setting up the party scene. Stringing orange paper lanterns across the yard. Setting out folding chairs from the truck parked on the side. In the center, two GIs stomped down the wooden square making a dance floor. Two more lanterns festooned the lamp posts at the entrance of the long dock.

The loud speakers released a blast of Woody Herman's "Woodchoppers Ball." Yahoos rose again as the music poured out, this time Glenn Miller's band chorusing about a gal-in-Kal-a-ma-zoo. Lelia took a deep breath and stepped into the yard with the ice water pitcher.

They wheeled around and surged forward. "Geee-juss!" . . . "Hubba, hubba" . . . "See what I see?" "All reet!" "This Grouper Hole babe, here she is in the sunshine . . ."

For once, Lelia dared open to their energy, look deep into glinting eyes, and know what they were saying behind their lively faces. She stood entrapped, encircled, letting them sway around her, picking up the juke box beat, singing about a "gal, a real pipperooo . . . from Kalamazoo," chorusing the words like a platoon of comic opera baritones and tenors, off-key and loud . . . taking away her pitcher, overflowing their paper cups, pouring water over each other's burr heads . . . She had to smile back, knowing they were drunk with remembering being twelve again back on some schoolyard playground . . . drunk now on knowing the war was over, whatever that would mean.

In their midst, she dared listen to their crazy lyrics and the ones they improvised about a long-legged, luscious babe, dark-haired water bearer, gold-flecked amber eyes, sweet plum lips, this Grouper Hole doll who eludes the touch.

Arms locked, they swayed in vocal glee, garbling their own lyrics about girls who were teasers and Precious Daughters, all those innocents waiting for Audie Murphy or Robert Taylor. One tenor rose, finishing for the rest, "But this one's a mystery, a girl who makes love to the man in the Moon."

She spun away, into the porch, back through the scattered tables into the small wooden bathroom where she threw cold water on her hot face.

In a corner of the barroom, Martha Critten dropped in a chair, propped new Oxford shoes up on another. "Elliot, do me a double bourbon while I catch my breath. Miss Queenie Elliot, bring it over and sit down."

Lelia brought the drink, sat down, and studied this woman. What have I missed knowing about you, Martha Critten? I always blanked you out.

"So. You finally showed up. What happened over there? Serves you right for living in the same house with that old murderer. But young stuff can bounce right back, can't they? How well I remember."

"I'm okay now. I'm here. About tonight –"

Martha looked weary but pleased. "Whole county's coming just like I said. Grove owners, social folks, big cheeses from downtown. They're going to remember the whole damn war ended with a party right here. They're going to have respect for yours truly and old Grouper Hole."

Stubborn pride. Was that it? To show off to the people who wouldn't otherwise come to this beach bar?

"Greet those old daddies, Miss Pretty. Show them some class, and keep the mamas away from the movie star. And rustle up something sexier than the skirt-and-blouse bit. Show some skin and leg. You were born lucky, girl. Long, lean body with the right padding and gams like Dietrich." She lifted one foot in the brown shoe. "See that? Once I had tiny ankles and curvy legs. Wore those itsy-bitsy shoes with godawful heels. Hell on the tootsies and the balance when you've got big boobs and little feet. These old clodhoppers are a de-clar-ration of independence, a thumb to the nose for the jokers."

"Jokers?"

"Men. You haven't learned that yet? Maybe you have – since you keep your distance. Even from Bubba."

Martha drained the glass and handed it over. "Remember the head table's the one up by the docks. That table's for Merrill and that Army Air Corps captain, Sweeling, who helps with the parties. And me and Bubba."

Martha pulled herself from the chair. "Now where did that Bubba go, damn that boy's hide. Doesn't appreciate what I do for him. You better get back to old Conch. He should have those cakes ready for the boys."

"Is that all?"

"Make sure those old biddies don't bother Mister Important at his table. He'll be pissed if they crowd in with those pesky Brownie Kodaks. Your job is to keep 'em happy and out of his hair. They'll see enough. He'll be front and center the whole damn night with the yacht sitting out there in the bay, lit up in all its glory."

Front and center?

The Schlitz clock over the bar said two o'clock. The GIs were gone, the party yard ready, the barroom in disarray. She had to get out. Going after another dress was an excuse.

"Look in on Hazel," Chuck said as he lugged crates of soda to the porch. "She's hell-bent on coming, but if she has a fever, make her stay in bed."

She ran out into the hot afternoon glare. First she tried to find Gil at the Bait House. Big Al scratched his head.

"Some fellow hired him to go off in the Gulf, dawn this morning. Nope, didn't see who, Miz Lelia."

At the Inn, there sat the Packard. And Francie, alone on the porch. Francie jumped up, pulled her onto the porch with an agitated welcome. "I got back but just for two nights. Mother's coming Monday to drag me back to school. What am I going to do? I can't find – it looks like I've got to rock here and go simply crazy."

"Help me tonight. I have the happy-greeter job for Evander Merrill's party." Yes. You stay with me, Francie and I won't have to tell you anything or worry about you. Stay in the light, Tingley had said.

"I've got to see someone."

"But I really need your help tonight. You'll have fun, I promise. More than two hundred people will be there, including officers from MacDill and Drew bases and the Coast Guard downtown."

Francie dropped into a porch chair and rocked absently.

"I don't know." She sucked in the full bottom lip. "I guess. All right. I couldn't sit here, for heaven's sakes. Wait a minute." She sprang up to riffle through a stack of newspapers in a chair. "Show you something. Me in the Social News page. I was sitting in a cabana at the Bath Club. Let me read the stupid thing."

In a mock cooing voice, Francie read, "Comely Miss Francine Welburn, daughter of Mrs. Elise Arnold Welburn of Charleston and the late Naval Commander Frank Welburn, has been spending the summer at Indian Rocks Inn as guest of her aunt Miss Mozelle Dickson . . ." She handed over the paper, unsmiling. "I'm saving it to show Mother. Proof I've been good." She tried to smile. "Do you think I'm 'comely?'"

"Mmmm – comely in the picture, tragic-looking now. But glowing. And you look older than that sassy kid I met on the train in May. Francie – that was meant well, don't cry on me."

"It's not that. It's just – everything." Francie flung the newspaper back on the stack. "Now that the war's going to be over, do you think people will stop hating each other? I mean, Americans and the Germans and the Russians and the Japanese and all?"

"I'm not sure." She saw the girl's genuine distress.

"I mean," Francie went on, "when you think of the boys you knew, or saw, who may be dead now, as well as all those on the other side. Now that it's OVER, will they stop blaming each other? The young ones, anyway, who didn't start it?"

"Be glad it's over."

"You'll remember me as a real ninny, a cry-baby."

"No. I'll remember you as my first real woman friend, and I thank you for that."

"Oh! How utterly dear of you to tell me that. And how awfully sad." The blue eyes glistened with tears and real pleasure. "You've helped me keep my sanity this summer. And I'd love to help you at the party. Lelia, do you know where I can find Gil?"

"No, Francie."

"That's all right." The smile was weak. "I only wanted to ask him something."

"Promise me you'll be over there at five. The crowd

comes at six."

"I will. I can't sit here. You're going to save my life."

From the Inn, Lelia ran down the beach road, through the shade of the tangled jungle, into the silent shadowed house. No, not silent. Hazel's angry voice, a hoarse cry, reached into the living room. Cheta stalked from the master bedroom, her dark face a sullen mask. She carried an untouched tray of bread and soup.

"Crazy woman in there. Don't deserve no help from me no matter what your uncle say."

"Cheta, I've got to find Gil, you know, the man with the *Strike*."

"Blues man. I know."

"Find him for me. You know the bayfront. Tell him to come to Grouper Hole." She was being calm. Focused, as Kali said. Not sure of anything, but open to knowing.

"I got grits to cook up. After I look after her upstairs. Every time Kali heals the poison outa of you, she has to get rid of it in herself. Don't look wild on me now, I take care of her. You go around dumb and dreamy like you don't believe nothing right in your face. I figgered you one white girl who'd be smarter than that. Don't look wild on me now, you got things to do or Miz Crit get on your tail."

Lelia found Hazel on her rumpled bed, whimpering, sweating in a satin slip, the topknot askew. Hazel looked up with bloodshot eyes, the voice a painful rasp. "Dammit. What time is it?"

"It's after three. The crowd is due by six. Chuck says he'd have to come for you in an hour if you're going. But he doesn't think you should. You must have a fever."

"Go early, yeah, like the goddamned hired help." Hazel groaned. "Whatcha looking at?"

"Drinking doesn't help the flu." The hot room was in shambles, a half-empty bourbon bottle on the littered table, no air coming from windows open to thick foliage. For all her impatience, she felt sorry for Hazel. "Why try to go?"

"I've got to see that hulking Sloan, face to face, that

double-crosser, leading me on, making me stick my neck out–"

"Making you do what, Hazel?" Her skin chilled in the hot room.

"To hell with that smiley-smooth Merrill. I'll sell this place to somebody else. He's not the only one with bucks. I have to go. Talk to folks at the party. Some old grove owner with the scrub land. They're gonna be ready to sell out and take mama someplace in an Airstream trailer."

Hazel tried to prop up but fell back, holding her throat, the whisper painful. "Know what I'm gonna do with the land? Plot streets and build houses. Morris told me that's what to do. Gonna put my daddy's name on one of those streets, like a joke on everybody."

"What did Sloan promise you?" Lelia asked. "What did he make you do?"

"Who cares, who cares? I had to shake you up, didn't I? Make you push on the old witch. And you didn't. Damn cool bitch, you didn't panic like you shoulda –"

"And the noises you heard – all lies, to push me, too?"

Hazel tried to sit up. The rasp was a plea. "At first. Now they're real. I swear on a stack of Bibles."

"And the seaweed, Hazel?"

Hazel moaned and fell back. "I had to do something, you bitch. I didn't mean for you to go off your rocker with that sulfa."

So it was sulfa in that herb tea. "I'll tell Chuck you're too sick to come. Stay here, Hazel." Out of my sight. I have enough to handle tonight.

In her own room, Lelia stood under the shower, blanking Hazel from her mind. From the closet, she took the peach chiffon Francie had given her and brushed back her wet hair. Obeying some impulse, she dropped the peach heels and slipped on sandals instead. She could run in the sandals.

As she hurried down the bayside road to the bridge, the Packard pulled out from the Inn, about to turn south. "Francie!" She ran to the car.

Behind the wheel, Francie waited in a cloud of pink

dotted swiss, curls awry, foot tapping the accelerator.

Lelia leaned into the girl's pink face. "You promised to stay with me tonight! It's almost time."

"I'll be back, honest."

"Don't go to him, Francie. Please. He's in trouble. It's not safe. People will be looking for him—"

Guileless blue eyes held a plea. "I know he's in trouble. But this will be the last time, and I've got to say good-by. I have to, Lelia."

The Packard pulled away, rumbling down the beach road, picking up speed. Lelia turned toward the bridge. Already across the narrow bay, party lanterns glowed dully over the waiting party yard.

GROUPER HOLE
August Saturday night, 1945

36

Glenn Miller's "String of Pearls" throbbed out over the waiting party tables and the wooden square of a dance floor. A couple whirled there under the orange lanterns, the corporal who'd come early to check the sound and his girl, her skirts whipping against his gyrating khaki legs.

At the tree-lined edge of the sand lot, Conch poked a stick at a beginning fire set under two lengths of bedsprings. Does Conch know? Lelia wondered, watching him work, intent and silent as some ancient medicine man beginning his own ritual. Whatever Conch knew, he always kept behind his sober silence.

Near the dock, orange bunting draped the head table. A stage set, all of it, for Evander Merrill, aging movie star, to preen before the natives on this night of celebration. The war was over. Reason enough for all of this. Why believe there was more at stake here?

Yet she wanted to cry out Gil, Tingley, where are you? Francie, it's getting late. Hurry, come back, wherever you went.

Two small Negro girls, proud in their red and white polka dot dresses, darted out the screen door. They ran about the tables on duty for Aunt Cheta, giggling as they delivered forks rolled in paper napkins.

The lanterns were brighter now against the fading light. *Francie, get here, in the light.*

Chuck shouted twice before she walked back to the screened front porch where he'd set up the temporary bar. The pool table was covered with oilcloth and stacked with paper cups. Tubs of iced Nehi grapes, Buffalo Rock ginger ale, Coca-Colas, and Budweiser beer sat on the floor. The two old fishermen, wearing limp dress shirts and ancient pants, had dragged out stools to watch, eager as kids ready to see a circus. They looked so dear and funny perched there, Lelia wanted to hug them both. Why not believe this was a happy party night? Cap'n grinned at her. "I swan – purty as a peachy hibiscus tonight."

Chuck waved his own drink. "Salud! Welcome to the verandah bar. Do I see concern, disappointment on Hibiscus' face? Did she expect elegance and aperitifs at this Critten establishment? Let's start the party. Have a drink."

"Bartender's getting drunk," Skipper said.

She'd never seen Chuck drink with sloppy abandon, "Chuck, I want to talk –"

"Fellows, she doubts the vintage of bubbly I am offering her sweet innocent lips." He wiped off a dripping bottle of ginger ale from the tub, and she took it, held the cold amber bottle against her cheek.

"Where's the Redhead?" Chuck said. "Thought she was to observe our event with her girlish giggles."

"Francie's an hour late, Chuck, and I'm worried. I can't stop thinking about those things Tingley told me. I tried to tell you before –"

"You think too much, my strange and beautiful niece. You also listen too well to clowns and weird old ladies." From the iced tub, he brought up two beer bottles for Cap'n and Skipper. "Take these two old coots. They're natural wits. They call it as they see it. No pondering the meaning of it all."

"Hear that, Skipper?" Cap'n said. "Joe College here admittin' it comes natural for some folks."

"What does?" Skipper glowered.

"Knowing how to get outa the rain, you old fool." Cap'n kicked at the tub on the floor. "How come you doing it this way? You oughta have the suds and soda pop separate. The teetotaler Baptists don't wanna dip in past a beer."

"An astute observation, fellows," Chuck said. "Ours is not to wonder, but to do."

"Some of those downtown, yacht-clubby fellas are going to want their martoonies," Skipper warned.

"No doubt." Chuck tipped the Wild Turkey bottle into his cup again. "Hey, Lelia, don't look so worried. Get the welcome smile working. That's your assignment, right? Francie will show. She's like these two geezers in that respect. Doesn't want to miss the action."

"We just come to watch," Cap'n said. "To see wimmen pester Handsome and ole J. T. Tingley get himself throwed out."

"Reminds me," Chuck said. "Dummy has to get the heave-ho, too, if he shows. Orders." He grinned at Lelia. "And he might show to get a look at you and the Redhead. Ever see his lost-soul eyes looking at you and your busty little friend?"

The ginger ale felt good on her tight throat. Over the amplified juke box beat, she heard a car on the road outside. The Packard hopefully.

"Where is Martha?"

"Fuming and drinking in the office at the moment." Chuck leaned against the wall. "She had to send Bubba for more ice. What the heck. She'll make a good buck tonight off Merrill, you can bet. Isn't that the bottom line on the ledger?"

"The visible one," Lelia said. "Hazel isn't coming, is she?"

"Dear wife is still sick as the devil and meaner than one." He grimaced over his drink. "Ever notice? Crit and Hazel are about as chummy as an old buzzard and a fighting cock hen. Yet both are imbued and fired with the same motivation and talent for single-minded pursuit of their aim. Big bucks. For self-protection, Haz calls it."

Chuck leaned forward, so intense her own chest felt his bitterness. "That drive, my dear niece, is one this man fails to have. Notice I say man with a certain protest as well as pride. Yet I bow to both ladies for their tenacity." His gaze swung away, stopping on the two old men, hunkered down on their stools, listening. Chuck turned back with a wooden smile.

"So, let's party. Hear 'em coming? If I weren't busy on this elegant verandah bar, I'd go watch our elder citizen-husbands take a look at you, Lelia. They'll be feeling around on the ground for their eyeballs. Go on, have fun. Pick out some first lieutenant who wants to take you home to mom and the family business. Don't take life so serious. Don't take anything serious and it won't get you."

Traffic noise hummed from the front brick road. Doors slammed. Martha Critten appeared from the barroom, a mass of faded pink cabbage roses stretching over the big breasts and fluttering in ruffles above the heavy calves and small ankles, the feet already swollen, stuffed into satin shoes. She stood there, fists on her hips, looking them over.

"Now that's more like it, Miss Beauty. Class and oomph all in one." Grouper Hole's owner heaved a long sigh. "Okay folks, let's get the show started."

Harry James' trumpet echoed over the dark woods and bay, a triumphant fanfare as the crowd poured in. Chevys, Fords and Buicks, nursed through the war, lined the grassy sides of the brick road, along with Army Jeeps and staff cars. Waiting at the side driveway entrance, Lelia strained to see a running figure in dotted swiss, but there was no sign of Francie. She forced a smile and began greeting them by rote, "Welcome to Grouper Hole and Mr. Merrill's hospitality . . ."

In they came, from downtown St. Pete and little Clearwater, from up and down gulf beaches and from the rural heart of the county, all of them streaming in, curious to see the movie star, ready to eat Conch's mullet, eager to share news so they could believe it – *the war, over.*

Their openness made her smile become real, her words genuine. Doubts about this party faded, replaced for now by their voices and the music beat floating into the night.

A cluster of khaki dress uniforms surged in, followed by gold braid and dress whites from the Coast Guard base in town. Their party-dressed dates curled proprietary hands around the crisp uniformed sleeves that led them in. Some of Francie's Bomb-a-Dears greeted her with little trills of recognition but swept on by, faces glowing with private triumph.

From familiar isolation, Lelia watched, wondering how it must feel to be like that, so carelessly assured, ready tonight for dancing and flirting rather than standing here fighting suspicions and worry about Francie, and anger for Gil.

A chubby blonde woman marched in, a Speed Graphic camera under one arm, a covey of ten women at her heels, chorusing explanations. They were from the Garden Club in town and Lonnie with the camera was here from the *St. Petersburg Times*. Lonnie was going to take the garden-clubbers' picture with Evander Merrill. They've named a rose after the movie star and they meant to announce it tonight.

"How nice," Lelia managed, remembering orders to keep the fans from pestering the host. She watched them chatter their way around the building into the lighted yard.

A rotund fellow in seersucker and string tie pumped her hand. "Well, aren't you pretty as a fresh peach. Didn't know Bubba Critten had young ladies working at this old bar. See, Bess," turning to the prim-mouthed woman at his elbow, "the party's gonna be real nice. I told you."

The brick road was dark now, lined with cars. Wafting into the night, Dinah Shore's voice crooning, "You'd be sooo nice, to come home to . . ." Still no Francie. A single lanky figure was walking toward her. Rumpled brown suit. Brockway. What did he know? Had Tingley reached him and would he believe Tingley? She moved toward him, eager to ask, but Bubba was there, blinking and whining a welcome, leading Brockway past her into the party yard. She pulled in a deep breath and followed.

Under the colored lanterns, chairs leaned at claimed tables. Guests moved around in clusters, voices raised over the thumping beat as the Andrews Sisters chorused their strident, happy nonsense.

No sign yet of the *Silver Fox* coming up the dark bay.

Francie, did you make Gil see you tonight? One last time? Get back here!

Across the yard, Brockway stood with four other men watching Conch spread fish over the glowing coals. At the bunting draped table, Martha Critten sat alone, waving signals now. She's drunk but watching everything, Lelia knew. She threaded through the crowd to Martha who leaned forward propped on her elbows.

"Keep circulating, you hear? That's your job. Keep 'em satisfied. They can't expect a movie star to show up right off. He'll ride in on the *Fox*. Grand entrance."

Martha waved her drink toward the crowd. "Look at that. The fancies. They've come partying at Poppy's. Yeah." She looked up, squinting at Lelia. "Whatcha standing there for? Get back to table-hopping."

Poppy? Who is Poppy? Lelia didn't ask. Chuck was calling, standing in the propped-open screen door, glowering over the tray he held, loaded with Orange Crush bottles.

"Do me a favor, Hibiscus? Take this damn tray over to those Garden Club dames. Next to the Barber Shopper guys in the red-striped shirts. They expect table service, would you believe." He turned back to the crowd standing around on his porch.

Three men in St. Petersburg Yacht Club blazers strolled out, laughing over their drinks. "Those two old fellows in there, the scrawny one and the big one? Now that's real beach characters for you. Probably can talk a fish onto the line."

Cheta appeared in the open screen door, arms folded, the usual throaty voice projecting into the party babble. "Hot pots coming through in a minute. Doan anybody git in my way."

Francie, where are you?

A khaki arm circled her shoulders. "Don't tell me you're on KP duty tonight, Lelia Beautiful." Pulled to the square of dance floor, pressed against his chest, she had to follow the man's steps until the beat changed, and she whirled herself away, slipping through the crowd.

Hands caught hers, drew her to the table. Martha was watching so she pretended to listen to the upturned faces talking to her.

"Do you jitterbug like that, Hon? That fellow up there. Why he's going to break his back! Crazy kids."

"Kids, you say. Some of these fellows were in the action."

"The bomb won the war."

"We should have dropped it on some deserted island first."

"You going to be glad to see Uncle Sam pull out of here?"

"Sure – if we get some paying tourists in their place."

"You heard about this new DDT stuff? We're gonna be bug-free some day . . ."

There. She spied Brockway in the tree shadows watching Cheta setting up the food table. Another hand grabbed before she could reach him. The man in the string tie beamed. "Look at this young lady, folks, couldn't she be some movie star herself?"

"What about that Conch. Is that colored cook eighty years old or what? He looks fifty. Guess those folks don't have any big worries to make 'em old like the rest of us. The fellow sure knows how to cook though."

"Wonder if those two little pickaninnys bringing around the ice bucket are his granddaughters or his own? You know how they are . . ."

"I don't think they like that word."

"Pickaninny? Well, why not? It means a cute lil' Negro child. And I'll be the first to tell them they look just darlin' in those red ribbons."

"Miss?" She was trapped again, this time at the table of red-striped Barber-Shoppers and wives. "Still haven't seen any movie star around here. And we're all set to sing."

"Reckon he has to make a grand entrance. Is that what he's planning, young lady?"

A man growled, "When that Chris-Craft is docked out there, don't expect him to let anybody troop onboard to look. I wouldn't if that 62-footer was mine."

"Who's the henna-haired dame up there staring this way? What's she doing sitting at the table for Evander Merrill? She's no Greer Garson."

"Martha Critten. She owns this place. The chubby fellow sitting down with her now is her son Bubba. She may look like Tugboat Annie, but that old gal has gotten her share of Uncle Sam's paychecks around here."

"'Moonlight Serenade!' Oh, Daddy, let's dance this one!"

Conch's iron bell clanged against the high clear exuberance of Benny Goodman's clarinet. The two pigtailed girls ran around tables saying, "You kin come on now."

Bodies heaved up from the borrowed Legion Hall chairs and began to form a line, murmuring with satisfaction at the food before them. Conch's roasted mullet. Hush puppies turned out nut brown and hot. Yellow corn ears piled high. White hearts of palm waiting beyond the huge pot of steaming grits. With butter. "How about that, butter!"

Cheta, with another bucket of corn, veered past dancers and tables, like a ship's figurehead plowing through a choppy tide. Moving back through, she stopped to put her dark moist face close to Lelia's. "Somebody called fo' you on the phone inside, screaming fit to kill."

"Hazel?"

Cheta pressed her lips. "Not her."

"Francie?" A hot wave of alarm.

"Reckon so. She goan call back if she can."

Francie's had car trouble. She wanted to believe that, but knew better. She ran to the porch.

"Did Francie call?"

Chuck looked up, slack-faced, shrugging. She wanted to scream at him. Cap'n wagged his brown head. "Can't hear thunder with all the racket."

A solid figure, in white duck pants and shirt, lounged in the dark barroom doorway, watching. *Gil!*

Both grateful and angry at the sight of him, she demanded, "Francie has called. In trouble. Where did you leave her? Where is she?"

Gil's casual stance froze. Every passion she'd ever seen in him, the tense energy in his shoulders, the hidden anger in his eyes, hardened, volatile, ready to explode. "What are you saying, Lelia?" His face darkened. He grabbed her arm. "Where is she?"

From inside, the bar phone rang faintly. Lelia pulled free, ran behind the plank, groping past bottles, grabbed up the black instrument. "Francie?"

At the other end of the line, Francie's voice quivered, "Oh, Lelia, oh God, I'm glad you answered."

Gil swung his legs over the bar, stood beside her now, reaching for the phone. She clutched it tighter, turning her back to him. "Francie, talk to me."

Gil's hand pulled her head close to his, listening as Francie sobbed on the line, "Oh, Lelia, what am I going to do? They're going to kill him, I know."

"Francie, where are you? Tell me!" She heard Francie's voice, faint against a background of garbled noise and music. She heard Gil's breathing as clearly, saw the pulse throbbing in his tanned neck as he demanded, "Is there another phone? Bubba's office?"

She nodded. "Francie, I'm going to another phone so I can hear you. Gil is on this one. Talk to him." She looked into his face. "She's terrified! Don't dare let her go until I can get back there and pick up."

"Get going. Francie – it's Gil. Talk to me."

Lelia plunged through the swinging door into the silent kitchen. Cheta sat cross-legged on the cleared off table, smoking. The closed office door was locked.

"Cheta – I've got to get in there!"

The girl slid down, went to the pantry, reached her long arm to the highest shelf and came back with a key.

The door swung open. The single light showed the cluttered cubicle of an office, Bubba's rumpled bed just beyond. Where was the phone? Yes, here on the desk, under the pile of papers. Lelia pushed some of the litter aside and lifted the receiver. Thank God, Gil's voice there, a soft command coming through clenched jaws.

"Get your breath and tell us first where you are, Francie."

"Johns Pass, inside a bar. Can't think of the name. Old men watching me, I don't know what to do. I'm afraid to leave." The whisper faded. In the background, muted jukebox sounds and the rumble of voices.

"Francie! It's Lelia. I'm on the other phone. Why can't you leave? What is happening?"

From the other end of the line, "Oh, Lelia, you're going to think I'm awful and Mother's going to kill me, but we were in the cottage. Tingley's place. We saw him leave. So we went. Two awful men came in. We had to hide in that terrible little bathroom. The men were laughing and talking about killing

Tingley, and they were reading all the stuff he's written. They read the part about *Karl*! So we had to get out of there –"

"Karl? Who are you with, Francie?"

On the bar phone Gil's terse answer. "She means Dummy. Francie, how close is your car?"

"Parked by the Peter Pan Diner." A sob. "That's a block away from here. I made Karl promise to go hide and let them follow me because he's the one they're after, not me. I made him." Her voice rose to a squeak. "Karl knows they're going to *kill* him like a dog on the street and no one will care, they'll just be *heroes*, and it's true, they'd do that. Ohhhh, Lelia!"

Gil bit out the words. "I'm coming after you, Francie. Now think where you are. Shanty Hogan's or –"

Francie whimpered. "That one. Where Tingley goes. He was here and gave me the nickels to call, but he went out looking for them. He told me to stay here and call you. I'm so scared. My mother's going to kill me, too, when she finds out." The hysterical giggle faded.

Lelia pushed the litter across Martha Critten's desk as Gil repeated his orders on the other phone.

"Francie, listen carefully. Stay calm. Stay there. Order a Coke. Tell the bartender you're waiting for your folks to come get you. Don't talk to anyone else. Don't leave –"

Under Lelia's fingers, under the glass on the desk, a smiling face looked up. A young Valentino. No, Evander Merrill at nineteen or twenty, bare-chested, black-haired, beautiful smile. Studio pose. Inscribed, From *Tony to Poppy*. That name again, Poppy.

"Francine, answer us," Gil said. "I'm leaving now. Tell me you understand."

Barroom noises filled the line from Shanty Hogan's. A different voice now close to the phone. *Oh, no, Francie, don't talk to anyone.* He sounded like Cage, the small swarthy man with Cracker. But different. Strange and cajoling.

Francie's voice again, faint, unsure. "Karl sent somebody to get me. Karl needs me and they're going to help us get home. I have to go." The line hummed.

Lelia hung up the phone, dumped the litter on top of it

again, and ran from the room, slamming the door locked behind her. Gil was there, catching her wrist with a hard grip.

"You can't go, Lelia. You don't know what you're getting into."

"I know and I'm taking Brockway with me!"

His grip tightened. "Forget Brockway. There isn't time. I need a car. Do you have Chuck's keys?"

"You can't go without me."

They ran to the porch, Lelia demanding the keys, a sleepy Chuck groaning they were in the car. A commotion held them rooted. Men had moved tables, making a path. The crowd stood, watching, faces curious, hands clapping. Bunny Berrigan's trumpet pumping out "Marie" like a fanfare for the convertible rolling into the party.

The driver, a plump Army captain, hopped out smartly, flushed with pride as if he was delivering General MacArthur into their midst. He swung open the door for his passenger. Evander Merrill stepped out, resplendent in white silk and blue ascot, silver hair gleaming under the glow of colored lanterns. He stood for a regal moment in his center stage, smiling faintly as hands clapped around him.

In the moment before Lelia and Gil ran to the Nash, they watched Merrill stop at the first table of upturned faces, take the hand of the nearest beaming matron, bend in a hint of a bow. Straightening, Merrill continued toward the head table where Martha Critten stood now, mouth pressed, glaring over the top of her glasses.

"He was supposed to arrive on the yacht," Lelia whispered.

"I can guess why he didn't. Hurry. I've got to be the one to stop them."

Together they raced through the barroom, out the building, across the road to where the Nash was parked.

JOHNS PASS
August, 1945

37

Neither spoke as the car clattered across the bridge to the beach side where Gil turned left, heading south toward Johns Pass. Beyond his set profile, Grouper Hole's party yard glowed across the bay, quickly giving way to dark mangrove shores and moonless night.

Eyes closed, face to the wind whipping in from the open windows, Lelia called up Francie's face, saw it startled, now angry, now incredulous with fright. The image faded. She watched the Nash's yellow lights pale against the road ahead. She was about to learn answers to so many questions that she might have known if she'd trusted both parts of her mind. *Francie, Francie, what's happening to you now? Who is Karl?*

Gil was a grim profile beside her, hands gripping the wheel, his quiet voice a crackling fuse. "If I've fouled up, if anything happened to her, to you – Lelia, you shouldn't have come."

"You were with her earlier? You left her to get in this trouble?" She knew it wasn't true even as she said it, the sound harsh, over the wind.

He flashed a tortured look before steering around a lone oncoming car. "That crazy kid. You seem to hold me responsible."

"I know Francie has had a lover all summer. She went to meet him tonight. I had reasons to believe it was you."

"What?" He groaned. "Lelia, I thought you knew what was going on with me. You seem to look into a person past the sham. I thought you knew the single passion that's kept me going these months – to make someone pay for what they did to Nancy."

She nodded. "I also knew Francie's vulnerability, her willingness. She was protecting someone."

"Me? Christ no. Not guilty on that score." He leaned over the steering wheel as if fueling the lumbering Nash with his own will. "I thought you understood even when I came across hard-ass."

She looked away to the dark gulf shore slipping past. Jealousy, denied or not, had blocked out what she might have known. "I believed your anger. But there was so much guilt with it. I had to wonder if the man you were looking for was yourself and you couldn't let yourself know." She watched his face tighten.

"I see. That crazy night on the beach, you floating in the surf. I went bananas a second, trying to undo the impossible. You're right, it was guilt driving me. I hold myself responsible for Nancy because we fought and she ran off into trouble. Then you had to wonder about Susie at the cabin. That poor kid kept running, didn't trust anyone by then. Ugly story. Tell you later." He kept braking for potholes, stomping the gas pedal to push the Nash on.

"What was Francie doing in Tingley's cabin? Who is Karl?" She knew and didn't know. *Fear blocks knowing.* Kali had said that.

"Your newspaper pal Tingley must have found out about Karl." Quickly, with irony, "Who is he? Karl and I do have something in common. The Navy. I was a Frogman, U.S. Navy, until six months ago. Came up too fast one time. Had to be put on medical hold. Karl – Dummy as you know him – is an AWOL German sailor. Swam in from a U-boat a year ago."

"Dummy? Not a deaf mute, but *German*?"

"A couple of others with him got caught. Old news now. Maybe you heard. This fellow managed to get to these beaches. Dug in awhile in that jungle patch around Hurricane House. Since then, he's been scrounging out an existence like any beach bum."

So Kali *had* known who he was. Outsiders recognize one another, she'd said. "You didn't tell anyone?"

"Why? I haven't been announcing who I am and what I'm about, either. Besides, when I made him talk, I found out he's no enemy of mine. More like a trapped, frightened kid."

So her sense about Dummy had been right. A haunted boy, happy only as he swam, agonized when he looked at Francie, and that time he'd run away on the beach, he must have been saying 'friend.' Poor Francie, feeling sorry for him, then loving him, always frightened to death of her mother finding out.

"I thought Francie was protecting you."

Just ahead a cluster of people straggled across the road toward the lighted Bath Club. Gil slowed, then leaned against the wheel, resuming speed.

"Those men – Cracker and Cajun – in your cabin that time. Are they connected with the yacht – or Martha Critten?" How many times had she ruled out that notion as illogical.

"Cracker is a hired creep. He made sure Susie didn't talk. No, you'd never see him on the yacht. You wouldn't have seen Cage because he's one of the Cajun crew members who keeps to himself. No shore scenes with Merrill. Jellybo is his kid. The grinning deckhand, short on brains."

"Does Evander Merrill know what is happening?"

"Not sure. I don't believe he's the power on that yacht. Just the dupe, with the money."

"Cracker and Cage went to Tingley's cabin –"

"To kill him or find out what he knew."

"And found Francie there with the boy – so they ran and she called. Francie wouldn't have left the bar willingly with either one of them."

"Here's Madeira. Look for Francie's car. Maybe Karl's hiding there."

The Peter Pan sign showed in the dark. Gil whipped into the diner's lot past the Packard. The big sedan was empty, its back door ajar. *They pulled him out,* she knew.

Just ahead, the palely lit Johns Pass Bridge arched over the pass between bay and gulf. Couched at its base, a low windowless building with a lighted sign, "Shanty Hogan's Bar."

Gil slowed. No sign of anyone on the street except for a pair of soldiers straggling out of the bar. And a lone man slumped at the shadowy curb, face buried in his hands.

"Gil, it's Tingley."

Gil switched off the motor. He jumped out and disappeared into the bar. On the sidewalk Lelia stooped down by the huddled figure.

"Tingley, it's me, Lelia. *Where is Francie?*" She shook his shoulders until the fuzzy head raised from his hands and looked up, a sad clown's face.

"Magnolia. I told you to stay 'way." The raspy voice was a whisper.

Gil burst from the bar. "She's gone. Left with someone." He scanned the empty street. "Get up, you sonofabitch! Goddamnit, you saw her in there, in trouble. Who did she leave with?" He kicked at Tingley's scuffed shoes in the gutter.

"Wait! Tingley look at me. Listen. You can get up and stand on your feet. You can think straight and tell us what you know. We've got to find Francie."

Gil grabbed the slumped man and pulled Tingley to his feet. "Who did she leave with, where did they go? Quick!"

"Jellybo. That weasel kid deckhand from the *Fox*. Promising to take her to the boyfriend, the little Kraut. I tried to stop him. Kid shoved me down."

"Go on," Gil demanded. "Which way did they go?"

"Headed toward the dock. Jellybo's arm 'round her like a lover, her little white heels dragging." He sagged against the Nash, hands covering the raspy curse.

Gil turned to run. She followed, down narrow streets deserted in yellow lamplight, past fisherman cottages, to the bayside docks. The *Silver Fox* stood out against the night, a single deck light shining. Together they reached the dock in time to see the yacht start moving.

Gil's fingers dug into her arm. "They've got Francie – they've got both of them. Moving north. Up the bay. Thank God, they're not going into the gulf."

"Then they're heading for the party. They have to be seen

before all those people. That's the plan."

"That's no ride to a party those two are getting."

"Would they dare?"

"Throw them overboard?" Gil's fingers loosened, but his voice smoldered. "Not on the way up the bay if they're smart. And Sloan's smart. The *Fox* has been in these waters all day. They'd have to dump them north of the party. Hurry!" He grabbed her hand and together they raced back to Shanty Hogan's. Tingley still leaned on the car, his back turned to the laughter of two sailors swaggering into the bar door.

"Get in," Lelia ordered Tingley.

Gil was already behind the wheel. "We don't have time to bother with that drunk!"

"Wait! He needs us. We need him." Lelia pushed Tingley toward the back seat, slammed his door and slid in beside Gil. With a grim nod, he spun the Nash around, heading north.

For silent minutes, the three strained forward, whipped by the wind and tormenting thoughts.

"Can we beat them there?" Lelia asked.

"By fifteen minutes if we're lucky."

She said aloud what they all knew. "We have to get them off that yacht." *Focus, focus the energy. There is power of will.* Kali's words. "How did Francie get into this? Do you know, J. T.?"

Tingley leaned forward from the dark back seat. "The bastards didn't want Francie. They had a different plan. But now they've got her, Magnolia."

You told me and I didn't believe. Fighting dismay, "Why didn't you tell someone who could have stopped it?"

"Who'd believe me?" Tingley moaned. "Everybody figures I'm a sore-ass about that bunch."

They swerved around a slow-moving car, the motion slamming Lelia against Gil's tense body. His steadying grasp on her arm stayed for a moment, an electric connection, before he gripped the wheel again with both hands.

"Okay," Gil muttered, "we have minutes to put this together. I know this much, the *Fox* meant to clear out of here, smelling clean, the boss still a hero – if that peacock Merrill is boss. They knew Brockway was going to deliver an invitation from the sheriff for some serious questioning." He glanced at Lelia. "We can thank the gadfly here for that. Reason why they hated your guts, Tingley. They felt you stirred up that suspicion."

"We're both on their kill list, friend," Tingley rasped.

"You worked for them, Gil," Lelia said.

"We watched each other. Sloan figured out who I was months ago and knew why I was around. I knew they'd try to set me up before they left for home port New Orleans. The *Fox* has been at Johns Pass all day, refueling, getting ready for the long haul. Okay, Sleuth, what else do you know?"

Tingley clung to the seat. "Busted up like I was, I couldn't get to Brockway until last night. He's no fool behind that long poker face. I told him what I knew of the plan."

"What's the plan?" Lelia asked. "We have to use their plan." She looked back. "I still don't see the *Fox*."

Tingley hung on to the back of the front seat, raspy voice fighting the wind. "What Cracker planned called for a pigeon, a dead girl to leave you with the rap for all three – doing in the first one, sorry fellow, your girlfriend, then Susie to shut her up."

"I know what they did to Susie – before they shut her up." Gil bit out the words. "Had her on the yacht."

"Cracker was to pull this tonight when the crew and Evander Merrill were front and center of the big shindig at Critten's place. They'd hired their pigeon – one of the old pros who work for Martha. They probably promised her some quick business with soldier boys if she'd wait on the dark bank below Clearwater pass. Aaw, Miss Magnolia, hate to say this to your pearly ears."

"Go on, J. T." Lelia studied the dark bay as they raced past. Still no lights behind them.

"This gal was going to be surprised by Cracker rather than any customers. Don't know how they were gonna get you there, Gil."

"They'd worked that out too," Gil muttered. "Some of my spray hood has been ripped from the *Strike*. Nice bit of evidence to leave at the scene. But Cracker tipped his hand when he tried to make me think one of Susie's friends was ready to talk about Nancy. He expected me to follow him tonight and walk into his trap."

"You didn't," Tingley said.

"Tempted to do some trapping myself. But big-eyed Cheta stomped up to the cabin, inviting me to a party. Urgent message, no explanation from Lelia here. See any yacht lights yet?"

"You would have ended up with a gaff in your back," Tingley said. "Cracker was going to be the hero who caught you. Now they don't need any volunteer pigeon. Martha's gal will sit up there in the bushes alone and find her way home innocent, but alive."

"Because they caught Francie in your cabin," Lelia said.

"And she becomes the pigeon."

"And that little Kraut becomes the fall-guy instead of you," Tingley rasped. "Only they can't leave until they get you, too, pal."

The roadside pines to their right gave way to an open view of the dark bay. Far behind them, a spot of light had to be the yacht.

"They'll have to dock at the party," Lelia said against the rushing air. "That's the purpose, to be seen. Or they can't –" Can't leave anyone dead she meant. She pulled in a ragged breath and mentally gave it to the face she was seeing – Francie's china blue eyes fixed with fear.

"If they come into the dock, they've already gotten rid of them," Gil said. "If they anchor in the bay, it means those kids are still on board."

"We'll get there before they do." She thought, *Stay focused. There is a place beyond fear.* Kali's words. "We'll get Brockway and go aboard and find them."

"No. They could be bound and gagged and stuffed anywhere, dead or alive. We'd look like fools and Merrill could do an indignant act, and they'd sail out of there clean and still do the job in the gulf."

Tingley pulled his head back from the open window. "We just passed a little 14-footer along the shore. Cracker, sure as hell, waiting to follow. He'll come in behind, ready to take them off. Party crowd won't see a thing. Cracker will take them up the bay, drop them off up there on the flats like they planned for the girl. While the party goes on, Lordy,

Now they could see Grouper Hole's lighted sand lot, the swing beat echoed across the channel. As the Nash reached the bridge, the *Silver Fox* was behind but moving toward them. The three of them fell silent as the Nash bumped across the bridge.

Lelia closed her eyes an instant to draw in a deep breath. *Dear God, nothing must happen to Francie. Or that boy. How do we stop it?* The exhaled breath left an exquisite urgency that was also energy. Was this Kali's 'magic' she'd been afraid of – or was this praying? It wasn't helpless pleading. It was a call for help released into some infinite listening space, source of all power.

Below, the party yard made a lively patch of orange light in the dark night. She saw it with the calm of a runner poised to spring. "We'll know what to do when we see what they're doing," and felt Gil's quick grasp on her arm in response.

He stopped the car at Grouper Hole's back door. With Tingley stumbling behind, they ran through the kitchen and dark barroom toward the lighted yard, where blatantly innocent music and voices waited for the appearance of the *Silver Fox.*

BAYFRONT
August, 1945

38

In the porch doorway, Lelia stopped, Gil's grip pulsating on her arm, as they scanned the party scene. At their feet on the doorstep, Cap'n yawned, "Where you been?" Chuck slept, head in his folded arms on the littered pool table. "Up A Lazy River" wafted over the unaware crowd.

Without speaking, they watched for the gleam of light to show on the dark bay. With grim patience, they waited until the *Silver Fox* came closer to know what it planned to do.

Lelia scanned the party yard, this stage set for Evander Merrill. She saw it with the clarity of slow motion. The crowd at the tables pushing back empty plates, talking, but restless. The four occupants of the bunting-draped table stood out in sharp relief against the dark, still empty bay docks.

Only the Army captain beside Evander Merrill was enjoying himself. Martha Critten looked windblown and drunk, twisting around again for some sight of the yacht. A morose Bubba got up and stalked away. The blonde photographer from the *Times* stood in front of Evander Merrill, causing him to look up with a false, twitching smile. Again, Merrill glanced over his tailored white shoulder to the dark bay. He looked agitated.

Gil let go of her arm. "It's coming. All lights on." They stood watching, breathing with the same rhythm.

Merrill turned back to the blonde woman with his movie star smile. He waved a languid hand toward the approaching yacht. She nodded and huffed back to the table of chattering

Garden Club women.

Francie is hidden on that boat! Lelia watched, blinking away tears.

The *Silver Fox* sounded its horn. Deck lights flashed off and on again. The crowd cheered.

Gil thought out loud, close to her ear, "All the deck lights are on and they're dropping anchor out there. The grand appearance. But they're launching the *Little Fox.* That means Sloan will come in to report a change in plans. They may want to get the hell out and dump their baggage in the gulf."

"How much time do we have?"

"Until Sloan gets Evander Merrill back out to that yacht."

Tingley bounded up, breathing hard. "I looked from the bridge. It's black as tar out there. And I swear that's Cracker's boat putt-putting along the shore's other side. Must be waiting until those stern deck lights go off."

"We can use the dark, too," Lelia murmured.

Gil squeezed her arm. In a breath he told his plan to get the *Strike* in position under the bridge. When the yacht went dark, he'd be out there.

"Take Brockway."

"No time. Just keep Sloan and Merrill from going back to the yacht. I don't want to have to handle Sloan, too." And he was gone.

With Tingley, she watched the *Little Fox* chug toward the dock, the first mate's hulking figure at the controls.

"Sonofabitch," Tingley rasped.

"I'm going after Brockway." Lelia left Tingley on the front porch with the sleeping Chuck. She ran past Cap'n on the steps and began weaving through the crowd. A soldier's hands tried to pull her onto the dance floor. She ignored Martha Critten who stood gesturing from the head table. Then Brockway was there, nodding comprehension, following her back to the dark front porch. Chuck still slept but Cap'n and Skipper watched, gap-mouthed, as Lelia quickly told Brockway what was going on.

"Believe me. They're both on that yacht now. Gil intends to stop Cracker as he takes them off. He shouldn't be out there alone."

"Stubborn fool, Gil MacLean." Brockway had listened, his brown eyes direct as bullets. "Okay. Two things for you to do, Miss Lelia. Call the sheriff's office. Tell him Brockway says, 'Here, not there.' They'll know. And keep Sloan and Merrill on shore however you can." He turned and was gone faster than she'd believed his lanky stride could manage.

Tingley said, "Lemme call, Magnolia. You go stir up diversionary action." He headed for the bar phone.

Keep them here, keep them occupied. That's what she had to do. She shook Chuck awake.

"Martha wants you to bring out more liquor from the bar. Stack a tray and get it out here. Hurry." To Chuck's grumbled questions, she said, "Ours is not to reason but to do. Just get down there and be charming to Evander Merrill, Chuck. Now!"

"What-all's going on?" Cap'n wanted to know. "Look at that old sonofabitch Sloan tying up that 16-footer when he coulda put the *Fox* right at the dock, high tide like it is."

"Where's the *Sea Bitch*?" she demanded of Cap'n.

"Bait house side of the bridge."

"You've wanted to get close to the yacht – now's the time! Take the *Sea Bitch* up close, in their flood lights. Shout. Ask them why they aren't coming in!"

Back from the phone, Tingley rasped, "That's good, Magnolia."

Skipper wagged his head. "I dunno. That meathead Sloan –"

"Listen – I need your help. Explanations later. Get out there and hold the attention of the yacht crew. Do anything."

"You two handle the boat," Tingley said. "I'll do the acting."

"Tingley, could you? Yes."

"Magnolia, you'd never find anybody who could do it better. I'm gonna help here if it's the last thing I do." The old grin flashed. "Let's go give the *Fox* some trouble, fellas. You ain't never going to have so much fun."

The three of them struck out through the barroom. Lelia

went back into the yard. *What to do*? Four Barber Shoppers clustered behind the movie star, clearing their throats, ready to sing as Sloan strode up from the dock, bulky chest molded by the his tee-shirt, head down, resolute. He stopped behind Merrill's chair to glower at the Barber Shoppers.

That was it. *Confusion*. She needed to create more. On her way to the head table, she paused at the Garden Clubbers' table. "Now's the time to get those pictures."

Martha Critten rose, unsteady, before dropping back heavily in the chair, a perspiring woman in wilted flowered chiffon, the moist face livid. "Where the devil have you been? Nobody follows orders!" She turned to Sloan behind her. "And you! Getting here late!"

Sloan stiffened. His cold gaze cut past Martha to Lelia with his knife-sharp command, "Get rid of these dames. Get them away from this table."

Chorusing delight, four women with Brownie cameras surged toward the head table. The Barber Shoppers, clustered behind Evander Merrill, began to sing. Lelia called to the woman. "You next. Of course, Mr. Merrill wants you to get your pictures!"

Sloan's thick fingers dug into her shoulder. She felt their fury. *You're the one who gives orders. Death orders*, she knew. *I have power, too; I am not helpless*. Something Kali said about confidence becoming power. She used it now, looking into his slate gray eyes.

The eyes narrowed. Sloan turned and stalked toward the dock. Leaving? No, signaling the yacht. Deck lights on the stern, angled away from the crowd, went out. The bow stayed lit, but the far side of the *Silver Fox* was as dark now as the black bay waters below.

She wanted to scream out what she knew to this crowd. No. Gil and Brockway would need the dark, need the time. The longer Sloan and Merrill stayed on shore, the more time they had.

Chuck was elbowing his uncertain path to the table. Watching him, Martha Critten half rose, screeching, "Nobody follows orders around here!"

Grim-faced, Chuck filled Captain Sweeling's extended glass but slammed down the other bottles and stumbled away, leaving the table in disarray. But Sloan had moved in behind Merrill. She couldn't stop him. His crew-cut head bent close to the silver pompadour. A quick message, but apparently enough. Merrill's dark brows arched, nostrils flared. He rose to his feet and announced, "We shall be leaving now."

Martha sputtered with angry surprise. Sweeling protested. Glancing down, king to courtier, Merrill murmured, "I'm afraid so, Captain. I believe we have partied enough."

"Not yet!" Lelia grasped Merrill's tanned, jeweled hand and held it. "Surely, you can't leave now – the picture – for the paper – with the yacht in the background!" Wheeling around, she saw the clustered Garden Club women, poised to advance with Lonnie and her bulky camera. She signaled them to move in.

"Let 'em get their damn pictures," Martha Critten hissed to Merrill. "*Remember* – you wanted your handsome kisser and the boat in the newspaper."

Sloan's hand clamped on the white shoulder. "We leave now."

But Merrill was trapped. Ten Garden Clubbers had surged forward to replace the Barber Shoppers. With flickering smiles of apology, they shoved aside the glowering fellow from the crew. In front of the table, Lonnie adjusted her camera, stooping, standing, calling out directions, each flash lighting a frozen-faced Merrill flanked by beaming women. The Barber Shoppers stood aside, waiting to do their second number from an old Evander Merrill movie.

Lelia looked beyond them to the half-darkened yacht. *Gil, be all right! Find Francie. Get out there. I'm trying to give you time.* Behind closed eyes, she saw his face and shuddered, saw him thrashing out there in the dark channel. She remembered dreams of Francie's wet face.

Voices echoed from the water. Now whoops and shouted curses. The music thumped on but the crowd stilled, faces turned toward the yacht.

The *Sea Bitch* rocked in the beam of a spotlight. Lelia let go of Merrill's icy hand and stared with the others toward the bay. From the upper deck of the *Silver Fox*, two crew members shouted down to the small boat. Over the music beat, a woman's voice squealed, "Somebody's hanging on the yacht!"

It was Tingley, midway on the wooden ladder, his foot caught. Twisting now, hanging there. To the crowd's *Ahh's,* Tingley plunged head first, arms flailing, into the lapping water.

The *Sea Bitch* churned closer, Skipper on his belly, long arm reaching out. Tingley's head bobbed up. He splashed toward the skiff, grasped for Skipper's hand. The two struggled, rocking the small boat until Tingley fell inside. From the party yard, cheers.

Watching, Lelia prayed, *Breathe, J. T. You must breathe.*

On the deck of the bow, the two figures kept cursing at the three men in the small boat. The thin one must be the captain. The other, she knew, was Jellybo. She didn't see Cage. Was he on the stern, in the dark, delivering Francie and Karl into Cracker's boat? *Gil, Brockway, where are you now?*

From the upper deck, a third figure turned a spotlight on the *Sea Bitch*. A chill told her yes, the slightly built man was Cage. His light played on the water, catching in its beam another motor boat. The *Strike*. Brockway, alone in Gil's boat, calling up to the crewmen. Their voices echoed faintly across the water to the party shore.

Dismay held her rooted, pulse roaring. The *Sea Bitch* chugged toward the dock, Skipper at the controls, Cap'n and Tingley waving their arms, singing, shouting. They were clowns putt-putting into the center ring.

The *Strike* whipped past them. Brockway threw a line onto the piling and strode toward the party yard before the rocking *Sea Bitch* reached the dock. People stood now, with half smiles, curious.

She wanted to scream at the deputy's casual stride. She made herself be still.

Waving lazily to the crowd, Brockway ambled to the bunting-draped table. He drawled into their blank faces, "Guess those fellows wanted to see that Chris-Craft up close for a long time, and maybe they had too much to drink tonight. I had to go after them." He stayed there smiling and nodding at Merrill as Martha shrieked toward the disembarking trio at the dock, "You blundering fools! You drunken bums, you stupid wharf rats!"

The crowd stood, entertained, watching the arrival. Skipper and Cap'n hung back on the dock, but Tingley limped toward them, a panting, dripping clown. To the crowd, he was a falling-down drunk, barking a raspy greeting, "J. T. Tingley, reportin' to the party. Didja think I'd miss it?"

Drunk with hard, determined exuberance, Lelia knew. Almost jubilant now, here center stage of his big story that hadn't gone the way any of them had known. She wanted to tell him, *now get away from Sloan, quick.*

The first mate moved toward Tingley, huge fists clenched at his side. She stepped in front of Sloan, surprising him, saying loud enough for the crowd's benefit, "They only wanted to see the yacht – like everyone here!" A few cheers rose.

She turned from his cold fury to Merrill's pale stare. She made her voice as cajoling as a fan's. "I know you don't want them thrown out, in front of all your guests!"

But Tingley had everyone's attention. Leaning against the bunting-draped table, his raspy shout reached out. The music had stopped now. "You gotta be pro-per-ly introduced to the hosts of this here shindig. This handsome movie fella in back of me now, who's been lookin' after lonely soldier boys the whole damn war? The man deserves full credit for *ever-thing* he's been doing. And Lordee, here's our Grouper Hole hostess who looks after 'em her own way."

He half-turned to Martha with a sloppy bow. "*Madam!*" He reeled back again, grin in place for his audience. "Now this big fellow Sloan comin' my way lookin' so unfriendly – you think he's just a first mate? He's a real clever bastard –"

The crowd saw Sloan stalk toward their clown. They gasped with the swinging blow, expecting the fall, only Tingley's knees buckled first. They watched the clown take the bunting with him, crumple to a wet heap of checkered pants and heaving chest.

Lelia reached Tingley the same moment as Brockway. The deputy looked up to drawl orders to the four gawking Barber Shoppers, "Get him inside the bar. Keep everybody else out except for the short, bald-headed fellow coming this way. He's a doc."

Numb, Lelia moved back as the men hoisted Tingley's sodden weight.

She wanted to follow, but Brockway was still there, spreading his hands sociably on the head table, long face in a benign smile, talking into Merrill's ashen face. "Best thing to do right now, to keep folks from leaving full of talk, is to stay right here and let them simmer down until I can haul this fellow off, out of your way. It'd help if you went on with your picture-taking, Mister Merrill."

Brockway straightened up, flashed her a direct look, and headed for the barroom. The look was not calm, and it promised her nothing. Brockway had been playing his own charade to keep Merrill and Sloan from returning to the yacht. To give Gil time. Gil, out there alone.

The crowd sank back in their chairs. Chatter resumed, muted. Sloan's hand closed over her arm. The eyes flashed their anger, like a snake's tongue. "You're an interfering bitch. Concerned for the stupid crowd? Perhaps it will please them if you come with us. If they notice." His clench tightened.

"It won't work, Sloan."

He blinked, stunned for an instant. She sent the words deep into his eyes, *"Francie will not be the one to drown, Sloan. You will. I know. I see it happening."*

His eyes widened before they narrowed. His grip left her arm. He backed away. "Witch!"

She felt a rush of pleasure. Had her loathing been so powerful? As quickly, the confidence ebbed.

Sloan turned to Merrill now, bit out some message, and bolted away. He was leaving, alone. At the end of the dock, Sloan bellowed with rage.

Again, the party voices hushed and turned to watch. The *Little Fox* bobbed free, away from the pilings. Skipper and Cap'n must have done that. Laughter from the crowd. Sloan stood a moment, poised, before he plunged and swam toward the small craft.

Now that the hulking man had left his boss' side, women drifted back to the host table, ignoring Grouper Hole's drunk owner and the puzzled Army captain. Surrounded again, Merrill sank back in his chair.

She had to get inside to Tingley and Brockway. But for an instant, Lelia watched what was happening here. She watched this man who used to be Tony in New Orleans, playing now the role he'd learned, that of Evander Merrill, continental lover. For a moment she watched the man perform his practiced role with a sad grace, his stage a makeshift table on a wind-blown waterfront for a bemused audience and half a dozen women pushing close. She watched, with a crazy sense of sympathy, as he made the eloquent brows rise, the resonant tones suggest intimacy held in check only by wistful courtliness, a hint of noble weariness, as one who has had, regrettably, so much adoration he must, reluctantly, decline what is being offered.

It worked. The women backed away, murmuring, apologetic but satisfied.

The arch poise faded to stark dismay as Merrill turned and watched Sloan scramble into the small *Fox* and roar toward the yacht. *He's abandoned.* At stake now, dignity and a graceful departure. Trim shoulders erect, Merrill stood. He directed a dull smile to Sweeling. The beaming officer rose with military bearing. The yard silent now, people stood, looking dismissed, gawking at the table where Martha poured herself another drink and Merrill stood alone and aloof, waiting for Sweeling and the car to take him to town.

A glance toward the yacht told her nothing. It waited there still half dark as Sloan churned toward it. She ran now to find out from Tingley and Brockway what was happening.

BAYFRONT
August night, 1945

39

The quartet of solemn-faced Barber Shoppers emerged from Grouper Hole's front screen porch. Lelia ran past them into the still, hot barroom. In the dim yellow light, she saw that Tingley lay on top of the bar like a body on a bier. The movements of the four men around him were halting, methodical, as though hurry didn't matter. The bald-headed doctor put down the bar phone. A sober Chuck lifted the fuzzy balding head as Conch slipped a folded towel underneath.

Brockway turned, nodded for her to move in closer, but his long face told her nothing.

She bent close. The grin lines etched deep were slack now. "J. T., it's Lelia." She spread both hands on the bare freckled chest, allowed a connection, and imagined her own breath going into his struggling lungs. The man had been sick and she'd sent him out there. Then that fall into the bay. Under her hands, his chest began moving, a tortured rise and fall. The doctor sucked in his bottom lip, nodded for Conch to cover the bare chest with another towel.

"J. T., you did it." His fingers responded, curling under her hand. "Tingley, hear me. You tricked them."

His lips moved. "Magnolia." His eyes tightened.

She glanced up at the others, aware of everything at once, the struggling chest, the silent men, the muffled outside sounds, Cap'n and Skipper waiting in the shadows, Cheta by the kitchen door, crooning something about black clouds always hanging over that noisy man's head. She knew what pulsed behind Tingley's mumbling now. Anguish over a lifetime of failed dreams.

In that moment, she knew this funny little man better than she'd ever known any of the Calhouns back in Bethel, knew that people don't just blunder into your life. They must be part of some plan never seen in its entirety, not while you live it. Just as she'd always known Gil MacLean without knowing his name, even though all logic asked why. *Gil – what's happening to you out there?*

But Tingley's hand clung to hers. A flash of a dream came back. Gil holding Francie, streaming with seaweed. All three of them in that dream. She looked at Brockway for answers. He had turned to murmur into the bar phone.

"Magnolia?" The raspy voice whisper was strong enough for all of them to hear. "We gotta talk . . ."

"Right here." She leaned closer.

The brown eyes opened. "Gil – how'd he do? What's happening?" The old rasp.

"He's out there," Brockway said. "You gave him some time."

Out there, in the dark, in the bay. She wanted to run, to find him, but Tingley's fingers tightened.

"Magnolia." Tears trickled from the corners of his clenched eyes. "Big story, like I promised. Too much for this old boy to handle. Drug my feet, 'fraid to fail. Always 'fraid to fail, know that, Magnolia? Every time, I got a good hand to play, I'd remember what my old man told me. Weak chin and no guts. I'd fold and pull out –"

His bloodshot brown eyes opened, squinted at the dark ceiling. "This time I wasn't gonna be a goddamned, bullshitting loser."

Chuck leaned in. "You've got guts, J. T., take it from a practiced loser. You have enough goddamn tenacity for both of us."

"Ernie Pyle would be proud," Lelia said. "You were after the truth, not just a Tingley by-line."

"Yeah. Right. Let somebody else write the damn story. I'm too tired."

They watched the frown lines on his forehead ease, the eye lids tense.

She leaned closer. "Tingley?"

The grin lined deepened. But not for them. He was seeing something, she knew, inside his head.

"Going up some kinda hill, Magnolia." The mouth curved. "No turning back now . . ."

For a moment, she followed him into that void of stillness, followed behind his rolling swagger until the darkness became strange and he was turning, waving her back. He moved on into it toward some pinpoint of light turning brighter. Then she was back, opening her eyes to this dim, hot barroom, flanked by these silent, hard-breathing men.

Tingley's eyelids quivered once more before they stopped.

The doctor nodded, as if to some inevitability.

At the kitchen door, Cheta moaned, "His spirit's leavin' now, floatin' right off."

From the shadows, Cap'n and Skipper shuffled closer, stopping at the far end of the bar. Chuck moved down to where they were, poured three shot glasses, pushed them forward, downed one, and walked back to help Brockway spread his brown jacket over the body, over Tingley's still face.

Cap'n let out a hoarse sigh. "That's a way I wanna go. On the dock, or in this here old bar, surrounded by my admirin' friends."

Outside, more doors slammed, motors hummed, and voices faded as Bubba burst in, shouting, "Mama's maddern' hell. He's going back to town and the *Fox* is pulling out –" Bubba stopped, mouth open, staring at Tingley's body on the bar.

"You have a death here," Brockway said quietly. "I order you to stay with the body, you and Chuck, until the ambulance arrives. Try to lock the doors. Keep everybody out."

Brockway touched Lelia's arm, breaking her trance. "Bait house."

She followed. They ran through the kitchen, into the clogged roadway, blocked a moment by the convertible as it swerved out of the party yard. Evander Merrill sat inside, chin raised, looking straight ahead. An imperial honk and the car moved on, disappearing down the brick road. With Brockway loping behind, Lelia ran again, past the parked Nash, down the weedy slope toward the dark bait house docks.

Above them more departing cars rumbled across the bridge. She ran the length of the bait house docks. Black waters lapped at the pilings. Brockway's long legs bounded along the dock behind her.

"What happened? Where are they?" she cried as he reached her, panting.

He squatted down to look through the pilings, and she did the same. She saw the *Silver Fox* moving out but still in the channel, a ghostly shape now, a single spotlight from the stern moving across the water. The yacht went dark.

"Are they looking for them? Why aren't we out there in the *Strike*, looking for them?"

He touched her arm. "You've done real good, Miss Lelia. Stay calm a little longer. That spotlight didn't find them. If it worked out like I think Gil had to do, they could be swimming in here – any time now. If it worked."

"Swimming?" That earlier image of Gil thrashing water, yes. Wind-whipped small waves slapped against the heavy pilings.

Brockway's drawl was a monotone, quickened now. "We followed the *Sea Bitch* out. Cap'n headed for the lighted water in front of the *Fox* to keep the crew's attention. Gil angled to the dark side. They must have heard our motor. They started swinging that spotlight around. Before the spot caught us, Gil went over the side and started swimming."

Yes, he'd have to do that. She waited, refusing panic, thinking *Gil, I love you. Did you ever know? I was careful that you wouldn't know.*

"I had to make them think it was just me out there, come to run the fellows in. Our commotion should have given Gil time to swim to the stern and meet up with Cracker and whatever was happening there. Gil could handle the old boy if he didn't have a couple others from the crew to deal with."

Francie, Francie, what is happening to you? A car rumbled over the bridge. Laughing voices in the night. *They don't know, don't know*, she thought. Panic rose and with it angry helplessness. How could praying, call it focused will or whatever, have any power over a windblown current in the dark bay? She forced out her confusion with the next breath. Maybe it didn't have to be against those elements but with them? *Gil, let this tide and wind help get you here, all three of you . . .* Panic again. How could Francie ever cope out there?

Brockway rocked on his heels, staring into the black bay. The wind had picked up lashing the pilings. "I've got a boat coming from Clearwater, but all we can do now is wait. We couldn't have gone before, Miss Lelia. That poor sucker Tingley was dying. I couldn't send some of those party fellows out in the *Strike*. It would have blown Gil's chances. That yacht would have hightailed it out, gotten rid of the girl and anybody else in the gulf."

Gil, Francie, Karl, where are you now?

Brockway's drawl was brusque with uncertain hope. "Gil MacLean is a Navy frogman, you know. Means he can swim like a fish."

"Listen!" The sound of heavy thrashing came from beyond the bridge pilings. She could see arms flashing, moving toward them. Two heads, close together. *Or three?*

With soaring joy, she sent them love as strength. The thrashers were under the bridge now, voices audible as they worked from the darker shadows toward the dock. Gleaming faces emerged. Gil and Dummy, no – Karl, with Francie's shocked white face between them. Hands groped up to grasp the bait house dock.

On their knees, Lelia and Brockway grabbed at Francie's white arms and pulled the girl up on the dock. Water streamed from what was once white dotted swiss. Francie slumped in Brockway's arms. Karl rolled himself onto the dock. He lay there gasping, "*Franzie, Franzie.*"

Gil's white-knuckled hands closed on the edge of the dock. She saw his face, looking up now, eyes glittering, exulting. He swung a leg on the dock and pulled himself onto the planking.

Whimpering, Francie turned from Brockway's arms to fall into Lelia's. Gil enveloped them both. They stood together, the three of them wet with stinking bay water, hearts pounding against each other's body. *I dreamed this*, Lelia knew.

Trembling, Francie backed out of their embrace, eyes wild, red hair streaming. "They swam all the way, with me in between them." At Karl's voice, she fell to her knees in his arms and the two rocked together.

"What happened out there?" Brockway asked.

"It can wait," Gil said. "Francie must be looked after. And remember your bargain. Get Karl into custody. No fuss. Otherwise, you'll have a lynch scene everybody will regret later."

Breathing hard, Gil watched the small gleam of light moving south, toward Johns Pass. "Bastard murdering crew is getting away, headed for New Orleans once they get into the Gulf."

"Without Evander Merrill," Lelia said and watched him swing around, surprised.

Francie fell back into her arms, sobbing, as Karl turned to Brockway. "I go mit you now." Trailing water, the young German followed Brockway's lanky figure down the dock and up the slope to the road.

Lelia turned to Gil. "She can't go back to the Inn, I'll take her to the house, to Kali."

"I'll go with you." He swept Francie up against his wet chest and together they climbed the slope.

The road was deserted now, only a van rumbling away with Tingley's body. Lelia shivered against the wet, feverish girl she held in her arms as Gil stomped the Nash into action.

They lurched across the bridge. Francie choking out fragments of the past two hours. ". . . pushed in this tiny space like *baggage* by that crazy boy Jellybo and the mean one Cage" – sobbing, shaking – "pushed us down into some little old boat in the dark with a horrible man waiting. Then this splashing and the boat rocking and Gil was there. Oh, Lelia, Gil was there! But then we were all in the water, and choking in black water, but Karl pulled me up and —" She stopped with a fixed stare. "All this happened because they found out about me and Karl."

They reached the beach side, the yellow headlights flashing on the Inn. Francie screamed, "No, I can't go there! Mother will find out, she'll know! I should have drowned back there. I wish I had."

"You're safe Francie, safe. Gil — your hands." She saw his bloody fingers gripping the wheel.

"Barnacles. Bridge pilings."

"Cracker?" She rocked Francie in her arms as they reached the tangled front driveway.

"We were four in that 14-footer for a few minutes, then no Cracker, then no boat." He threw her a quick look. "Later."

"They'll find me," Francie whispered, on the edge of hysteria. "They want to tell my mother."

Gil ran the car close to the house, got out, swept Francie out as Lelia ran ahead up the stairs, leading the way to her room. As Gil carried Francie in, babbling against his chest, Lelia ran into Kali's room.

"My friend, Francie," Lelia said. "Help her, Kali."

GULF NIGHT
August, 1945

40

Midnight. Still in the damp peach dress, Lelia paced between dark windows and the bed. Under the faint bedside light, Francie slept, wet red curls against the pillow, face flushed like a child's whose fever had broken. Not fever but hysteria. Kali's voice had been barely perceptible, the touch light, but in time the wildness in Francie's eyes eased, the sobs subsided.

When finally the girl slept, Kali had turned from the bed and whispered, "The memory will be nullified. It had to be so. This night was crystallizing into guilt and fear of her mother's wrath. I leave her with you now."

Lelia paced back to open windows. A restless surf rolled below. *Francie may not remember. But I will because it's not over, not for me, not for Gil.* Gil had stalked Nancy's killers too long to give up now. Where had he gone?

The yacht crew was out there in the gulf somewhere. Evander Merrill was abandoned to leave the best way he could. She could still see his proud profile inside Captain Sweeling's car driving out of the party yard. Yes, the vain little man was an excellent actor after all. But a murderer? No answers.

All through this wild night she had remembered what she'd heard from Kali, to keep the body calm, mind focused, open to knowing what to do. Now, confusion roared in her pulse, wild as the thudding waves below.

Gil, did you go back to Grouper Hole? With the wind picking up, the party yard must be a chaos of tables and torn lanterns, the people gone home, knowing nothing of what happened except that the party suddenly fell apart and maybe that drunk fellow died. *Poor Tingley*! She thought of his body, jostling toward the morgue under Brockway's brown coat. Did his face look as she'd seen it months ago in that flash Knowing – brown eyes staring, clown grin frozen? *Tingley, you didn't get to write your big story, but you were a part of it.* That business with the boat and coming ashore pretending to be drunk, holding Merrill there, cost you, Tingley. But it gave us time.

And why was Martha Critten involved? What did that browsy woman have in common with the fastidious little actor? Even if they had known one another long ago in New Orleans when she was Poppy and Merrill was young Tony getting a break in movies.

By morning when she woke up sober, Martha Critten would be planning her own vengeance on all of them, Gil, herself, and Cap'n and Skipper. But tomorrow, who would believe what happened tonight? If Francie did remember being trapped on that boat or pulled through the dark water by Gil and Karl, Francie would have to live with it rather than let her mother know she'd had a lover all summer. In beach darkness and in that sad little cabin in Johns Pass.

And Karl – eventually, a story in the paper would say a young German, escaped to this beach a year ago, had managed to live by pretending to be a deaf-mute beachcomber. A curious footnote to the end-of-war stories. That's all. No connection with the item that would come after they found Cracker's body along the bay shore. Lelia stopped cold, thinking how it might have been Gil's body. But it wasn't. Be thankful for that.

We did so well together tonight, didn't we, Gil? But not good enough. We stopped them yet they're getting away. You didn't get your satisfaction, did you? And hate leaves no place for love. Distrust shouldn't either, yet all this time, Gil . . .

On the bed, Francie still slept like the exhausted child. Her own pulse soared. She ran out of the room and down the stairs. On the dark beach, she could scream into the roaring gulf.

Scudding clouds gave the sands a moment of hazy light. Then darkness again. She ran along the surf's edge, the peach skirt clinging, salt spray stinging. A scream stayed caught in her body, unable to release itself. She wanted to comfort Gil. She wanted to be comforted. She imagined him walking toward her now along the curving beach. But clouds raced, the dark shadows melted, and she was still alone with phosphorus-edged waves that reached and called her in.

The clinging wet dress came off in a single pull. She waded into an oncoming wave. It crested against her and receded, leaving her breasts gleaming. The gulf was a warm swirling womb, its rhythm building toward some kind of birth. She had only to rock with its ebb and flow, be a sea-born creature, almost free, even as her toes still clutched soft sands.

This sea-self looked back at the dark shape of jungle hiding the house. On the shadowed shore, a man's silhouette now. Gil? Or a wish momentarily visible? The man ripped off the shirt and white pants and kicked away shoes. Another wave came, rocking her. When she opened her eyes again, shifting light shaped the man, this beautiful shore animal, moving toward this sea creature of herself.

Another wave rose, sweeping over, falling around her. His head surfaced, foam sighing around the two of them. He was real. Close now. The heat of his body radiated to hers. The half-light haloed his head and shoulders, shaped the plane of his face and glinted from his eyes. His hands slid around her waist, and the rhythm of the sea moved her against him. Together they rocked in the waist-high water, baptized by waves.

"*Lelia, Lelia, Lelia . . .*" His moan a supplication, his breath hot against her wet face and streaming hair. No need for words. The light in his eyes answered every question in her whole being.

Her hands moved over the hard mold of his chest, his shoulders. His arms slid around her, his hands cupping her hips. She curled around him as the current rocked them.

His head bent, seeking, and she lifted hard trembling

lips that softened and opened under his. When she pulled away, legs anchored around his waist, his hands bracing, it was to lean back, arms wide, to look up into infinite night sky.

He pulled her back, mouth against her ear, "Lelia, for so long, oh, God, I've watched you, I've wanted you but I couldn't let myself love again, not until –"

She curled around him, cradling his head against her breasts, her sea-self nourishing this other creature whose pounding chest might have been her own.

For curious moments, she rocked against him, watching the heat bloom and expand in her body . . . spreading along the same channels at that other, that private happening, the silver fire that had wakened her on certain lonely dawns . . . or like the red glow once feared and blocked for all those hidden reasons . . . Now it rose, unhurried, spreading into every nerve fiber, the core of her body grasping to be filled.

For an instant, she pulled back to cup his face and search his eyes. His arms guided them a step deeper out of the breaking waves into the quieter swells. Again he pulled her to him. Braced, she arched back, giving herself to the water, and to him, not hurrying now, neither hurrying, because there was no such thing as time.

The red glow spread, beyond thought, beyond choice; in warm, lapping waters, they rocked, bodies melded. The waves kept coming. His moan was a gift and a beginning of her own.

From some other space, she heard the faint, high wail like the cry of a wild bird, winging above the gulf's soft roar. Only when it rose and faded did she realize the sound had burst free from her open throat, releasing into the night.

By morning, storm clouds darkened the beach and turned the choppy waves metallic. In Lelia's room, Francie sat slumped on the side of the bed, in a borrowed petticoat, making fitful sighs, deciding if she should borrow the blue dress or the gingham.

Lelia turned from the window. "You're only going to the Inn and it's about to pour." *Francie, Francie, don't you remember anything about last night? I remember every-*

thing. She turned back to the window. This morning the gulf was angry. Last night the waves had been warm and wild. At the memory, some of the aching pleasure suffused her again.

"I know," Francie was saying. "I can't wake up and think. Awful, awful dreams. And I've got to get back to the Inn and wash my hair before Mother gets in this afternoon." She looked around at the gray morning as if it held some answers. "Lelia, I feel so *strange* and *sad*, you know? You saw Karl last night, didn't you? So you know."

"I know about Karl." She watched Francie pull on the blue dress. Her face emerged still puzzled.

"You and Gil brought me here because I was crying so hard. I must have done something stupid and crazy last night to be on that dock. I was trying to hide Karl, wasn't I? It gets mixed with the awful dreams. Did you give me a pill or something? I must have slept like the dead. What will happen to Karl, Lelia?"

"He'll have to be held a while, but he'll be safe. The war's over. Do you remember him going with Brockway?"

"They walked away up that slope. He didn't look back." Francie flung herself back on the bed. "I'm so tired! And Mother's coming. She'll be taking me right back to town, the train's tomorrow. So I've got to go." She struggled up. "I'm not going to say good-by."

"Are you all right, Francie? Truly?"

"I don't know, I guess. You haven't scolded me. Did I spoil your party? You look so, well, kinda tragic this morning but beautiful. You are, you know." At the door, she looked like a waif wiggling bare toes under the long dress.

"I'll never forget you or this summer – or Karl, never! I'm not saying good-by because I'll be back sometime, but by then it'll be with some husband Mother has approved. Oh heck, I'm going to cry all over again." She went out, bare feet thumping softly on the stairs.

From the window, Lelia waited until Francie emerged from the house, then started running across deep sand, down the deserted beach without looking back.

Lelia turned from the window. Gil, where are you? I have to know what's happening, too.

Kali's door was closed. She ran downstairs but stopped short in the foyer. Hazel stood leaning against the living room doorway, clutching the silk wrapper, thin hair spiked her small sharp features. "Bitch!" A painful whisper full of venom.

"Hazel – is Chuck still here? I have to see him."

"No, Bitch, he's back over there like a good boy to clean up the mess." The thin mouth spewed obscenities.

"Hazel, you're ill."

"But not blind. I saw you, hell, I watched him carry you back out of the water, up to the house. Then left you, ha." Hazel winced and clutched her throat.

"Go back to bed, Hazel. You don't know everything that happened last night. And Chuck doesn't know." Only Gil and myself know. And Tingley, only Tingley's dead. Brockway knows but what proof does he have to show?

"Got your ticket now," Hazel rasped. "Hot Bitch pretending to be an innocent. On two scores I got your number, playing me for a fool, playing Bonnie for a fool, double-crossing us with the witch upstairs. But you didn't fool Bonnie."

"You have a fever. You sound delirious. I'll find Chuck –"

"I'm gonna fix your train, Bitch Honeychile, Yours and Kali's. Today, tomorrow, it's gonna happen. I've called the sheriff's office. They're coming."

"How could you do that, Hazel? You're sick, no phones here."

"Got myself over to the pavilion yesterday afternoon. I'm sick, all right. Sick and tired of waiting, besides I've got to get out of here. I just told the sheriff to send somebody out to cart away a mad old hag, take her off to the hoosegow or loony bin, I don't care. Just so it's now!" Hazel turned and lurched across the musty living room toward her bedroom.

Lelia stayed rooted until she heard the door slam. *Don't fall apart on me, Hazel. I don't have time to humor you now.*

HURRICANE HOUSE
August, 1945

41

Rain pounded the house with a vengeance of its own, bending palms, turning the front yard into a lake.

Lelia slammed the front door and leaned against it. Impossible to get across the bridge in this deluge. She looked up. Standing at the head of the shadowed stairs, Kali waited, a still silhouette in a wine red robe, long hair falling loose about the shoulders. *I've dreamed this*, Lelia knew. That night before moving into the house she dreamed this.

"Come. We must talk." An invitation with the sound of finality.

Lelia climbed the stairs. *Gil, I want to find you, but this is what I have to do.*

She followed Kali into the room where the French doors rattled with blowing rain. Stormy gulf sky darkened the room. "The girl is safely back at the Inn?"

"Yes, before the rain started. All she wanted was to get there before her mother came." Lelia sat down on the leather stool to study Kali, seated now in the wing chair by the bookwall. Again, this lean, erect woman with the shadowed eyes might be some ancient priestess, but now the thin purple lips trembled and emotion played behind the poised face. Watching, Lelia told Kali how Francie had left without seeming to remember what had happened last night.

"And you, Loa? The etheric energy shows a different balance. The night taught you something?"

There was too much to try to tell. And at this calm

moment, she didn't want to think of Evander Merrill and Martha Critten. "In the past twenty-four hours, I had reason to use what you told me about power, about going beyond fear. Only I found I was praying. You never called it that."

"You opened yourself as a channel to infinite power." Kali was smiling. "Prayer is the usual word for that opening."

"You never said . . . and I thought –"

"I reached into some evil power? Because my words were not those you learned in Bethel? Words limit what is unlimited. There is one power, and many words for God conceived by the human mind. The divergence they cause becomes arrogance, then cruelty, one people against another. The Kahunas had long taught wisdoms known by the few. Then the missionaries came to the islands and perceived these simple words and fire rituals as profane, not sacred. The knowledge had to be hidden and disavowed – to outsiders. What was left in view became amusing history, a caricature of the what had been hidden. But you were speaking of last night."

"I learned, almost, what it's like to die. And what it is to love, totally. I almost lost myself in both."

"To surrender the small cautious self to discover the greater." Kali smiled. "Yes, a paradox that defies logic."

Lelia looked out to the rain-swept balcony. Where was Gil? At this moment Kali was ready to tell her about Bonnie, everything about the Elliots. She wanted only to go find him. Didn't she already know about Bonnie? No, there was still so much to know. As swiftly, she remembered, I've promised myself to leave here. Even Kali was saying now, ". . . leave here for the present." But Kali meant out of the house, to the mainland, away from danger. Hazel was the danger, Kali was saying.

"Hazel? She can't force you out! No matter what you have to tell me, I won't allow her to hurt you."

Kali's hands went up for a moment to cover her face. She lowered them as quickly. "I have waited so many years for what you have just given me." She rose, went to the bookcase, and returned with a thin leather folder.

"Lelia Elliot had been taught too well to doubt her mind,

so when you came here you saw me strange, equated as dark, as evil. Yes, Loa, there is evil in the world, when the heart allows it. But you must know why I seem dark to you. I have been alone so long. Solitude can comfort and open the mind, yet when the heart is insulated with its guilts, the energy becomes dark."

The long fingers spread over the leather folder in her lap. "Your coming caused exquisite pain. But I could not tell you what you demanded to know. It would have confirmed your fears."

"I found out what I had to know, Kali. Why doesn't it seem real?"

"Because you are open to truth and you haven't found it yet. To understand about yourself, about the Elliots, you must hear my story first. It is time you knew."

The only reality at this moment was the dark velvet voice and the droning rain that sealed them in this room as Kali spoke.

"After our father's death in San Francisco, I planned to take my sister Maylene back to Hawaii, to the Hana coast. My teachers were there, my work, and the beauty she knew and needed. But the Elliots came."

As Kali described them, Lelia could see them. Don Elliot, an intense young man, an artist, and Bonnie, a fragile beauty, restless and impulsive.

"It was she who swayed my sister to return to Florida with them. Bonnie had left an infant in this house with servants, to her husband's concern. Bonnie saw my serene and beautiful sister as the perfect docile nursemaid to take home to Florida."

"Against your wishes. So you came, too."

"Maylene was like my child. Our mother had been a gifted young woman, taught by Marriminde herself. She had died young. Maylene was left in my care. As I have told you, my father was a rare soul and tireless scholar."

"Phillip Seaton, the Englishman, whose library I have been reading in this room, I know."

"He was more than a scholar. He was a seeker of truth, lost

in dogma and ritual. He sought the Elixir of the human spirit, so illusive to a world of troubled souls. He had searched over the world before he found his joy on the coast of Hana. Yet his rearing of us was an experiment and not wise."

Kali nodded toward the rich leather of the library shelves. "I was to learn all he had researched, Maylene was to live unschooled, unconditioned by any teachings. She grew up on our beautiful shore, a child of nature, happy, spontaneous. But when father had to bring us to San Francisco, she was at risk – eighteen then, wise in her way, totally innocent of other realities. When the young couple from Florida delighted her with their offer, I could not stop her. I had to follow to bring her back to the life she needed."

"But you stayed."

"We didn't leave that first year because we were both happy here. Don Elliot had taken Bonnie away to the south of France. We were very content to care for the child – Charles – and this house. This coast is not rugged as our native shore, but it had its own kind of beauty."

"And Dr. Miller came visiting."

Kali nodded, smiling. "In those days, these gulf keys were quite remote from town. This house was an oddity. Mainlanders called it a rich man's folly, which would surely bring the wrath of God in the form of a storm. They called it 'Hurricane House' and so it was known. No guests came. Except a young doctor. Yes, that was Andrew Miller."

"But he said Don Elliot came back alone. Where was Bonnie?"

"In a sanatorium, in France, where she had been before."

"A manic-depressive." Strangely, she could say that without accepting the implied curse. "I guessed after talking with Dr. Miller and seeing the painting in the studio. Go on, Kali, tell me."

"So you saw a glimpse of her extreme moods. Also she hated living here and being a mother and wife of a man who wanted only to go to the tower room and paint for long hours. She had married to get away from the Canadian father. The second year, Don Elliot – your grandfather – returned from

France without Bonnie."

"And you were happy here, all of you. Dr. Miller told me." Hibiscus on the table. Laughter. Don Elliot working in his studio, free to paint as he wished.

"Very happy. For a short while. Andrew was in love with Maylene, of course. In a way, both of us." A faint smile. "But he expressed it only by gravitating here, watching from his shy loneliness."

"But Don Elliot fell in love with your sister, didn't he?"

Kali looked toward the gray rain, her voice a whisper. "My sister was love itself, an exquisite child. About your age but unlike you, Lelia, she was so open she was defenseless. She turned toward Don like a blossom to the sun. She knew nothing of hurt or betrayal."

"And Don Elliot hurt her?"

"No. I betrayed her."

The low answer held so much remorse Lelia felt it in her own chest. "Go on."

"Maylene talked happily of having a child. She expected a child with all the naturalness of a ewe on a hillside in spring. I had to save her from this before Bonnie returned. I told her she must go back to Hana."

The dark eyes burned into Lelia's for a moment. "Don Elliot was a beautiful man, Loa, loyal, too loyal, with no heart to hurt anyone. He held himself responsible but he took that upon himself. He sacrificed his art and therefore himself for Bonnie."

"How did you betray Maylene – forcing her to leave?"

"There was not time. I made him love me instead."

"*Made* him, Kali?"

"With the cunning a woman knows, with the power that I knew, until it was something beyond my own control and plan. By then, I loved him from the depth of my soul."

Lelia glanced back at the seascape over the alcove bed. "You are the figure in the paintings, aren't you. The ethereal figures are Maylene. But the strong ones are you. Go on, Bonnie returned –"

"She had been gone eight months when Don left to bring

her home, by ship and by train from New York. It was agreed, Maylene and I were to be gone before they returned."

"But you were both here when Bonnie came back?" Some Knowing tried to surface "Why hadn't Maylene left?"

"She was ill. And the child – your father – was an infant in this house."

"My father –?"

"Was not Bonnie's child."

Lelia was quiet. Bonnie had come home and found a baby in the house. Maylene's child?

"We hid him as long as possible, weeks, in Maylene's room. We cared for him there and feared every moment his cries would be heard. They would have been except this was September, stormy, the wind loud. We were sealed in with our pain and our danger. Bonnie stalked the house, sensing something and growing more ill."

"How did she die – you can tell me."

"I must tell you about death, yes."

Still holding the leather folder, Kali rose and went to the rain-swept French doors. "Bonnie was a danger to all of us. Even to Charles who was four. But a greater danger yet to the baby, to Lee. The afternoon it happened, I went to Don in the tower room. By his easel, his last painting. The one he had done out of his own anguish. Bonnie had ripped it with her nails."

"I saw that canvas." She walked over to the rain-swept French doors and looked down on churning, gray surf as Kali told what happened in this house, on that beach down there, forty years ago.

"We agreed, there in the studio, that Maylene and I and the baby must leave the moment he could help us get away from the house without Bonnie seeing, without anyone else knowing. Then we looked down as you are doing now. The same kind of surf. We saw Maylene down there. Because I knew my sister would be helpless before Bonnie's anger, I had tried to keep her hidden in her room, cruel as it was to make her care for the baby there."

As Kali murmured the story, Lelia could see it happening on the foggy beach below.

"As soon as we saw Maylene, there was Bonnie running from the house toward Maylene sitting on a small boat beached on the edge of the surf. Don and I ran down the stairs. I remember Charles, who was four, looking up from where he played some lonely game."

"You ran to protect your sister." She saw them down there on the gray beach. Two women struggling at the water's edge. Now three figures.

"We reached the path in time to see Bonnie pick up an oar and strike Maylene who fell back into the boat. We saw Bonnie push the boat out to the surf."

"And you ran into the water . . ."

"I swam for the boat. Don wrestled with Bonnie until she escaped him and then he was swimming with me. The boat was small. It had capsized. I swam and dived again and again, Don with me, trying to find Maylene. I imagined her face coming to me and receding, pushing away, as though she preferred the sea to life. When she was gone, we realized at the same moment Bonnie would have run back into the house. She would find the child. We got upstairs in time, just in time."

Kali leaned back, eyes closed, long fingers still holding the leather folder. Lelia settled again on the stool as Kali murmured, "We managed. My heart cried out to Andrew for help. He came the next morning, not knowing why. A fisherman had just found Maylene's body, washed ashore. Andrew was of great help."

"And you had Maylene buried as Bonnie Elliot. Dr. Miller testifying, making it official. Why?"

"For the child's sake. And Bonnie's. She had murdered my sister, but Don could not allow her to be taken away. If we let the world—and her father—believe Bonnie Elliot had drowned, then everything that had happened here would be buried, too. Bonnie's father would accept Lee as his grandchild and provide for him just as he would do for Charles."

"But that family picture – the one of Bonnie with the baby on her lap out there by the banyan."

"Another cruelty of mine. But the picture was necessary. I had Maylene pose in the flowered hat. The photo had to be seen in the newspaper because mainlanders learned of the child, and we couldn't let them know Bonnie was not here. No one ever knew the young Mrs. Don Elliot had been away in a French sanatorium."

Lelia leaned forward. "Why was it cruel to have your sister pose with the baby?"

"Let me read something I treasure," Kali opened the leather case and took out three yellowed envelopes. "For Don, my name was still Kala. Here, see."

The first, a short note, addressed to Kala from France, the handwriting strong and beautiful, with Don Elliot's name on the bottom. Lelia read: "We have arrived. Difficult but accomplished. Bonnie is back where she is happiest and cared for. I will stay in the village close by. In your wisdom, you must agree we have done what is necessary."

Lelia looked up. "He could take her back there, without anyone knowing?"

Kali nodded. "A steamer out of New Orleans, Andrew Miller gave her sedatives so she went quietly." She handed Lelia a second letter, dated six months later.

"Dear Kala," it read, "Do you send me strength? I believe you do. Every fiber of my body and soul reaches back to you, and my tower room easel, even to that house that holds so many harsh memories but gave me, too, some months of deep happiness. Whatever else has happened, and however it began, and in spite of how it ended, know that I loved you. I'll always love you. But I must stay here. What paintings I can sell in the village allow me to keep Bonnie where she is."

Lelia took in a breath and forgot to let it out. "Kali, who frightened my mother? Was it Bonnie's anger, taking form?"

"Loa, read the third letter. It came after your father had left for the Navy, an angry eighteen-year-old."

Don Elliot's handwriting, still that of an artist, showed fatigue. "My dear Kala: Do I hear from you less because life is unhappy for you in that house? I have allowed myself to realize what we have left you to face. I realize why Lee does not return your love and why both he and Charles must hate me. They believe I abandoned them. Perhaps we were wrong the way we chose to protect them. But how could I let Charles know his mother was and still is insane, and a murderer?"

Lelia turned the yellowed page, her heart pounding. Don Elliot's fine scrawl continued, like a voice reaching her:

"But you must tell Lee at the first time he returns to that house. Tell him he was born of love and is loved. Tell him all of it and why you have stayed in that house, letting others think ill of you, and of me. Bring him back, Kala, and tell him that. I know your quiet power; I feel your presence reaching me across time and space. Pull him back and tell him the truth."

Lelia folded the letter with trembling fingers. "He didn't come back until he brought a bride, did he? What happened that night?"

The dark purple lips softened. "He was so – so handsome and grown-up when he came in that night. And abrupt with me, a face out of an unhappy childhood. I knew he was unsure, too, of loving anyone, even this frightened girl at his side. It was no time for such a talk with me. I went upstairs as he wished. But later, in that dark night I walked the beach as was my custom, gathering seaweed to dry for kelp. I walked with my heart overflowing with need to speak with him. When I saw him standing on the open porch, I walked toward Lee, to tell him what he should know: that he was born of love and his father still loved me and his father was not a man who ran away from responsibility but the opposite. He had meant to protect both sons."

"You, Kali! My father was your son, not Maylene's. You are my grandmother." The truth of it spread like new blood in her veins.

The dark eyes turned luminous. The low voice continued. "I came to the porch and saw him there, as though he'd heard my heart calling to him. I remember the bare chest, the white pants, the open, listening face. He needed to know what I wanted so to tell him. I went toward him, saying that word I had never said before, aloud, to Lee Elliot."

"Son," Lelia said. "You said 'Son, I must tell you . . .'"

"Yes. Then there was his bride, her white shocked face,

and her screams to deal with."

"You never told him, then. He left not knowing?"

"There was no time. The girl – your mother – was hysterical before she fainted. Andrew Miller had stayed, fortunately. He came from the other end of the house and took care of her. He took both of them in his car, immediately, back to town, to his place."

"Where Tarrant came and took her home. Didn't my father come back here? Didn't you tell him then?"

Kali's face was a mask of pain. "I looked out. I thought I saw him on the beach. Then no more. I hoped with every fiber he had left, gone away, though no one ever knew."

"There's something you're not telling me, Kali?"

"That night – I saw, I thought I saw her out there. A woman like Bonnie. When I looked again – no. I suffered then that my fear had created her, imagining her vengeance on my son. I had to believe he had left, safely gone away. I called to him all those years, from my heart I had called."

"Did he hear? Did you ever feel an answer?"

"Not until you came, Loa. As you see, answers come but not always the way we demand them to. Perhaps my son's child heard me –"

"Yes." Those nights in that lonely child's room in Bethel. Yes, the sense of *Come to me* like a thought felt in her head. Later she'd tell Kali. Later when she could speak.

"You have freed me, Loa. My only wish now is to return to Hana."

"Someday, Kali You can't give the house to Chuck and Hazel and walk out!"

"No. To you. I leave the house to you, Loa. Do with it what you will."

From the hallway, a shriek pierced the room. Hazel stood there in the orange wrapper, eyes wild. "Oh, no, you don't give this house to that little bitch! It's mine! Hear that, you witch. Mine!"

AUGUST RAIN

42

"I knew it! You've been in cahoots with that woman all summer," Hazel wailed as Lelia led her back downstairs across the living room and toward the bed where she fell across the rumpled sheets, whimpering. "I saw her eyes, spooking me, pushing me out of the room."

"I took your arm, Hazel. We came down together. Does Chuck know how sick you are? I'm going to bring you some juice or tea. Chuck brought you aspirin. You should be taking it."

"Miss Innocent, playing me along, telling me to be patient." Hazel coughed and rolled on the bed, moaning. "I know your tricks. Bonnie knows, too."

"Listen, Hazel. Bonnie is not buried out there. It's someone else who wanted to die and would not want to come back into this house. Your fever's talking. And you've been drinking and not eating this food Chuck brought." Cold food waited on the littered table, stuck with cigarette stubs.

"She's here," Hazel hissed. "I tell you. In that cat sometimes. I've got to get up from here and find Merrill or Sloan. They want this house. Gonna buy it with Crit – for some kind of private hotel."

"Evander Merrill has gone. The yacht has pulled out. They won't be back. There's more but I can't explain it now."

"Nooooo!" She sat up, eyes bloodshot, wild. "Get that cat outa here."

"Don't Hazel. The imagination is powerful. You mustn't

imagine Bonnie is here. Nalo, get going, you're not wanted in this room."

"Believe me, Lelia, sure as it's ripping my throat to talk, Bonnie watches me. She stands here like a shadow sometimes, whispering fancy gibberish."

"What does she say, Hazel? Does she tell you to throw Kali out and sell the house and get rich?"

"No. You don't want to believe me, I know Chuck wouldn't but I swear, I think she says *'my lene'* and other stuff. Fancy talk that sounds like French."

Stunned, Lelia left Hazel. In the kitchen, she set out a tray, made Kali's pot of tea, sliced the bread. What am I doing? Trying to be normal. Kali, you can't mean you're leaving. Tell me Bonnie is not in this house.

She carried the tray upstairs and set it on the pedestal table. Kali came from the small dressing room behind the wall of books. The long hair was coiled and pinned in a bun. Except for the face, she might have been any old woman in a plain black dress that stopped just above the heavy shoes. Kali nodded her thanks for the tray and sipped the tea for a moment, eyes closed.

Still disbelieving, Lelia looked at what Kali showed her, taken from a lacquered box. An abalone necklace and a strand of pearls. Now a small roll of green bills that gave off a musty odor.

"From my crab traps," Kali explained. "Traps lowered in the bay many a night, pulled up by morning, then rowed across the bay to bait houses. It paid taxes and bought staples. A portion was always saved for the time I would be forced from this house or until I could stop waiting for a son who never came."

"Kali! You can't go. You're –"

"Old?" An indulgent smile. "You will learn."

The necklace and pearls went back in the black velvet envelope and with the money, into a small leather pouch.

"This raincoat," Kali murmured, holding up the garment that whispered with age, "belonged to Don Elliot." She held it to her face a moment.

"But there's more you have to tell me. You are my grandmother."

"This strange woman is your grandmother, true. I can't leave you still doubting what kind of inheritance flows in your own veins – but you must see why I couldn't tell you when you first came. Until you saw for yourself, such an admission would have proven your worst fears. As the preacher told you – *cunning gifts of the devil.* It was he who marked Lelia Elliot."

For the first time, Lelia threw her arms around Kali's shoulders. She felt the quivering energy there, saw the strong face close, dark eyes shimmering with tears.

"You are a beautiful creature, Lelia-Loa. You have the delicate curve of Maylene's face, the rich color of my own hair as a girl in Hana, and the fine brow of your father and grandfather. You have the eyes of Marriminde herself."

Marriminde? Lelia stood back, agonizing with questions. "What happened to Bonnie? Is she still alive in France? And is he alive, my grandfather?"

Kali looked toward the balcony. "The rain is lessening and I must go before dark." But she drew up the wheelchair and sat down at the pedestal table to explain. Bonnie had died five years ago in the sanatorium, still sane enough, or mad enough, to be vengeful. Don Elliot's letter to Kali had been mailed by someone else, six months later, by the person who was handling his paintings.

"I knew when Don was gone. I felt his presence as he left his body."

"Why didn't you return to Hana?"

"I waited these years in stubborn hope Lee was alive and would return. I called to him until I gave up to bitter melancholy that darkens one's soul and lessens one's powers. Until Lelia Elliot came, hiding confusion and fear about her own gifts. You forced me to open again, to all the remorse from the past." The strong face softened with a smile, "Of course there is no healing when pain is hidden."

"Kali, you called my father and I heard. As a child, I heard that call like a whisper in my mind. I know I did but how?" The logical part of herself had to know.

Kali stood. Even in the plain black dress and tied-back hair, the face was still the inscrutable priestess. Lelia repeated, "I have to know how –"

"Some things are beyond delineating. They cannot be explained, only experienced and believed or not. Consider. We live on an unbounded sea, a living universe of waves and vibrations, in which all things are connected though we are unaware of this connection, except perhaps in moments, a rare moment in a lifetime for most. The sea is the source of all energy. Your eyes tell me you ask for a name. For this source there are as many words as there are names for God."

"But to feel – or hear – someone else's thoughts?"

"Consider. If waves and vibrations carry meaning, perhaps our minds are bombarded with messages. Of necessity, the mind must close off, block out. Or it may hear but interpret according to one's own conditioned beliefs. When a clearer message is perceived, it is called intuition, ideas or intellect. For some, this openness is called genius. And yes, for a body in disharmony, it becomes madness."

"When I heard that whisper like 'come to me,' I was a child, alone in an upstairs bedroom in Bethel, Alabama."

"A lonely child who was open. You knew to hide your gifts of perception even as you were taught to fear them. Loa, how it has grieved me these months, knowing my yearning must have reached you. And learning how I must have traumatized my son's bride. For this I have suffered remorse.

"But Kali, you couldn't have known I existed. You called to Lee Elliot."

"Love from the depths of a heart carries a power and magnetism. I don't speak of magic. Perhaps the urgency of my need to reach Lee found its way to you, as a part of him." Kali began packing the leather pouch with the cheese and bread Lelia had brought up.

"But you can't go! You've just given me a gift, my sanity back, and I have to know more." She watched Kali's long fingers touch the dull glow of the crystal ball, telling it good-by, watched her sigh and gaze about the room, murmuring, "I shall take the seascape with me in my mind." Kali turned back and

Lelia felt the cool electric touch of the long forefinger tracing her cheek. "Your lovely face is stricken, but these are the eyes of Marriminde, the gold flecks in the amber. I take that memory too."

Helpless, Lelia watched Kali pull on the ancient raincoat.

"I must go. It is my choice. The rain has lessened, but a storm will come by tomorrow. Hear me now. In the base of this crystal ball, I have left you papers, the deed to this land. My signature says it is yours. But you must leave this house and go to the mainland before dark. You must stay until it's safe to return. Andrew Miller will find a place for you."

"But you?"

"Once over the bridge, there will be tourist cars heading for town. There should be a train out yet tonight."

"I can't leave now. Hazel's so sick she imagines Bonnie talks to her. Tell me, Kali, is Bonnie's energy still here? Is this why you want me to leave?"

"Some things cannot be proven or disproved, Loa." The strong face tightened, denying alarm. "Let the storm cleanse this place. Find Charles and send him back to care for Hazel. She has drawn Bonnie to her, with her lust for this house and her desire to be like Bonnie Elliot. Leave, Loa, Hazel is the danger."

The ancient raincoat crackled under Lelia's embrace. She stood back. "Marriminde. Tell me who she is."

"The most honored of all Kahuna teachers, my own grandmother. Loa, you come from a long line of such women. They were healers of the spirit as well as the body. Had I told you this was your legacy when you first came, you would have heard it as a curse, not the gift it is."

"Then stay and teach me now!" She followed Kali into the hall.

"You will learn. When the soul is awakened, the mind will seek truth and find it. Life is the teacher."

They opened the front door to a slow gray rain and wind-blown trees. From the porch Lelia watched as the raincoated figure disappeared toward the front road, Orion trotting along-side. Back inside the foyer, Lelia closed the door and leaned against it, listening to silence and the faint roar of waves. *Bonnie, you aren't here. Only in Hazel's mind are you here. Stay out of mine.* From the bedroom, Hazel cried out.

GULF NIGHT
August, 1945

43

Leave, Kali had said. But Hazel was sick, crying out, louder than the rain.

Half way across the living room, Lelia stopped. The wail from the master bedroom had turned to cursing. No, Hazel, I won't listen. She ran upstairs instead. To do what? Not sure, not sure. She dropped into the high-backed wheelchair to deep breathe and cleanse her mind. The wind pushed at the French doors with the stench of seaweed.

Chuck shouted from downstairs. With relief she ran down, following his wet tracks into the kitchen.

"Lelia, thank God," when he saw her. "I walked this over. The damn Nash is out of gas. Chowder in the Ball jar here. Heat it up for me? I just had a session with Haz. She ordered me out. Make her eat something and take these aspirins, will you? I've got to get back."

"What's happening over there? Have you seen Gil? Has he told you –?"

"The place is a tomb. A total wreck. Conch and I are cleaning up. Maybe everybody's heard about Tingley. Christ, that poor guy. After all those crazy hi-jinks last night, no sign of Cap'n today to explain. No Gil."

"Then you don't know."

"If you're pointing out I got stupid drunk, save it. I'm paying. Feel like hell. Crit is so uptight about the mess and Merrill taking off – don't think they've paid the bill yet – she's talking about selling the joint to me, and I want to be over there, listening. She'd sell on time, of course, and get it back if I can't make it pay. What's wrong, Lelia? Dammit, stay here out of this rain. I've got to get back over there. I've got dry clothes in the trailer."

"Hazel needs you."

"Bull. She needs to cool down, and she'll do it without me. Heat the chowder, okay? Haz says she doesn't want to see my face. And I can't handle hers right now."

Chuck wheeled to go, but paused, a twist of a grin on his tired face. "No, Gil isn't around. But you should see Bubba. Actually being cocky today, giving Mama an order or two."

Hazel looked at the bowl of hot chowder, wailed, and turned over to clutch her pillow again. Lelia fled the room and trudged upstairs. A wind gust reverberated through the house. Where are you now, Kali? Did you get away? And Gil, why haven't you come back? The last thought hurt.

In Kali's room, she dropped into the wheelchair and listened to the wind. It came in gusts now, flailing the house. The green Tiffany lamp flickered and went out. Power gone. Hazel would be frantic. She made her way downstairs into the musky air of the living room to look for candles in a desk drawer. Something watched, her skin knew. She kept her back toward the portrait eyes of Bonnie Elliot. *I refuse you, Bonnie.* Kali was right. Imagination makes fear real. A movement on the loveseat froze her attention. The Siamese's crystal eyes gleamed back. The cat sat crouched, paws holding down a lizard. Nalo, it's you. Keep away from Hazel.

Again the cry from the master bedroom. She found the candles, lit one and stuffing the others with matches in the pockets of the chambray skirt, went in. The candle's light penetrated the hot stale air. Hazel's face looked skeletal. She sat hunched up against the carved mahogany headboard in her red satin gown. Hot as it was, Hazel clutched a pillow in front of her.

"Where have you been?" A hoarse whisper. "What's going on? They come yet to get the old spook? I wanna see it happen!"

"I brought you some light. The power is off." She found metal holders encrusted with old tallow, lit two more candles and set them on the ornate salon desk. The soft light gleamed against the curved back of the desk, decorated with small rich squares of oil paintings. A very old French piece. The antique music box shone darkly. So much in this room was French. Hazel wouldn't know Louis XV from old-and-fancy. But Bonnie's possessions must have been feeding Hazel's imagination all these months.

"Chuck, baby. I'm sorry I ran you away. Get the hell back here," Hazel whimpered. "You got a lulu of a hangover, I know your game. You wanna sack out in the trailer. Lelia?" Feverish eyes tried to focus.

"I'm leaving you some light in the bathroom, too."

In the pine-walled bathroom, the smell of rain-lashed palms blew in the high windows. A black Palmetto roach scampered over the edge of the high porcelain tub and disappeared under the gilded claw feet. She left two candles on china plates to flicker light over Hazel's make-up clutter. Shadows threatened to move when she remembered, *My mother was once in this room. She undressed for her marriage bed here.*

Hazel was slapping the bourbon bottle back down by the bed. "Don't gimme that look. Stuff helps my throat. What's going on? You look funny."

"A storm is about to come in from the gulf."

On the bed, Hazel stilled. The white face framed by wispy hair looked strange, the colorless mouth sunken, trembling. No wonder. Hazel's lower plate, one half of Fascinatin' Hazel's perfect smile, lay in the mess on the table. In the sweat-stained satin gown, she curled around the pillow and moaned. "It's Bonnie. She doesn't want us in her house. She'll make me go back upstairs again."

"Make you what? Take the pillow away, Hazel. Tell me."

"Bonnie wants that woman upstairs killed. Wants me to do it. I know it's Bonnie. She whispers in a fancy Frenchy way. Says *that will finish it, both of them.*"

"No, Hazel. Don't. You've been sick a week. How long has

it been since you slept?"

"Can't sleep. She's always here now, watching. Look." A hoarse whisper. "Watch how the shadows move."

"The air from the window moves the flame – makes the shadows pulsate." *I must stop her, must stop myself from believing her.*

Hazel's sunken mouth was muffled against the pillow. "I wanted to get Kali out of here, see her get dragged out screaming like an old hag. But Bonnie's not satisfied with that. If I want her house, I gotta do what she says. My last chance for Hazel Mae not to be left the fool, ending up with nothing. Bonnie wants me to do her dirty work, but what the hell, everybody else has double-crossed me. You. Sloan. All of you."

"That's fear talking, Hazel, not voices from the dead. You're imagining ways to get what you want." She made the words sound calm. If Hazel guessed Kali had given her the house and left, the sick woman would be wild.

"Hazel, you've got to sleep. Aspirin will help more than bourbon." She sat on the edge of the bed, trying to touch the feverish, thin arm that jerked away.

"Can't sleep. She'll come if I do. Just like the devil. My daddy knew about having truck with Satan, warned me." She tried to sit up. "You're so goddamned smart, Lelia, do you believe in the devil?"

"I believe –" What did she believe? "I know this, that thoughts and desires can be so powerful they can heal or kill. And it can be someone else's thoughts you take in. Or your own wish turned into a scheme. Let it grow and it takes root into some force to possess you." Yes, Bonnie had been in her own mind, drawing her into madness that time she was ill with herbs and Hazel's sulfa. "I'm going back upstairs."

"Ha, tell you something, cool bitch. Bonnie hates as you much as she hates that woman upstairs. Says you're hiding a baby in this house, says she'll get you again like she did before. You had to come back here, didn't you? Don't look at me like I'm crazy. Go tell Kali that. Make her explain that."

"Stop it!" Lelia sprang up from the bed. "Play your radio – no, the power's off. Wait –"

The music box wouldn't be Hazel's radio swing, but it would be a sound other than the wind out there. Under the raised lid, small bronze wheels, intricate as a fine clock, engaged with a faint initial scrape. A delicate melody began, like viola strings and chimes blending, the melody echoing clearly from another time and place.

"There, Hazel! You'll have music and light to sleep by." She had to leave this room. "Tomorrow we can talk. And decide what to do – about the house. When Chuck is here."

The music box's soft chiming followed her out.

Halfway across the darkened living room, holding her single candle, Lelia stopped with a jolt of dismay. The music box was French. The melody issuing from the exquisite gears was not a lilting nineteenth century waltz but an ethereal lament, haunting as a woman's cry from another plane of existence. She might as well have left Bonnie's voice for Hazel.

Gil, where are you? I need you. With a consuming weariness, she climbed the stairs to the upper floor that was achingly empty of Kali's presence.

Chuck didn't come. Still hadn't come at midnight. He must be staying in the trailer. In the morning, she would wade out of here and send him back to handle his wife. Plans. None of them felt real.

Carrying a lighted candle, she padded into Kali's room to try to read. The damp air held a chill. From the tapestry bed, she picked up a folded dressing gown, slipped her arms in the big sleeves, wrapped it around her, and with a book from the shelves, dropped into the wheelchair left there by the pedestal table. She rubbed its arms as Kali had and opened the book but watched candle light shape the crystal ball instead. She had no desire to reach out now, open the bottom, and see the deed. In the morning, they would deal with that. She'd have to tell Chuck and Hazel the house was hers. Hazel would be wild with anger, but she would tell them they could stay.

A sound from downstairs froze her hand on the page. She rejected the image it flashed, but listened without breathing. Hazel was too weak to get out of bed. Had the French doors blown open?

Kali's voice whispered in her mind – memory or a message? *Leave, Loa, leave where you are now.* She stood, took the candle, went back to her own room, snuffed out the light, and dropped across her own bed.

She listened again. Only rain. No, a sound on the stairs now. She sat up, rigid, hearing with her entire body, the way she'd done as a child. Bonnie's eyes flashed in her mind. No, I won't let you be real. Bonnie couldn't be out there, moving along the hall now, *unless Hazel and I have given her substance.* Fear made real.

The sound bumped toward Maylene's old room. *Searching?* Now back to Kali's doorway. She heard the cry, low, animal-like, from a closed throat. A hard object bumped into the hall. Now slow steady thuds of that object falling down the stairs.

With wild anger stronger than fear, Lelia sprang from the bed and stood in her own doorway staring into the dark hall, silent now. She moved to the head of the stairs and looked down into the grainy darkness of the foyer. At the foot of the steps, a glint of metal. The wheelchair, one wheel still spinning.

Someone moved down there. A shimmer of color showed in the dark, like silk, like the kind of Spanish shawl that draped Bonnie in the portrait in the tower room.

The shawl-shaped shoulders bent over the spinning wheelchair. White arms flailed the air. The guttural cry was anger at not finding what she wanted to find, a broken body, tangled with the chair.

From the top of the stairs, Lelia waited for the hard-breathing figure to look up. When it did, it would see her as Kali up there, standing in the long robe. Kali, meant to be in that chair pushed down the stairs. The figure moved. The face that looked up was stark and white. A madwoman's face. Hazel's face or Bonnie's? Either or both.

She forced her legs to move, slowly, surely, down the steps. She spoke to the crouched figure just as Kali had calmed a hysterical Francie, as Kali had spoken to the wild-eyed Hazel at the door. The words came of their own, softly spoken but powered with confidence.

At the last step, she shoved aside the chair, and made herself touch the silk shawl covering the bony shoulders. The face looked up with the mad eyes of Bonnie Elliot.

"Look at me, Hazel. Look close. It's Lelia. I am telling you Bonnie has gone. She is not here any more. We are here, alone together."

GULF STORM
August, 1945

44

The night passed in howling darkness. Now, in trackless, gray time, an angry surf rose, pitched forward, surging over the seagrapes, sucking back, to hurl again, closer each time. This gulf she loved had turned violent, an angry god, with a vengeance all of its own.

She watched from the corner bedroom windows of her room where she'd taken Hazel who lay curled on the bed, in a fetal position, still in the red satin gown, crying out as each gust of wind battered the house.

Lelia paced the small room, bare feet knowing each tremor of the floor. Hot air crackled. Her pulse beat a crescendo against her eardrums. What day was this? Tuesday? Kali's departure on a dark Sunday afternoon might have been weeks ago. The party Saturday at Grouper Hole, Francie's rescue, Tingley's dying, then, Gil, and the gulf, an unreal lifetime ago. Where was he now? She stopped pacing to draw in a long breath to calm mind and senses. Could she reach him as Kali had reached her?

Gil, why didn't you come back to me? She saw his face, dimly, as tense, involved in some struggle, but from far away. Another wave pounded. Already it was too late for anyone to reach the house. Chuck hadn't returned. No one could now. If so many trees were down, the bridge to the bayshore must be out. They were trapped here. Hazel, curled in rigid fear on the bed, feverish eyes following her movement. She paced the small space of the bedroom, calling out silently to Kali. Did you get away?

For an instant, the high cheek bones, the luminous dark eyes flashed in her mind. Hear me, Kali, I have to talk to you. Last night I used what you taught me. When the storm came, Hazel believed she was Bonnie. She became Bonnie. Somehow she'd found the same shawl as in the portrait. From the closet maybe. But it was Bonnie's face who looked at me, whispering gibberish. Kali, I used the mana power, the confidence.

I got Hazel back into her room. But I couldn't leave her there. The front windows blew in, scattering glass. It was Hazel who screamed, not Bonnie. I had to bring her up here. She was clinging, submissive then, leaning against me, clutching her flashlight, whispering, *"See how powerful she is, dead or alive."* She meant Bonnie. Hazel kept whimpering, *"She won't let either one of us have her house until we get rid of Kali."*

That was last night. But now, Kali, now, Hazel is crawling to the floor, crouching in the corner. I can't fight them both, the storm and Hazel. She whimpers now. Her long red fingernails are wrapped around the flashlight. Her white face is a mask. The eyes glitter. Bonnie's eyes. Only fear holds her down, but fear will give her Bonnie's strength.

Leave her? Yes. I can go into the hall. Already there's water lapping below. The French doors down there went earlier. Wind moans through the house.

Kali, I'm in your room now . . . pushing the library chair against the balcony doors, the table against the chair. The madness I always feared is here now. Not in me, but ready to stalk toward me. Do I wait for it to come? I hear you say, Go beyond fear, but at this moment, I see only a dark abyss.

In the dark, Lelia struck a match to a candle. In the flickering flame, opened the drawer of the pedestal table, drew out paper and pen and took them to the corner of the bookwall, away from the French doors rattling against the bulwark pushed there.

She crouched there on the floor, the candle in the corner, paper on a book. She would put down things she needed to say and try to hide the page in the base of the crystal ball for someone to find . . . At this moment, she would focus only on the moving pen . . .

I, Lelia Elliot, age twenty-one, on this night of August 19, 1945, write this to stay sane. The gulf roars closer to the house as I write. It is too late for anyone to reach us.

We wait our separate ways. Hazel cries out with each crash and gust. She was enraged and frightened and ill, but now she is an animal clawing at a trap. During this dark, hellish day, her frenzy has became mania, her eyes Bonnie's. She will come looking for me to vent her anguish. She clutches a flashlight. It will be her weapon. She is ill but strong with fury. She will not know what she is doing.

I huddle in this corner, against the bookcase, away from windows, waiting for storm or madness to reach this room first.

My body trembles. But my mind is strangely calm confronting the inevitable. Even curious. Is it always this way? Do you have to stand at the abyss before you look back and see that life is a gift never fully claimed?

My face is wet. Am I crying? Not from fear of dying but with an angry passion to live. Chuck, if you find this in the base of the crystal, everything there is yours but with another gift from me, for the taking. Forgive the past, forgive Kali for her lonely wait here. That's all you have to know. And Gil, if you ever see this, I loved you. Did you know?

A roar, the candle flickered out as the French doors shattered over the chair and the table. Something huge and wet thudded into the room. The pale beam of Hazel's flashlight found the tree limb in the middle of the floor. The beam moved on, searching.

Lelia stood up in the dark corner, trying to track Hazel's movements over the roar of her own pulse. For an instant, the weaving flashlight caught Hazel's white face and wild eyes. The beam moved on, searching the empty alcove bed, then back to the broken glass and the tree limb on the floor.

Downstairs, another crash. Now a soft lapping sound,

heard because the world had stilled suddenly. The air felt like a held breath before the final scream.

Hazel whimpered in surprise, the trapped animal, aware of silence as a new danger. The eye of the storm, Lelia knew, we're in it. From the quiet eye of her own storm, she watched for Hazel's movement. She watched from a deep, still place that had no time for fear. She knew to move forward. The corner would be a trap.

The light found her as she moved toward it. For a moment, the thin figure lurching forward might have been a frightened child, stumbling toward comfort, arms up. Closer, the face was a wild creature moving in to strike.

The flashlight swung. Ready, Lelia moved aside and sprang forward before the next blow to embrace Hazel's body and flailing hands. Fury radiated from the tensed body Lelia held tight against her.

"Hazel, Hazel, Bonnie's gone. Chuck will come. Let go, let go."

For in instant Hazel stopped struggling but in the unreal quiet, stiffened again, with new strength tore loose, dragging, then whirling them both into the hall.

On the landing, they struggled, rage against focused will.

"Hear me, hear me, Hazel."

But fury didn't hear. It twisted them both around and suddenly there was no wall. Together they plunged backwards into black air.

The descent was endless, dreamlike, the only reality a steady thud of blows . . . the odors of musty carpet . . . sharp sting of fingernails in her arms and Hazel's high, faint wail.

At the bottom was the abyss, after all. A wet dark pit. No, she could see dimly there was something beyond. Noises impossible to place. A faint light bright, faded again into blackness.

Hands tested her arms, her legs. Arms scooped her up against a solid, hard-breathing chest. She imagined Gil, even the warmth of his breath, close to her face.

Harsh male voices rose and fell around her. She opened her eyes then, and saw it was Gil crouched on the wet floor, holding her to him. The bright light came again, sweeping the darkness along with footsteps thumping down the stairs.

"Nobody else up there."

Gil's chest throbbed against her face as he said, "Look over there. In the corner."

Lelia turned to see, too. Hazel cringed there, one leg turned crooked, her eyes glazed and fixed in their light, the slack mouth mumbling.

The man behind the light muttered, "Must be the one we got the call about the other day. Said we'd find a crazy old woman. Careful, boys. She looks like a case all right."

She felt Gil lift her, carry her in his arms through water, the front porch covered with water, then into a boat. Gil's boat, rocking at the doorstep. In the hushed quiet, she heard a steady sloshing sound. Now the wind stirred again, like a warning. Someone muttered, "Hurry."

They were in the boat, motor roaring, moving them away from the house when she forced her eyes open once more, searching for Hazel. A flashlight beam swept past the figure wrapped in a blanket. The face that looked out was not Bonnie's. Not even Hazel's. The face of an old woman, eyes blank and wild, mouth sunken.

Lelia thought sleepily, *Hazel — this is what you asked for, for them to come and take away a mad hag of an old woman. And it is you.*

Gil's arms held her against his warm chest. Blackness flooded in again. She let it come, without questions, without fear. In the darkness, someone called. Not Kali. But the ancient woman with the glistening hair who waited on the strange shore.

MOUND PARK HOSPITAL
August, 1945

45

The room was a sterile cubicle, her aching body heavy against the bed. Someone in rustling white held her wrist. Then the voice called again through the darkness, and she heard it like a memory or melody, pulling her to its source.

She followed the whispered call into some weightless space, turning back only to look down on the room, on Lelia Elliot's body, dark hair spilling over the flat pillow on a narrow bed.

Again, the other called, drawing her from the movement below, away from the corridors and scurrying figures in little starched caps. She drifted by choice toward something nameless but always sought.

She ran now barefoot over springy grass, along a rugged bluff under blue infinity, moving with the weightless exuberance, trying to find Kali, to hear Kali, calling to her, you forgot to tell me the most important secret of all. Now she was running alongside the waves, iridescent, blue-green, rolling white-capped onto pristine sands . . . Hana, this must be Hana. On the open shore, a figure waited, a woman with long hair, silver bright in the sun, waiting as she had in so many dreams that must not have been dreams.

Coming, I'm coming . . .

She moved effortlessly along wet glistening sands, straining toward the woman with the flowing white hair so bright in the sun . . . The woman turned, the face as old as the sea and as ageless, the eyes shining like dark jewels, polished by sorrow and joy and time.

She knew this was Marriminde, Kali's teacher, the grandmother, the Kahuna, wise woman of the sea, Marriminde, the woman on the shore who had always waited. And now, so close, the light was too bright as the hand reached forward to touch her temples as Kali had done, sending cool, electric energy moving along nerve paths. *Let me see you, Marriminde. Tell me that last secret I wanted to learn from Kali. No, don't fade away . . .*

Water dripped somewhere like a metronome. Lelia opened her eyes. A lavatory, against a white wall. Someone in rustling white moved about the bed. Light from a window was a dull glare. The rustling stopped. A round face bent close, smiling.

"Well, look now. Our Sleeping Beauty's awake. You've had us worried, Honey Bun!"

Her left arm was heavy, in a plaster cast. She wiggled her legs against the smooth bed. Her body was sore and tired, but it moved at her will. Not as before, in that place where she'd been, some other reality replaced now by this static room. She accepted the thermometer in her mouth, closed her eyes again. The nurse's solicitous chatter went on, expecting no answer.

"No telling how those beaches look today, storm veered back into the gulf and the sun's out. You're lucky, Hon, just that fractured arm. You young ones can take a fall and not crack up like the rest of us."

The nurse extended a plump hand. "Now! Let's see you get up and walk. Show Annie you're good awake. We'll just make a trip down the hall and by time we get back, your oatmeal will be here cooling off. And your company'll be back. Some company! A tall silver-haired gentleman, a Yankee, I think, then a Navy fellow. Every nurse on the floor stopped to look at that one. Ready to get up and walk some for me, Honey?"

She allowed herself to be guided down a green tile corridor. From open doors, pale faces stared from high beds, slack faces, not knowing about that other place. Then there was a mirror and her own wild hair framing a pale oval, the eyes still trying to remember that other place.

The nurse was there again, hustling her back down the dull green tile, helping her back into bed, voice purring, "You did take your time coming round, Honey, but you're fine except for that arm. Think I'll try sleeping that long and find out if it makes me look like some angel on a church window."

She wanted to lie still, go back, find that joy in body and mind, that effortless reaching toward the answer to everything, but the nurse's chirpy greeting made her look toward the door. Gil stood there. Was he real? Yes, but different. The clipped haircut, the Navy officer's uniform. Something else. The smoldering fuse he'd hid from others, but not her, was gone. In its place, an easy vitality.

He nodded to the departing nurse and pulled the chair close. His mouth curved the way she always knew it should. Under sandy lashes, the blue gaze searched her face. He picked up her right hand and pressed it against his cheek.

"Hello, Lelia Elliot."

"I thought I dreamed you, too," she said. "The boat at the door. Was it last night?"

"Twenty-four very long hours ago. You were lost somewhere. I watched."

"You've been here?"

"Counted every green tile – when I wasn't checking on the things you would want to know, once you decided to come back. God, but I suffered guilt for not getting out there before the storm."

Guilt. She didn't want guilt left over from their night in the gulf. She found her voice. "Tell me everything that's happened. I don't remember anything except – Kali left, and the storm came, and Hazel and I were alone." With Bonnie. She shuddered.

"Hazel is here, too, Lelia. In the psycho ward, bad case of hysteria, but she's coming back, meek as a repentant sinner. She needed food for one thing. Bourbon's a lousy medicine for flu. Hurricanes don't help."

"And fury, and fear, mixed. She was losing her house." She didn't ask, And where were you Gil?

His fingers traced her cheek. "I have so much to tell you.

Not in the order of importance, but to finish about Hazel – Chuck was there when I looked in this morning. He had a rough time of it, too, trapped on the mainland. But the guy looks gratified. Hazel's holding on to his hand."

"Yes, he needed her to need him." She saw concern working in his face. "Go on. What else are you afraid to tell me? It's about Kali, isn't it?"

"You do look into a guy's head, don't you? There was a car that went over in a flooded ditch. The couple in front was injured, but the old lady in the back seat drowned. That's all I know. But someone had seen Kali on the road earlier."

Her throat closed down on the cry. "She wanted to get to a train in town. She meant to get back to Hawaii."

"Sure. Maybe she got away." He didn't sound sure. "Lelia, there's more to tell you, but right now I'm going to look for Dr. Miller and get you released and take you out to the beach. You'll want to see what's happening out there."

She looked away, shuddering. "No."

"You do. And you should see before I tell you the rest of it. Trust me."

Gil swung out the door, the tailored white shoulders radiating some measure of relief. Lelia sat on the side of the bed, dizzy and unsure, watching him go. The man was so imbued with responsibility. Fine, but she didn't want his attention based on duty or guilt.

The second shift nurse, a skinny girl with black braids, breezed in, white shoes squeaking on the green tile. She set down the large flat box on the bed with the beaming pleasure of a gift-bearer.

"Somebody's got a pretty new dress to wear home, I bet. The store called us to find out just what you needed."

The card said the blue dress and the rest of it were from Morris Alderman. There was a note too, on top:

My dear Lelia,

I have talked with Gil MacLean about my Nancy. I am aware of what you two prevented Saturday night. I am most grateful, for my daughter's sake. Gil will tell you more. I am returning to Boston. Not knowing the condition of Hurricane House on the beach, I invite you to stay at the Vinoy Park Hotel until such time you wish to make other plans. The hotel will expect you.

— Morris Alderman

She was dressed, arm in a sling, when Gil returned, Dr. Miller following, neat and gray as she remembered. Andrew Miller's dry voice made her heart leap.

"You'll want to know Kali got as far as my house quite safely before the storm broke. She left Orion with me." He smiled, sharing her relief. "No, I couldn't make her stay. You know Kali's strength. She made me promise to send someone to check that you had left the house."

Downstairs, Dr. Miller handed Gil the keys to his coupe and waved them away.

From Mound Park Hospital, they drove down streets strewn with tree limbs, past small store fronts still boarded up. Yellow pine boards reflected the sun. At the wheel, Gil explained how he and Brockway and another man from the sheriff's department in the *Strike* got across the flooded bay to the door of the house.

"We brought you and Hazel to town in a Jeep, rough ride, but you were both out of it. My boat?" He flashed a quick smile. "I don't need the damn thing now."

There was so much more to hear, and she knew it would come. He was having to tell it his way. She felt his energy radiating next to her, vital now without the anger but still contained, waiting to make his explanations. The Navy whites must mean he was back on active duty and would be leaving. The thought hurt like a loss of something just found, but she refused any disappointment at that moment. Leaning back, eyes closed, she listened to Gil tell about their trip back to the mainland and into town even as she reached again for a glimpse of Hana's coast. It was a dream memory now yet something waited there, some final secret she needed to know. Phillip Seaton who had sought the Elixir of Life had found it there. What was it, Kali? You left without giving me that answer.

Doc Miller's little coupe moved through leaf-strewn streets, turning west toward the sun, a red ball still high over the clear August sky. Already the breeze was drier, with the feel of September. Gil was saying again, "It was hell not being able to get back out there sooner than I did."

"During the storm, I called to you, Gil," she murmured without accusation.

Quickly he told her where he'd been. New Orleans. At dawn that Sunday, he'd caught a flight out of MacDill Field over in Tampa, an available space hop to Barksdale Field, not knowing about the storm until he got into New Orleans. At MacDill, the sergeant had told him what he'd suspected. Two hours earlier a Captain Sweeling from Special Services had requested and gotten available space for two, claiming he had some important star with him who needed the flight.

"I knew where to begin looking once I got a cab into New Orleans. An old friend, Yellow Willie, best jazz piano man in the Quarter, knows the underbelly of that town. He told me where to find Poppy's house, off Rampart Street."

Lelia nodded. "I know. Martha Critten must have been Poppy years ago. She had a friend Tony Van. Maybe he was already using the name Evander Merrill. What did those two have in common?"

"Tony Van and Poppy had a history of doing each other strange favors. Years ago he bought that house off Rampart for her. You know what kind of house, I take it. It was a favor for naming him in a paternity suit." He flashed a twisted grin. "Tony was getting his start in movies – he needed to clear up some rumors about his love life that would have killed his screen lover image."

Gil swerved around a fallen tree and went on to explain. Martha was still half owner of the house with an old gal named Effie who ran the place. Gil had found Merrill hiding there. "And while I was at it, I found the two missing local daughters – live ones – sent there by Martha. Those scared kids hadn't worked out for a bordello. It wasn't too difficult to scare Effie into letting them go, with bus fare home."

"You saw Merrill. What about Sloan and the others?" She

watched his profile, grim but without the old anger.

"I found Merrill down the hall in a suite of rooms, Victorian trappings like something in an old movie. Lelia, he was sitting there in a silk robe, a frightened, pathetic old man but still playing the indignant role to the hilt. He kept promising me Sloan would show up any moment and put my lights out."

"What happened?"

"Someone coughed in the next room – beyond the beaded curtains. It was Sweeling, drunk. Out of uniform you might say. Lelia, Nancy was on that yacht and she must have seen something, Merrill with some young officer. Nancy wouldn't have cared if Merrill was gay or a lush. But she would have laughed at the guy. Discovering his little secret cost Nancy her life. Also Susie's. She'd slipped onto the yacht that night. She saw Sloan – saw it happen."

"I never felt he was a murderer – but just a vain little man."

"Right. Sloan and Cage took care of the dirty work. And Cage's idiot son, Jellybo."

"They killed – just to protect Merrill's screen lover image!"

Gil nodded, the old bitterness there again. "Two women drowned – and Francie was about to be the third. But not only to save Evander's miserable little image but to protect their own meal ticket. The whole crew, leeches all of them, were living off Merrill, so they had to clear the yacht of any suspicions. Martha Critten hated Sloan but helped with their plan because she wanted to get rid of Susie, too."

"Martha hated all men," Lelia said. "Susie must have known too much."

"Right. People on this waterfront could look the other way about Martha's maid-for-hire business but white slavery traffic to New Orleans? Once that was out they'd have come in a posse to torch Grouper Hole before the sheriff could bring the handcuffs."

"Poor Tingley," Lelia murmured. "He was so close to putting it together. If the third murder happened while Merrill was 'front and center of the crowd,' they could have left a day or so later free of suspicions."

"You were in their plans, too, Lelia." They were passing wind-lashed orange groves now. "Bubba told them you could look in their eyes and know what was going on. Poor Bubba, he knew what his mama was doing and stayed scared. But he was right about you." Gil flashed a smile. "Thank God, you have a guardian angel looking after you since I did a lousy job."

"Somebody did," she murmured. "I know about Cracker. But what about Sloan and Cage?"

"Lelia, the yacht was midway between Florida and New Orleans when the storm cut across the gulf. They never made it into port. I got to tell Merrill that in New Orleans even before I learned it was true. He looked like a sunken old man."

She took in a sharp breath. "I told Sloan he would drown. Maybe I cursed him. No. He did it himself. But you still have more to tell me." She touched the white sleeve of the uniform.

"After we see the house."

"Gil, I know why Merrill and Martha wanted Hurricane House. They had plans. Is it still standing?"

"We're about to find out."

OPEN GULF
August afternoon, 1945

46

The old brick road leading to the bridge appeared to be a lane covered with pine straw and limbs. Saws hummed and workers shouted, clearing the country road of felled trees. A roadside ditch had become a canal, sluggish with debris-laden water. Gil stopped the car. They got out and with Gil bracing her arm cast, they walked to what was left of Grouper Hole, flattened, collapsed on its foundation.

"Looks like a surge of high tide filled it, pulled back, and left a pile of lumber," Gil said. "Moby Grouper and Chuck's bar, the whole works in that mess. but the trusty old bridge, look. They've got it connected again."

Ahead, sightseers scattered along the bridge. With Gil's hand bracing her arm, they walked onto it. Bay water roared below, the air clean and new. Pelicans swept by.

"Look who's coming," Gil said. "If my eyes don't deceive me, here's proof old water rats are immune to hurricanes."

On the bridge, Lelia threw her good arm around Cap'n's scrawny shoulders first, then embarrassed Skipper by a pat on his long face. Below, three men hammered down new plankings as Big Al climbed the embankment, grinning. He nodded at Lelia's arm cast.

"Lucky. That was a mean storm. I heard Kali got out and kept going." He pumped Gil's hand. "Navy man, they tell me. Scott Gilford MacLean, Lieutenant Commander, U.S. Navy. Nothing new, being a hero, huh."

Cap'n beamed at Gil. "Look at this gen-u-wine U.S. Navy

officer who's been running a 17-footer around here all summer."

"Conch?" Lelia said, heart in her throat. "And Cheta?"

"They been over there digging in that mess for his best boiling pot. He's got hisself a new job," Al said with Cap'n adding, "You heard about Martha? She got a ride out with a couple of folks and ended up in a ditch. Drowned deader 'n a mackerel. I saw them drag her out. You want to know how red henna frizz looks coming outa mud?"

"No," Lelia said quickly. Martha. Yes, it was you in the ditch. Not Kali.

To questions about Bubba, Cap'n reported, "Been hopping around here all day, bossy as his mama talking with the fellow who's gonna buy that bayfront." Skipper added, "Bubba hasn't sweat a drop."

Al explained, "Some fellow was here soon's the sun come out, talking about buying what's left. Gonna build a drug store kinda place they call a sundry store with bathing caps and lotions and junk like that for tourists. But Conch's gonna cook the eggs and hamburgers." Al scratched his head and looked solemn. "Guess that old Hurricane House is still standing but don't know much more. You better go see. Sure you can walk it? Can't drive over there yet."

Yes, she could walk it. Together, Lelia and Gil crossed the bridge onto the sand-filled bayside boulevard. Between the battered and deserted Pavilion and Inn, the beach was strewn with debris. Without speaking, they hurried down the sandy road to the entrance to Hurricane House, Gil bracing her arm as they climbed past tangled limbs.

The house loomed against the blue and gold sky, exposed without its framing palms, staring down with shattered glass eyes. So much of the jungle was down, the gulf could be seen, gleaming like silver. The porch was piled with sand and ripped of its screening. Still silent, they crunched into the dark foyer. White sand lay thick where she and Hazel had fallen.

Gil cupped her face in his hands. "You're a strong one, Lelia Elliot. So is this house – but it won't be easy looking at it now. Are you okay?"

She nodded. "There's one thing I have to see first. In the

living room."

He followed her into the dank shadows, jumbled with broken chairs and soaked couches, scattered with shattered porcelain. The wall where Bonnie's portrait had hung was ripped and bare. The frame lay face down on a broken Tiffany shade. Gil lifted it up. The canvas had been scoured by sea water and sand. Only a faint scarred image remained. Where the painting had fallen, Nalo lay, body rigid, fur matted. Lelia backed away. Gil gripped her arm.

The soggy stairs creaked under their feet. At the landing, she hesitated. With Gil's hand warm on her arm, they stepped over shattered glass into Kali's room. Yes, it had happened. The French doors ripped open, the whole balcony gone, leaving a gaping open wall.

"I have dreamed this," she said quietly.

But unlike the dream, the gaping hole didn't open to darkness, an ending of hopes. Beyond the ragged opening, a peaceful sunset gulf rolled in from the endless arc of horizon. Storms would happen again out there, she knew, but the sun would return. The gulf would still roll in, wiser than the people on shore.

Gil was plodding around in the mess at their feet. "Good Lord, you got out just in time. The force came right through here."

But the seascape at one end was safe and the library wall at the other. *Can you hear me Kali, do you know?*

"Look, here's something." Gil pulled up the overturned table and lifted the heavy crystal ball. The wet wood base fell loose in his hands. He handed the folded papers to Lelia.

"It's the deed," she murmured. "Kali told me it would be here."

"I knew about the deed," Gil said. "Doc Miller told me the house is yours. Kali planned it that way. Lelia there is more I want to tell you. It hurts like hell to say this but –"

He would tell her he's leaving. She felt herself pulling back, closing off his energy, to protect herself from the loss. Without letting him know of course.

"Look, Gil. Here's a note attached. Kali's handwriting.

Lines copied from Rainer Marie Rilke. She always said words limit the truth but poets at least cast some light." His restless eagerness still came to her like a heat beside her so she folded the papers and let him slip them in his pocket. She felt strong, she felt whole, without the need to hide behind any shield. The gaping hole showed her a moving gulf and golden sun. "So tell me."

"First, about this house. Morris Alderman has asked me to convey his message. He wants to provide the money to restore the place, if you choose to do that. He says the funds would have been his daughter's inheritance."

She felt surprise and joy. "I could make this house beautiful again! I could give Hazel and Chuck some of the land, let them build a motel." The joy faded to appreciation.

He ran restless fingers through his close-cropped hair and looked around the room, frowning at the littered floor, the seascape painting, the books. "Doc Miller told me about Kali being your grandmother and who she was. Told me all that while we waited for you to come back from wherever you were in that bed. You called out to Kali. So I know you won't be satisfied until you go to Hawaii and find her, if she made it there, and with the war over, that's possible. One more thing."

His hands went up to her shoulders and dropped again to hold the cast on her arm. "I know how strong you are under that beautiful, serene exterior. You could walk away from here, go there and stay. You also have this house to come back to. I don't want to stop you from doing what you have to do. With Nancy, I tried to possess her. Fought her choices. A mistake. I've learned better. I want you—but I want you happy. Because I love you that way, Lelia. That's what's hard to say. I know you have these choices. My own is for you to love me. There it is. Even if it hurts, I want you to do what makes you happy."

She touched his face. Traced his warm jaw. Saw the truth of what he'd said shining out of intense blue gaze. Would she have known if she'd opened to know? Perceptions always came mixed with one's own hope and fear, she knew that now.

"Yes," she told him. "Those are things I want to do." At

that moment all the alternatives felt like warmth and freedom flowing in her veins. Her life. Not Bonnie's. "What about the Navy? Do you have choices?"

A smile played on his lips. "I could have a Navy wedding next week and be out as soon after that. Lelia, I've loved you from the first moment I looked at you. But I didn't dare let myself feel or show it. I had vowed retribution for Nancy and I had to keep my hate fine-tuned. That's past."

"Those people took care of their own retribution," she heard herself say, not wanting to hurry this moment. "The crew, Martha." The gulf rolled in below, golden now in the late sun. People walked down there, staring up at the house. His eyes waited.

"My choice," she said, "is all of the above if you want to do it together." With her good hand, she traced the lean plane of his jaw. "Find Kali. Come back, reclaim this house. Yes, I love you, Gil. I love you more for knowing about choices."

He pulled her close, careful with the arm. "All of it. And why not? My beautiful, strange Lelia, do you know what I see in those amber eyes? Everything. My life. Are you willing to have that Navy wedding before I get out of these whites?" She murmured against his warm chest, met his eyes again, unafraid of the impact.

He turned her suddenly toward the gulf. "Look at that would you? A littered beach turning gold. Somebody's trying to tell us something." A path of purple and gold shimmered across the water, coloring the sands.

"At this moment, Lelia Elliot" – he squinted into the glow – "I feel like a man who has just discovered what it's all about. Probably the oldest secret in the world but it feels new. Tell somebody that it's love – totally loving – they'd give an indulgent nod. Unless, of course, they'd just discovered it themselves. Or remembered."

"Gil, do you know what you said?" Delight made her laugh.

He grinned. "I said I love you and it feels good. And scary. And lets me know I'm alive."

"I have to tell you this! Before I woke up in the hospital,

when I was still unconscious, I was running along a shore. The Hana coast, I'm sure. I was trying to reach someone who was supposed to tell me this wonderful secret. Some have called it the Elixir of Life, no less. Kali had told me it's something you have to find out for yourself to believe. And well, you just said it. Wait – hand me Kali's note."

She looked at the note he handed over. "The Rilke lines. There's something here Kali wants me to see. And you. She would have known about you, too. Yes, listen to this." She read aloud in the bronze light, *"To love is good, too, love being difficult . . ."*

She leaned back into his warm arms to read the rest of it:

"For one human being to love another; that is perhaps the most difficult of all our tasks, the ultimate, the test and proof, the work for which all other work is but preparation."

"Go on." His chin nudged her cheek. "I hear you."

"Love is a high inducement to the individual to ripen, to become world for himself for another's sake. It is a great exacting claim upon him, something that chooses him out and calls him to vast things. . ."

"The fellow's saying it's not easy." Smiling, he turned her around again. "We'll work on it."

With a finger, she touched his curved lips. In the next moment, she would open her own to his. But in this breath she had to tell him, "There's a place I want to take you to. I know we'll find it in Hana. There's a high grassy bluff overlooking an ocean. And a special beach. I want us to run along that shore, and remember what we found."

The End

ABOUT THE AUTHOR

Author Marian Coe's characters come from the imagination, but the setting of *Legacy* is real – Gulf of Mexico beaches of 1945, along the Pinellas County, Florida, shore. She first saw this open, still-natural waterfront as a young reporter in 1958 as the postwar influx began. During twenty years as a staffer with the former *Evening Independent* and *The St. Petersburg Times*, Coe talked with those who had known St. Petersburg during Florida's second "boom" – the Forties when thousands of seniors sunned themselves on downtown green benches and hotels and beaches overflowed with young servicemen during World War II, an experience that would draw many back in the Fifties and Sixties, looking for the good-life-in-Florida.

The character of young Lelia Elliot was inspired by the writer's longtime studies in mind-sciences and potentials of human consciousness. Other books by Marian Coe reflect that interest: *On Waking up* (1979) and *Women In Transition* (1984). Cover art was done at Coe's request by her husband, artist Paul Zipperlin who, like writing friends, knows her characters well. All of whom – including son David Coe, a writer in Santa Fe, New Mexico, and daughter Carol Abdo, an art history student at Cambridge University, England – have encouraged her to stop rewriting *Legacy* and release it.

St. Petersburg Ti[mes]

ST. PETERSBURG, FLORIDA, WEDNESDAY, AUGUST 8, 1945

ATOM BOMB DES[TROYS] 60 PCT. OF HIRO[SHIMA]

Florida Man First t[o] ... Most Secret War ...

BY WILLIAM F. TYREE

GUAM—(UP)—The first atomic bomb dropped on Hiroshima completely destroyed an area of four and one-tenth square miles—60 per cent of the city's built-up area—and wiped out five major industrial targets with a tremendous blast which obliterated the city in a cloud of boiling smoke and flame, it was disclosed today.

An announcement by Gen. Carl A. Spaatz, commander of the strategic air forces, gave the news that had been anxiously awaited for more than 24 hours.

THE SINGLE atomic bomb had wiped out more than half of the city of 343,000 in a terrifying explosion which ... said equaled a raid by 2,000 B-29s.

Fukuoka, a city of approximately the same ... Hiroshima, was hit last June 20 by Superfortresses ... dropped nearly 1,000 tons of bombs. ... 1.3 square miles of the city—approximately 20 p... of it.

The single atomic bomb dropped on Hiroshima ... out 60 per cent of the city—4.1 square miles—... aged a wide surrounding area.

... within the four and one-tenth square mile area ... destroyed.

The force of the great explosion ... damage outside the "completely destroyed area." ...

It was obvious that a crippling blow had been ... Hiroshima, located on the southern section of ... of Honshu about 400 miles southwest of ... supply depots and factories producing large ... machine tools and aircraft parts are in the ...

No More Fighting for Veterans of Two Fronts

Army to Transfer

PLANES POUND WAKE ISLAND, JAP SHIPPING

V-J Day Celeb[ration] Okeh—Provide[d] ... Are Within Rea[son]

Liner Queen Mary Sails For New York With Troo[ps]

Tropical Storm Gains in Fury

JAPS ACCEPT ULTIMATUM

Ford Lays O[ff] ... Test Strik[e]

Damned Clever, These Japanese, but W[e Want No] Any Compromise With The Emp[eror]

Will Florida Allow 'Eden' To Vani

By GERALDINE DALY

one has said "Books, like friends, should be careful-
" Those which take you through Florida ...

St. Petersburg Times

THIRTEEN

TION TWO FRIDAY, AUGUST 17, 1945

MacDill Is Sprayed With DDT---

This B-25 is spraying the army's powerful
secticide, DDT, over the entire area of Mac-
ill Field.
The spraying was classed as an experiment
determine possibility of eliminating mos-
uitoes, which began to swarm the huge air
eld shortly after prolonged rains had provided
reeding grounds for the pests.
Mosquitoes have virtually disappeared since
he spraying. However, experts

entific means to
on mosquitoes at
rails for several
Attracting wh
men and civilia
swooped back an
as 50 feet. The
bright yellow

Highway Traffic Problem Looms, Officer Says

St. Petersbu

SECTION TWO THURSDAY, AUGUST

---FILL 'ER UP --- AND NO

ON WILL SHATTER PAST RECORDS

ida Faces Stiff Post-War Travel
npetition, Says New York Expert

should reap a substan-
e of the post-war travel
careful preparation is
ow, according to Lorent
manager of the Florida
of New York, who has
St. Petersburg
week during
the state. With his
ails from London
as three brothe
armed services.
the Tides hot
soon as wart
are removed
services are
the American
k loose on a
will shatter
of the past,
More, who sa
recreation
ten billion
stry, and all
will share

-THE WAR
nce almost
vincialism of
the America
Newspaper
of the gre
has made
conscious to visit areas
anxious to
sons, brothers and
and fought
will see

Tourist Influx Seen If War Ends Quickly

CITY RETURNS TO NORM
WILD CELEBRATION OF V

As Gas Ra

"Fill 'er up!"
That order, a dream of filling
rationing, swamped local static
news that gasoline rationing la

LET US OUT OF
HERE - WE'LL
HAVE YOU
ARRESTED!